Return to Treasure Island
The Lost Journals of Sir James Hawkins

Capt. Julie,
to the adventure!
and to slaying!
yer dragons!
John O'Melveny Woods
August 2010

John O'Melveny Woods

intellect
Publishing™

An Intellect Publishing Book

This is a work of fiction, based in part on the original work of Robert Louis Stevenson. Names of additional characters, places and incidents are the product of the author's imagination or are used fictitiously. Any resemblance to actual persons, living or dead, business establishments, events or locales are entirely coincidental.

Copyright 2008 by John O'Melveny Woods
ISBN: 978-0-9729761-3-8

Cover design and artwork by Craig Attebery
www.craigattebery.com

First edition: 2010

This book is an original publication of Intellect Publishing

A portion of all proceeds from this book is donated to campkorey.org

Intellect Publishing
P.O. Box 8219
Kirkland, WA 98034
www.IntellectPublishing.com
For enquiries:
info@IntellectPublishing.com

Printed in USA

Dedicated to rekindling
the excitement and childlike
wonderment still within
all of us.

Foreword

I have always been a fan of great storytelling. As a boy, it was books that inspired me to dream. They invited me into worlds far beyond my California bedroom and introduced to me characters that would become my friends for life. In the canon of classic literature, among my favorites was Robert Louis Stevenson's *Treasure Island*. The harrowing adventure of young Jim Hawkins and his encounters with Long John Silver lives in my heart as one of the greatest tales of pirates and bounty ever told. It was with genuine trepidation, skepticism and more than a bit of outrage that I began my journey with the novel you now hold in your hands.

I can hardly express to you, Dear Reader, how happy I am to share with you, that all of my fears were unfounded. *Return to Treasure Island* is in fact a first-class sequel to the original. John O'Melveny Woods has skillfully brought us back into the life of Jim Hawkins in the most successful way imaginable. He has created, in seamless fashion, a remarkable adventure for the characters we all know and love and in the process, introduces us to a few new ones destined to make an indelible impression on young and old alike.

And so, it is my extreme and joyous pleasure to introduce to you as good an adventure tale as has ever been told, and as Long John himself would say, "You can lay to that!"

LeVar Burton

RETURN TO TREASURE ISLAND

Prologue

Affidavit of Nathaniel Hawkins:

Due to a forced sale to pay the inheritance taxes owed after my Mother's passing away, I, Nathaniel Hawkins, great grandson of Sir James Hawkins, was charged with cleaning out and removing much of the family's heirlooms and furniture in their estate located near Elgin, Scotland.

On the twenty-first day of June, 1998, I was supervising the workmen while they were moving a rather large bed from the master bedroom (rumored to be the personal bed that Sir James had slept in) when we made an amazing discovery: Concealed beneath this bed lay a large wooden trap door. The workmen tried to open it, but it was locked.

Unable to find a key for the over one-hundred-year-old latch that secured this mysterious door, I hired a locksmith who used an acetylene torch to cut through the cumbersome steel hinges. After it was removed, I peered inside with a flashlight. To my astonishment, the door concealed a room that was, until this date, unknown.

The room was fifteen feet square and covered in cobwebs and dust that accumulates with the ages. I carefully made my way down a rickety set of wooden stairs and discovered musty bookcases filled with leather-bound books and small nautical artifacts—periscopes, compasses and charts. Paintings and wooden crates were neatly piled against the walls. In the middle of the room, stood an Early American accountant's desk, with an inkwell and oil lamp smothered in cobwebs. A captain's chair, in perfect condition except for the layer of dust that covered it, sat directly behind it. Next to the desk's table, on the floor, lay an old seaman's chest.

I proceeded to clear the dust and cobwebs from the desk's surface and thereon discovered a two-page letter on parchment, written in the hand of Sir James Hawkins:

To whomsoever may discover this letter, greetings.

I had at the first decided that the chronicles of my most spectacular second adventure, which almost cost me both life and limb, would never see the light of day, owing to the fact that I had promised my readers in my first narrative that I would never again get taken into such a fate.

However, upon considered reflection, and the realization that my years in this world are finally approaching their rightful close, I have decided to leave intact my completed manuscript, written and based upon my original journals, notes and maps made during the adventure. It is my hope and belief that someday these materials will be discovered and, if found worthy, published posthumously, thereby saving me the embarrassment of having to go back on my word, especially now that I have been knighted by Queen Victoria.

I shall die happy knowing that if I should be fortunate enough to still have any living relations at that time, they will have come to know more about me, and share, in this roundabout way, a period in my life which caused me to mature greatly—and to also realize how close they came to never being born at all. I relish the fact that in some small way they may experience the thrill of one of the world's greatest treasure discoveries.

One last item of business. The journals and manuscript are contained in the trunk from the Hispaniola *located in this room. Look further into it. There is a reason you have made this discovery, and I have anticipated it.*

Signed,
Sir James Hawkins

The manuscript and five leather-bound journals were found inside the chest, along with the original handwritten notes and story as penned by James Hawkins during his adventure.

Attested to this 21st day of December, 2008 by:

Nathaniel Hawkins

RETURN TO TREASURE ISLAND

Editor's Note

With the full support of Nathaniel's family and the remainder of Sir James Hawkins' heirs, this project has been worked on relentlessly for the past three years, and is now ready for publication. I have included the original manuscript, exactly as written, and also reproduce herein many of the marginal notes, maps, drawings and thoughts to help supplement his narrative and undertaking.

The only addition is the inclusion of a separate Journal found inside the chest that Sir James must have thought not important enough to include in the original story. It is the colorful narrative, as told him by Long John Silver, of how he came to know of the existence of this most magnificent treasure he calls The Pharaoh's Gold. This Journal is now the first Chapter, and sets a tone for the entire adventure. I believe you will agree it is worth including.

It is hoped that the reader, through this recently discovered manuscript, will share the sense of wonderment, adventure and terror that Sir James Hawkins experienced as a young man. I feel fortunate and honored to have been involved in bringing to the world this epic tale of his return to Treasure Island.

John O'Melveny Woods

John O'Melveny Woods
April 25, 2010

One Final Note: I have included an appendix that contains certain verbiage used in this book in order to clarify their meaning and context for the modern-day reader.

Return to Treasure Island

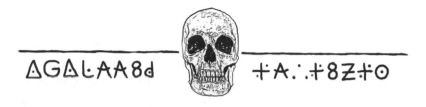

Chapter One

The Missing Journal

Written on Friday, the twenty-second day of the sixth month in the year of our Lord 1862.

I have asked Long John Silver to relay in detail how he learned of this most amazing treasure, in hopes that writing will divert my mind from our dire predicament. I am setting it to paper exactly as told me.

--- --- --- --- ---

Well, Jim, me boy, 'twas a funny ways I found out about this here treasure, it surely was. No stroke of thinking nor fore-planning could have prepared this poor soul for the story told me by that pathetic twig of a mate that came to inhabit the same dingy cell as meself. No sir.

As you are awares, I was in the Admiralty Jail, awaiting a most unfortunate outcome. One night I were awakened by the jailers' shoutin' like hungry seagulls and the sounds of 'em draggin' someone toward me cell. When first he was thrown in by the Guvner's men, I thought for sure he would be stiff as a board in a few hours' time, that's how bad he looked in the little light that came in through them bars from outside the cell. Couldn't have been more than five foot in length, and didn't weigh no more than a few fingers' worth of stone, if even that. I had no guess for his years, but he looked aged. His eyes sunk in, and the scraggily black beard that covered his face looked like it contained bits and pieces of all his past year's meals. Truly a dismal sight to these old eyes. By the talk of the jailers, I surmises he was a very important prisoner for the Guvner, and that all their waggin' tongues was about how they was goin' to drop the floor from the gibbet beneath him as soon's they could. I figured if they didn't do it that very evening, they'd miss a good chance for sure, and you can lay to that.

But shiver me timbers if it didn't appear as if the hand of the Lord reached out and gently touched this wretched soul, for he stirred awake about midnight and crawled from the floor onto a bunk and fell in. I'm a guessin' he didn't see me at first, being dark and all, but after his eyes got used to the pitch, he whispered:

"Who are you? What ye be doing here?"

You can imagine how startled I was Jim, believin' he was a dead man only waitin' to find it out.

"John Silver, me mate," I replied to him.

Although it was dark as Hades in there, I could have sworn I seen a smile spring up on that mate's pitiful face.

"Would that be *Long* John Silver, eh? The same Long John Silver that crewed as the quartermaster and sailed with that despicable Captain Flint. Be ye the same one?"

"Aye. That'd be me, by thunder," I told him. "And who be ye?"

"Jasper. Jasper Jennings."

There was a long pause, with him gasping for a breath. Then he raised up real sudden on his elbow and just stared at me. Spooky like. His long gaunt face just lookin' straight at me. And then, as if he heard the damndest yarn ever told, he broke out in a tremendous laugh… and continued laughin', getting louder and louder, and I'm a wonderin' to meself what in tarnation is all that dang funny? But as happens when you least 'spects it, I caught the feelin' of laughin' from him and we both were just rollin' in our beds, laughin' as if the king himself tole a tale of jesters and clowns. After a spell we both started to slow down and he started to coughin' and gasping for air again.

Finally, he sat straight up in his bed.

"Of all the miserable scallywags in this world," said he, "I'm a cursed to spend me last few hours with ol' Long John Silver. If that ain't the Lord's way of telling me my life ain't worth a farthing, I don't know what is."

And then he let out another huge laugh.

Well, I'm a guessing that was his way of sideways insultin' me, but it didn't work. The kiss of death upon him was sign sure enough that he wasn't long for this world, and I figured I'd at least humour the poor wretch until Beelzebub came 'round to pickin' him up and takin' him home.

"Yea," I told him, "that is a stroke of pure bad luck on your part, that's a fact." And I lay back down and tried to get some rest.

"They say I'm to visit the hangman on the morrow," he sighed, "and I'm afraid that day will be a short one."

"That's s'posin' you even make it till then," I replied.

"Oh, I'll make it, to be sure. I wants to look that mangy Guvner right in his beady eyes as my last breath is wrenched from this poor body, cursing him and his family every minute I gots left. And I will too, you can be sure of that."

Then he just quieted up for a spell.

"Silver," he started again, "I was hoping…well I don't know what I was hopin' for. Someone besides the likes of you, I'm a guessin'. Aye, I was hopin' to tell someone a secret before I goes on and sees which way me soul is a gonna travel outta this place. But the luck of the cards has given me you, John Silver, and that's the hand I gets to play. Can I be a trustin' you?"

3

Well Jim, this here got me interest perkin' up real high right 'bout now, so I asked him:

"What's the secret?"

"You gotta promise one thing and one thing only," he told me. "And on your word of honour too, even with what little of it I've been hearin' that you—"

"Now, now there, don't you go off offendin' me propers, mate," I broke in. "By the powers, you don't really have any awares of me, except by reputation, which can be the truth or it may not be, that's a fact. But let me tell you somethin'. I meself is scheduled to be swingin' from the hangin' gallows in a few days time, I am. So this here little secret of your'n might only last that long, if'n even that."

The mate got up slowly, all wobbly like, and hobbled over and sat himself down on the bed next to mine.

"There are some mates of mine who are goin' to try and break me out of here," he whispered, "but the devil's luck, that damn Guvner moved up me hangin' to the morrow instead of the day after. These mates, they are s'pose to spring me on the morrows eve, they are."

"Well then, of course I can be a trusted to be keepin' a secret, and you can lay to that," I told him. "Pray tell, what are ye talkin' 'bout?"

"You need to make that promise, Long John," he went on, "a promise that you'll keep."

"Aye, a secret and a promise," said I. "Shiver me timbers, mate, what is all this skullduggery about?"

"A treasure."

He looked 'round the cell slowly and then fixed his eyes on me directly.

"A treasure, the likes of which no one's ever seen before, and that's for sure. So do ye promise, Long John Silver, on yer word of honour?"

"Well of course'n I do, my good mate," I said. "Of course. Why didn't you say so in the first place?"

"Say it."

"What's that?"

"Say that you—"

I quickly held up one hand and placed the other over me heart, all affy-davy like.

"I, John Silver, do promise to be keepin' your secret and promise to… by the powers, mate, what 'tis it I am promisin' to do?"

"To take part of the treasure to me family so they can live out their lives comfortable like. So go on, say it like that."

"I, John Silver, promises to take part of that treasure and give it to yer family so they'll be comfortable and all. Now, is that okay mate?"

He let out a big sigh.

"Yea, that's what I was wantin' to hear," said he.

"So I made me promises of keeping a secret and all, matey," I went on. "Now what is this about a treasure?"

"Not a treasure Long John. *The* treasure. A king's treasure. No, that's not 'xactly it. It's a great pharaoh's treasure. Thousands and thousands of pounds of gold and jewels in all kinds of shapes… cats, kings' heads, chariots. You've never seen anything like it, and that's a fact."

"Nay… and you've laid your sorry eyes on it, have you?" I asked him.

"Not only seen it, but helped acquires and bury it myself, I did."

"And where would that be?" I pondered aloud, skeptical like, for at this point I couldn't tell if I were listening to a crazy man's rant, or if his tale be real.

"I'll tell you in good time," said he. "First I want to give you this paper with me family's whereabouts upon it."

Jasper pulled a crumpled paper out of his pantaloon's pocket. He grabbed me hand and placed the paper in me palm and slowly pressed me fingers 'round it, he did.

"You've got to keep yer promise, Long John. It's for them I am a dyin'."

He gasped a few more times, tryin' to be catchin' his breath, and then started talkin', real low like.

"You ever heard of a certain captain name of Redbeard?"

Jim me boy, that got my ears waggin' to attention real quick like. Just thinkin' about that man gave me the shivers. That there Captain Redbeard was one of the most nefarious, ruthless seafaring men that ever sailed the seven seas—with a worse reputation and feared more than my ol' Captain Flint by a couple fathoms, he was by thunder.

"Of course," said I to him, "but I thought he was killed good and fair a whiles back by me old captain—"

"Nay, he wasn't," this ol' mate Jasper responded. "I'm thinkin' now Redbeard faked his death through a most fortunate set of circumstances, he did. I know it, because I was there when it happened. Although I just got the truth of it a little whiles ago. 'Twas me being his first mate that led to all this in the first place, it was. It's not important right now how the rascal did it, but I swear he was as alive until a fortnight ago as you or me... I reckon... Aye, 'cept maybe more so seeing as our cases is looking for the worse, I'm a fearin'."

"What does Redbeard have to do with that pharaoh's gold yer speakin' of?"

Jasper slowly leaned back against the wall behind his bed and spun his tale.

- - - - - - - - - - - - - - -

"It all started up nigh ten years ago in Pirates Cove," Jasper began. "One of me mates was 'proached by a certain wench who offered to sit and have a few pints with him. He told her nay, 'tis his desire to be remainin' alone, and just as like a spurned dog gets, she starts a yellin' at him somethin' fierce about how she knows somethin' he'd gladly pay dearly for and goes on a tauntin' me mate about it. Well, then, ol' Captain Redbeard heard all the fuss, and intrigued like, he suggested they go and have a drink together.

"She took him up to her room and commenced to tellin' him that only the night before a certain 'upstanding' first officer from Her Majesty's admiralty took too much of the grog and stayed late into the evening in the parlor with her. This officer started to braggin' 'bout how he's on some sort of a 'secret' mission on behalf of who knows what. And how they are s'posed to deliver these priceless objects of gold to, and this here's the stranger part of the tale yet, to no one other than President Abraham Lincoln's main general where they will be a smelted all down and used to help win their war against their Southern States. This officer told her there's a 'secret' deal between this certain group and Lincoln, and when their North wins, they'll be a new allegiance 'tween their countries.

"Turns out, to this wench's misfortune, she didn't realize exactly who she was a spinning this story to, which of course, was Redbeard himself. He got the name of the ship and the officer. Of her fate after that, I can't be sayin'. Poor lady.

"After this, Redbeard hurried down to the docks, checked out the ship and real quick like finds me and relays all what's just happened, including it's a gunners ship and carries nigh forty cannon on double decks. Then he tells me that he's wantin' to take her wares.

"This gets me real concerned, Long John," said Jasper, "for although I'd been with Redbeard a half score of years, we'd always done what's smart and profited good from it... pickin' our ship's and cargo real careful like, that's for sure. But this was somethin' different."

"'Why do you care about that ship?' I asked Redbeard. 'It's a suicide plan if ever I heard one, and plain folly tryin' to attack a ship like that—we're outgunned and outmanned.' That's what I said for sure.

"Redbeard then tells me this ship sets sail the next mornin', and that he has a plan he's figurin' just might work, but we need to be quick about it, and departs at once."

Well now, Jim, I too was most curious 'bout this and I interrupts his tellin' me his tale at this point and I asks him: Why in all the world would Redbeard take such a risk to carry out such a dangerous and reckless deed as this, bein' that it seemed certain to fail?

"That's just what didn't make sense about 'is actions, Long John," he continued to tell me. "Redbeard was always kind of secretive like, especially about a certain tattoo he had—looked to be of a golden circle with some kind of triangle and eyeball within it. Tells me once that it had somethin' to do with a high soundin' group called the 'Knights of the Golden Circle', and that these here knights sorely wants the South part of that America to win the war; and that he would surely risk hide 'nd hair to either get that treasure or make sure it never reached its destination.

"Well then," Jasper continued. "We sail out that night and places ourselves about ten leagues out, square where we figure this gunner's ship will be sailin' past us, and then we waits for our chance. We lowers our colors and looks right smart like a merchant ship of some sorts. When our bow's mate spots that other ship's approach, we lights us a huge fire right on the deck, we does, with a couple of old sails we was repairin', and covers it up all over with wet grog. Clouds of smoke start billowing up and if I ain't lyin', next thing you know, that ship tacks toward our way, thinkin' we was going down, fallin' full sinker for our ruse.

"When they sails within a stone's throw of our stern, we drops doors on that side and fire away all ten cannons at once. Their ship is caught completely unawares. Then our crew, led by Redbeard himself, grabs ropes and swings over, and I tell you Long John, I never have seen such a frightful sight. Within a few minutes, bloodied men and body parts is fallin' overboard and their ship's a listin' from our cannons' second barrage to her old side belly.

"I goes over on the second rope volley and Redbeard yells at me to find the treasure. I fights a couple of lowly scallywag officers, quickly dispatch them to their maker, and continued runnin' down to below decks. When I reached the ballast room, I don't see nothing 'cept some large rocks.

"Then, all sudden like, the ship lunged forward 'bout twenty degrees, and one of them rocks rolls and pins me foot as water starts rushin' in. I can't move. I starts to panic and wondered if I were headin' to Davy Jones locker, when I hears a loud cracking noise, and then a door flies right open from the jolt. And there I sees it, Long John. The most beautiful face as I ever laid me eyes upon. It looked golden and oriental like, with some sort of an elegant headdress. It took me breath away and I lost me fright. After a few minutes, Redbeard and a score of me mates reached the hold I was in. I shouted and pointed to the fabulous treasure which lay behind this statue.

"They started unloadin' it and takin' it straight up the hatch, whilst two of me mates freed me bloodied leg so's I could help. There was so much of the bundt that we had to anchor-tie the two boats together to keep that ship from sinkin'. We finally offloaded the entire treasure in two days time, we did, and we watched as we released her lines and she finally gurgled down to Davy Jones's locker.

"We set our sheets full and sails for a week, finally makin' our way behind Skeleton Island."

"Aye, wait a moment mate," I quickly interrupted. "Are you tellin' me ye went to Treasure Island with this Pharaoh's gold?"

"Aye I am, Long John. A bit of the irony, isn't it?"

"Shiver me timbers, mate, you've no idea," I replied, "so be on with yer tale."

"Well then," said Jasper, "we was two weeks offloading, inventory'n and creatin' the most elaborate way of burying it as

9

you've ever heard tell or laid eyes upon. I asked Redbeard why this was so, and he told me that only one of his fellow mates, bein' a Knight of the Golden Circle, would be able to be findin' it this way. I helps him make a map, all pretty like, and we are ready to depart when I notices some of the crew is missing, I do indeed. When I asked Redbeard as to their whereabouts, he told me fifteen of our here-to-fore most trusted crew had been conspirin' to come back on their own and steal the Pharaoh's treasure, so he helped them meet their maker at the treasure site—in a very sinister way, as no doubt you've heard tales of.

"Later, when we was back in Pirate's Cove, Redbeard is recognized and called out by yer ol' Captain Flint, and the fight of all fights breaks out. Redbeard stabs Flint in the face with his knife, and you know that's how he lost his eye. 'Twas a vicious one, it truly were."

"So I heard meself," I told him. "But I thought Flint killed ol' Redbeard and fed his carcass to the fishes below, 'tis what I heard."

"Aye, so a story grows after the hundredth time of telling it, don't it? Truth is, Redbeard ended up being pushed back onto a pier and fell in the drink, after being cut up a great bit by Flint's cutlass. He never came up. But funny enough, as I mentioned earlier, I am sure I saw him not more than two fortnights ago in London leaving on a merchant ship bound for those United States. I swear it 'twas him, for sure."

"So tell me Jasper," said I, "where 'xactly is this mysterious treasure located on yon Treasure Island?"

"Aye, that is the question, ain't it Silver? The map herself was destroyed in the fight when Flint grabbed ol' Redbeard's jacket offin' him in the scuffle and threw it to the flames burnin' in a firepit… with the map inside it."

- - - - - - - - - - - - -

"So there's no map?" I queried Jasper.

"I didn't say that, did I John Silver? What I'm a sayin' is that the map *he* had was destroyed in those flames. I 'appened to 'ave an exact copy, I do… made it over the course of three nights when he was asleep and not lookin'. When I saw that he was drowned or at least pretendin' to be dead, I figured I was on me own, so I sets out to get a crew together and go back an' get it meself—since I alone am the one who know'd how to find it without losing it all over ag'in.

"But I figured it be safer to lay low for a spell. So I bides me time, spendin' most of it with me family and such. When I finally think it's been safe enough time to waitn', I comes back to Bristol. Through some old friends of mine I ends up makin' a deal with a certain captain, cuttin' him into the treasure. A deal with the devil it was, knowin' his reputation. But he was the only one I could get in contact with that could do the job. So he instructs me to go out and scout up a crew."

"And who would that thar captain be?" asked I.

"You'll find out soon enough. Anyways, that's when the tides turned against me and I ended up in this here hell hole."

"What are ye talking about mate?" I queried. "When all what happened?"

"Remember that certain important officer that let loose with all the talk to that wench about the ship and the secret mission I tolds ya about?" he asked me.

"Aye, I do," said I.

"Well, turns out 'twas the Guvner's son hisself, he was. One night a score of days ago I got to drinkin' in this local 'stablishment, which my little woman says will be the death of me, she does. Sure as the sun rises, me tongue gets a little loose and loud after a few pints. When one of the officers in there toasts the memory of this Guvner's son, I spit out loud and one of them starts to givin' me a hard time. I makes sure that he has a good case of the bewares by tellin' him we took care of the Guvner's son none too swift and I'll do the same to him too, and that's for sure. Well, this officer takes grab of me with a couple of his mates and proceeds to beat the story out of me about how Redbeard sunk the ship and all. By the time they tell this all mighty Guvner the tale, it seems that I alone was the pirate that seared his son through the gizzard, all personal like. You can bet I didn't tell them nothin' about the treasure, John Silver, and you can take that to the book.

"So I goes and sits through this official hearin' about me wrongdoin', and the Guvner hisself condemns me to die and has a good hearty laugh about it too, he does.

"They had me in another jail for a fortnight, givin' me no food nor water and beatin' me real regular like every day. I'm a guessin' the Guvner tired of this and they moved me here just this very evenin' to be gallowed in the morn."

Well, Jim, I thought about this story for awhile, and then I asked him, "So where exactly be this other copy of the map, Jasper?"

"Remember yer promise to me, Long John. You must give part of that treasure to me family."

"'Twas a promise I made, and one I'll surely keep, by thunder," I told him.

The mate painfully took off his shirt and gently untied some threading near the pocket over his heart. Then, slowly, a small patch opened off'n it, and there, inside, shined a golden coin, with the head of one of them Egyptian Pharaohs on it.

"Take this," he said while he handed it to me. "Go to the Quiet Woman in Pirate's Cove and ask for Blue Bell. This coin will get you yer map, 'tis a fact."

"And once I be getting this map?" asked I.

"There's *two things* you must know about if you be ever to succeed," he said.

And then me boy, he told me specific instructions of what to do, sort of like an insurance policy, said he, to be sure that no one tried to cut me out of the deal. You already knows one of them.

After that, me and Jasper just sat there. Nay, neither of us talkin' in the least for quite a spell.

"Ya know, John Silver," he finally said, breakin' the silence, "'tis not true that I'm fearin' of dyin'."

"Nor I," I replied to him, "and you can lay to that. But I've got a burnin' question for you, Jasper," I continued. "Just how do you know there be a rescue attempt the morrow night for you?"

"I got the awares through one of the crew that I scurried up before this unfortunate incident occurred. They sent word through another misfortunate soul in the jail that the morrow they would break me out of here. My new captain arranged it. The Guvner, that twisted soul, don't want to wait for the preordained time of my demise. He just told me that the morrow morning he will watch me die like a scurvy dog, he did.

"But ya know what *is* true, Long John?" he continued, "I'm just despisin' the fact that the filthy Guvner will have his hand in it. That's why I'll be cursin' him while he watches, and laughin' knowing that he'll never get his dirty hands on that thar treasure, nor lay eyes upon his son ag'in."

He stopped speakin' for a while, then became pensive in demeanor and finally stared me straight in the eyes.

"If you die the day after morrow, John Silver, then the secret goes to yer grave and no one will ever find it. Even if they know where it is, they can never get to it without the proper knowledge. So it don't matter. Either you gets it and helps me family, or no one ever finds it, and to the devil with it, I say."

The mate looked more gaunt-like than ever, and told me he needed to get some sleep. He slumped down into his bed and starts to snorin', all gentle like.

When the guards arrived in the morn, his face told the tale. The color of life had left it, and the Guvner would not be havin' his day.

- - - - - - - - - - -

13

And that, my boy, is how I came about to learnin' of this most incredible of all treasures, the Pharaoh's Gold.

.∴8GZ⅃82✝ ╳∟A.∴✝∟✝⅃

Chapter Two

Three Buccaneers

It's been nigh three years since I put pen to paper and described, in detail, the particulars of my first adventure to Treasure Island. Without warning and through a chance set of circumstances, the underpinnings were put in place that led to my next escapade with Long John Silver and that, for me, accursed island. I have decided, through much thought and overcoming immense trepidation, to relate the details of this second most fantastic and harrowing adventure. I promise to keep nothing back, including the exact location and bearings of this island, since, as you'll soon learn, there is no longer any reason to keep its location secret.

However, much more precedes that revelation.

The past three years leading up to this had been a wonderful time for my mother and me. Dr. Livesey and Squire Trelawney both generously agreed that a portion of the treasure we had recovered was rightfully due me, especially owing to the fact that my actions had put in place the means for all of us to escape with our lives from that lawless island. Through this endowment, we have been able to live a somewhat comfortable life in spite of the scarcity of travelers eating and lodging at the Admiral Benbow. I myself have been traveling back and forth to

Manchester, mostly at my mother's urging, attending the University of Manchester to become what she often referred to as a more "culturally rounded" young man. As such, it was necessary that I become schooled in many subjects such as history, geography, the life sciences—this last one at the bequest of Dr. Livesey—the defensive art of fencing and philology; all of the foundations required if I were ever to attend a more advanced university when my years and temperament permitted. In a word, I was on my way to becoming a young gentleman in the eyes of the more civilized world of the British Empire.

Yet, that was all to change, and by a queerer set of circumstances I could not have even imagined.

It was a particularly cold and wet afternoon in late March. I was through with my studies and helping my mother serve some of our more loyal local patrons. They seemed to enjoy her cooking almost as much as they enjoyed clamoring on about the various goings on with the neighboring villages, and of course, endlessly discussing all of the political shortcomings of the Crown and her Parliament.

I remember the moment vividly: three men boisterously entered the Admiral Benbow and made their way to a table near the far back corner. Their manner of appearance was what struck me—as well as the other patrons, judging by the hush 'round the room upon their entrance. The biggest man—twenty stone I guessed—was a peacock of a man. His wizened hands sported a ring with a shiny bluish stone, framed with dirty yellow unkempt fingernails. His clothing was atrociously patched, seemingly made of old rags of various sorts. An attempt at a full beard fell far short of covering the numerous scars that sported his face, while his mad dog eyes darted about the room at a fantastic pace. Long and matted hair fell clear round his neck.

The next man was the mirror opposite of this one, as far as weight was concerned. Tall and lanky, he reminded me of a walking broom handle. He had a long narrow face, sunken-in eyes that looked nowhere and a scraggly beard that I could see through to his skin. When he talked I could discern no teeth. His attire too, looked to be from the ragman's cart.

The last in this trio was an anomaly, wearing an almost new looking blue suit, with a large cape flowing over it. Of medium build, he walked with a slight limp and used his silver tipped cane to clear the area in front of him. His face showed the years of hard sea faring that mark a man's travels, and yet he still had a certain spark in his eyes that seemed out of place with the other two—as though he knew something that was very important indeed. All of them wore three-pointed hats that were the unmistakable fashion of seafarers—both pirate and swab.

The three men sat down and shouted their drink orders to my mother, who was also tending the bar, and chatted on amongst themselves. I don't know why, but seeing them immediately caused my mind to wander back to the crew of the *Hispaniola*, of which I had no doubt it was a similar ship they must have served on throughout the years. They were bickering good humouredly amongst themselves, but from my vantage point I was unable to hear of what they were speaking.

I delivered their drinks, and just as I was walking away one of them asked me how far it was to Bristol.

"About two day's journey by foot, a day shorter by horseback," said I, "if the weather holds and you stick to the main road."

"Good, good," the one who reminded me of a peacock said. Then the properly dressed one spoke up, with a very high tethered singsong voice:

"My good lad, I hear tell that this is the inn, the very inn indeed, where old Billy Bones met Beelzebub hisself. That's what I heard."

"Is that a fact?" asked Mr. Peacock as he furled his eyebrows. "Is that so, boy?"

Hearing the name of Billie Bones sent shivers down my back that shot clear into the ground. I stood frozen for a moment, this so startled me, for my mind was remembering a thousand thoughts, and yet none of them brought any remembrance of the three men that sat before me. My hands started to tremble slightly without any recourse; for I remembered how it was through my meeting that very Captain Billie Bones, as he insisted I call him, that brought me into contact with Long John Silver and almost cost me my life.

"What's the matter with you, boy?" the proper one spoke. "I asks you a question and I expects an answer from you, lessen, of course, you ain't got a brain to answer with."

They all started laughing. The skinny one snorted like a pig, with drops of spit drooling from his toothless mouth as he leered out of those yellow sunken eyes, while Mr. Peacock's belly jumped all around his chair. The proper one grabbed his cane and tapped it upon the table, as if to get their attention.

"Do you have an answer for us yet?" he asked me, while winking to his mates.

"Yes, sir, I… I do," I replied. "Yes… this is where the captain… died, sirs."

"The 'captain' is it? Oh, that's how it was? Captain, eh?" the skinny one told the group in a mocking way.

"Aye, I guess he gots the Queen's stamp on that one, he does," said Mr. Peacock.

They started laughing again, only this time more boisterous and annoying than before. I took my leave back to the bar, when the proper one picked up his glass and ostensively pounded his cane on the table for all to hear while he stood up and eyed our guests, sporting his glass high up into the air like the Queen's solicitor himself.

"Let's all take a drink to Billie Bones—"

"*Captain* Billie Bones," the skinny one who sounded like a squeaky mouse piped in.

"Yes, to Captain Billie Bones. May he rot in Hades and a curse be upon his soul for not lettin' us catch up with him before he goes and dies."

"And not getting our share, don't forget that," Mr. Peacock added.

"Yes indeedy, for stealing our shares. Curse you to the devil, Billie Bones."

"Hear, hears" followed as they seemingly inhaled their drinks, while the frothy foam of the ale ran down the sides of their mouths and dripped from their beards. This continued for a good couple of hours, them shouting their drinks to my mother and me delivering them to the table. I suspect the annoyance caused by their escalating toasting and voices compelled the patrons who normally stayed into the night to take their leave early. Soon, they were the only ones left. I caught bits and pieces of what they were saying to each other from my position at the bar. It seems they had been traveling for a long time…from somewhere or other far away. I couldn't much make it out. At times they purposely hushed their voices so as not to be heard. Finally, my mother told them this was the last round for the night, and I delivered their drinks.

"Well, me mates," Mr. Peacock said. "'Tis time we be makin' the most important toast of the night, and that's a fact. Let's put glasses together and give a toast to the reason we be makin' this here journey."

"Aye," said the proper one. "'Twill be a good day indeed to see that scurvy dog swinging from the gallows at the end of a rope. I've been waiting for this day a long time."

"And I'm square on that too," added the skinny one.

They all rose up from their chairs and held their glasses high. The proper one made the toast:

"To John Silver… may he perish and rot on the end of a rope like the wharf rat he is."

"And may he sees our smilin' faces as the life slowly drains out of him as he swings from the gibbet!" shouted Mr. Peacock.

At first I suppose I didn't truly comprehend what they were saying as I walked back to the bar. It was as if my mind wouldn't let me cognize what the words meant. But this was fleeting; for before I knew it my heart was racing and pounding in my head. They were speaking of Long John Silver being hung! I dropped the tray I was carrying away along with the glasses, and a resounding crash echoed throughout the inn. The three buccaneers, startled, quickly turned their attention toward me.

What they witnessed must have been a pitiable sight; for I was trembling outwardly, like a Shepherd's dog on a winter's night, with the tray and all the broken glass scattered on the floor about me. They started to laugh out loud, slapping each other on the back.

"Ain't that just a sight?" the skinny one snorted.

"A scared ships' mouse, if ever I've seen one," laughed the proper one.

"Hey boy," Mr. Peacock said. "How's about you get us all 'nother round before you break all them glasses."

I quickly bent over to pick up the mess, but truth be told, my attention was not in it. Long John Silver. It's a name I was sure I would never hear again as long as I lived. I hadn't thought of him for quite a long while, as if my brain had created a rock wall through which memories of that man would not be able to pass through. And yet, at that very same moment, the very mention of his name flooded me with thoughts so rapid and vivid I could scarcely keep my balance.

They continued to laugh at my awkward attempts at cleaning up when my mother came to the rescue and shooed me to the bar, where she had lined up another 'final' round of drinks for these strange travelers. I shakily delivered them and the proper one threw down ten shillings.

"Will that cover some rooms for the lot of us tonight, boy?"

"Yes sir," I replied.

"And these here drinks?"

"Yes sir, this will do fine, sirs."

I picked up the money and started to leave when I found myself turning back, not entirely of my own accord.

"I beg to interrupt, sirs, but might'n you have just been speaking of *Long* John Silver?"

"Mighten' we?" mocked the skinny one while they broke out laughing.

"And mighten' *you* have heard of him?" asked the proper one, narrowing his brow.

"Heard of him only," I lied.

Mr. Peacock pushed himself up from the table again and looked at me squarely with a sinister glare.

"You can be bet'n it was, *boy*," emphasizing that last word, "and it be of no concern of yours, and that's a fact, it is."

"But I thought I heard you talking about his hanging."

"Aye, indeed we was," he continued, while sitting back down and adjusting his jacket cuffs. "He's due for the gallows rope in seven days time, he is. We've traveled through most of the Queen's land to be able to spit on him as he does his final death dance on the gibbet."

"Hear, hear to that," the other two shouted.

"I did hear he was a scoundrel, but why are they hanging him?" It was as if I could not contain my question.

"High falutin' words for a boy there," the proper one started in, banging his glass upon the table. "A 'scoundrel' indeed. And that's the least of it. He's one of the most vile, evil men that ever walked the earth, and that's a fact."

"And don't be forgettin' his bein' the quartermaster for that wicked Captain Flint," added the skinny one.

"He's stolen from widows and orphans, and even played a trick or two on the lot of us," Mr. Peacock said, "depriving our poor selves of the rightful share of a certain… *investment*…we all were s'posed to be possessin'."

"And because of that we, well, we now has no financial means available for our future," the skinny one cried as his face grimaced, giving the impression his eyes would almost pop out.

"To hell with you, Long John Silver, you one-legged… what was that the boy here said… scoundrel?"

"To the one-legged scoundrel," they all toasted.

"May Beelzebub make him most welcome!" shouted the proper one.

These now drunk buccaneers finished their drinks and slammed their glasses on the table. Mr. Peacock ordered me to show them to their quarters. The proper one then proceeded to tell me to take their horses to the livery so they could be warm for the evening, which was some distance, since we no longer liveried any horses ourselves. They insisted I perform this activity only *after* I delivered their bags. I could hear them shouting and continuing their boisterous activities even when they were into their rooms and I was already down in the tavern below.

Truth be told, I didn't mind the walk with the horses, as cold and miserable as it was. In fact, the chill and sting of the rain pouring down seemed to clear my mind a bit, being as I could not take it off the fact that Long John Silver was scheduled to be hung in a week's time. Memories flooded my thoughts of having made a promise to him three years earlier to do all I could to help him avoid such a terrible fate.

After I returned to the Benbow, I retired to my bedroom and lay there, wondering what I could do, if anything, to help him. I was not expecting to get a good night's sleep, and was not disappointed. A kaleidoscope of remembrances and images danced about my mind that evoked feelings and fears I had not experienced for almost three years. And try as I might, I could not shake the image of Long John Silver's lifeless body dangling on the end of a rope. I prayed that the restlessness would finally turn to slumber and that in the morning's light I would know the right thing to do.

I could not have predicted in the least the turn my life would take in the next few days.

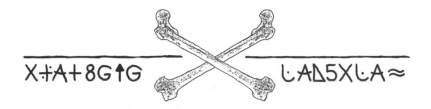

X✝A✝8G↑G   ⌐A⎊5X⌐A≈

Chapter Three

A Strange Note Arrives

The storm that had enveloped our coast the previous evening was still raging when my mother came to wake me up for my morning chores. I must have appeared a sore sight indeed, for she commented on how ghastly I looked and that I had better try to take a nap later that day before my evening's lessons. I felt as I suspect one of those "Haitian" zombies I'd read about might: going through the motions of my duties and responsibilities, yet all automatically and without feeling, for I was deep in thought trying to wrestle an answer to the question that vexed me the entire night before.

The three buccaneers were down in the inn eating their porridge breakfast when I entered. They looked none the worse for their drinking the previous evening. After I ran over to the livery and returned with their horses, they quickly packed up and left; heading out into the storm to their rendezvous with Long John Silver's demise. Watching them ride off I stood paralyzed by the urgency of my dilemma.

It was at times like this that I most missed my father and his sage advice. His passing had been hard for both my mother and me; perhaps more so on her since she was left to finish raising me on my own these past two years. And truth be told, I had little time for grieving. Even with the cushioning effect of my part of the treasure to help financially, my mother relied upon me extensively for helping her with all the day-to-day activities of running the inn, as well as the other things a man would usually do around the house. And as much as I cherished my mother, when asked for her advice, she would always seem to edge toward the less dangerous side, at least for me, of any decision. Whereas, my Father would listen objectively, ask pointed questions and then give his measured opinion, regardless of its effects upon me. I felt if only he were here, he would have been able to help me uncover the right thing to do. However, I was on my own, struggling to come up with a plan. I knew whatever decision I made would rest squarely on me.

My direction of thought was interrupted by my Mother, who told me that there was a man in the front of the inn who *insisted* that he see a certain *master* Jim Hawkins at once. I found this very strange—especially the term "master"—and rushed at once to meet him. He was standing just outside the front door of the inn, the rain pouring upon and then trickling down the back and sides of his coat. He wore a buccaneer's hat, but truth be told, I don't remember any distinguishing features of his, other than he was missing two fingers, his index and pointing, from his right hand. This was due to my observing he held a small leather pouch in it.

"Can I help you?"

"Would you be Master Jim 'awkins?" asked he.

"I would."

"The same Master Jim 'awkins that sailed on the *'ispaniola* on her last voyage to Treasure Island?"

"The same. Why sir, do you ask about that?"

"'Twas made to promise to make certain that no one else would be given me charge, accidental like, and them was the words that I needed to 'ear before I gives it to you."

"Give what to me?

"Why, this 'ere."

24

He opened the leather pouch and pulled out a folded note. He started to pass it my way, when he abruptly stopped.

"I was told there would be a little 'gratity' for me troubles getting this 'ere to you, in the rain and all."

"Just who is this from, and what is it about?"

"I can't rightly tell you, seein' that I was only asked to deliver it. But the swab that 'anded it to me said you'd know the sendin' party quites well. Said it 'twas urgent no less, he did."

"One moment, sir," said I, as I quickly got a quid from the register and brought it back.

"Aye, that's what this poor messenger was 'oping to be makin' for this terrible journey through the storm and all."

He handed me the note, tipped his hat, and with a crooked smile backed away and disappeared into the pounding rain.

I must admit, curiosity had gotten the better of me. For all I had known, this could have been a trick by a gypsy to separate me from some of the Queen's treasury, receiving a blank note for the looking. Yet I had a feeling this was not of that ilk.

Sitting down near a lamp in the inn, I slowly opened up the note. My guess was right. My eyes darted to the bottom of this letter to see who the sender was…

John Silver.

Dear Master Jim Hawkins,

I'm a hoping this letter finds you well. I'm putting ink to paper, Jim, to get a few things off me chest. I am in deepest hopes you receive it. You know, Jim, in spite of all that has happened between us, I can't help but be thinking how you grew on and influenced me in a good way, and how in the end I felt of you as a father feels for his very own son. In that vein, I wants to tell you, from the deep of my heart, how sorry I am for all the hurt and misfortune that I may have caused you. I've had a little time to think as of late, and just wanted you to have awares of that.

As the devil's fate dictates, I am to be hanged the 27th day of March, for crimes they seem to think I am at the bottom of. I know that if you could, you would do everything possible to help me, but I am not asking that of you. Fate has played a cruel trick, and I believe's me time has charted its course, and I'm afeared near run out.

Again, me deepest sympathy's and heartfeltest sorrys, my boy, as to anything I has done in the past that in any ways was harmful or hurtful to you. Them weren't my intentions, and you can lay to that.

Good bye me son,
Signed,
John Silver
Admiralty Jail, Bristol

My hands trembled, while the sound of my heart pounded loudly in my head as I set the note down. There could be no doubt at this point that what I had learned from the buccaneers was true. It was also true I had made a promise to put in a word for the turnaround of his nature so this fate might not befall him. He was spot on about that. This note seemed clear that he was not asking for any such help, that it was too late. However, was I not supposed to at the least try? Or rather, was I simply to wish him well in the afterworld and continue on with my life? My thoughts turned to what, if anything, could be done? Why would anyone listen to or believe me? But maybe, I reasoned, maybe it would be twice as good if I could also get someone they could not in the least doubt... someone such as Dr. Livesey. He would be the perfect advocate, since he was witness to all the good works Long John had finally accomplished, not the least of which was to save my life from the bloodthirsty pirates on Treasure Island who, without his intervention, would surely have diced me up into fish bait. And of the doctor's fair and reasoned nature, well, there could be no questioning.

As I was standing behind the doorway, lost in these thoughts, my mother approached me.

"Who was that at the door, Jim?"

"I'm not sure Mother."

"What did he want?"

"He gave me this note."

I picked it up and handed it to her. As she read it, her hands began trembling and her eyes started to tear up. She let it fall to the floor as she grabbed her breast.

"That horrible man, how could he write such a note to you?"

"Mother," said I, "I think he just wanted to apologize—"

She shook her head and frowned.

"Jim, you are still young. This man is evil, and knows how to manipulate people. From all the stories told me by Dr. Livesey and Squire Trelawney, this is just what one would expect from his kind. You must never see or speak about that... that hideous man again, Jim."

"Mother, I believe you are getting upset for naught."

"Promise me, James Hawkins. Promise me you will do nothing to help this despicable man. I will not hear of it."

"Mother, please."

"Promise me, now!" She started to cry, and I reached out to hold her.

"I promise, Mother," said I as I pulled her closer to me.

"You were almost killed because of him, Jim, and I couldn't bear the thought of your being in danger again, especially now since we've lost your Father."

"It will be all right, Mother. You will not have to worry."

I held her for a few moments in my arms, after which she straightened herself and went back into the kitchen. A few minutes later, I went in to see her and made an excuse that I needed to see Dr Livesey for some advice on a matter relating to my studies (you may remember he accompanied me on the *Hispaniola* to Treasure Island on my last adventure). I was anxious to speak with him regarding this current news about Silver. Quickly I made off on the one-hour journey to his offices.

It was mid-day when I arrived. Dr. Livesey was still taking his meal, and generously asked me to join him.

"You look very well Jim," said he. "I am so glad you came by. I have wanted the chance to congratulate you on your victory in the regional fencing competition. I heard you gave those Oxford boys a good drubbing."

"I was very lucky."

"I think it was more than that," he said as he winked. "And how are your studies going?"

"The sciences are the hardest, as you forewarned me, Dr. Livesey, but on the whole, I am excited and challenged by them."

"You are a very bright young man, Jim Hawkins, with your whole world before you. A world of unlimited possibilities. If you continue to study in earnest, you may accomplish anything you set your mind to. Maybe even become a knight." He gave me a wink. "Yours is an enviable position, especially by this old man whose possibilities are nearing their end."

"That's not so, sir."

He waved his hand to stop.

"It's not a sad state of affairs, Jim, only an observation. The world of the future belongs to you, and that's the way it should be. And with your endowment, you can have that future."

"Thanks to your intervention on my behalf."

"More than happy to do it." He settled back into his chair. "Now tell me, what brings you to visit me at my office—especially on a frightful day such as this?'

I pulled the note out and handed it to him. He read it while wiping his mouth with his napkin. His eyebrows narrowed, as he comprehended what it said.

"This is interesting, indeed. Are you sure it is true, this part about his being hanged?"

I relayed the story of the previous night and the conversations with the three buccaneers while he listened intently, asking a few questions here and there, and then thought for a few moments.

"Do you have any idea why he is being hanged? What his crimes are?"

"No sir, I don't."

"Well, I cannot believe it has anything to do with what we knew his crimes to be. Captain Smollett and I made a pact, once he escaped, to speak nothing more regarding him, nor the egregious acts that he committed throughout our journey. This must be of another matter altogether."

"Regardless of the circumstances *or* matters concerned, we made a promise to him to testify on his behalf—"

"That we did, Jim. That we did. But the fact remains, this must be of a matter unrelated to our trip, and therefore, it stands to reason that anything we could possibly offer in evidence or vouchsafing his character would be irrelevant."

"What are you saying?"

"I am saying that there is nothing to gain at this late stage of the proceedings, especially in the light that he is to be hanged in a few days. He's obviously not changed his ways and, in some perverse way, is getting what he has deserved more than once over."

"He saved my life, Doctor, and that counts for something."

"I agree. I was there. However, as he states in this letter, it is too late to make a difference. So I suggest the best thing to do is let fate fulfill her quest and we continue on with our lives."

"I cannot believe this is coming from you, sir. I mean no disrespect, but I beg to point out again that we made a promise— *you* made a promise—and I believe that we have an obligation to fulfill that promise at all costs!"

"As a magistrate myself, I would not even consider hearing from any character witnesses after a decision has been made, especially one of this seriousness. I don't expect the one who presided over the trial of John Silver will feel any different, Jim. Sometimes we just have to accept the inevitable. That's what I think you should do."

"It's not inevitable. Not until the end," said I. "The fact that he has apologized shows he can change."

The doctor did not reply.

We both sat there, silently staring at our plates. I did not know what he was thinking, but my mind was racing at full gallop, and anger welled up from somewhere deep inside me. I could not understand why a man of such integrity would not fulfill his promise. I tried to put myself in his position, and it did no good. If I were in a jail cell waiting to die, I reasoned, I would have wanted Dr. Livesey to at least try to help. Yet, he was unwilling to do even that! So be it. I picked up the note from the table and carefully folded it and put it back into my coat.

"Thank you so much for your advice, dear Doctor. I wanted to get your opinion on what I should do, and I thank you for it."

"Take my word, Jim, it is for the best. He is a bad influence." He stood and walked with me toward the front door. "It was only a chance set of circumstances that forced him to save your life and try to make amends for what he had done. His kind are the way they are by their very nature. Like a chameleon who changes his colors, Silver can sound and act like you or I, but deep down he is not, and even he cannot change that. In the end, the world will be a safer place when he has left it. You must trust me on that."

I bid my farewells and left for the long walk home in the rain. I must admit what the doctor said made sense. Long John Silver was known throughout the colonies as a notoriously evil man. Even I had seen him mercilessly kill an unarmed man. That could not be denied. What I could never agree to, however, was that he could not change. Even the Bible said that if you really desire it, you can change. In that area I thought the doctor to be wrong. More troubling though, was his reluctance to do anything to help, in spite of the promise he made directly to Long John Silver. The doctor was a man I greatly admired, and in many ways, one that I have tried to emulate in all areas of my life. But this incident gave rise and cause for concern. My father had always instilled in me that a promise made was a promise kept. *"That's what separates us from the lowly forms of animals,"* he would tell me. *"They can't make or keep a promise... but we can. Be sure to never make a promise you can't keep, and keep every one you give your word to."*

As to why the doctor was acting the way he was, I could not guess. I must assume it to be a character flaw that I need to be careful about in the future, especially when words of honour are concerned. I could see too, in a roundabout way, that being angry at his manner and opinion had brought unexpected energy and clarity of thought which was new to me.

I was now able to clearly discern that my choices in the matter had been whittled down to simply one: was I going to keep my promise to Long John Silver and try to stop his hanging, or not? Am I as good as my word, or not? It was black and white—no gray area in which to squeeze a little white lie out of, or try to rationalize to myself that I need do nothing. For that was a choice too.

It was all, or none.

I felt as if my departed father had sent me a message... one that I needed to hear. And I knew with unwavering certitude what the answer to my question was.

As to the promise I made my mother? That was troubling. It was made in the moment, and although I tried to be sincere with her, it was more to stop her from hurting than an honest reflection of how I really felt. I reasoned that it was more urgent to keep my promise to try and save a man from certain death. After doing all I could to accomplish this aim, at the very first opportunity I would make my amends with Mother, and hopefully keep her trust in future matters.

I took advantage of the remainder of the walk home to formulate a plan that would accomplish the completion of my promise to Long John Silver.

I was going to Bristol.

Chapter Four

The Plan

It was late in the afternoon by the time I reached the Admiral Benbow and I was soaked with an icy coldness that reached into my bones. My mother was busy preparing the evening's fare and took no notice of my arriving, or at least I thought so at the time. I hurried upstairs, peeled off my wet clothes and started a small fire in the hearth to warm myself.

To say that I had concocted a plan at this point would be putting a rose petal on the actual weed that had sprouted up within me so far. The best I could say about my "plan" was that it needed a little more "work". Once my teeth stopped chattering, I started to reason with myself.

Firstly, I thought, it wouldn't do to take the main roads to Bristol, since once I was missed that would surely be the first place anyone would look—especially my mother or her agents, which I had no doubts she would enlist to try and stop me. Additionally, I would be on foot, and whoever's charge it would be to find me would either be on horseback, or perhaps using a buggy or wagon. There was no way I could get to Bristol before I would be overtaken and discovered on the road.

No, that was not a possibility. An alternate route was needed.

The countryside between where the Admiral Benbow was located and my destination was separated by a large and hostile mountain range to the east. Therefore, this necessitated most people taking the longer more westerly route around them by availing the main road that follows the general coastline, and then heading inland at LeSalle and continuing southward to Bristol. But then I remembered another option. Before the main highway was created, there was an old one-horse cart road that followed about the foothills of these mountains, and had been used for hundreds of years. This would take me as far as Edburg, wherein I could easily take side roads and eventually arrive in Bristol. I calculated the additional time of taking this more indirect route as a day, maximum. That would still leave me ample time to see if there was anything I could do for John Silver once I arrived.

But there were other issues that seemed to me even more pressing, not the least of which was the weather. If it remained as it was, which was extremely likely, it would be vexingly difficult to make that trek. And what should I wear to keep this miserable wet and cold off of my bones?

I was obsessed with these thoughts as I finished my afternoon chores and bade leave from my mother to go upstairs and work on my studies. Once in my room, I pulled out the trunk old Billy Bones had left and started rummaging through it. With these supplies, I reasoned, I should be able to make the trip comfortably. I started to inventory them and then made a list of what additional supplies I would need.

I bounded into action. Within the span of no more than an hour, I had surreptitiously gathered from throughout the inn all the additional items that I could think to bring, and laid them out upon my bed.

Before me were the following:

- ✓ 2 pounds 3 pence, which was all the money I had in my room saved from my working at the inn.
- ✓ A compass.

- ✓ A spyglass.
- ✓ A walking stick.
- ✓ Billy Bones' oiled whale skin outer coat and boots.
- ✓ A small medical kit.
- ✓ A hat.
- ✓ A pocket knife.
- ✓ A cutlass.
- ✓ 2 pair of knit socks.
- ✓ A candle lantern.
- ✓ 3 candles.
- ✓ A lamb sack water bag.
- ✓ A striking flint.
- ✓ 2 ink quills.
- ✓ An ink stone.
- ✓ 4 writing journals.

I also needed to leave my mother a note, so as not to worry her in the extreme, and start to offer an apology. Truth be told, this weighed heavily on my mind, and the thought of her worrying about my decision hurt me to my core.

The rain continued to pour down, with the addition of lightning and thunder. I wanted to finish my lessons for school. Yet, try as I might, I could not keep my attention focused on this task before me. My mind kept going over the reasons why my plan would not work, and at each objection I would work out a new detail or two. What if I got hurt? Bandages should do quite nicely. What if I should get lost? I would carefully retrace my steps until reaching the last known place with which I was familiar, and then continue from there.

However, all of these were truly just masking a much larger and greater fear that I did not want to face: would I have the courage and fortitude to even begin the journey? Had I the certitude to embark without returning in an hour's time scared out of my wits? I didn't want to address these questions for fear I would accommodate these concerns and lazily accept the easiest of the answers, which centered about not going, using the logic of the good doctor, and find myself snug in my bed and assured I was in the right.

No. I pushed away all thoughts in this direction. I must go. There can be no further debate, I told myself.

The chattering noise of the inn below started to diminish, and I knew the appointed hour of my journey approached.

I heard a knocking on my door.

"May I come in?"

It was my mother's voice. I grabbed a blanket and threw it over my supplies, scurried to the door and opened it.

"Yes, Mother?"

"I need your help cleaning up later tonight."

"Yes, Mother, I will be down shortly."

I was trying to block her viewing the obviously lumpy bed with all my provisions lying upon it under the blanket.

"I also wanted…" she continued, "I wanted to say how sorry I am we argued about this whole John Silver incident."

"Yes?"

"I do not like to be that way with you."

"Yes, Mother, thank you."

"Are you all right?" asked she. "You look a bit piqued in the cheeks."

"Very well, Mother… I am just finishing up my studies," I lied. "I'll be down in a short while."

She turned about and I shut the door. I lastly remembered that I needed foodstuffs for my trip, and made note to procure them later after cleaning the inn when everyone was fast asleep.

- - - - - - - - - - - -

It was late evening by the time I had finished helping my mother clean up downstairs. Since then I had been in my room, stealthily packing everything into my knapsack and making nervous movements just to bide my time.

When all appeared safe, I crept out of my room and down the stairs, which tonight seemed to relish their ability to wake up the horses in the corrals a mile away with their squeaking. I crossed over through the hallway at the bottom and tip-toed into the kitchen area where I would find the salted meat that I most needed. Suddenly, I heard a noise and instantly knew that gait – it was my mother coming toward the kitchen. I hopped into the storage area and leaned as far against the wall as I could, hoping to avoid being caught in this most inexplicable situation. She walked past the kitchen door and up the stairs toward her room. I was sure she would be able to hear the pounding of my heart, but as good fortune reared itself, she did not. Upon hearing the door shut, I grabbed the biscuits and meat, and crept back up to my room.

- - - - - - - - - -

Whether it was wishful thinking or an actual fact, the intensity of the weather seemed to diminish. The hours ticked away and felt like days. I had tried to rest, but my mind would not cooperate. Thoughts darted about inside my head like so many fireflies in June. When the bed shook from the nervous twitching of my leg, I could wait no more. I decided that it was now the appointed hour of my leaving. I gathered my things, which were packed and ready, and started down the stairs. At the bottom, I went to the bar and placed the note in the coin box where I was sure mother would find it the next evening after counting the day's wages.

She would not miss me until then, since I had made up a yarn while we were cleaning about my going off early to school and being back late, which I felt doubly bad about doing.

I opened the door of the inn and slipped outside. The sign was flapping about in the wind. It was still cold and wet, although the storm had subsided to a degree. The lightning still made itself known, only less often. I donned my cap, lowered my head and struck off down the main road.

The night was pitch black, and the only way I could be sure of my direction was the illumination from the bolts of lightening flying overhead, which seemed to now start coming in quicker succession. I knew the general direction and where I was to cut off from the road. This, coupled with years of familiarity, allowed me to make a good deal of progress using the electrifying luminescence nature had provided me.

When finally the area where I was to turn my direction eastward toward the mountain arrived, I pulled in my jacket tighter, and ventured forth into the milky blackness of the unknown countryside.

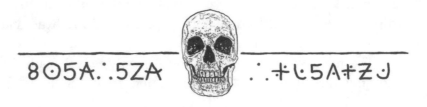

8⊙5Α∴5ΖΑ   ∴✝Ϲ5Α✝Ζ⌐

Chapter Five

The Journey

With the gift of hindsight, I could see that leaving at that time of night in such a frightful storm was an unprofitable decision. However, even with that perspective I really had no choice if I were to get to Bristol before the appointed hour of my friend's demise.

The old road for which I was searching, if one could rightfully call it that, was by my dead reckoning another hour's journey to the east. It was arduous traveling by the light of those lightening bolts, and frightening when they subsided for a few moments, for blackness swooped in to make my trek more perilous.

As the precipitation was not torrential, the going, although slow, was made with great facile. Another hour passed when, in the darkness, my foot slipped from beneath me, and all at once my world spun topsy-turvy. I found myself sliding at great speed down a long embankment with no way to stop. My speed accelerated, and I was unable to make out anything. I could feel rocks and brush slap into me as I headed into an unseen abyss. Finally, I slammed lengthwise into a tree, upside down, my forward movement violently arrested. I was covered head to foot in mud, and immediately felt soreness start to envelop several places in my body. I stood up, checked for any obvious mayhem to my limbs, which good fortune proved none, and searched for and found my knapsack not more than a few steps up the embankment, caught by a bush on the way down.

The next burst of luminescence revealed that I had landed right atop the old road I was searching for.

I continued along for what I estimated to be another labourious ten miles and decided to take refuge under a large conifer tree that offered me limited, yet tolerable, shelter from the storm. Tired to the bone and genuinely sore, I sat and reviewed my progress, and was satisfied with the fact that I did not let my fears grow and sway me from continuing with my quest. As I rested there I watched the lightning create sinister shadows within the flora of the area, dancing about the sky and ground. Using my flint on some dry needles I found under the tree I finally was able to light a small fire and warmed myself. I nestled a small blanket from my knapsack about me, and fell fast asleep.

I awoke the next day early in the morning to a gray and overcast sky. After a cold breakfast of biscuits and meat, I set about to use this break in the weather to profitably make up time.

Near the end of the day, I had traveled a great distance, and suffered no setbacks to my journey. By my reckoning, I was perhaps halfway to my destination, and was ahead of my mental schedule. I stopped to reconnoiter the area, and afterwards sat down to eat and rest. I was still quite sore, and wanted to not push myself beyond endurance. I was quite sure of where I was, for I could see the small hamlet of Hamstead to the west.

I wondered if my mother found the note I left her, and how she would feel about it. I went over what I had written in my mind:

Dearest Mother,

It is with a heavy heart I must leave you this note, yet I trust you will understand that I must do all within my ability to save Master Silver. I beg you to please not interfere with my

decision, and with all hope I desire you to know I will return after
doing so to continue helping you with the inn.
    With dearest affection and love,
    Jim

Truth be told, my heart was at odds with my actions and in sympathy with the hurt she must have felt. Yet I found my resolve sturdy and in the right.

I could almost hear her summoning the doctor and showing him the note, pleading with him to search me out and save me from fulfilling my duty by bringing me home straight away.

After eating, I set about to cover some more distance before the storm again grew in intensity. The darkness started to increase and soon enveloped me. I lit the candle in the lamp and continued ahead. The winds from the storm increased and I had to re-light the lamp with the flint several times with great difficulty. Suddenly the rain started pouring down with increased ferocity. In equal measure, the lightening and thunder appeared. I pushed forward, the lamp going out in the storm being replaced again by the bursts of light provided by the Almighty. The gale force winds were blowing northerly, which impeded my progress to a great extent since my direction headed me directly into them. Finally exhausted, I spied a tree with rather large foliage, and squatted beneath until I could catch my breath, and perhaps wait for the storm to subside before moving ahead further.

I am not sure if my memory and description of the following events can give a full picture of what occurred within moments of leaning against that tree.

I had not even finished removing the strap from my knapsack when, within the next moment, the world around me glowed with the light and intensity of the sun. Everywhere I looked was illuminated. My eyes involuntarily squinted, while the hair on my head and the back of my neck stood straight up on end as if trying to jump off my body. Sparkles rippled all around, like an intensely starry night, dancing about up and down my body, while the ground cracked and roared with a horrifying pitch. The loudest boom I had ever experienced quickly followed. It shook my body to its core while violently propelling me up off the ground and throwing me about ten feet away. Immediately orbs of flaming lights raced up the tree where I had just been sitting, and in the blink of an eye it burst into flames, engulfing it within moments and sounding like the roar of a large beast. Another large boom followed and the top half of the tree, seemingly cut in the middle by some invisible force, came falling down and landed almost exactly where I had been sitting, flames jumping hither and yon.

My ears were deeply pulsing inside my head from the explosion, and my senses and bearings were for naught, since I was completely dazed and not sure of what had just happened.

Suddenly, not fifty feet from my new position on the ground, I witnessed a huge bolt of lightening strike another tree, followed by a deafening explosion, and it burst into flames. I realized at once what had happened to me, and I was want to wait around to see if my luck would hold thrice.

My heart was pounding so hard I fancied it would leap from my chest, yet I found the strength to jump up and run. "Get away from this accursed place!" I screamed at myself. The rain was a torrent, covering me in a deluge of water. I could barely see where I was going. But truth was, I didn't give it much thought. I was scared out of my wits and running like a spooked jackrabbit, darting left and right with no aim. My only thought was to pray that I would not be struck by the lightening.

Boom! Another strike to my right, and by the light I was able to see and jump over a hedge that lay before me while I dodged another large tree that blocked my path. This last strike gave wings to my feet and urgency to my flight. I was beginning to want for breath and my legs were growing tired and weak. And yet I dared not stop until I was able to find safety in some form of shelter from this storm's fury.

Suddenly, in the distance, I spied what appeared to be a light flickering in a grove of trees. As I ran closer, my hopes grew as I could make out that it was a fire. Relief coursed through my body as I straightened and guided my aimless running toward this promise of warmth and refuge and safety from the wrath of this storm, caring not to whom it may belong.

As I raced through the cluster of trees I tripped over a downed trunk, fell over, and slid on the mud for a good while, ending up not more than a yard from the fire. I lifted my head and could see shadowy figures of men, obviously startled, jump up and away from me, no doubt not believing what their eyes were clearly showing them and wondering who, or what, this uninvited visitor might be.

Tired and panting, I lay there deathly still, trying to make out the bodies that were scurrying about. I was unable to understand any of the words they were speaking, for my ears were still pounding from the force of the thunderous explosions. Their voices seemed as echoes in the distance.

I pushed myself up and rolled upon my back, and could see three figures with cutlasses drawn, staring quizzically at me. And what a sight I must have looked, being covered head to boot with mud. One of the figures slowly started toward me with caution abound, and finally got close enough to touch my panting chest with his cutlass.

"What 'ave we 'ere?" said he.

It took a moment for my eyes to adjust to the fire's light. However, by squinting I could start to make out the face of the one with the cutlass perilously close to me. And a frightening face it was, indeed. A cragged, wizened face with a scraggily sparse beard attached. His mouth revealed great spaces between yellowish extended canines, a large pointed hook nose, all accentuated by a black patch on his right eye. Under his whale skin jacket he wore pantaloons with a shirt and a kerchief wrapped around his head. His one ear sported a silver loop which bore the sign of a skull. Crossbones were tattooed upon his neck, the same side as the patch. A pirate, without a doubt. His scowl sent shivers through and through me.

"Looks like a sowed pig, if'n you asked me," shouted one of the others.

"A pig in his muddies pen," the third said.

The two started to laugh, causing the one holding the cutlass on me to break out into laughter too. Quieting down, he moved in closer as the rain dripped from his hooked nose onto me.

"Who be ye, my little swine?" asked he, "and what bizness has it that ye be droppin' in so unexpectant like upon me and me mates? And be tellin' us straight, now."

I tried to answer, but found no voice within me to speak. It was as if I could not move my tongue or my mouth. I wanted to tell them I meant them no harm, that I only wanted to be away from the lightning and warm myself with their fire and then be off, but these words would not come forth. Instead, I could only stare helplessly at this hideous pirate, unable to state my case.

His eyebrows furled as he watched me struggle with a myriad of facial gestures, unable to give a satisfactory answer to his question. He looked over toward his mates.

"Might'n be a dumb mute, perhaps. Seems a bit short on the words. Check him to be makin' sure he's no weapons," he told them.

The two other pirates appeared and removed my jacket, finding my knife inside.

"Looky here, all right," one of them said. "The little sow has a dagger, he does."

"Pick him up," the one-eyed pirate ordered.

They wrestled me off the ground and held my arms firmly to my sides.

"Can ye talk?" shouted the one-eyed pirate. "Do ye have a tongue?"

I tried to speak, but try as I might, my speech still failed me, and only unintelligible grunts were to be heard.

"Hmmmm" he spoke to himself. "Look at this sow's clothes. They all be burned and singed, yet I might'n not remember him touching the fire. Looks like he jumped in and out ag'in, he does."

They laughed. He leaned in and smelt me, his nostrils flaring like a bull in springtime. Now, for the first time, I also started to smell, and the acrid odor of my own burned flesh reared itself.

"This'n here is a strange one, he is. A burnt muddy sow of a lad, if'n he's anythin' at all. Comes flyin' in here like a spooked partridge, too. Check him twice to see what els'n the mate may be shorin' up."

As they loosened their grip I made a decision. I surmised that no good was to become of this encounter and that if I had the chance, I should make flight. I yanked my left arm away and tried to wrest the other one away with all my might. This caught my captors unawares, and for a moment I was free. But alas, the one pirate grabbed hold of my arm and violently drew me back, and try as I might I was unable to break his grip. In my struggle I swung around and into the other pirate whose grip I broke from, and almost fell into him.

"Oh, I think he likes you, Barton," said one as they laughed.

This seemed to anger him greatly, and he pushed me with full force toward the one-eyed pirate, who promptly pushed me back. With sinister smiles, they started to push me between themselves in a sort of macabre game such as we used to play as children. They started laughing and shoving me harder, all the while I tried to protect myself as best I could while being thrown hither and thither like a child's spinning top. I became greatly disoriented and knew not where I was, the images becoming a blur as they pushed and shoved me between them, deriving great pleasure all the while from my misfortune and pain, judging by the intensity of their laughter.

44

After a particularly fierce push from the one-eyed pirate, I flew past the other two and into and atop the fire, the force carrying me through to the other side. Sparks flew everywhere. I fell down with great force when one of my feet slipped from beneath me. A great pain shuddered my head as I landed full force upon the muddy ground and a large rock. I felt warmth dripping down the side of my face. Weakness coursed through my body, and I found not the fortitude to move a limb. I lay still for what seemed an eternity until a boot lunged into my side.

"Looky what you did, Bart. You killed the little sow, you did."

"Is he a meetin' his maker?"

"By the look of the blood, he's surely due to soon."

"What should we do?"

"It's of no business or concern to us, mates. Fetch me spoils from him."

"It bein' *your* spoils, now, is that the way it is? I'm thinking we've all 'tributed to his demise, and we all shares in the spoils of that misfortune of his, and that's a fact."

"Equal it 'tis, then."

My eyes grew heavy and faint as I felt their gnarly hands rummaging my pockets and then pulling off my boots. When there were no more spoils to be had, they began ruminating amongst themselves.

"Shouldn't we bury the poor sow?"

"Bury, humffff! That seems a might bit of labour. The wolves will make quick work of his bones in no time. But I say we move along an git a new camp, so as not to spend the night with his ghost hovering 'bout us."

"Aye, I sees your point."

Darkness was swirling in my head as their voices slowly grew fainter and the light from the fire faded. I could barely feel the rain pounding upon my head and body. I tried to hold onto a thought, any thought, but they danced away as my mind seemed to spin into a large black netherworld.

Finally, I could hear them no more, nor the rain, nor anything. A curtain of numbness lowered itself on my thoughts, and I slipped away into a pit of darkness, until I finally felt nothing at all.

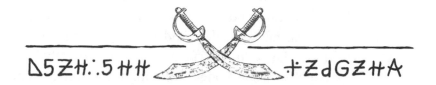

Chapter Six

A Chance Encounter

The first sensation I became aware of was gentle warmth encasing me, as if lying within wisps of heavenly feathers. I remained in darkness, and moved not for fear of the pain returning, which so gripped my last remembrance.

I also at once realized that I could hear no rain, nor any sounds of the forest. A strange sensation, thought I. Although my head was still pounding within my ears, I gradually became aware of some sort of... angelic humming echoing from afar.

Was I in heaven, resting peacefully upon a cloud with celestial beings singing in the background? I struggled to take inventory internally, trying to sense my limbs. They all seemed to be accounted for, although I had no idea what I was to feel being in this angelic state. Can you even feel your body in heaven? If I am dead, why does my head still hurt so?

Whilst these questions and more occupied me I felt the gentle, cooling sensation of water gently being dabbed upon my brow, which greatly startled me.

I commanded my eyes to open and let my fate enter my sight. At first all was a blur. Blinking profusely, I slowly gained focus and beheld the most beautiful vision I could ever have imagined.

What struck me first were her handsome brown eyes—eyes of empathy and care and of understanding and depth. Her dark hair flowed past her shoulders and seemed illuminated by the light that filled the room. It surrounded a classically oval shaped face, perfectly proportioned with high cheekbones and silky smooth skin that seemed as if it belonged on one of those very expensive porcelain china dolls. What enchanted most was her gentle smile; so natural it looked as if it were a permanent part of her. It sent tantalizing shivers through my body, causing my fingers and toes to tingle. She was holding a cool cloth and sponging my forehead.

"Are you… are you an angel?" asked I groggily.

She continued to smile while still dabbing my forehead without offering a reply. She finally set the cloth on a table next to us. I reached up and touched her hair, gently twirling it around my fingers, and I could hear her catch a breath. She grabbed my hand and set it back down on the bed, although still holding it.

"Am I dead?"

"No… you're certainly not dead." says she. "My name is Chloe. And I can assure you I've never been called an angel. You can ask my brothers about that."

She winked, released my hand and quickly exited the room, where I could hear her speak.

"Mother, he's awakened."

"Oh my goodness," her mother responded. "That is very good. Much sooner than the doctor expected."

Into the room walked a stately woman who I knew to be her mother, for she bore the same gentle smile.

"How are you feeling today, young man?"

I started to talk and found my mouth was very sore, but this time the words cooperated.

"Well, ma'am, to tell the truth, I am not sure of what or how I feel."

I tried to sit up and became aware of a large bandage about my head.

"I seem to have all of my parts, but I am confused about how I ended up here, wherever here is."

"That's not surprising," she told me, "imagining what you must have been through, I am sure. If it wasn't for Chloe, I am afraid the results would have been much more dreadful. Chloe, see if our guest would like a little broth."

"Yes, Mother."

I nodded agreeably to the suggestion, suddenly realizing I was quite ravenous. Her mother smiled at me again as she left the room. My wonderment at my good fortune increased as I searched these surroundings, trying to glean a clue as to where I might be. It was a simply decorated room, with a few dolls on a table and lovely pink curtains framing the window. A girl's room, I guessed. My throbbing head persuaded me to wait and ask some questions of Chloe, rather than get up and venture about.

She arrived shortly with the most delicious smelling broth. I could not muster up the strength to feed myself, so she gently fed me spoonfuls of the elixir, which I must admit was not unagreeable in whole or part to me.

"What is your name?" asked she.

"Jim, ma'am, Jim Hawkins."

"I don't believe 'ma'am' is necessary, Jim Hawkins. Is your Christian name James?"

"Yes, it is."

"Where are you from, James?"

"North country."

"Mother wants to send word to your family about your—"

"No, that won't be necessary, Chloe," I interrupted.

"Won't they be worried about you?"

"They… they are visiting relatives, and will be meeting me in Bristol."

I hated to lie to her about it, and promised myself not to do so again.

"Where am I? And how, pray tell, did I arrive here?"

"You're at my house, of course."

I stared at her, hoping to elicit more.

"Oh, of course. Our house is on the old West Front Road, about ten miles from Bristol. We used to supply lodging and food for travelers years ago, but since the new highway we have been selling dairy goods twice a week in North Bristol."

She picked up the cloth and dipped it into water, and then gently pushed me back onto the pillow and lightly started to dampen my forehead.

"You are a very lucky young man, my James Hawkins. It just so happens that after those terrible rains and such, my Mum recruited my little brother and me to search out for some chanterelle mushrooms near the edge of the hills not too far from here, in an area where they usually pop up after a storm."

She set the cloth down, stood up and walked over to a dresser where she picked up a pitcher with water in it and walked back to the bed. She gently poured it into the bowl she was dipping the cloth in.

"Whilst I was looking about, I saw your foot and leg sticking out from behind a tree. At first I was frightened, for I was not expecting to see anyone. Finally, curiosity overcame my trepidation, and I quietly peered around from behind the tree. My, my, what a frightful sight you were, indeed. Covered in crusty mud, dried blood all about your head, no boots or jacket. I slowly crept up to you to see if you were alive or dead, although I feared the worst, for my thoughts were already heading in that terrible direction. After pushing you with my foot several times, gently I might add, I discerned no movement. I bent down and listened to your chest as I had observed our doctor do on many an occasion, and it is then I heard a slight sound.

"I raced back to the farm and dispatched my father and brothers who brought you back here in one of our wagons.

"We sent word for Doctor Glickman while we cleaned you up and tended to your wounds. After an examination, the doctor stitched a gash on the back of your head and told us to tend to your needs and see if you awaken. If you did soon, that would portend well. He is the one who bandaged your head.

"I knew that you would, and begged my mother to let me stay by your side until you did. And you have finally come 'round."

Something about the word *finally* caused my memory to explode with thoughts, and I leaned up quickly in spite of my head pain.

"What day is today?"

"Why it is Thursday."

"No, I mean the date."

"The twenty-third day of April."

"Oh, thank providence," I whispered as I lay back.

I had been out for only two days. I tried to calculate how much time was left, but it only increased the discomfort I was already feeling. I knew there was still time enough, and that would have to do for now.

"We're all wondering what happened to you, James Hawkins?" queried Chloe.

I relayed the night's adventures, sparing no detail I could remember, and in the process puffed up my role in the sordid affair, although only in small measure.

"Pirates," she said. "Well that makes sense. Ever since the new highway, the only types of visitors we get are the scallywags and buccaneers that traverse the old road, stopping in to replenish their supplies. But tell me, James, why were you there in the first place?"

"Please be so kind to call me Jim." I felt it was important to me for her to do that. She smiled.

I told her my version of the adventure to Treasure Island with Long John Silver, and why I was traveling to Bristol to save him. She seemed to enjoy the tale, and I began to act out some of the parts, making her laugh. However, this tired me and I lay back down when finished. I was unsure whether she believed me

51

or not, for even I, upon hearing it retold, realized what a yarn it could sound like.

"Well, *Jim*," she said, emphasizing my name. "That is quite an adventure. I think you should get some sleep and see how you feel the morrow. The doctor says—"

"I must leave tomorrow, if I am to save him."

"Yes, yes, you must leave tomorrow. I understand that," says she smiling, "but today you will rest. When you feel hungry again, ring this bell and I will bring some food."

She brought up the covers to warm me and tucked them in. I watched as she walked through the room and gently started to close the door, looking back and smiling directly at me. I found myself feeling strangely after she left. It was as if a warmth had left my body. And I found myself wanting to please her by resting. This was most confusing to me, and I wanted to know why. However, while pondering the answer to this question, I fell fast asleep.

- - - - - - - - - -

At mid-day I felt much better, and was allowed to sit up in the chair downstairs next to the window. I sat there and watched Chloe as she tended the animals—chickens, geese and ducks. She performed a myriad of chores, each with a breeze of joy and humming all the while. Every so often she would stop, look over toward my window, and smile.

She was nothing at all like the girls I had known at university. She seemed an amalgamation of a delicate and beautiful china doll, farm hand and nurse, only in proper balance and harmony. I felt toward her not in a sisterly way, and knew not what to make of this.

I did need to think about renewing my travels to Bristol, and post haste, for I had calculated the time and discovered that the dreadful event was approaching in three days. I realized that if I did not leave by the morrow I surely would be too late and my trip would have been in vain. I hobbled back to the bed upstairs and fell into a fitful slumber.

That afternoon I was feeling much refreshed and Doctor Glickman had been gracious enough to come by the farm and check up on me and redress my head wound. He told me I was a lucky lad indeed, for had it not been for that mud caking up my head wound, I surely would have expired due to bleeding.

Before dinner I helped Chloe gather some milk from the barn and had a chance to observe her up close. Although appearing to be as a farm hand, this was deceiving... for she was more, almost flowery. But this flower proved tempered and accustomed to hard work and responsibility. She was different from any young woman I've ever met. I found myself in numerous instances entranced, and for the life of me, without words.

"What do you think of me?" she suddenly asked.

I didn't know what to say.

"What's the matter Jim, cat got your tongue?"

She teased playfully as she ran off to her next obligation. I did not want to leave her presence, but I found myself tired and begged to go and get some rest before the evening meal.

For dinner I was aware that she was all dressed up in a dark, silken green dress with lace at the neck and a matching petticoat like one I've seen my Mother wear on special occasions. She looked very fine in her dress. It must have been a special occasion, for I noticed the looks from her younger brothers as they nudged each other and laughed.

The dinner with her family briefly diverted me from my trepidations about the journey ahead. They were fine people and made me feel as one of their own. And it was not unpleasant regaling them with the tale of my pirate adventures—and watching the wide-eyed astonished looks on her little brothers' faces... especially during the fighting scenes.

After our meal, Chloe and I bade our leave and walked outside along the trees that lined the road leading up to her farm.

It was one of those rare English spring evenings when the warmth of the sun remained late into the night. As we walked along the road, I became aware of a most pleasant smell, and asked Chloe about it. She shared how her mother had planted lavender bushes all about their farm, and that this time of year they were at their most succulent. The scent was intoxicating. The twilight sky shed enough light for me to appreciate how lovely Chloe was, and I found myself wanting to reach out and hold her hand. Nervousness kept me from doing that. Chloe must have been aware of how I felt, for she commented more than once regarding how shaky my hands were.

Soon it was time for sleep, and Chloe walked me back to the house and upstairs to my room as I bade goodnight to her family. She made a fuss about my comfort and my getting into the bed and staying there, and sat next to the bed holding my hand until I appeared fast asleep. Then she stood up, bent down and gently kissed my forehead and left. I wasn't asleep, and I was glad it was so.

- - - - - - - - - -

The next morning I was awakened by a nightmare of Long John flailing at the end of a rope, and found the hairs standing upon the back of my neck. In the distance I heard a song that reminded me again of the serious and dangerous nature of my self-imposed obligation.

Chapter Seven

A Ghost from the Past

"Fifteen men on a dead man's chest,
yo ho ho and a bottle of rum."

It had been more than three years since I'd heard that old pirate's song being bellowed from Billie Bone's mouth, and yet I felt it as if it were yesterday. I jumped out of bed, peered out the window and saw an old wagon pulling up toward the farm. Four buccaneers sat upon it, singing that wretched song. I gazed as they weaved their way closer to the house, and then observed Chloe's father approach them.

"Mornin', gents," said he.

The way their wagon was situated when stopped prevented me from making out the face of the one who was holding the reins, nor could I see the one sitting next to him. The other two caused me no remembrance of having seen them before.

"Mornin', Cap'n," the man with the reins in his hands replied.

"What brings you to these parts?"

"On our ways to Bristol, we be. A bit low on provisions and grog, too, so we's hopin' we might'n get a bit from you."

"There's no grog here, but the provisions I can be of help with. Wait here and I'll be directly back."

As if my neck hairs could rise any more, they did when I observed Chloe strolling up toward those buccaneers. As she walked past them from the barn and made her way toward the house, their leers followed her like dogs eyeing a soup bone.

And then I saw the face of the driver. Oh my God, could it be? My fright reared itself so quickly I froze. My mind raced to make some sense of this. His gaze, now off Chloe, slowly moved toward my upstairs window, and for a moment it seemed we locked sights. I reacted instantly by shutting the curtains and running back to the bed.

This new event definitely brought to mind the escalated dangers that lay before me. What could he possibly be doing here? How did he get here? Where is he going and why?

A knock on the door startled me back to my present surroundings and Chloe entered the room.

"Did you see those buccaneers?" she asked.

"Chloe, close the door quickly and come here," said I.

She did so and walked over and sat upon the bed.

"You must stay away from those men."

"But why?"

I grabbed her arms.

"Chloe, that pirate, the one who is driving the wagon?"

"Yes?"

"He is none other than Morgan, the pirate I told you we left marooned on Treasure Island. A truly vile and despicable man, with no remorse or conscience in the least. The other one I think is Gerry Merry."

"What?"

"I'm rock sure of it. I don't think he saw me, for if he did I would no doubt be dead right now. But this you can believe; he is ruthless and dangerous as a snake and would not hesitate to hurt you or your family."

"I must tell my father," she pleaded.

"No, that may give them a thought that he knows who they are. It is more likely they will do no harm if they are not provoked. I do wish I knew what they are doing here."

"They simply asked for some supplies, Jim. Maybe that is all they want."

"Of that I have grave doubt. The fact that he is still alive... they must be up to something—"

"I know exactly what to do," she said.

Before I could say anything she rushed out the room, slamming the door behind her. I next heard her speaking to her father in muffled tones, and looked out the window to observe her shooing him into the house. She grabbed the bag of foodstuffs, walked up and handed it to the men in the wagon.

"Thank'n you missy," said one of them, who gave her a leering smile.

"What do we owe ye?" asked Morgan.

"Two pence."

"Fair enough, if'n you ask me." He lightly jiggled the reins to wake the horses as he nodded to one of the others.

"Where are you heading?" she asked in an innocent way.

My heart was pounding like a bass drum at the fair.

"Well now, miss, we're off to see a scoundrel pay his rightful dues, we is. It's been a long journey that will end the day after the morrow with him dangling at the end of a line like a mackerel."

They looked at each other and laughed. One of them took out a coin and flipped it to Chloe, who caught it in her right hand without missing a beat.

"Thank'n you kindly for the food, miss," Morgan said.

He shook the reins. The horses jumped to life and off they trotted. Chloe stood and watched until they left sight, then turned and hurried back to my room.

"Oh my, Jim Hawkins, those are truly awful men. I believe they are going to see your John Silver hanged."

"I must leave at once," I stated.

I rose from the bed and started to pace about the room, unable to arrest my energy in the matter.

"The doctor said you should wait—"

"I mustn't wait. I cannot wait. Time is my adversary and is growing worrisomely short."

"You weren't stretching the truth about these pirates, were you?"

"Did you suspect my tales?"

"Well, maybe just a little. But that is not important. It's only that I have a feeling it will be very dangerous."

"I, too, have that concern. But my motives should not expose me to such. I have only two goals to achieve: the first is to search out and find John Silver and set his conscience free; and the next is to contact the proper authorities and plead they let him live for having saved my life. After that, I will go back home."

"You simply must not go until you are well."

I found my hands grabbing Chloe by the arms and staring directly into her eyes.

"Chloe, I will leave within the hour, and that is that."

Her crestfallen brow betrayed how hurt and angry she was with my decision. I released my grip and turned to stare out the window. I was starting to doubt it on my own, but resolve crept in and reminded me the reason for this journey and the folly of giving myself up to it not succeeding. I will confess here, that it was important to me how Chloe felt, and I was sorrowful she was not pleased with my decision. I had so wished that I could make her understand. But there was no time.

Reluctantly, Chloe gathered some old clothes and a pair of boots from her father, which suited my stature well, and her mother packed some foodstuffs for my journey.

An hour later I bade farewell to her family. Chloe and I made off for the old West Front Road. She shared with me a shortcut her father sometimes used that I could follow that would shave some time from my journey.

"Your parents aren't meeting you in Bristol, are they Jim?"

"No Chloe, I did not tell the truth about that, and I feel bad for having done so. But I swear all the rest I spoke is on faith true."

"I believe you."

She reached into her pocket and pulled out the two pence coin the buccaneer had thrown her.

"Here," she said while pressing it into my hand, "you will need this if you are to get back home."

I looked into her eyes, and a feeling came upon my chest and heart that was both joyful and painful. Without a first thought I leaned over and kissed her on the lips.

She did not react, nor did she pull away. I thought my heart would burst, and kept my lips on hers until she finally unlocked our kiss.

And then she slapped me.

"You are very impetuous, Jim Hawkins, thinking you can take advantage of me, just before you are leaving on such a dangerous journey! I might never see you again. You might be... you might never come back!"

I didn't know what to say, nor how to respond. I found myself speaking with no forethought.

"I am sorry to leave you, Chloe. For... I... I do truly want to stay."

"Will you stop here again.... on your way home?"

"I promise you Chloe, I will come back."

I quickly kissed her again, and started running toward the road. She ran after me and finally started laughing. I knew I could outrun her, but took care I didn't go too fast. She caught up with me. I stopped, and she gave me one more hug.

"You be careful, Jim Hawkins," she said, "and be sure and come back to me."

"I will," I shouted, as I sped off at full speed

"I'm going to marry you someday, Jim Hawkins!" her voice echoed in the distance.

My heart raced at the thought.

Chapter Eight

The Escape

I made my way to Bristol allowing myself neither rest nor the luxury of any stops along the journey. A heightened sense of urgency gave wings to my feet. My thoughts alternated between the journey ahead and the convoluted and confusing feelings I felt toward Chloe. I knew I'd neither the time nor constitution to continue this internal battle, and so brushed them aside as best I could.

True to her word, the shortcut I traversed caused me to reach Bristol before evening arrived, and soon I entered the town and found myself on Noland Street. I made some casual inquiries about the whereabouts of a certain "scoundrel" they called John Silver, and the local townspeople were not stingy in their pride at having the pleasure to be the host of his demise. Because of this, I knew both his hour of execution, which was the day after morrow at mid-day, and further, that he was being kept in the Admiralty Stockade, which was on the southern edge of the town near the fish warehouses. I was also able to find the office of the town magistrate and made straight away for it.

When I arrived, it was closed. A sign inside said it would open again the morrow. I pounded on the door, hoping someone was still inside. A young man in military uniform opened the door and peered out.

"Yes, what is it?"

"I am here to see the Magistrate."

He stood at attention while only his eyes perused me up and down skeptically, as he undoubtedly took in my mismatched clothes.

"About?"

"John Silver."

"I am working late. His Excellency will not be in until the morning. What is this matter regarding John Silver?"

"I'm here to help him escape the gallows. That is all I can say until I see the magistrate."

He smiled to himself.

"Escape the gallows? That will take a miracle. He is scheduled to hang at mid-day the day after morrow."

"I have information that may have some bearing upon that decision. What time will the Magistrate be here in the morning?"

"About nine o'clock." He started to close the door and stopped midway, as if remembering something. "Who shall I say has called?"

"Jim. James Hawkins. Will you see that he gets my message and desire to meet with him?"

"I will. Good day, Mr. Hawkins."

I was now left with no other option than to spend the night and plead my case in the morning.

Bristol was a typical fishing town and port located on the western shores of Great Britain. Its population in past years had grown in great number. It was a juxtaposition of shanty shacks and fish processing houses on the one hand, and the modern beginnings of a civilized city on the other. It seemed odd to walk down the streets and see these types of dwellings side by side, with no rhyme nor reason. The people were the same. The rogues and buccaneers all tended to congregate toward the water's edge, where many a grog shack and tavern catered to their every whim, no matter how vile their debaucheries. In the town proper were the newer upstarts and proper citizens, and here you found hotels, barristers' offices, very few taverns and all the trappings generally associated with the gentry class.

I took stock of my limited funds and decided, after a reconnaissance of the area, that suitable accommodations of that gentry's class were not in my budget, and resolved to find them elsewhere. As luck would have it, there was a large stable near the Admiralty Stockade, and I found that it would serve my purposes, having spent many a night in the stables at the Admiral Benbow Inn and suffering no ill effects.

Having secured, in a word, my night's lodgings, I decided to wait for darkness to fall and see if I could stealthily make my way down to the stockade and at least speak with Silver, even if through a window opening.

After a few hours' rest, I awoke and started toward the docks. As darkness set in, gas streetlights burned along with the many candles flickering within the windows. The combination cast eerie shadows on the walkways and down the various alleyways. It was almost as if I had been transported into a different world; one inhabited by characters of dubious ethics and intentions. My progress was impeded numerous times by people who attempted to lure me into nefarious establishments with various promises of pleasure.

I took note of my stomach and decided I needed to eat something to satisfy the groaning that I'm sure everyone I passed could hear. Not paying much attention to where I was located, I suddenly found myself in front of the Spyglass Inn, John Silver's old establishment. I crept up to the door and peered in. It still had the same appearance as my first visit, nearly three and a half years ago. Red curtains scantily covered the windows, with tables scattered about and overflowing with buccaneers. I half expected to see John Silver burst forth from the back room, and glide from table to table with his most charismatic attitude and spouting fallacious niceties. But no, it was not he who appeared. Rather, it was a wretched looking man—gaunt, tall and with eyes that darted endlessly from side to side. He was walking from table to table, speaking to the patrons. I entered and sat down.

"What will it be for ye?" asked the lanky man.

"I've got two pence. What can I get for that?"

"Two pence, is it? We's got a stew that will satisfy you."

"That will be fine," I replied.

"Grog?"

I shook my head no. He showed no emotion, one way or the other, and disappeared into the back. He returned shortly with the stew, which either because I was thoroughly famished, or it was well made, smelled and tasted delicious.

After the meal I made my way through the alleyways of Bristol and reached the area where the Admiralty Stockade was located. I decided to wait in the shadows of one of the fish warehouses while my eyes adjusted to the darkness and I could get my bearings.

My eyes finally made out a number of shadows lurking about directly in front of me near the back wall of the jail. I was unable to clearly hear words spoken, but could easily discern they were speaking with someone within the jail through a small window. One of these shadows carried something shaped like a small goatskin pouch, and slowly backed up from the jail, hunched over, while the rest quickly scurried behind him. This shadow then set down whatever they were carrying, and began to strike a flint repeatedly. Without any other notice, a flame as if from the end of a cannon erupted on the ground and slowly snaked its way toward the jail. I watched in astonishment.

As the flame reached its destination, I had the horrifying realization of what was about to happen when…

A deafening sound, as if from a dozen cannons firing simultaneously, shook my entire body and threw me to the ground. A huge pillar of flame and smoke bellowed out from the jail's sidewall and engulfed the sky. Charred bricks and mortar aflame rained down in abandon over the entire area. I could faintly make out the sound of screaming and shouting. My ears, already sore, were now revisiting the pain of the days before. I pushed myself up from the ground where I had fallen and stumbled out from the safety of the shadows with a curiosity and desire to observe all that was occurring.

Shadows of men rushed toward the frame of the jail that once held a solid brick wall and entered through the opening the explosion had created. Other shadows were running out of the jail toward the countryside. I then observed that the men who had gone inside returned again, helping someone walk quickly within their grasp. Then, horrors. They were rushing right in my direction. A myriad of options crossed my mind. Should I run? Lurch back into the shadows? Announce myself? Seemingly as if an hour had passed, they were so close that my actions would have been of no consequence.

As they got closer, I stepped aside and saw that the man in their midst was none other than John Silver, hobbling on his crutch. I observed he was being shoved more than once, rather than moving on his own volition, by two buccaneers, who were also yelling for him to hurry up.

I followed closely behind and witnessed how they pushed him into the first wagon, of which I could now see that there were two waiting. The men started to pile into it. Shots rang out from the direction of the jail, and I could feel the balls whizzing by us through the air.

The rest of the men filled up the second wagon, and I found myself jumping into it too. I just jumped in: no plan, no reason. I've no idea why. I bowed my head down to cover my identity.

The horses were whipped, and we started off down the road at a swift pace. The shots grew dimmer in volume as we traveled deeper into the forest, and any hope of reversing my flippant decision to join these shadowy figures diminished with each second that passed.

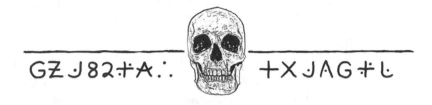

GZ J82⊹A∴   ⊹X JΛG⊹L

Chapter Nine

Meeting an Old Friend

The next passage of time was both frightening and seemed as if it would never end. We were bouncing and rolling about over rutted roads in the dark of night at breakneck speed. It was difficult to keep from being bruised by the lurching and swaying of the wagon. I lost all sense of bearing and was unable to get even a glimpse of where we were heading. I hung on for dear life. None of the men in my wagon took notice of me or were speaking to each other. The fierce and laboured breathing from the horses' strenuous output could be heard, as well as the cracking of the whips that kept them at their pace.

Finally, the two wagons slowed down and stopped. I peered out over the wagons' railing and could observe a small clearing with a fire in the middle. A couple of buccaneers were waiting with pistols drawn until they recognized who was arriving. The men jumped out. I remained in the back of the wagon, crouched low behind the sideboard.

And then I clearly saw him, hobbling on his crutch toward the fire. It was as if we were parted only yesterday, he looked so similar. Tall, lanky, his long brown hair hanging to his shoulders beneath his three-pointed hat. His face showed more aging, yet it was hardly noticeable. He had a slight shadow of a beard

67

growing. And his smile. It seemed to light up the area it was so broad and cheerful. He looked around the men and waved his arm in a regal way.

"Aye, me mates. 'Twas a fine job of ye blowing the outerds of that there jail, it was," said Long John. "Almost blew all of me innerds along with it tho', and you can lay to that."

He brushed debris from his clothes in an overtly animated manner while the buccaneers laughed.

"Was a close call, that's for sure," one of the buccaneers quipped.

"That's not the half of it," Silver continued, "but that tale's for another day, it is. We've not much time to be wasting here, so I suggests we rest up and keeps our heels to the gallows whilst we make plans for getting off this infernal rock. Who be in charge of this fine group of scallywags?"

"He has not arrived yet," said one of them.

"You made us a promise, John Silver," stated another, "and we intends to be collectin' on it. It's why we took you along with us instead of lettin' you rot in that jail."

"Aye, a promise I made and a promise I'll keep. You'll be paid tenfold for your troubles, just as ol' Jasper promised ye, I can attest to that. What I knows will—"

A pistol shot rang out. Down fell one of the men, firing his flintlock pistol into the ground as he met it, blood oozing from his neck. Another shot quickly followed and another buccaneer screamed and fell down, clutching his chest. Shouting filled the air as six or eight men surrounded Long John and the others, cutlasses and pistols drawn. One of these men shouted for the others to not move, or face the consequences.

Out of the shadows stepped Morgan. Morgan the pirate. Pistol drawn. He slowly sauntered up to Long John, raised the pistol toward his head and stood there, head arched back, face in a scowl. The fire's crackle and crickets chirping in the background were the only sounds I could hear besides my heart pounding voraciously within my head. A scornful look turned into a sneering smile as Morgan stood there, Silver at his mercy.

"You do remember me, yea?" asked Morgan.

An eternity passed in my mind. Silver broke out into a great big smile.

"Well, fancy this. Morgan! Morgan hisself 'tis. By the powers, you can't be 'magining how glad I am to see you still alive and kicking, and that's a fact. How is it—"

Silver stopped abruptly as Morgan thrust his arm forward and pressed his pistol into Silvers' throat.

"Long John Silver. Always a way with the words, you are. This time, they won't be of any use."

Silver raised his hands in a surrendering gesture while leaning on his crutch.

"Morgan. Morgan, me good friend. How can you say that about ol' John Silver? I didn't want to leave you on that island. You can lay to that. The captain and that doctor were taking me back for the gibbet, that they were. They was the ones that left you and Gerry to die. I tried reasonin' with 'em, telling 'em that it would be the Christian thing to do, to bring you back and all with us. But nay, they'd be having none of it, they wouldn't. If it were up to me, I would have—"

"Enough, Silver," said Morgan as he shook his head. "This tale is becoming tiresome. Tell me now why I shouldn't kill you where you stand?"

"I'm a bit in confusion, Morgan. Why would ye be wantin' to send me to the reaper after helpin' escape me out of jail?"

"I had nothin' to do with that. I came here to watch you hang and die on the gibbet like the scurvy dog you are. 'Twas then I heard scuttlebutt from the wharf rats that this jailbreak was in the works. We laid low at this spot this afternoon and then followed these scallywags until they sprang you out. 'Twas my hope you'd be blown up in the process, based on the way these boat rats placed the charges. But nay. You beat back the reaper again, and here we be."

He lowered his pistol and slowly circled Silver, eying him as a predator does its prey.

"But this is an even more fortunate turn of events... being that I've been dreamin' of nothing else but yer dyin' at me hands for the past two years."

Morgan stopped and stared stone-faced at Silver. Then a bemused look graced his face.

"Wondering how I got off that accursed island, John Silver? Are ye?"

"Morgan, me hearts full of fair sailin' winds at yer good fortune of having gotten off that—"

"Always the talker. Thinkin' big soundin' words and praise will *mitigate* what ye've done. It'll do you no good this time, Silver."

Silver stared perplexedly at Morgan as if searching for an answer.

"Surprised I know of such a word, eh Silver? I've a lot of surprises, especially for you."

Morgan holstered the pistol in his sash and pulled out a dagger, reflecting the light with it that emanated from the fire.

"We made a raft out of palm trees, and used our pantaloons for sail. We were in the trades for a couple of weeks until provisions were gone and all seemed lost. We looked up, and all miraculous like, a merchant ship from the East India Trading Company was seen in the distance. We used the shots from the pistols to signal them. Remember them three shots you were so kind to be leavin' us? They heard them and picked us up. A bit ironic that was.

"And the whole time I am thinking of only one thing, John Silver. How I am going to kill the most treacherous, lyingest, dispicablest, vilest human being I has ever had the misfortune to run in with. Painfully. Slowly. Ah... my nights lit up with pleasure as I runned it over and over again in me mind.

You'd 'ave thought from my outward appearance I was thinking of lilies in the springtime."

His men started to laugh mockingly.

"Morgan, me friend of friends, I be saddened you'd be thinkin' of yer good mate John Silver in such vile and nefarious ways, I am. I've always considered you a mate indeed. And you can lay to that. And 'specially at this time, Morgan, when the treasure of a lifetime be waitin' for us to just go and get her. Snatch her right up, we can. Surely we be able to work this out my friend, can't we?"

"What's this 'bout a treasure? Another one of yer stinkin' lies to buy yer wretched self a few more minutes of life? I ain't believin' none of what comes out of yer lips again, Silver."

"He speaks the truth," one of the surrounded buccaneers said. "'Tis why we escaped him in the first place." The others murmured affirmatively.

"He's lied to all of you. There be no treasure on that island. I spent over a year on it, and nothing was ever found. He and his supposed 'captors' left with all that was there, and for all I know profited from it with the others that took it."

Silver started to relax. I could see it in his frame. He hobbled over toward Morgan, and leaned into him.

"All of what you speak 'tis true, Morgan, 'ceptin' the sharin' part. But hears me out. Those devils did abscond with the treasure, I'll attest to that. But the treasure we were lookin' for was only a pittance compared to the real treasure buried there. A treasure so vast, that it be beyond all 'magination. The treasure of kings and pharaohs, 'tis."

Morgan starred at Silver distrustingly. His facial features relaxed slightly.

"I'm ears for your tale," said Morgan as he lowered the dagger. "Be forewarned. Me patience be thin with you."

"Me old dear cellmate told me 'bout it," Silver continued. "Said he was with Redbeard when they looted the *Isabella* and killed all aboard her. 'Twas a secret cargo that they found. Full of gold and jewels the likes of which neither man nor maiden has witnessed before or since. Came from the great Middle East, said he. Redbeard buried it on Treasure Island in a secretive way, and then killed all the witnesses. We knows Red Beard was killed in Pirates' Cove, so it still be there, waiting for us."

"If Redbeard killed all the witnesses, how did this mate know where the treasure be?" asked Morgan suspiciously.

"Me cellmate Jasper was his first mate, Morgan. He made a copy of the map. Once Redbeard was dead, he was putting together his own crew to go gets it, which is these mates here, I'm a guessin'. Unfortunately, this mate who told me the tale was 'rested for killing the magistrate's son on board the *Isabella*, and scheduled to get rope choked the morrow."

"Why would he entrust this treasure to such a trustworthy, upstanding member of the Crown as you, of all people?" smirked Morgan.

His men laughed again.

"Didn't want the secret goin' down to Davy Jones himself. I promised him if'n I 'scaped out in his stead I would be sendin' some of the proceeds to his dear family. Tonight's jailbreak was planned by him and these buccaneers. But as the fates sometimes dictates, he died of sickness only this morn, and they brokes me out instead."

"Died more'n likely at *yer* hands, I'd be guessin."

Morgan walked around the fire, his eyes fixated on Silver.

"You've spun quite an interesting yarn, John Silver. A *coward's* tale, if ever I've heard one."

"Morgan, by the powers, I am tellin' you the straight up truth. You've got my full affy-davy, my word of honour, on this. Shiver me timbers, man, I pleads you to just ask these mates."

Morgan turned his attention toward the other captives and eyed them as they stood still, most of them trembling with fear. He looked down at his dagger and flashed it again in the dancing lights of the fire. He walked closer toward Silver.

"Ya know, Silver, as good as this tale of yours sounds, I'm a bettin' that, like most everything you spew out, it's covered and spun round a lie. So I'll just be gettin' my sweet revenge and findin' me own treasure elsewhere."

"Hold on, Morgan. I can prove me tale," Silver shouted. "Don't go rushing to a bad judgment on the slimmest of evydense. Let me shows you something first."

Silver reached into his pocket and pulled out a gold coin, holding it between his thumb and forefinger and moving it in the firelight, creating a beautiful flickering golden glow with each twist.

Morgan reached over and yanked it out of his hand, eyeing it carefully in the firelight.

"What's this?"

"Part of the treasure the old man be givin' me for proof. Let your own eyes tell the tale, Morgan. You can see the Pharaoh King's picture on the coin."

"Aye," said Morgan, still dubious. "A Pharaoh it looks to be."

"That proves the tale, don't it? With this coin we can get the map that will lead us straight to the treasure."

"And where be this supposed map?"

"Pirate's Cove," Silver replied, almost smiling.

"Aye, it would be there, indeed. And how do we get it?"

"He shared with me how to do it. That'll be my little secret, for safety's sake and all."

"That be your take on what's to be?"

"Aye. And Morgan, if'n it ain't there, then I'll be the one handin' you the dagger and begging you to thrust it into my heart, and you can lay to that. Because there is treasure aplenty waiting for us, enough that we will never be having to do another bit of workin' in this, or ten, lifetimes. I'm askin' you to not let this treasure's location die with me here. I mades a promise to ol' Jasper to help his family. And you know me, a promise made is a promise kept."

"Aye. I remember a number of yer promises nigh three years ago, I do."

Morgan turned and addressed the captive men.

"Is what he's sayin' ringin' true?"

"Aye, we were recruited by Jasper to get a ship and sail," one of buccaneers started. "Paid us half our wages with gold, he did, with promises of more gold to follow. After the magistrate's men grabbed 'im, we was given a note, all secret like, that laid plans for his breakout along with the black powder canisters. When we got inside, we only found Silver there. He tells us that Jasper is dead and that he knows where the treasure be. We'd never seen the coin before, but his tale rings true. I says we need 'im if we're ever to find that treasure."

The other buccaneers mumbled agreement amongst themselves.

Morgan paced around the fire, seemingly deep in some sort of thought, talking out loud to himself and almost shouting at times. Finally he stopped and shook his head.

"I'm not sure how ye always seems to end up in the crow's nest, John Silver, but the winds seem to favour you on this one."

"Morgan, I tolds you, I've always had yer best interests in mind. If I could 'ave I would 'ave slit the throats of those leavin' you on that despicable island and turned stem to stern and picked you up, and you can lay to that. 'Tween us here we've almost a full crew. We can get to the island and split the bundt up amongst us all, and no man's the poorer for it."

"And who will lead this crew, John Silver, you?"

"Me? Oh, no Morgan, I'm not for that. No, as you can see," he winked looking downward, "I don't have the sea-legs no more for captainin' anything. Never was cut out for it. No. I'm thinking it 'twill be you that leads us to this king's fortune, *Captain* Morgan."

"Jasper told us he already had a captain paid for, that he'd be meeting us here after the escape, said he," offered one of the buccaneers.

"Looks like them plans 'ave changed," replied Morgan.

"Who be this?"

A loud voice shouted from behind me, as all eyes turned my direction. I felt a set of hands grab the back of my jacket and careened through the air like a dead partridge. I landed not ten feet from the group of buccaneers.

"I caught him spyin' on us from inside the wagon," the voice continued.

Morgan looked over and down at me with the same attention as one would give an insect passing by, and turned back toward Silver. Then I noticed a sort of recognition. His face squinted. He turned back to look down at me again, quizzically this time.

"It can't be," said he to himself.

Then a smile. Diabolical in nature. Fearful in intent. He stepped closer, and stared raptly upon my presence.

"Would ye be a certain Jim Hawkins?" asked he.

I was frozen with fear and dared not answer. I tried to avoid John Silver's stare, but he caught my eye and immediately recognized who I was.

"I believe it is, Morgan," Silver volunteered. "Fancy that. Young Jim Hawkins, landing in our camp. Like a pheasant falling out of a tree. Seems providential, don't it?"

"Looks like I'll get me quest for blood this evening after all. Pick him up," he ordered his men.

- - - - - - - - - -

Chloe's Diary: 25 April, 1867

I have had a most unnerving experience. Earlier today some men came by our farm, and while purchasing some supplies let slip that the previous evening a certain pirate named John Silver was broken out of jail. My heart sank while hearing of this, for I couldn't imagine that young Jim Hawkins had anything to do with an outlandish act such as that. Upon further listening, I learned that the authorities were looking for a certain young man that was making inquiries about John Silver the night before his escape.

"Did you, per chance, learn who this man was?" I asked of him.

"No. Only that he hasn't been seen since the escape."

"Aye to that," said the other. "They want him for questioning."

"Yeah, questioning," the first one added. "You know how that Magistrate is. Likely as not he'll hang the poor lad first as question him."

My heart flew into my throat upon hearing this news. I was scared and felt helpless to do anything about it. How can this be? Could it be my Jim who is being accused of such a treasonous act? There must be some mistake.

My chores the rest of the day were meaningless, as I thought of the horrors that may be inflicted on him at this very moment. After dinner I made a decision. I am going to wait until Mum and Father are asleep, and I will venture to Bristol to see if I can offer any assistance in finding my Jim and clearing up this matter. I am unable to stay here and know not of his fate. If he has gotten mixed up with these pirates, either through his own volition or not, then I fear the worst may have befallen him. I also know that I would never forgive myself if I were not there. I feel as in a nightmare, unable to awake.

- - - - - - - - - -

Two of Morgan's men picked me up and held me firmly by both arms. Escape was a futile dream. Morgan walked toward me and held out his dagger in a menacing manner.

"You're going to die like the coward you are, Hawkins. 'Tis your traitorous actions that stole our ship from under us and left me and Gerry to die on that island. There's no Doctor Livesey or Captain Smollett to protect you now, boy. And I promises to make it as slow and painful a death as I can."

He raised his dagger. I braced myself for the painful jab that was sure to follow, and heard myself cry out, *"No, please don't"* as it raced toward my chest. At the last minute I closed my eyes and prayed to the Lord to make it quick.

"Arghhh!"

I heard a loud scream as my eyes quickly opened. I observed Long John's crutch handle wrapped around Morgan's wrist, holding it from going any further than the few inches it lay in front of my chest. Morgan was struggling and shaking, trying to free his arm. He finally stopped and turned around.

"What are you doing?" he shouted at Long John. "Let go of me arm you mangy dog! I'm going to skewer this little mackerel and there's not a thing yer goin' to be doin' about it, you hear me John Silver?"

"Aye, it's a fine idea yer got there, Morgan, a fine one indeed," said Silver. "Would do it me very self if 'twer me this lad had a hand in strandin' on that accursed island. Yes indeedy. It surely would do this world good to let the likes of his do goody kind savor the cold taste of a dagger's steel skewing his gizzards, I grant you that."

He hesitated and looked around at the motley crew surrounding the fire.

"But I be wonderin'—"

"You wonder what?" asked a now frustrated Morgan.

"Aye, I be wonderin' if'n this here guppy might not come to value in future times if we needs someone of his kind."

"Speak your mind plain, John Silver," Morgan snarled.

"That I will, Captain, that I will."

He hobbled around Morgan and almost got between Morgan and myself.

"I'm supposin' that we'll be needin' a ship and wares and such to undertake the journey back to that treacherous island. And bein' as we've got no ship I'm awares of, I thinks we could make good use of a lad like this in case something goes awry while we's acquiring what we needs."

"Go on."

"Well then, I've got no personal care for Hawkins hisself here. He was part of thems that chained me ups for the ride to the gallows nigh near two years ago. The facts is though, he's a friend of that Captain Smollett. In me eyes, he'd be good fodder in case we gets into a delicate sityation and needs to trades our way out. Then again, maybe it's of no matter and we're lucky enough to haven't any needs of him, and that's a fact too."

"He was mighty partial by that, Captain," said Morgan, thinking out loud. "You're speakin' right there, John Silver."

"Then again, Captain, I could be all wrong and carving him up here all slowly like would be the quickest way to—"

"Aye, I'm not takin' to that now," Morgan interrupted. "We will need a parlay chip casin' we do run into any English Man-o-wars, and he's as good as any, I reckon."

Morgan side armed his dagger and stared at me with a hateful look that sent shivers down my back. He stepped within inches of my face and held his stare.

"You be in charge of him and keep the little 'squire man' out of my way, Silver. And mark me words. If you and he be planning anything, I will cut you both up, personal."

"Wouldn't think of it, Captain," Silver replied. "As I said, all the same to me if you kill him now or later."

Morgan stormed off as Long John turned toward my captors and ordered the men to let me go. I shook loose of their grips and looked directly at John Silver, who met my eyes with his.

Then he winked at me as a slight smile crossed his face.

Chapter Ten

Narrative Continued by Chloe:
Captain Smollett

27 April, 1867

I arrived in Bristol before the early morn without any major incident. Although tired, I was able to inquire as to the location of the magistrate's office, and fully satisfied myself that I would be there when he arrived. I sat down on a bench in front of the office and went over in my mind the afternoon before, when I learned of my Jim Hawkins being accused of helping those awful pirates. It seems as if a bad dream. And yet, after having saved his life once, it may be true that it was only to prolong the inevitable destiny that he was facing. Death at the hands of the authorities—or worse, buccaneers. Although these thoughts and more were only swirling about my imagination, the thoughts were nonetheless painful.

- - - - - - - - - -

After the men who conveyed the news about the jailbreak left the farm, I implored my parents to come with me to

Bristol to see if we could help with searching for Jim. My father was particularly adamant:

"Chloe, we are not even sure it is this Jim Hawkins these men are speaking of."

"Father, I know he is in trouble. In my heart, I know something is amiss. I am unable to explain to you how, but I know."

"Even if it were he, there is nothing we can do. It is in the hands of the authorities. He may be in grave trouble. We mustn't interfere."

"Father, if it were me would that be your answer?"

"Of course not. But 'tis not you, and no amount of worrying will help. We must let the authorities—"

"Father. We must go to see if we can help."

"There is nothing that we can do."

"Then I will go myself!"

"I forbid it. It will come of no good."

"Mother, I implore, please tell him to let me go."

"He is right, Chloe. We would only add to the confusion and chaos of the incident. We must place our trust that he is not involved, and that all will work out."

"He needs me, Mother, I, I don't know how or why, but I can feel it."

"Chloe," my father said, "you are to stop this at once. I have spoken and that is the end of it."

- - - - - - - - - -

Suddenly my memories were disturbed by the sensing of another person standing near to me. I looked up and saw a towering man, with a captain's hat and uniform, peering down at me. He sported a close kept beard, and I could see he had brown eyes.

"And who might you be, madam?" he asked.

"My name is Chloe Dowling. I'm waiting here to seek an audience with the magistrate."

"A fateful coincidence. I have just arrived to meet with the magistrate myself. Would it be acceptable to you if I sat down?"

"That will be fine," I answered. I thought the company would help relieve some of the worry that was coursing through my mind and body. I was tired and hungry, and desired nothing more than to stay awake until I could learn of any news regarding the prison break and Jim.

"My name is Captain Smollett, of the ship *Hispaniola*."

Tingles started shooting up my spine. Smollett? Could it be?

"The *Hispaniola*?" I asked. "The same ship Jim Hawkins was on, with that despicable pirate John Silver?"

He seemed a bit startled with my question.

"Indeed, madam. The same. And how would you know about this?"

"I'm Jim Hawkins' fiancée. He told me the whole story about you, Long John Silver and Treasure Island."

"Fiancée? Pray tell. That is certainly news to me," he said.

I explained to Captain Smollett the entire story of how it was that I chanced upon Jim and brought him back to the farm after the pirates almost killed him. How his injuries were life threatening and that, through the doctor's help and my nursing, he was brought back to health. And how he agreed to stop back at my farm on his way home.

"Then I, and his Mother, owe you a great deal of thanks, Miss Dowling," he responded. "She has been extremely worried, and is greatly responsible for my having sailed down here to search him out. Do you know where he is?"

"Have you not heard?" I asked.

"Heard? Heard of what? I only arrived in port an hour ago and came directly here."

"Oh, Captain Smollett, it is awful." I fought to hold back the tears that I could feel welling up within me. "There was an escape two nights ago from the Admiralty Stockade. John Silver was one of the criminals that was broken out. Some men came by my farm and relayed how the magistrate believes that a young man may have had a hand in it and are searching for him to question. He has not been seen nor heard from since that night. I am without doubt that it is my, *our* Jim Hawkins, they are speaking about, for he said the entire purpose for his visit here was to speak with John Silver at the stockade. I do not know how he is involved, nor where he is at present, and fear the worst may have befallen him!"

The thought overwhelmed me and I was unable to hold back the tears. I could not bear to think of what may be his fate, and was regretting his loss even at this moment.

"I can attest, Miss Dowling, that the idea of Jim having anything to do with activities such as you describe is preposterous. And further, if he is mixed up with those pirates and they harm him in any way, there will be no place small enough for them to hide from my vengeance, which I can assure you, will be merciless and swifter than the hanging gallows. You mustn't worry about that."

"We must find him," I implored the captain.

"Yes, assuming he is... yes, you are right," he continued, "all stops must be pulled to begin a search at once. If my guess is correct, this is not the sort of operation that would be unknown by others of their ilk. Perhaps a few guinea spread about the docks could loosen up lips to help us in our search."

He stood up with a fervent intention.

"Miss Dowling, it seems as if the Greek Goddess Moira has brought us together with the same intention. I suggest we join forces in our search of... uh, your *fiancé* and my friend. However, I do think it prudent to find out what the Magistrate has knowledge of, and assure him that he is mistaken as to Jim's involvement in such an affair. I can only assume that if he is involved in any manner, it is against his will, and must be treated as such. The magistrate may not know it, but he very well could inadvertently bring Jim into harm's way. Let us wait until he arrives and can question him before we start our search."

- - - - - - - - - -

I am writing again while waiting for Captain Smollett to finish his meeting with the Magistrate, who only arrived a few minutes ago. Their voices are growing louder in intensity with every passing minute. I can hear the captain tell the magistrate that it is inconceivable that Jim would be involved, and swore an oath to Jim's integrity in all matters. The magistrate relayed how more than a dozen of his best soldiers took off after the pirates and were slaughtered mercilessly while on the chase.

The magistrate then told Smollett that because of the serious nature of these crimes, he had ordered additional troops that would arrive the morrow and immediately start their search to track the pirates down. Captain Smollett implored the magistrate to wait one more day so he can make some inquiries, explaining the predicament and peril that may await an innocent man. Finally, the magistrate relented and gave Captain Smollett until the day after morrow noon before he sets out for the pirates that destroyed his jail and murdered his men.

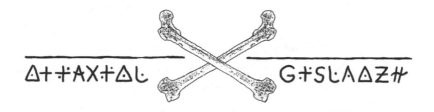

Δ+⸸AX⸸Δᒪ   G⸸SᒪΛΔZ⸸

Chapter Eleven

Narrative Resumed by Jim Hawkins: The New Captain

I surveyed the lot of buccaneers around the fire and could not describe a more mish-mash, sorry looking group of miscreants. Not one of them could have cleaned up to be worthy of a chimney sweep. Scars and dirt caked on them like bark; tattoos covered them like flies around a dung heap. And their clothes! It seemed the more contrasting and offensive to the eyes a group of colors together could heave on a viewer, the more likely it was these pirates would be wearing them. Dingy, loose fitting silky shirts graced their upper bodies, whilst their pantaloons were of a much coarser material resembling a sheep's hair blanket. Again, the contrast of colors was startling. A blue top with purple pantaloons. Gold atop red. Most of them swashed a kind of striped sash round their waists, which held their pantaloons up and provided a place to attach their cutlasses and knives. Round their throats, many of them had an additional piece of cloth tied in a knot, which sufficiently contrasted with the rest of the outfit as to assure total offensiveness to the senses.

And the smells. I sincerely wished I could stifle my nose, they were so abhorrent. This crew of buccaneers was by far the motliest and most dangerous group of criminals I had ever encountered in person or whimsy. However, this was the least of my worries.

Thankfully, whether intentional or not, John Silver had been able to buy us some time. His reasoning to Morgan was on solid footing, his logic unarguable. Yet, I could not dismiss the thought I entertained deep in my mind: the chances of the Queen's Navy not sending these rogues to a well-deserved watery death because of keeping *me* hostage seemed remote, at best. However, their belief in such an outcome would keep me alive, at least for the time being. I turned my mind to other matters.

Escape was not an option for two reasons. The first, and most obvious, was that I had no idea where I was. It would be pointless to run off into the night and end up in a direr predicament. The more immediate reason was even more complicated to me. I knew I would be risking John Silver's life too, not that I was too concerned in this regard. After all, I reasoned, his bluff, if it really were one, almost cost me my life.

Morgan had been pacing about the fire for at least an hour's time, studying the gold coin Silver had given him, and mumbling to himself loudly. Nothing coherent. At least not anything that I was able to discern. I dare say he must have been at a crossroads inwardly. His earnest desire to kill John Silver had been capriciously yanked from beneath him; and now his outward frustration and disappointment at not having been able to skewer me. Both of these outcomes due in total to one of man's oldest and deadliest sins—*greed*. It was clear that John Silver was clever enough to rope him into his scheme based upon it.

Truth be told, the idea of another treasure such as the one John Silver described brought up that same unpardonable sin within me too. Ancient pharaohs and the mysteries of the Middle East were subjects that were simply words to me on paper as a schoolboy. Now, these antiquities were promising to show themselves to me through the untold wealth of this mysterious treasure. I imagined being able to peer into the eyes of the statues of gods and rulers that were last seen and worshiped by heathens more than 3000 years ago! It was humbling. Perhaps even the great Queen of ancient Egypt, Cleopatra, had worn some of the crowns or necklaces that we were about to set off and discover!

Rumours had come of great cities partially covered in sand within that region of the world. There were varied descriptions of structures, such as a huge lion with wings and a pyramid built of stones bigger than a house that had been relayed back to the West through Napoleon's conquests.

Perhaps this treasure was a part of that history?

Morgan finally stopped his pacing and called the buccaneers to surround him.

"Mates," said he, "I have been cogitatin' on this treasure, and I am only able to arrive at a single plan to get us there, and in haste. We've to steal a ship, pure and simple. And as far as I can reason, the only place we can do that is where we just left."

"Beggin' your pardon, Morgan," said one, "but it's seemin' to me that there's heaps of trouble waitin' for us if we return there."

"No doubt, the magistrate has sent word for more troops and the likes to tries and finds us," offered another.

"Aye, I've been thinkin' like that too," said Morgan. "But then I reasons: would this magistrate think we'd be back agin so soon after our deed? I thinks not, says I. No. I'm a thinkin' he believes we'll try to travel over to the Dovers and we either have a ship waitin', or we're planning on borrowin' one. That's what I thinks."

"I thinks you're right as rain on that one Morgan, yes I do," said Silver. "Mates, this magistrate's thinkin' must be that we're running high tail away from Bristol, not circlin' back. This here's a real gem of a plan, and you can lay to that."

"As I was *sayin'*," Morgan went on, emphasizing that last word. "What we needs to do is circle back and find us a fair runnin' ship."

"With cannon," another quipped.

"With cannons," Morgan continued, "that will make it to Pirate's Cove. Once we've arrived, if the ship will do, and her sails is strong, we'll keep her. If not, we'll be able to negotiate another suitable vessel."

"Morgan?" asked one of the buccaneers, "how comes yer makin' up the plans here. Don't we get a vote on it too?"

"Well there scabby, that there's a good question. Yes, indeed. A question that needs answering, and that's a fact. Now, I could come up with all kinds of the queen's talk 'bout how this and that is a fact, and 'splain it out to you. I could do that. Or, I could pull out me trusty cutlass and lob off one of yer ears. An seein' as I'm feelin' a bit peeved from all the evening's activities and disappointments, I'm leanin' toward yer losing yer ear."

"'Twas only a question, Morgan. I meant no offense."

"No offense taken, mate. I'm speakin' square with you. But your point is sound and I've been puttin' thought to that too. So I'm offerin' meself to be captain. We know the code. So we needs to vote on it. And that's what I'm demandin'; a vote, here and now."

"That won't be necessary," came a booming voice from the dark. We all turned toward the area where it emanated. Presently, out of the shadows of the trees, a commandingly tall figure atop a horse slowly approached the fire, stopped and dismounted.

"Who be ye?" asked Morgan, "and what 'av you to say in this—"

This silhouette reached the ground, turned around, walked into the fire's dancing light, and faced Morgan directly. I've never seen a quicker change in stature than Morgan's as he transformed from the cocky stand of a Sunday morning barnyard rooster to a shrinking shouldered grouse. His hands started to shake noticeably.

"I... I... am beggin' yer pardon, Steele. I had no awares it was you who be speakin'."

"Captain Steele," he bellowed.

Hushed and whispered tones shot through the men like wildfire. Slowly, everyone, including myself, started to step away and distance themselves from Morgan. I looked to Silver for some direction on what to do, but his eyes were transfixed. Captain Steele pulled out his cutlass and rested it by his side. Slowly he surveyed the buccaneers, including the two lying dead on the ground. He made a sort of double clicking sound with his mouth, and within moments, a half dozen men on horseback trotted out from the darkened trees, pistols at the ready. They surrounded us.

"Where is Jasper Jennings?"

Silence.

"I asked a question."

Silver cleared his throat.

"Well, you see, Captain Steele, sir," he started. "Jasper is no longer with us, he ain't."

"And you are?"

"John Silver, sir."

"Ah yes, the quartermaster to Flint, was it not?"

"Why shiver me timbers, Captain, sir, I be flattered that ye've had an earful of someone as insignificant as me."

"Don't be. It's not a reputation you should wish. Is there more to this story of Jasper's demise?"

Silver seemed to stumble. I'd never seen him at a loss for words. His neck got quite red; his forehead started sweating profusely. The crackle and popping of the fire seemed to grow louder while the flames cast dancing shadows everywhere. A sinister vision indeed.

"Ah, well, yes, Captain, sir. You see," Silver continued, "this very morning, right in me cell, he died, he did, before the magistrate's men were to hang him this very day. Very peaceful 'twas... and of course, it be of natural causes."

"Naturally," Captain Steele replied sarcastically. "So tell me, Silver, am I to grow old and gray listening to you spin this yarn, or is there more knowledge relating to the point of my question in this narrative of yours?"

He grew noticeably angry and seemed to be shortening of patience.

"There's the matter of a certain map that was rightfully part of his estate," Steele continued.

"Yes, sir, there was. Is. That be right as rain, it be. He told me personal about it. And how to get it, too, and you can lay to that."

"So you know of it?"

"Yes."

"Exactly where it is?"

"That's a fact."

"Tell me more."

"Nothing more to tell, Captain, sir. He gaves me a gold coin with a pharisee image on it and 'structions on how to gets it. The map, I mean."

"Where is this coin?"

Long John looked over at Morgan, and Captain Steele followed his gaze.

"I has it," Morgan said, "and as I sees it, thems that has it has the right to it—or at least a part of it."

"Oh, I see, *Captain* Morgan I think it is you were about to be named?"

"That be right, and you can—"

Morgan had started to regain his upright stature during his reply to Captain Steele, when Steele suddenly lifted his cutlass and reverse swung it around his hip in an wide arc. In one fluid move he swung it by Morgan's head, and completely severed his left ear and some hair with the blade's pass. Morgan screamed, dropped the coin and fell to his knees as he grabbed the side of his head. Steele stomped on Morgan's shoulders and he fell further to the ground, sprawled flat out on his back. Captain Steele dug his right boot into Morgan's chest.

"I heard a few moments ago you were partial to cutting off someone's ear. Now you know what it feels like." He turned toward one of his men. "Hand the coin to me." They picked it up and tossed it to him.

"It appears, Morgan, it has now come up for debate who actually has the right to possess this coin."

Steele lifted his boot off Morgan and studied the coin closely for a few moments. Then, he flipped it up in the air, caught it, and turned his gaze toward Silver.

"Are you prepared to 'share' this information, regarding the map's location, with us, Silver?"

"Absolutely, Captain. You can lay to that... of course, it be behoovin' to me not to be disclosin' that there information 'til the 'propriate time and all, as I wants to be part of the crew that finds, *and* shares in it."

"Attend to this man," Captain Steele ordered, pointing to Morgan. He was still on the ground, whimpering and crying, holding the side of his head. One of Steele's men dismounted his horse and came over with a ship doctor's bag and started to clean the wound.

"Silver, you know of who I am. I suffer fools lightly, and traitors the less. Having the likes of you to depend on goes against all of my instincts, and yet it seems we've no other choice. Fate has dealt her hand, and we must play it. I could perhaps torture it out of you, but if misled the treasure will be lost forever. But hear me clearly, Silver, if there is any villainy in this matter, I will hang you by your thumbs from the foremast, skin you alive and watch the crows pick your bones clean. Map, or no map."

"Oh you can be sure, Captain, nothing of the sort be 'volved in this. Jasper mades me promise to save a portion for his family, he did, and that's all I intends to do.... 'ceptin', of course, a little portion for me troubles."

"But of course," replied the captain.

Steele walked around the fire slowly gazing at the men, and then turned back to Silver.

"Jasper told me we need to sail to Cow's Island and retrieve the map. Is this so?"

"That be an error, Captain, and not bein' what he told me. He said it was to be found in Pirates Cove, and you can lay to that. That's the God's truth or so help me, you can cut me down where I stands."

"Well, Silver, it appears you've passed the first test for honesty. I hope it didn't upset your constitution too much by telling the truth."

By his tone of voice, there was no answer expected to be forthcoming from Long John.

GL✝35X△⋏ ✝J53∴✝XL

Chapter Twelve

The Seaman's Oath

"**M**en, I want to be very clear, so I advise you to take heed and listen closely with both ears," Captain Steele began. He looked toward Morgan and smirked slightly.

"I was commissioned by Jasper Jennings to captain a ship and crew to find this treasure. He was to fund it with his gold, and gave me a down payment. When he hired you men, he was acting on my behalf, being that I am unwelcome in most of the Crown's colonies. Since Jasper was arrested and, apparently, died of *natural causes*," he looked to Silver at this comment, "we do not have him to guide us. But, we have someone in his stead who knows where the map is and how to get hold of it.

"Some of you know me. Some of us have sailed together. Others by my reputation alone. A reputation, I must say, that is true in all ways. I have been a privateer and buccaneer for over twenty years, and had my fair share of successes. And you can be sure, any man who crossed me is no more. The reason I signed on to this venture is due to the fact that I believe after we take this treasure, my days of sailing the seas for profiteering, and all of yours, if you so wish, will be over.

"The obstacles are great. The chances for success are in doubt. The plan I have devised will bring the entire English Navy chasing our sails. The price for our heads will be unprecedented. I'll need every man here if we're to make this voyage and be successful in our endeavors. However, if any of you do not desire to serve under my command, you can sign blood oaths to silence and be on your way. It matters not to me.

"If you do join me, then I promise each and every one of you shall benefit in equal shares of this plunder. By reputation you know that with me, a promise made is a promise kept— honour above all else."

He fell silent as he surveyed the lot of us with his granite gaze.

"Be aware, I am now funding this venture on my own, and as per the rules and codes, mine will be the greater portion. However, for those of you not familiar with its contents, it is said to be the largest treasure ever accumulated on this Earth. A fantastic treasure from the most precious of old world Egypt's greatest riches. A horde of gold, diamonds, precious stones and silver. Jasper was there when it was taken from the *Isabella*, and said it could be worth millions of pounds.

"However, anyone who does not pull equal share on this voyage will be cast aside. I expect hard work, and unwavering loyalty. Villainy will be met with a long and painful death, I promise you that. My word is final; my orders immutable. Our code will be strictly enforced, and you will be expected to sign oaths and articles to these terms which will spell out the shares due you.

"You may speak your mind freely now, and we'll take a vote. The captain I am and will be. These are my terms. I need to know herewith and now who will be counted on for this voyage." He looked over at Long John and smiled. "We already have a ship's cook, and I have a trusted quartermaster and doctor. All other positions are open to the best man.

"Tell me square now, where do the rest of you stand?"

One of Morgan's men shouted: "I say we vote to join now, and work out the dooty's later!"

94

"Aye, that sounds like a good plan," said another.

"I'm with you, Captain," came from the others.

"Me too!" I found myself shouting as loud as I could.

To a man Morgan's men swore a loyalty to Steele. The rest of the buccaneers that Jasper had hired all quickly assented. Steele faced his gaze upon Morgan, who was sitting on the ground with a head bandage.

"As to you Morgan, you are on board against force of will."

"I'd sooner die than join you," he whimpered.

"And you will. But not tonight. You have no choice in the matter. The only reason I didn't kill you is I need every skilled seaman I can get, and it seems we are already two short because of you. But I make this promise to you: if you prove to be loyal, an equal share you will also receive. If not, you will suffer the dire consequences. Do you agree to my terms?"

Morgan sat there and said nothing. Captain Steele reached for his cutlass.

"Do you agree?"

"Aye, I do," said Morgan.

Steele looked to his quartermaster. "How many do we have?"

After counting, he told him twenty-four men, total.

Captain Steele turned around and sat upon a half barrel next to the fire seemingly lost in thought.

His stature was immense—even when sitting. He was at least six feet and a half, quite lean, and held a very stately gait—upright and proud. His clothing was regal. By that I mean he wore black, well-fitted silk pantaloons, with a black satin sash. An almost opalescent lavender silk shirt lay beneath his tailored black leather jacket, with lavender cuffs protruding from the sleeves. This was crowned with a brown-skinned Buccaneer's hat. His face was rugged and his hair a dark auburn. His beard and mustache were two inches long and well manicured. His lips were thin and white teeth shown between them. However, the most striking point that the eyes were attracted to is the large black patch over his left eye, held in place by black lacing tied round his head. He had enormously bushy eyebrows that hung over both his patch and eye. If this were a different occasion and time, I would have taken him for gentry instead of buccaneer.

"We've no time to lose," the captain began. "I know where a ship can be procured, but we must act in haste. Every moment counts and we've mountains to accomplish. My men and I have purchased precious time with the Magistrate's soldiers' blood. We ran into some of his men following you and dispatched the group of them. But, it will not last long. Soon they will re-supply and become a formidable challenge. If you will agree, I will have all the contracts drawn up for our voyage once we are aboard the ship.

"In the meantime, I need two volunteers who are quick on their feet and agile of mind."

Two of the men who arrived with Steele came to the fore and offered their services. I was not privy to what the captain and two buccaneers spoke regarding, but after a while they took off on their horses in the direction of Bristol.

By this time it was mid-morning, as the sun had been up a couple of hours. Most of the men were in small groups of two or three, sitting and talking as if they either knew each other, or were getting acquainted. From what I was able to discern from the general conversations, most of the men were aware of each other by reputation or through friends of friends. Long John made his way to where I sat, hobbled down from his crutch and settled next to me on the ground.

"How ye be doing, Jim me lad?" asked he.

"I've been better."

"That a fact, 'tis?"

"What do you think?"

He scooted closer to me over the ground.

"Yes it 'tis, it 'tis indeedy. Seems the fates herself has brought you and me together again, and I be thankful for it, for the sight agin of you is warmth to me heart, and that's a fact, it 'tis. So tell me, Jim me boy, what have ye been up to these last few years?"

"Not that it is of matter to you, but I've been studying at university in Manchester, while helping my mother at the Admiral Benbow."

"University be it? Pray, what 'ave you been studying there, seamanship?"

"Hardly. Mathematics, science, anatomy, philology, fencing and writing."

"And do you like this here learnin'?"

"I do. It has opened a whole new world for me. I plan on becoming a doctor of medicine when I graduate."

"A doctor, 'tis? Well shiver me timbers. Don't that take the prize. My Jim, a doctor. Well, I wishes ye all the luck to being a mighty fine one, indeedy."

"Silver, you told Morgan it was of no matter to you if he killed me, to murder me at his fancy," I burst out. "I do not think your wishes are quite sincere."

He leaned over and whispered to me.

"Nay, Jim, you can't be thinkin' that? I hads to do it. Let him think I don't cares 'bout yer welfare. Don't you see? He would have killed you if'n I hadn't planted the seed that I did. It were me plan all along."

I just sat there not responding. I could not. My blood was, in a sense, boiling. I knew I was feeling and acting as a child would in this instance. And yet I cared not. Here I was face to face with the man I had risked life and limb to try to save from swinging on the gallows. Yet all I could think of was how angry I felt toward him, and how foolish I had been to lie to my Mother and ignore Dr. Livesey's advice. Something within me changed. Now I could see the truth of it. Silver would have traded me in for his life. I risked mine for his for naught. How stupid I had been! I could not muster the fortitude to even look at him straight again. The wink at the end negated nothing. Morgan could have just as well ignored him, and I would be dead.

Now what am I to do? Perhaps I can escape at a later time? I am not sure. I have made an oath to stay with the crew. Duty bound, with buccaneers, no less. I also admit to myself the captain has painted a good canvas of the rewards that awaited me if I continued on with the voyage. I thought of Chloe, and how we could live our lives together if I did go on. I realized the riches I had acquired from my first adventure to Treasure Island, although providing a comfort, would expire in short order in caring for my education and Mother's old age. There was not enough to raise a family and maintain an assured future. I needed time to think this through.

"You aren't angry at yer old Silver now, Jim, are you?"

"I don't want to talk about it. So how about we do not."

I started to rise.

"Come now Jim, don't go off like this."

I jumped up and went over to the fire and poured myself a cup of broth, which was cooking in a large kettle over it. I looked up and realized that Captain Steele had been watching the two of us the whole time.

He was still staring at Long John.

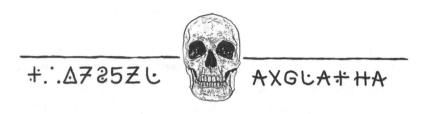

Chapter Thirteen

Narrative Continued by Chloe:
A Lead in Bristol

I have had nothing else to do but wait, and so I have decided to continue chronicling my thoughts and adventures on the captain's stationery to while away the hours. It's now been three or four since he left the ship. I would guess near the midnight hour. All is quiet and I am very tired and ready to fall asleep, although I promised myself I would stay awake until word of my James reached me.

- - - - -

After leaving the magistrate's office earlier this morning, Captain Smollett and I made our way down to the wharf and started to wander through the *seedier* side of Bristol, an area of about eight hectares just north of the main pier. He relayed that most of the known and wanted buccaneers, privateers and seaman looking for work have congregated here for well over one hundred years. It was dotted with various taverns, eateries and warehouses.

We traveled by foot from establishment to establishment, with names such as The Seven Stars, Jolly Sailor and The Rose and Crown. I must confess, even the odd visits throughout the years of a multitude of misbegotten souls to my family's farm, had ill prepared me for understanding how these men live and behave in such depraved conditions; and especially how different they were from my brothers and the neighboring menfolk.

Captain Smollett was extremely gracious in inquiring if I wanted to wait outside each time he decided to go into one of the taverns and make his investigations. I declined. Not for lack of fear upon entering them, as that feeling did arise when I passed each threshold. Rather, I desired having no regrets in my search by not exhausting every possibility, even if it exposed me to the sneers, lecherous smiles and the horrendous smells of these men, if only it might lead to finding my James.

We visited one particular tavern located next to the wharf that overlooked the water called the "Spyglass Inn". The captain shared with me how, many years before, an enemy ship fired a cannonball that shattered a hole through the thick walls, and hence thereafter this hole was used to spot other advancing ships. He also mentioned it was owned by John Silver and that is where he and Jim first met. I despise that man even more after having been there and again realized he was at the root of my present troubles.

Many of these buccaneers we met in the taverns seemed interested in what the captain had to say, and most especially after he mentioned there would be a substantial reward involved, but none of them could offer any solid hope or knowledge of the whereabouts of John Silver or James. It became a discouraging trek through the last of these places, and by perhaps two in the afternoon, we decided we should take a meal on Captain Smollett's ship. We were in the captain's quarters when we heard a knock on the door.

"Yes?" asked Smollett.

A crewman peered around the door, half stepping in.

"Sir, there are two uh... men... here to see you."

"What about? We are eating and I've no time for frivolities."

"Yes sir. They say they have some information regarding the persons you are looking for."

He quickly wiped his mouth with his linen napkin.

"Send them in straight away."

"Yes sir."

He closed the door and the captain looked to me, a glimmer of light in his eyes.

"I was hoping that by spreading the word of a reward through this abominable district that someone would come forward. This could be a fortunate break for us."

There was a light knock on the door. The crewman opened it and two buccaneers entered while looking about the quarters. They were poorly dressed, and the stench had already reached over to me before they were fully inside.

"Gentlemen, do you have some information for me?

"Well, Captain," responded the other one, "we heards you was lookin' for a certain person or persons that recently made their escape from the Admiralty Stockade, and we comes straight away to do our dootys and sees if we can be of some service to you."

"Your duty, is it? Very well. What is it you know about this *certain person or persons*?"

"Well, you see, Captain, we was minding our owns business a few days back, whens we was approached by a couple of mates we'd know—only casually, mind you—and theys propositioned us for going on a sea farin' voyage. And of course, we was inclined to do that, since it had been awhile since our last sea engagement, and our funds be growing low."

"Go on."

"Yes. Well then, these mates told us that they has to take care of some certain business by escaping their mate out of the Admiralty Stockade, and then afterwards we would all meets up and then take off on our voyage."

101

"And where were you to meet up with these 'mates'?"

"Well then, Captain, that there's the spanner in the works. We are supposed to see them in a few hours and then they plans on tellin' us wheres to meet."

"Then we'll meet them with you and find out—"

"No, Captain, I think that would definitely spook them away, since they knows us and if'n anyone else were there, they would be sure to scamper off and then we'd have no chance of learning where it is."

"What do you suggest?"

"Well," started the other, "we thinks it wise to meet with these mates, find out the location, and then come back and relays it to you. That's what we thinks."

"An admirable plan."

They seemed to not notice this last comment while they both perused the inside of the quarters.

"You've got a beautiful ship, Captain," he went on, "and that's a fact. Who be the owner of such a fine and beautiful seafarin' vessel such as this?"

"That would be Squire Trelawney. However, that is no concern of yours."

"A squire's ship, is it?" said the one.

"Oh, we understand, Captain," the other said, "it's just that we, as we mentioned, is out of work, between seafaring jobs, so to speak. And being that we is planning on telling you about this other job of ours, we most likely will be needin' to find new work, and so we was just inquirin' about that possibility."

"There is no work here."

"Oh, we understand."

These two buccaneers continued to stand there, admiring the room and not saying a word. The captain looked them over for a few moments.

"Is that all, gentleman?"

"Well, not exactly," the first one continued. "There is the matter of someone saying there might be a 'reward' for this type of information. Of course, we wants to be doing it for our civic dooty, likes I said before. But if there should be a little something for the troubles we are going through?"

"Yes, yes. I promised a reward, and you shall have it. How long until you are to meet your mate?"

"I should think within a few hours, Captain."

"Then meet me here directly after you have discovered this location. I will get the magistrate's men to join mine, and we shall go out and meet them straight away, before they have a chance to escape."

"Sounds like a splendid plan, Captain, a real fair sailin' idea."

They continued to stand there, not moving.

"Be off with you," said the captain." I will not pay for anything until I receive like in kind. When you return, I shall pay you half. You will accompany us to this location you speak of, and *if* it proves you both to be truthful, you shall have the rest. Of this you can be assured. But if this is a farce, then I shall have you whipped at the foremast. Now, be off."

"Yes, Captain, we will return shortly."

They bent over in a sort of bow as they walked backwards toward the door, and then opened and left through it.

"Oh, this is excellent news," say I. "Do you think they are telling the truth, Captain?"

"I've no way to tell. But the fact that they want the reward suggests to me they may be on the square and level. But, we are to take no chances. I am going to the magistrate's office and see how many men we can get to go with us. Based on his men being killed when earlier they encountered this group, I think it wise to show up in force. If it transpires to be an ambush, we will deliver a striking blow to them. That is why I wanted those men to hear about my going to get the extra men. If there is treachery planned, they will more likely than not, miss their appointment with us. If they do show, it will be another indication of their truthful intent, as far as they can be truthful."

"I've no time to lose. I will return shortly. If those men return, have them wait for me upon the quarterdeck, not in my quarters, and I wish for you to remain here until my return."

He grabbed his hat, and as he was leaving added:

"Wish me luck, Chloe. We've needed some this day, and it seems to have arrived most fortuitously."

Captain Smollett was gone about three hours, and the two buccaneers did return, just before sunset. The captain came aboard the *Hispaniola* and spoke with them for a few minutes on the deck, and then returned to the cabin. He called in his first officer.

"I have almost a full regiment of the Magistrate's finest men meeting us here at the docks. Those buccaneers say they know the exact location and are willing to lead us there themselves. Get the crewmen ready to leave within the next hour. They are to be fully armed with pistols and sword."

The first officer left and Captain Smollett went to his desk. He reached into a lower side drawer and popped open a lever that caused the letter drawer in the upper left to open. He pulled out a leather satchel and from inside this he removed a few golden doubloons and put it back in. He pushed it into place, and then closed the lower drawer.

"When do we leave?" asked I.

"There is no *we*, Chloe. You are not to accompany us."

"But of course I am. If my Jim is with them, I want to see him as soon as I may."

"Chloe, it is not a request, it is an order."

He grabbed me by the shoulders and sat me upon a chair.

"These are ruthless and vicious men we are going to meet. With a complement of almost sixty men, including most of my crew, I am still uneasy about a successful outcome to our potential encounter. I cannot, and will not, be responsible for any harm, of any sort, befalling you. You heard what the magistrate said they did to his men already. I will return in haste upon the successful conclusion of our endeavor, and if... *when* Jim is found, bring him straight away here to you. But you must stay here, safe and sound."

I realized that argument would fall on deaf ears, and it was not lost on me that what he spoke was in my best interest and out of concern for my welfare.

"On your promise then, you'll return with haste?"

"On my promise, Chloe. After all, I am Jim's Godfather, and as such could only want to see him reunited with his fiancé."

He kissed me on the forehead and then went out and met the two buccaneers on the upper deck. I could see him hand them some coins. He shouted to the crew and spoke; I was not able to discern his words. However, all of them nodded their heads in assent, went below decks and returned with their jackets, cutlasses and pistols in plain view. The captain gave an order, and they all disembarked the ship and left, except one mate, the same one who came in earlier and introduced the two men who stayed behind to stand guard on the main deck.

- - - - - - - - - -

I just heard a strange sound, almost like a muffled cry or perhaps a cough of some sort, followed by a most strange gurgling noise on the deck. The ship is starting to move as if someone might be boarding. I must sign off now and see if it is the captain. If so, I am in hopes of the good news he brings.

Chloe

Chapter Fourteen

Narrative Continued by Jim Hawkins:
A Ship is Taken!

"**M**en," Captain Steele started, "our future is waiting for us in Bristol. We have devised a plan that is sure to work, but we must be on the quick to implement it. This ship's crew and the magistrate's men will be on their way to meet us here this evening. We must make this camp look as if it is occupied. So I need you to grab brush and stuff it under your blankets, and we will need the fires brightly stoked, so gather some more branches.

"After dusk, we will leave for Bristol, taking the southern road using the wagons and horses. I expect no resistance at the ship, but we must be prepared, so all pistols will be loaded, and cutlasses to the ready. Once the ship is taken, we will use longboats to row her out and set sail at once.

"The quartermaster will assign temporary duties until we are at sea, so see him at once."

- - - - - - - - - -

About an hour earlier, the two buccaneers that Captain Steele had sent into Bristol had returned. They conferred with him for quite awhile before they remounted their horses and raced off.

Hearing the captain's words caused my heart to start thumping with excitement, and yet I knew not what my actions would be. Upon entering Bristol, I should surely be able to find a chance to escape, especially since it would be nighttime and taking a ship should involve a certain amount of confusion for the crew.

Yet, I also wanted to go. And I did not think it was simply greed. It seemed an adventure. One in which I could make my fortune, and then live the life I had only daydreamed about. The fear of this decision did not dwindle as the hours wore on while waiting for darkness to arrive. I could see Silver look over at me constantly. However, I pretended not to notice, a childish action I was ashamed of whilst doing it. In spite of my anger at his actions, I realized in my heart that I was exceptionally glad to see him.

- - - - - - - - - - -

It was an arduous trek to Bristol in the wagons. I elected to walk a good portion of the way, for the swaying on the buckboards did not set well with me in the dark. We only used a small lantern to lead us at the fore. It took near five hours to get there, which would put it about the midnight hour, I guessed. The moon was obscured by cloud and fog.

We left the wagons on the edge of town and slowly snaked our way in small groups to the wharf district. Once there, we regrouped behind a warehouse, while the quartermaster made gestures for us with his hands to move forward with stealth—and haste. We rounded the warehouse, and I could barely make out through the fog the silhouette of a ship against the dock. It was a large, three-masted affair with her sails stowed away. We crept up along the dock until very near the gangplank. The captain motioned for us to stay put, and he stood up and started to walk alone to the gangplank, and then boarded it.

"Ahoy," said he, softly. "I have a message from your captain that is most urgent."

"Stand to and board," was the reply.

Captain Steele met this mate at the top of the gangplank. They spoke a few words, and then he pulled out a knife from his sash and plunged it into the mate's throat. A sickening gurgling sound ensued until he fell onto the dock with a dreadful thud. Captain Steele motioned to the quartermaster. Suddenly we heard the sound of horse's hooves galloping and stopping in the fog. The men drew their swords and stood at the ready. From out of the mist appeared the two buccaneers that were leading the group of men to our camp. They walked up to the captain and the three of them started laughing.

"Let us go!" shouted the quartermaster.

We all jumped up, ran onto the gangplank and boarded the ship. As I reached the deck, I felt a certain familiarity with the layout, but quickly pushed it aside. We had all been assigned tasks, and we needed to perform them with precision and haste.

I knew then, by nature of not having tried to escape, that I had made my decision. I prayed it was the right one.

Upon boarding, the crew found their way to their various assigned duties and sprang into action. I noticed that Captain Steele shouted for Long John to come at once to his new captain's quarters. They disappeared inside, slamming the door.

It was decided one longboat would do to take us out into the harbor. I assisted the men who were lowering it. The mooring ropes were pulled back into the ship and the long boat was released and floated with a dozen of the crew to the ready to row. The fog was quite thick, and if not for reference to the docking it would have been difficult to discern which way to start. The long boat was attached to the stern of the ship by a bowline, and slowly, arduously, the men rowed and the ship started moving away from the dock.

Captain Steele finally appeared from his cabin, with Long John near, and using his compass directed the operation, since sighting was not an option once the pierings disappeared. The fog was still a hindrance. I was assigned at the camp to be an assistant to the ship's cook, since I had no skills as a mariner. This meant, to my displeasure, a good deal of my time would be spent with Silver. In the meantime, I was at the beck and call of the quartermaster, who had me assisting the crew moving various ropes from their tie downs along the rails.

Two of the mates appeared above decks and reported within hearing distance that the ship was fully provisioned to reach Freeport and that a full compliment of powder and balls were aboard. Steele seemed exceptionally pleased, as I also knew this would expedite our journey.

After almost an hour, we pulled out of the wall of fog and were able to take our bearings. We had cleared the harbor. The captain conferred with the mariner, and they picked a course heading. The night was cloudy and winds were less than ten knots SSW, as far as I could tell. The captain ordered full sails raised. I helped the mates as best I could and heaved with all my might on the various ropes. Finally, the sails were pulled into place. The four-quarter lanterns were then lighted, and I could see the sails full of wind and feel the ship start to cut into the water.

I started to go below deck and noticed the name of the ship carved above the downway stairs, and I knew instantly why I had that earlier feeling of familiarity, what the French sometimes refer to as déjà vu... a sense of one having experienced the same event before. I was now on Squire Trelawney's ship, the same ship I had traveled to Treasure Island upon the first time.

The *Hispaniola*.

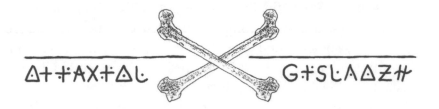

Chapter Fifteen

Narrative Continued by Chloe:
Captured

I hardly know where to start. The nightmare I have been living these past few hours is indelibly etched within my mind as though I'll never be able to entertain another thought again.

I heard what I thought was Captain Smollett and his men coming aboard the *Hispaniola*, so I peered out through the window of his quarters. The heavy fog obscured the figures and I could not make out whom it was that came aboard. Instinctively my hand rested on the door's brass handle, ready to open it. A breeze parted the dismal grayness and suddenly I could see the new guests clearly; and what I saw shook me to the core and gave rise to great concern for my own safety. Pirates were boarding her! I searched for but could not see the crewman who was charged with guarding myself and this ship.

I panicked. How would I get off this vessel? What if they found me out? What would they do? Calmer thoughts started to flood in as I surveyed my predicament. I needed to first of all hide myself in hopes of making use of the additional time to formulate a plan. I rushed into the starboard drawing room and closed the door. Just as I did I heard the captain's door open from the main deck and heard a man's voice issue some orders about releasing bowlines and being quick about it. I sat down on the bench near the outside window and tried to open it. Pry as I might, it would not budge. Upon close inspection with my hands I could feel some nail heads that were holding it closed. What was I now to do?

Suddenly, the door opened behind me and in the doorway stood a tall man holding a lamp. A frightful looking man with a short-trimmed beard and black patch covering his left eye. He had a pistol drawn and aimed at me.

"And whom would you be?" asked he.

I could not speak. I dared not speak. There was no reaction within my voice, even if I had willed it to do so. I was frightened beyond all remembrances. He just stared at me quizzically.

He backed into the main quarters. I could then hear him walk toward the door, open it and shout for "Silver" to join him at once. Now my fears escalated, for I knew it could be none other than that despicable Long John Silver who without a doubt lay at the root of everything bad that was happening.

The sound of his crutch thumping on the floor became clearer as he reached the captain's quarters and entered. John Silver asked this man if everything was all right.

"No they are not. Come here with me," he commanded.

They both peered in through the door with the tall one still holding the lamp, and for the first time my eyes laid upon Long John Silver, leaning on his crutch with a half crooked smile, leering at me.

"Who be this, Captain?"

"I was hoping maybe you could shed some light on that very question."

"Not me. I've never laid me eyes upon her before, and ye can lay to that. Although…"

"Yes?"

"This is Squire Trelawney's vessel, and I knows that even though Smollett be its captain, he's no family to speak of. Least wise that I've known 'bout. Have you asked her who she be?"

"She doesn't seem to be able to speak. Is that so, miss?"

He stared directly at me. I decided not to speak, for to do so would be no better for me until they have made their intentions known.

"See what I mean?"

"Yes, I does, Captain. Most strange, indeedy. Well, as I were saying, perhaps she be the daughter of the Squire. A fortunate fact, if'n it be true."

The man Silver was calling captain stepped into the drawing room and Silver quickly followed. They sat down directly across from me on a bench.

"The squire's daughter. Is that who you are?"

"I'm not saying anything to either of you." This just blurted out of me.

"Ah, she does speak," said Silver. "Well, Captain, if she be who we think, as I said, circumstances be with us. For as sure as the tides rise and fall, you can bet no ship of the Crown's would ever fire upon us, knowin' she were aboard, and you can lay to that. Most fortunate indeedy."

The captain seemed to like what Silver said, for a slight smile graced his face.

"I think you are right, Silver. In fact, I would bet on that as a fact."

"And, Captain," Silver continued, "if'n she be or be not, she will still fetch a pretty price in Pirates Cove. And bein' captain, she is yours until then."

Silver winked at the captain.

"Whatever you may think, Silver, I am not an animal, nor do I trade in human flesh," he replied sternly. "I despise it with all my essence as barbaric and inhumane."

"But of course, cap'n, by the powers, I was only suggestin' it were an option. Of course, only if you be willin' to do them things as captain of this here ship. I meant no offense, nor harm, in the comment."

"We do have a problem, and that is the crew," the captain continued. "We cannot afford to let them know of her presence aboard. Discipline and order must be maintained. So I will devise a way to accomplish this. In the meantime, get out above deck and help the men get us on our way. Before we shove off, come back in here. I will have a letter written to Captain Smollett letting him know of our intentions to keep the squire's daughter from all forms of harm as long as we are not interfered with in our voyage. You make sure it arrives on the docks and is secure for him to find."

"I'll tend to it right away, Captain, when you be done, of course."

Silver used his crutch to stand up and started to leave the room.

"Silver."

"Yes, Cap'n?"

"I am trusting that you understand the order I just gave you. No one is to know of her existence aboard this ship. If they find out, I will hold you personally responsible, and I am sure you remember the description of the fate I have planned for you for any treachery you may perpetrate upon me or this vessel?"

"Aye, Captain. You've got ol' Long John's affy-davy on the matter."

"I thought so. That is all."

After he followed Silver's leave with his gaze, he turned his attention to me.

"Do you have a name?"

I decided not to answer, for I wanted not to give the impression of intimacy in any way to this, this captain.

"My name is Captain Graham Steele. I am now the captain of this vessel. As you heard me mention, I am not a barbarian, nor a man who will take advantage of this situation, unless forced or provoked to do so. You can understand that I will consider you a prisoner of mine, and as such you will not be given free rein of the ship nor anywhere outside my suite of quarters—both for my command's sake and, more to the point, for your safety. In return, I expect you to obey my orders, and do not try to escape, although that would be fruitless on your part, being that we will soon be out to sea."

He got up from his chair and started to leave.

"Did you murder Captain Smollett and his men?"

He stopped and turned around, bemused.

"As I mentioned to Silver, I am leaving him a note. So no, I did not."

He reached the door and turned back toward me, again.

"I realize you are frightened, as a daughter of my own would be in such a position. I have no love for who your father the squire is, nor his position within the Crown. But as I have already stated, my manners in this matter have not been compromised, and my word is my bond. I will lock you in this room until we have set sail and will start to arrange the other matters regarding your unexpected stowage aboard *my* ship."

He set the lamp on the table next to the door and then closed it. I heard the key turn within the lock.

I am not sure what my fate will be. I will continue to write, if time and circumstance allow.

GL✝35X△Å   ✝J53∴✝XL

Chapter Sixteen

Narrative Resumed by Jim Hawkins:
First Leg of Voyage

We made good time after leaving Bristol, even though it was a cloudy night, and there was a real danger of collision with other vessels. The captain's orders were to make haste with full sail at all costs. The next morning we could see that the coast of England was behind us, and we were heading south by southeast, toward Gibraltar.

Within two days we had passed the Mediterranean Sea, and as best as I could reckon our position was about one hundred miles to the South of the northern tip of Africa, also known as Algiers. The captain made known that we would take on supplies and stores at Freetown in Sierra Leone and then sail due west to take full advantage of the trade winds that would fill our sails and deliver us to our next destination, Pirate's Cove.

Life about the ship had gotten into a comfortable routine with very little effort. These were seasoned crewmen. To a man, they took to their jobs with vigor and seriousness. As I have already mentioned, my assignment was an assistant to the ship's cook, John Silver. I also drew lookout watch every third evening.

During the voyage from Bristol to Freetown, the captain made good on his word and had drawn up, for all the men to sign, Articles for this voyage, including me. These were fascinating, for I had no conception that buccaneers lived by such rules and guidelines. For instance, spelled out in detail were each man's duties aboard ship, punishments for different offenses and what percentage of the final treasure discovered would be distributed to each crewman. There were twenty-four men aboard, not including the captain. This amounted to a three percent share for everyone, while the captain maintained that he should be given an additional twenty-five percent share for leading the voyage and having to use his funds to purchase the stores and such to complete it. There were no disagreements to these terms.

The contracts also included passages such as: *any man that shall snap his arms, or smoke in the hold without a cap to his pipe or carry a candle lighted without a lantern, shall be subject to "Moses's Law", being thirty nine stripes on his bare back.* Also, every man that lost an eye, or a leg or an arm would be compensated according to his loss, and further, if any man died, his heirs would receive his portion. I listed my mother and Chloe as heirs.

One thing did seem out of place. I noticed there were no written Articles proffered to Silver. When I asked Silver about why, he told me:

"Ah, Jim me boy, that is the Cap'ns doing, alrighty. You sees, once a contract is signed, it is in stone. He told me that untils it be determined that the knowledge I have in me possession from Jasper be valid and all, there be no contract for ol' Silver. However, I has his affy davy that once this here treasure be found, due to my helpfulness, then a share will be mine, fair and square. I has nothing else to leverage, so I'll be takin' the man at his word."

This made sense to me, and therein I let the matter lie.

We arrived at Freetown on the third of May, according to my journal. Taking stores and water aboard took only a day. I stayed aboard ship and tended to the maintenance that the quartermaster had assigned. We left the following morning under clear skies and warm trade winds west by southwest. As I witnessed the dark continent of Africa start to disappear behind me, I knew that there was to be no turning back. I had now teased destiny, and she was to have me see this quest through to the end. A sense of adventure, the likes of which I had never felt, crept upon me. Suddenly, standing at the fore of the ship, the wind blowing through my hair, the sun shining on my face, and the excitement of the crew, all combined to make me feel comfortable on my own, for the first time in my life.

The voyage to the Southern Americas was estimated to take three weeks. The trade winds fared well, and the weather was favourable. I learned from the crew that this time of year could be the most dangerous for mariners, due to storms within the Caribe that could appear with little forewarning and devastating results. However, we had no choice in the matter; we had to reach Pirate's Cove to get the map. Each of us were warned of the danger in the Articles, and each swore his word to accept the results.

A council of buccaneers was formed to meet once a week and discuss any business of the crew, which included grievances and ship's duties. This group consisted of the quartermaster, mariner and four of the crew who were voted to this position by the others. I enjoyed the solidarity of being an equal member who had a say in what occurred on this vessel. Captain Steele was always accommodating and respectful of the men's wishes, and except for his being in the position of captain, he was in all respects an equal part of the crew.

Unlike the stories I've heard throughout the years as to the ruthless and cold-hearted nature of quartermasters, ours was an anomaly on many levels. First and foremost, he was an Afrikaner. He stood almost as tall as Captain Steele, but his body was much more massive—huge muscles rippled his deeply darkened skin. He had a rounded face with dark short-cropped hair and piercing brown eyes. Perhaps his most distinguishing feature was his smile, which covered half his face and exposed the whitest teeth I have ever witnessed. Although sparse in showing itself, when he was in a jovial mood, it was difficult to not share in his enthusiasm. He and Steele seemed to have an unspoken communication between them, for often Steele would simply look to Tafari, for that was his native African name, and he would spring into action. Of his loyalty to Captain Steele, there could be no doubt. As importantly, Steele held him in high regard and showed him more deference than any of the rest of the crew. Tafari could be stern, but I never observed him to be unfair in his implementation of orders or duties.

With great difficulty, I managed to avoid becoming engaged in any conversations of consequence with Silver, in spite of the fact we worked side by side every day of the week. I could see that he desired to make it not so, but I would purposely and with intent let him know, through actions and deed, that idle chatter was not what I wished to become engaged in with him. I am not sure if this factored into a cause behind the grumblings from the crew in reference to their food—the main complaint being too much spice within it. However, I noticed Silver dropping more and more of the powders he kept for this purpose into the various dishes whenever I would go out of my way to avoid his gaze. I continued to feel childish about my actions, and yet something within me would not let me accept that I might be wrong about his intentions back at the camp.

Part of my duties were to serve the captain his meal in his quarters, a luxury afforded no one else on board. I brought in his food, set it on his table with no words spoken, and then left. When he rang his outside bell, I hurried up decks, knocked on his cabin door, entered and removed the dishes. Steele had a ravenous appetite, for he ate at least two men's portions consistently.

On one occasion, as I was leaving with the dishes from his quarters, he stopped me outside his door.

"Hawkins, is it?"

"Yes Sir."

"I understand from John Silver that you are an educated man. Is this so?"

"Well sir, I attended University for the past two years."

"Where?"

"Manchester."

He thought about this for a few moments.

"I would like you to join me for supper tomorrow evening. Five bells."

"Respectfully, Captain, I must assist Silver with the crew's meals."

"I will speak to Silver about this matter and he will make do as he can. That is all. Return to your duties."

I relayed to Silver what the captain had requested of me, and he seemed surprised out of proportion to the news of the invitation.

"Are you sure he be wanting yous to join him *in his quarters*?"

"Of course I am. I heard him say it himself. Five bells."

"Strange," I heard Silver say to himself.

After I finished my duties I went above deck to listen to the ocean and the wind whistling through the sails. I especially liked leaning against the rear railing of the ship to watch the wakes veer off the hull. It was a favourite pastime of mine, and I cherished it. I would feel the wind against my face while I closed my eyes and visualized Chloe, running after me and shouting her intentions of marriage. Memories of our being together flooded my thoughts, and it seemed as if I could smell the lilacs of our last evening together. I wanted to relive these moments every chance that I could, for I feared I would forget her image if I forsook it for too long.

That evening I was on rear deck alone. It was church quiet. Most of the men were asleep, and only the helmsman and myself were above deck. The moon's light upon the ocean's rippled surface appeared as if a thousand little fires were dancing about the horizon—creating a wondrous pathway toward that brightly shining orb. I became mesmerized by the serenely peaceful and magnificent beauty of this vision.

Perchance something caught my ear. At first it was as though I heard a faraway noise, a murmur of sorts. The wind playing tricks on my ears, thought I. Yet, there it was again. A soft, almost crying sound. I knew not what to make of it. I've heard tell from various seafaring men that there are mistresses of the sea, called sirens, that call out and beseech mariners to lure them to their death. In university I learned that these rumours usually referred to the order Cetacea, genus Phocoena—what is commonly called a sea porpoise. And all of these tales were just that—yarns from old sailors. Yet, I could clearly hear a soft crying somewhere out there in the ocean.

I decided to take heed and leave the railing. Although not a believer in superstition, perhaps caution in the middle of the sea was a more prudent pathway than finding out that I just might be mistaken about those rumours.

As I left the upper decks and started toward amidships, I could feel a presence nearby. I turned to see Long John standing by the fore rails, staring over toward me. He motioned for me to join him, which I instinctively, and yet reluctantly, did.

I stood next to him for a few moments, while he lighted his pipe and blew the smoke out into the wind gently breezing by.

"A bit of the irony, 'tis it not, Jim me boy? On the same ship together again and heading to Treasure Island. Seems like the fates have been at work, it does. I gets a real good feeling about this. Yes indeedy. All is above board and ins the open this time. No skullduggery. And if'n we keeps our noses to the wind, we'll end up rich beyond our wildest dreams. 'Tis all I've wished for and more, and you can lay to that."

"Is that what you wanted to tell me, Silver? How enchanted you are that we both share the *Hispaniola* together again?"

"No, Jim, 'tain't all what I wanted to say."

"Then why don't you get on with it?"

He took another puff from his pipe and lowered it to the rail.

"What do ye know about this here captain, Jim?"

"I've never heard of him before, if that is what you mean."

"I've heard stories, well, and this Captain Steele be a tough one, that he is. Has no tolerances for anythin' not in line with his ways of thinkin'."

"I've seen that already—with Morgan."

"Aye, Morgan was a lucky one, he was. Circumstances be different, and he'd be bait this very evenin', he would, and you can lay to that. Jim, ye know I think gold's dust of you, gold's dust, and that's a fact. Yet as I sees it, you can't be dyeing an old sail blue and expects it to be taken as new as a silk scarf. It's always to be what 'tis. And that there is yer Captain Steele. I's worked under swabs of his type, before and after the mast. They's been under me eyes day and night. And I tell ya straight he be one to keep an eye on, I do's. He be like one of them scorpions you hear tell 'bout in them lower latitudes, with a deadly stinger on 'is tale. No matter what he tells you, he'll always be a scorpion; and sure as the tides he'll end up stingin' ya good and dead."

"Maybe what you say is so, and maybe not, Silver. What I do know about him is he has been fair in all his dealings with the men, and the men who know him respect him. That is more than I can speak about on your behalf. And please know that I do not appreciate your attempts at dishonouring my opinion of him."

"Jim, me boy, I be only trying to—"

"You never give up, do you, Silver? I know what you are trying to do. I am not a fool. Maybe your intentions are fair and good, and maybe they are self-serving. I cannot judge that point as yet. In either case, I am old enough and with years a plenty to take care of myself. I am not the young Jim you remember. You will do wise to not relent and give birth to your old ways, for I will not be able to offer you any more assistance from harm on this voyage."

"I meant no harm or ill will, Jim, and if you took it to be so, I am 'polygizn' this very instant. 'Tis not my intent in the least. You and me's the only ones to knows each other, Jim me boy. All the rest has their mates. Every once in a while ye needs someone to watch yer back, so to speak."

"Like you did for Tom on Treasure Island? Before you killed him in cold blood by stabbing him in the back?"

"Well now, that be an unfortunate incident, it surely was. And ye can bet I'm not bein' proud of me actions back then, and that's a fact."

"I am sorry Silver, I do not care to take your counsel on this matter, nor of anything more on this voyage. I beg you to let us work in peace, and hold your tongue from proffering any more of this *friendly* advice you seem to possess."

I left the railing and immediately felt bad for my conversation and actions with Silver. I was feeling uncomfortable, and just wanted to get away from him and not listen to any more of his disparaging narratives against the captain. I was indeed confused with his intentions, and while falling asleep below deck in my hammock, tried to unravel the underlying motives that accompanied his wanting to speak with me about this matter. There were always hidden meanings and intentions with Long John Silver, and if history proved to be a true and faithful indicator of the future, his actions always involved, as their end result, *treachery* and *death*.

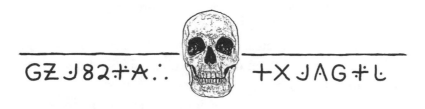

Chapter Seventeen

Dinner with Captain Steele

The next day I finished doing what I could to help Long John with the evening meals for the rest of the crew, and when five bells arrived I rushed upstairs and knocked on Captain Steele's door.

"Enter."

Upon entering I had cause to remember the captain's quarters with exactitude. All was the same: the ornate oak desk and dark leather chair, the map pedestal in the far right corner, the teak dining room table upon which we were to take our evening's fare. Even the musty smell.

"Sit down at the table, Hawkins," said Steele, motioning and pointing.

He was absorbed with some business on his desk. Another knock on the door signaled Silver's arrival with the fare. He opened the door and hobbled in on his crutch with a large plate of food precariously balanced.

"Begging the captain's pardon, I were wondering if ye be needing yer extra portion this meal?"

Silver continued over to the table and sat the tray with bowls and meat stew down upon it.

123

"I would like something extra to eat *later* this evening, after Hawkins leaves."

"Of course Cap'n. I'll see to it."

Captain Steele closed the desk roll top with a slam and met me at the table. We sat down to eat and he said nothing for a goodly time. I was not at ease, and my wondering why he requested my company for this intimate occasion grew as the minutes ticked on. He was a very methodical and thorough diner with impeccable manners. Determination and deliberateness seemed to rule his every bite, as he slowly raised them to his mouth. He took a drink of wine and carefully set down the glass.

"I, like you, Hawkins," he started, "attended university. First in Glasgow and then finishing my studies in Oxford."

"Oxford sir? How marvelous that must have been. I've only heard about it through my friend, Dr. Livesey. His descriptions have given rise in me in the most desirous of ways to attend that prestigious institution. He described it as full of huge libraries and great stone buildings with Grecian columns adorning them. And the ivy-covered hallways are said to stretch for miles."

He measured my words, and continued eating.

"Indeed, it is all that you say and more. It seems like a different lifetime ago that I was there. Compared to…"

He wiped his mouth with a napkin and set it down.

"I desired your company for the purpose of being in the presence of another educated man, Hawkins. Tell me, what were your studies at Manchester?"

"Well sir, I specialized in the sciences, which were my favourite: mathematics, chemistry and botany. I also studied philology, philosophy, astrology and Latin, in addition to my physical studies of fencing and gymnastics."

"Who was your professor in botany?"

"That would be Professor Sitchin."

"Short gray beard, squinty eyes?"

"Why, yes he was."

"He's a good man. Knows very well his subject."

"You know him?"

"Yes."

"But how?"

"It's not important. Tell me, did you study the Greek philosophers?"

"Plato and Socrates, and later Pythagoras."

"What did you think of them?"

"In what way?"

"Their methodology of reasoning."

We discussed this subject for the next hour without a break in conversation for even a large breath. The captain stressed the importance of deductive reasoning and how it could be applied to all studies, and in all problems of life and business affairs. His grasp of issues was intriguing; his manner of bridging philosophical concepts into examples of relevance was without equal to any of the professors I had studied under in university. I caught a glimpse and began to appreciate how the diversity of concepts of which I had been learning about were interconnected, although it was a fleeting insight. Captain Steele had a command of the English language that enabled him to make very fine distinctions within the subjects we discussed, and I found myself wanting to simply listen to all that he had to say. Finally, he stopped and became what I would call introspective. Silence ensued.

"Begging your pardon, sir, but why, with your education and knowledge… what I mean to say sir, is… it's clear you could have made your fortune in any field you would endeavor. Why did you, you know, become—"

"A buccaneer, Hawkins? A common pirate?"

"Yes sir, but I meant no offense."

"It is true that I was blessed with a formidable education. And my family has good and solid roots in… *had* roots in the gentry class. However, to answer your question, it was not I who made the choice. It was forced upon me."

"I do not understand?"

"Ah yes, they would not teach this in your university, I am sure."

He stood up and started to pace the floor around the table.

"I started as a privateer. A fancy name for a legal pirate. With all the privileges and status it entailed. I was charged with pillaging any ship not under the Crown's protection and returning with the spoils, of which I would receive a percentage—all under seal and permission of his Majesty the King. Of course, these goods became respectable once they passed through the accountant's hands, and as far as the rest of the world would know, were not tainted with the blood of those that formerly possessed them. This is a gentleman's secret that is not often spoken of."

"I have heard of such things in my parents' inn."

"Then you also know it became a contentious issue once peace treaties were signed among our various European countries' monarchies, yes?"

"Yes sir. But I still do not understand why you would end up—"

"The circumstances and actions preceding my metamorphosis from privateer to buccaneer, as you call it, are of a personal nature and will not be discussed. It was an unwelcome transition. A stroke of a pen forced my entry into this position, and it will be dealt with at the appropriate time. Justice will be served, in cold portion. Yet, as in all endeavors I have been faced with, I have wholeheartedly embraced this life, and have strived to be the most successful buccaneer the world has known. In this regard, I have made it my business to make all merchants, especially those involved with the king, and all his gentry and squires, pay dearly. And pay dearly for it they have. No ship, nor king or country has been beyond my vengeance. I have found myself doing things… I thought no human was capable of against another."

He stopped his pacing for a few moments, then sat down and took a sip of his wine.

"It seems the depths to which one must reach to perpetuate this fame and lifestyle are of an unfathomable nature. No one can judge me without full benefit of my circumstances. That is all I will state on this matter."

He again seemed to be remembering some far off event, and became lost in his thoughts. He finished his remaining meal in silence. I knew not what to say, I was so in wonderment at his story. Who was this man? What had happened to him to cause so much anger and hate toward the world?

"Hawkins," said he, interrupting my thoughts. "I want to ask you, as an educated man, is this the fate that awaits you? Is this the life you have envisioned for yourself?"

I had not anticipated this question and found myself short of words and searching for an answer. He was not probing me for quickness of reply, and I took the time to reason it within.

"Truth be told, Captain, I am at a crossroads. I enjoy my studies and the promise of an educated gentry life; one which I think fits well with future plans for a career and family. I had always envisioned this outcome, using a close friend of the family, Dr. Livesey, as a role model. But since embarking on this journey, I have started to entertain ideas—ones I never imagined would enter my mind. There is much to be said of this nomadic life upon the oceans. Much that is appealing to me. In my innermost thoughts I, at times, can envision myself roaming the seas and living as I please. I think I have a heart for it."

"Ah yes, the seduction, at least at first, is intoxicating and elating."

"However, sir," I continued, "I have met a girl who is also weighing on my mind, and one who I am sure would not approve of such a life. And I would not wish it upon her either. I have decided against making a decision regarding the permanence of my plans until after we have discovered and parceled out the shares of the treasure. In this way, I will be able to make my decision based upon the underlying soundness of my desires, rather than out of fleeting glimpses of a future I am quite unsure of."

"Your share will no doubt assure you of a future of your own making. Very few men at your stage of life are given that opportunity."

"That is not lost on me, sir, and my appreciation of it is great. But I can't help but wonder, sir."

"Yes, Hawkins."

"Well sir, knowing what you know now, if you were me with these same future possibilities, what would your decision be in this matter?"

He got up, walked to his desk, picked up a pipe and stuffed it with tobacco. He slowly lit it from the lamp and drew long on it.

"We are from different worlds, Hawkins," he said, blowing the smoke slowly out of his mouth. "Everything I had is now gone. You have a future with the possibilities of a family and love. My fate was handed to me much differently than I had envisioned when I was your age. I can no longer picture these possibilities."

He drew some more on the pipe and then sat back down at the table.

"There are times when only you can make the decisions that affect your future course. You can be whatever you will yourself to be. It is all the same. Most men do not know they have a choice, and remain in the bondage of their prejudices and beliefs. You are at a crossroads, one that is seductive. Socrates suggested that if you are to know anything, one must know oneself. I suggest you make your decision before the treasure is parceled. Once in hand, it will be difficult to walk away from this life."

I admit I wanted him to be more definitive in his answer. However, he was right. I was feeling seduced by the excitement of discovering a fortune, by the camaraderie of the crew, by the freedom of traveling about the oceans at will, even about the violence I once abhorred. This was offset by the life I could visualize spending with Chloe sharing the fortune that awaited me at Treasure Island. A king's ransom that could afford us anything in life we could want for. I begged leave of Captain Steele and told him I would think about all that we had spoken of.

On the way back to my quarters, I walked past the kitchen and relayed to Silver that the captain was available for his extra meal portion.

"You be all right, Jim? Ye tends to looks a bit worn."

"Yes, Silver, I am fine."

I reached the door of the kitchen that led to the sleeping quarters and stopped. Captain Steele seemed so different from the warning Long John had given me, I thought. Perhaps he's been wronged in an unfair manner. Maybe he'd started these types of rumours and stories to remain in control of his men and ship.

"I think you are wrong about the captain, John Silver. He's not the man you think he is in the least."

"Jim, I can be a lot of things, and you may call me any one of thems you likes and takes yer fancy. And if'n it makes you feel better, I will be sayin' no more 'bout it. But this I'll say: be on yer guard. A leopard with no spots still can give an awful gash, and you can lay to that."

Chapter Eighteen

The Plank

Life aboard the *Hispaniola* had fallen into a rather tranquil routine. Hours gently rolled into days, and days became the same. But for my journal, I would have completely lost track of the dates. The ocean's waters were smooth, the winds were blowing favourably, and there was nothing to do other than our jobs and then sit with one's thoughts and try and contain the anticipation we all felt as we moved closer and surer to our destination—first to Pirate's Cove and then on to Treasure Island.

It had been five days since I dined with Captain Steele. Although there were no outward signs, at least not overt ones that I could discern, I felt more comfortable in his presence. He showed no favouritism. No smiles, or knowing nods. But I felt a certain specialness, nonetheless. I was approached by Quartermaster Tafari, who informed me that my presence was again requested by the captain for the evening meal.

Although I see now how misplaced my feelings were, I did let my ego get the upper hand and felt puffed up as a rooster. I considered the invitation, and myself, in high esteem.

After arriving promptly at five bells, I found Captain Steele playing a game of chess on the table next to his desk. Actually, he seemed to be studying it more than playing. He invited me into his quarters, and inquired as to my abilities in the game.

I answered his inquiry in the negative, having never learned to play nor had the time to do so.

"It is the game of kings," he told me, "and once you learn the rules, it is the greatest teacher of forward thinking strategy that you could ever be exposed to." He recommended I learn how to play and practice it studiously when I returned to university.

The rest of the evening was intellectually challenging, with topics ranging from philology to politics. I found myself completely enthralled with the breadth and depth of his knowledge and understanding of such a chasm of new and diverse subjects. He seemed particularly fond of botany, which was my weakest subject. However, after his sharing the wonderment and scientific nature of the flora and fauna that inhabited the islands we were to visit, and also of the other mysterious lands he has sailed to, I vowed to myself to be more diligent with this subject in the future.

One exchange between us near the end of the evening did cause me some discomfort, for it hit me unawares and surprised me at its interjection into our conversation. It started off innocent enough. We had been discussing philosophy, and our flow of thoughts turned toward the true nature of men.

"You must understand, Hawkins, that there are certain types of people that are incongruent—it is as if they are two. Whilst speaking platitudes to your face, their other half, the interior one, is working out the details of your demise. Your Long John is one of these types. To be a leader, you need to be able to see that side. Actions are what count. Not flowery words. And there is only one thing those of this ilk understand: strength coupled with fear. Any attempt at negotiation is considered a vile and exploitable weakness by these types of men. I made that mistake once and it cost me part of my sight.

"Half of my crew are also of this ilk, because this type of lifestyle seems to favour them. However, once they commit to loyalty, they are the best mates you could ever hope for. Leadership involves the ability to distinguish the subtle difference between intent and action. Words are of no value and must be ignored. *Always* look toward the actions they take. They'll steer you true."

He paused at this juncture and took measure of my reaction. I did not respond, for I felt it more of a lecture than a question.

"Could you explain the nature of your and John Silver's relationship?"

"Begging your pardon, Sir?"

"I am asking you to explain what loyalties there are between you two. As captain, I need to know to whom and where your loyalties lie."

"Captain, I am not sure how to answer. I signed the Articles, and pledged my loyalty to you and the crew. I have known John Silver from my last trip to Treasure Island, and consider him a, a… I *did* consider him a friend at one time. But no more."

He listened intently to my response.

"Jim, I need to know I can count on you. If Silver gives up Jasper's secrets, and they lead to our successfully locating the treasure, then all should end well. However, I believe it his nature to think he is smarter than most, and in this case even of myself. His very presence has caused tension within the crew. It is not his fault. It is simply an ingrained part of his way of doing things. He could choose the good, yet I believe he cherishes the evil way of accomplishing a task. I cannot rule out the possibility that he will try and sway the crew to grab the larger portion that I lay ownership to. My responsibility is for the entire crew and their shares. If, and when, he gives up his secrets, I will have a decision to make as to his fate."

"You told him he would be signed to Articles once the treasure was found," said I.

"That will be based upon *his* behaviour and actions. And it is those I will be looking at, not his words. Will I be able to rely upon your loyalty in this matter?"

"Yes Sir," I responded, "you may rely upon me."

I avoided Silver after my dinner and went straight to my bunk. It was a quiet evening, and I wanted to just lay alone and be with my thoughts. What was the captain trying to tell me? Was he planning on not honouring his word to John Silver? I tried to wade through these thoughts, when a horrifying event occurred that shook me to my very essence.

- - - - - - - - - -

I must mention first that one of the buccaneers, Ripley, had taken a slight liking to me, for every once in a while I would add an extra portion of meal when he asked. We had friendly relations, and on the whole I liked him very much. That night he was into the grog when off his watch, and after exceeding what was normal for him, he became quite drunk. After he had finished his measured allotment from his goatskin pouch, he made the fateful decision then and there to go down to the storage room and procure some more on the spot.

I could hear him shouting at Ben, who had the assignment that night of standing guard at the storeroom. What was said between them was unintelligible to me, and truth be known I didn't pay much attention to it. However, the sounds of a scuffle broke out, with both of them shouting and screaming at each other, and suddenly a blood-curdling scream erupted from below deck. Then silence.

I jumped up and started down the hatch stairs toward the storeroom and was met by a couple of other crew members at the bottom. In the shadowy light of the lanterns held by these mates, I could see Ben laying face down, his blood sloshing on the floor beneath him in a macabre rhythm with the ship's swaying. Ripley was sitting slumped against the mid-ship post with a bloody dagger in his hand, cursing to himself about how *"no one was going to tell old Ripley when he can drink or not, and to the devil with he that says different."* I had the feeling he was unawares of the severity of his actions, based on the blank stare of his eyes.

"What goes on here?" came a booming voice.

We turned and saw Captain Steele bounding down the stairway.

"Captain," stated Quartermaster Tafari, who had arrived the same time as did I, "it appears Ripley has gutted Ben who was trying to avert him from raiding the stores for more grog."

The captain's face turned noticeably red in the flickering lamp's light, and his lips pursed as he surveyed the downed seaman lying in his own blood, the semi-broken door and Ripley sitting with dagger in hand.

"Pick him up," the captain demanded, and two of the crew forcibly grabbed Ripley and stood him on his feet.

"Stealing and killing, is it? It has come to this on *my* ship?"

He backhanded Ripley squarely across the face. His head bounced against the mid-ship post. Blood started to ooze from his nose and mouth. The captain then grabbed Ripley's shirt and pulled him almost off his feet. He turned around and took measure of the rest of the men who were now crowding the hatch and looking in.

"I've told you seamen that I will tolerate no treachery on this ship. Now this sorry soul will suffer the consequences of such an act as this."

He threw Ripley violently to the ground. Steele's face pulsated with an anger I'd not seen before; it was red as a vine-ripened tomato. He opened his lips slightly, and spoke with his teeth clenched together.

"Bring him topside at once."

The two mates again picked Ripley up and then pulled him clumsily up the stairway as we all poured out onto the deck behind him. Ripley was struggling and shouting for them to let him go. Captain Steele walked into his quarters and a few moments later exited with his cutlass in hand.

"Drop the plank," he shouted, "and bring Ben's remains up here at once."

"But, Captain," one of the men pleaded, "Ripley here's drunk and not awares—"

"Do you want to join your friend?" Steele shouted back.

"Drop the plank," this same mate hurriedly shouted at the rest of the crew, "and be quick about it."

Murmurs and loud whispers erupted at those orders. I tried to get near Long John so as to ask him what this all meant, but he was too close to the captain to accomplish that wish. One of the mates opened a side rail that is usually used for disembarking the ship when we were in port, while another two brought the gangway plank and set it down with about three feet extending beyond the ship's side. Two crewmen placed a large piece of wood at the other end, laying it over the plank in such a way that by their hammering wooden pegs into it, it stopped the part extending above the ocean from tipping over the ship's side.

Ripley was now slouched onto his knees upon the deck and still shouting to himself. Blood covered his face.

"Stand that swab up!" scowled the captain.

Once they did, the captain commanded two other mates to bring Ben's lifeless body over to where Ripley was standing. He then ordered another mate to get a rope and tie them together, with their backs to each other. He got a rope and wrapped it around the two of them, starting with the neck and ending up at their knees, and tied it off in a knot.

Ripley was still under the grog's influence, for even while they held and tied him, he was wavering back and forth, as if he were about to fall down not of his own volition. Steele approached the two tied up together, while three mates struggled to hold them up.

"Move him to the plank," he ordered.

They did so with great effort, since Ben's body was now a great hindrance. They finally set them on the plank just at ship's side and remained there holding them.

"Ripley, you know the penalty for your actions this evening. The code is clear. I'll not tolerate nor condone it. I told you I am the captain, and I will always enforce our code. As such, I sentence you to the same fate as you befell upon Ben. An eye for an eye, a tooth for a tooth. Have you anything to say?"

Ripley slowly looked around at the crew assembled on the deck and scowled. He returned his gaze toward Steele, squinted and looked directly at him.

"You're a pig's ass, Captain Black-Eyed Steele," he spat with a special emphasis on the black-eyed part. "To the devil with you, say I."

"To the devil is it?" Steele screamed exploding with rage.

He raised his cutlass high and toward his back.

"You tell him hello for me, you scurvy dog of a man! For you will surely meet him first!"

He swung it forcefully, and it sliced across Ripley's gut. He let out a frightful, blood-curdling scream. His innards started to leave him, while at the same moment Captain Steele raised his right leg and yelled, "Let him go!" to the men who held him. He used his boot to shove the both of them, now tied as one, off the end of the plank with great force, and they fell into the water, making a great splash. They disappeared from sight, swallowed by the dark green abyss of the waters. The ship did not alter its speed and we were a good distance away from their briny grave before we could draw breath.

Then silence.

The captain's nostrils flared in and out as he turned back and surveyed the crew, where not a sound could be heard.

"This is what happens to anyone who dares to challenge my authority or breaks any of our codes. There's worse than this that can befall each of you. This scoundrel got off easily."

He stormed about the ship's deck, walking in a circle, and then came to an abrupt stop.

"Clean up this mess!" he screamed to one of the crew, motioning to the blood and innards that had dropped upon the deck, and then he walked back and into his cabin.

The crew quickly and quietly dispersed. I felt weak and queasy in the extreme, as my stomach churned relentlessly. I ran to the side railing and all the day's rations, and then some, came forth violently from my insides.

Long John disappeared below deck and quickly returned with something in hand while I leaned against the railing.

"Here, take a bite of this here, Jim; it be settlin' yer innards."

"What is it?"

"Ginger root. Now do as I say and bites into it."

I did, and within a few minutes, my queasiness had settled. But the horrifying scene was still indelibly etched within my mind.

"Why did he murder Ripley?" asked I.

"'Twasn't murder, Jim, 'twas the enforcin' of our code. Pirates we be, and rules we have. And he broke one of the most serious of the lot."

"He was drunk and didn't know what he was doing."

"Aye, Jim, that be a fact," said Silver as he looked around and then whispered. "We needs to be hushed until we can talk in private."

This caused me great confusion and unrest. Was this the same Captain Steele I had dined with only hours ago? How could he change so drastically? I quickly went to my quarters and forced myself to try to sleep, although it was not sound, nor restful. I woke up continuously to the sound of Ripley's screams.

The next day seemed to never end. Most of the crew was obviously shaken up by the previous night's event. No one spoke about it, nor even mentioned that Ripley and Ben were no longer with us. I finally had a chance later that night to be alone with Silver whilst finishing the cleaning of the dinnerware. I did not eat supper that evening, nor did most of the crew. My heart was not into the task, and I felt a kind of numbness throughout my body.

"You could have helped Ripley," said I to Silver.

Silver sat himself down on a barrel, rested up against a side spar of the ship, and pulled out his favourite corncob pipe. I noticed a couple of other mates were watching he and I. They had been friendly to us, and this caused me no concern.

"That's a fact you're speakin', Jim Hawkins, indeed 'tis. And it were a huge burden on me heart that I felt whiles watchin' such a…"

He looked up toward the main deck's stairs, and I suppose satisfied himself no one else was listening.

"As I were saying, it pained me heart dearly to the core to watch such a senseless act of killin' as the captain performed in front of us all last evening, and you can lay to that."

"Captain Steele would not have harmed you if you had come to his defense. He is well aware you have the key to the treasure's location."

He lit his pipe and inhaled deeply.

"That be a fact too, 'tis. He surely would have had that to be considerin'. And it's true that he would be as surely cuttin' hisself and the crew if'n he gutted me, and I doubts that would be his actions. But treacherous thoughts of my interference in his authority would surely enter and settle all cozy in his mind, and he would be plannin' me demise once the secrets I holds be revealed. But 'twasn't only me I was thinkin' of Jim. No indeedy. It was of you."

"I doubt that."

"Now, now, Jim, hears me out. You sees, well, the captain knows that you and me—we's a special relationship, he surely does. And cuz of that, he has been more affable to you, knowin' that I have a special liking to you and such. And me bein' a sort of a key to unlocking the treasure's whereabouts. Well then, Silver, I thinks, if I get's mixed up in this affair, and the captain later on decides that he's gonna send me down to Davy Jones' locker, well, then I won't be there to provide any leverage with me special knowledge to keep him from doin' the same villainous act to you. And I has another thought in that regard. What if he uses you to spring the secret from me, knowing me special feelin's for you. Tortures you even. I couldn't stand for that. Do you see that? Do you understands how old Silver felt about it? You do understand, don't you Jim, me boy?"

"It was just awful what he did. A bullying and lawless display of cowardice," I responded. I looked around and saw the two mates listening. "And I don't care who hears me."

"There, there Jim, I understands hows you feels," Silver replied in hushed tones, "but you must be prudent in these matters with ye voice. Anger knows no bounds, even if'n there be a fondness for ye."

The two mates listening walked over. One of them looked around and then told me this was nothing compared to what old Flint did to his crew members. The other mate reminded him that Redbeard was the worst of the lot.

"You tell em, Long John. Tell him what a monster that Redbeard was."

"You sailed with Redbeard?" asked I.

He re-stuffed his pipe with tobacco and lit it slowly, looking at the mates and then me.

"'Tis true, I sailed with Captain Redbeard nigh half a score of years ago, 'twas. I was a man before the mast, the ship's cook I was then, yes indeedy. Had both me legs back then. Everyone thought Redbeard got his name from the strikin' color of his hair and beard, but likely as not 'twas for another reason altogether. He was the most ruthless, merciless and cunning pirate who ever sailed the open waters, and you can lay to that. And he seemed to like it as not the more blood spilled in the brutality of the acts he perpetrated. Fact is, he'd kill or murder anyone who got in his bad straights or disrespected him in any manner, and that's a fact. And not just fair and gentlemanly like, neither. No sir. There be tales of his butcheries that are legendary, and some that will give you nightmares for the rest of yer natural life."

Silver slowly looked around, leaned in and lowered his voice.

"Once, when I was on his ship, he was off the coast of one of New Providence Islands in the North Caribe, 'twer. He and his men rowed to shore in a long boat with a chest of the bundt in tow. A day and night pass while they be on this island. Come the next morning only he, Redbeard, is rowing in the long boat back to the ship's side.

"That evening, as I were servin' he and his first mate their meals, I had the chance to be overhearin' their talk. They's laughin' and banterin' back and forth. I hears ol' Redbeard as clear as you and I be sittin' here talking right now, and that's a fact.

"Redbeard told his first mate hows he found out whilst devising a suitable restin' place for this chest of his that the men he broughts with him was planning larcenous intentions toward his treasure and he himself. That day he ties all six of them up and drags them, one by one, to the sandy side of a beach. He commences to diggin' six holes in the sand, each to the depth of a man. Throws each one of them in, one by one, he said, and covers them with sand up to their necks, leavin' their heads stickin' up out of the sand. And that's all. And then he really gets to laughin' whilst he told how he waits until the tide rolls up and covers them up, wave by wave, as they be screamin' for their lives, until late in the night when's they're all drowned. Then he told his first mate how he watched the crabs start to eat their heads the next morning, he did."

"I heard tell," one of the mates started, "that one time he had half his crew on shore with him diggin' some sort of 'laborate system of water for buryin' and hidin' his treasure, when he commences to skilletin' the whole group and dump them all on top the chest they just dug the hole for."

"Fifteen of them, is whats I hears, all on top. A dead man's chest, it was," said the other mate.

"He was a bad one, that's a sure," said Silver. "It was right after I hears that conversation that I makes it my business to end me days with that bloodthirsty buccaneer the next time we arrived to port, and you can lay to that. And, I might as well add, that it was not on any favourable terms that I left. If he were still hereabouts my life would surely be in danger. It's a blessing for sure he no longer is around to foul the waters with his murderous deeds, and you can lay to that."

"That's a sure one," the other mate added. "At least Black-Eyed Steele here sticks to the code, and you can trust that a share promised will be a share gotten. Even if he's a temper that fears a shark."

"Aye, that Captain Steele is a tough one, he is," said the other mate. "Sailed with him two dootys, and profitable they were. But he's not to be crossed with. If a ship is flying private flags, then he takes the bundt and let's 'em go, 'lessin' they puts up too much of a fight. But if the ship be showin' the Crown's flag, or in any ways is connected to the gentry of the Crown, then there be no mercy for her. All hands are dispatched and she is sent down to Davy Jones."

I for one did not care one way or the other about Redbeard. But the stories somehow lessened my, by now, inward growing disdain for Captain Steele and his actions. I was not even sure why. I still felt he had murdered Ripley without court nor jury, and I could not reconcile this with the man I had been having dinners with these past few weeks. I decided to put it out of my mind, if I could, until I had a chance to think it through more thoroughly.

"I am getting tired," I told the three of them. "So I'll see you in the morn."

"Goodnight Jim, me boy," said Silver. "Remember what 'tis I said about havin' your best interests to heart."

I did not respond, for I could still hear Ripley's frightful scream in my mind and was sure that sleep would not be forthcoming this night and for many nights to follow.

Chapter Nineteen

The Whale

Three days had passed, shrouded by the somber mood aboard the *Hispaniola*. To a man, excepting Long John, the effects of the death of Ben and, in my opinion, the murder of Ripley, lingered and placed dampened clouds upon the enthusiasm over the adventure we had embarked upon. I, for my part, was still at odds with what I had witnessed. Meals were not taken, for they would not cooperate and behave inside me. I performed my duties, and that was all. Silver was his usual, cheerful, merry self, dancing about his duties and wishing everyone good day. In this case I longed to have some of that merriment avert me from the thoughts that seemed to flood my mind; thoughts of murder, death and how easily life can be taken.

Captain Steele approached me yesterday and inquired about having another meal together. I told him I preferred to eat with the other men in the crew. He did not seem bothered by this and replied that if that is the way I felt about the matter, then there is where I belonged. He has not spoken to me since.

The next afternoon, after the men had finished their mid-day meal, I went above deck to feel the sea breeze upon my face, hoping it would help me to stay awake. I was exceedingly tired, for my sleep lasted not more than two hours the previous evening. After feeling a bit more invigorated, I returned to the mess to help Silver finish cleaning up.

"Captain!" shouted one of the men atop the crow's nest. "Call the captain right away!"

"What is it?" shouted back Quartermaster Tafari. "Enemy ship?"

"No sir, I am not sure what it is, but there be a sight never before seen by me eyes out there."

I heard the first shout and ran up from the kitchen, while Silver didn't seem to be bothered about it.

"What is it?" asked I to one of the mates already on deck.

"Not sure, lad. Seems like a whale off the starboard side of the ship."

"A whale?"

I ran over to look, and could barely make out anything. Finally, my eyes rested on an object quite far off into the distance, which looked to my mind to be just a dark spot on the water, with something raised above the water line. I guessed it could be a whale, although I'd never seen one before, leastwise not in person. My only references to the beastly fish were to be gleaned from book pictures in anatomy classes at university, with the different varieties: humpback, gray and orca. In point of fact, it was not a fish at all, rather it was a mammal. The captain arrived from the helm and looked toward the direction the man in the crow's nest was pointing.

"Give me the spyglass," the captain ordered Quartermaster Tafari, who handed it to him. He looked at it a goodly time, and then slowly lowered the glass. I greatly wanted to view one of those monsters of the deep, and remembered that I had eyed another spyglass in the crew's quarters. I ran below deck and returned with it as fast as I could make my body move. I aimed it toward the spot where I thought I saw something before and focused.

The incongruity of what I witnessed is difficult to explain, and one which I was totally unprepared to experience. Through the spyglass I clearly saw, surrounded by the vastness of the ocean, two men walking atop the whale. At least I thought it was a whale. It looked to be about a dozen or so lengths as long as the men were tall. However, at one end there appeared to be a sort of rounded horn, in the shape of an arc that was connected to the whale at each end. Unlike a horn, it was dark gray in color and looked to contain a pattern resembling factory gear teeth on the top side of it.

One of the men I could see clearly. He sported a full beard of dark hair, and wore a sort of Asiatic head cap, the type my Indian professor wore and I believe is related to what is called a "fez". My first thought was perhaps they were stranded on a shoal, their ship having sunk or capsized, marooning them atop its keel. Then the strangest thing occurred. A sort of round cover opened upward and through it ascended another man. How did he do that? I lowered the glass and peered toward the captain, who no doubt witnessed what I just had. He also looked confounded, having lowered his spyglass about the same time as I.

He walked to the upper deck and then over to its railing. I ran up and stopped next to him.

"Captain, did you see—"

"Indeed Hawkins, I witnessed it."

I looked again through my glass, and the last man who joined the three of them had a spyglass in his hand and was looking directly at us. Chills surrounded my neck, and I could barely hold the glass in place.

"Cannons to the fore!" shouted the captain.

"Who are they?" asked I.

The captain resumed his peering into the glass.

"They're of this world. Men like you and me. As to who or what they are, we'll soon find out."

The crew readied ten cannon to the starboard side, and prepared them to fire. Another group of men went below decks and brought back powder bags and balls. I judged we were sailing about ten knots with sails full. It was a smooth sea. And yet, as time moved forward, ever so slowly it seemed, these strange men on their whale kept up with the ship, and remained in the same position and distance from us as when we first sighted them.

"What be all the ruckus?" Silver asked me as he surfaced from the kitchen. "'Ave we comes upon an enemy ship?" He looked around and didn't notice the 'whale' on the horizon.

"No Long John, it's the strangest thing. There are three men on a whale just a few leagues away from us."

"Shiver me timbers if that don't be a fisherman's tale I've heard before," he said. "Lend me yer glass, Hawkins."

He spied through it in the direction we were looking and studied them for a moment.

"What do you know of this, Silver?" asked the captain.

"Arghhh... nothin' at all, Captain. 'Ceptin' of course scuttlebutt from the wharf rats, and maybe a bit or two that I reads in the papers before I was unjustly accused of a heinous crime."

"Go on."

"Well, sir, tales be told that there is this here sea monster... a whale they calls it, that has been sinking Man-o-wars the last couple of 'ears. Seems it can also tell the difference 'tween one of them Crown's battlers, and a merchant ship. I heard tell a couple a merchants 'ported seeing a giant whale—just like this one, but nothin's come of it. They say it spits fire and can sink an ironsides, that's what they said, by the powers. The Crown has a price on anyone who destroys her. Coursin', it on'y be tales they be telling."

"Now that he mentions it, Captain, I've heard tales similar in nature at one of the port stops we've made," Quartermaster Tafari said, "but I too laid them up to myth."

"Well, she is no monster, and is definitely not a whale," stated the captain.

"No whale likes I've seen before, and you can lay to that, leastwise not with a trio of men riding 'top o' her," said Silver.

"Pull fifteen degrees leeward," Captain Steele shouted to the helmsman, "and make it quick."

He looked again through the glass, while the ship dug into the wind and the *Hispaniola* laid into her new course. I grabbed the glass from Silver and observed the whale again. It continued to keep the same distance and followed our turn. The three men were still atop of her.

The captain lowered his glass.

"Maintain course," he shouted to the helmsman. "Powder the guns, and get ball ready," he yelled to the master gunner.

"Get about and stuff in the powder packs with a full charge, and then set the balls within!" the master gunner yelled. The gunners scurried about and fulfilled the order with great haste.

"We'll follow along until they either make a move, or darkness approaches," Captain Steele told Quartermaster Tafari. "It will be a cloudy night, and we'll be able to move under cover of stealth and be done with whatever that thing is. If they move toward us, then the balls will do our speaking."

"Mates, I want you all back at your stations now," yelled the quartermaster. "No more gawking over the rails."

"But, Captain, what is it out there?" asked one of the men.

"It's a sea monster, that's what it is," shouted another.

"There is no sea monster, men, and that's all you have to know now," Captain Steele told them. "We'll be quick with the guns if it becomes a threat. My orders are to sail this ship, and do it with full haste. Now, go back to your duties and be prepared for any potential siege."

The men started to murmur, and I could not fault them. I was scared. And fascinated. How could men be standing on top of something so low in the water? How did it move? Who were they? What did they want? Importantly, what was the captain going to do if it did attack us?

It took less than an hour to find out.

"Captain!" shouted a mate from the forward crows nest, "it's moving closer to us."

Steele peered through his glass, as did I, and to be sure, it had taken a turn inward and was closing in toward us. There were no men upon it to be seen.

"Man the cannon. Be ready to fire on my orders!" Steele shouted.

"Man the cannon, men, and be to the ready," relayed the master gunner.

I observed this whale as it moved in closer. The bone-like part of it with the gear shaped teeth that protruded from one end was now heading straight toward our starboard side. It had already halved the distance between us.

"Fire cannon!" shouted Captain Steele.

The roar of ten cannon firing was deafening. Smoke rose from the side of the ship while the cannons lurched back on their wheels and were stopped in a jerking fashion by the ropes tied to them to arrest their escape. I watched through the glass as the balls headed toward their target and started to splash near it. I witnessed—and heard—two of the balls hit it dead on. However, they bounced off and hit the water. When I say heard, I mean it was a clunking sound, like a hammer hitting an anvil.

RETURN TO TREASURE ISLAND

"What the devil?" the captain said. "Reload and fire again at will."

The gunners sprang into action, and within a few moments another volley of tent shot were fired. Again, only a few hit their target, and promptly the balls bounced off it as well, as if they were rubber balls hitting a wooden sidewalk, while the others missed their mark and splashed into the ocean.

Suddenly, this beast started to speed up toward our ship. And then, its eyes opened up, and we could see them lighted, glowing. And bright lights they were. One on each side of that strange gear-like arced bone on its front. A large wake was emanating from the front and sides of the beast.

"Fire again, and make your shots count!" yelled the captain.

The gunners worked at a feverish pitch, and within moments another volley was fired off. This time I could see that almost all of them hit their mark. Again, to no avail. I looked toward the captain and could see from his facial expression that he too was as unbelieving of what he was witnessing, as was the crew, who now had stopped their duties and were standing and observing the thing as it approached the ship. It had picked up speed and was now within viewable proximity.

"That be the darndest thing I ever be seein', and you can lay to that," muttered Long John to no one in particular.

I, for one, was frozen in my place. What could I do? Where could I go? I wanted to run, but there was nowhere to run to. And truth be known, I couldn't take my eyes off that fiery-eyed beast as it raced toward us with seemingly malicious intent.

It was within fifty yards of the ship when suddenly it disappeared below the surface of the water. A watery wake still led toward the ship. I ran over to the railing, leaned over and could actually see it going beneath our vessel through the clear azure tinted waters. I ran to the other side of the ship, and again as abruptly as it had disappeared, this beast returned to the surface about fifty yards out and continued traveling in that same direction.

"Man the guns on the port side at once!" the captain shouted.

The gunners moved to the other side of the ship and started to drop bag and ball into the cannon. The monster continued straight away from the ship, and at about the same distance as from the other side, about one league, it turned west and started to parallel our course, keeping an equal distance as before.

"What does it mean, Captain?" asked the gunner.

"If I were a betting man, I would say we have just been warned. Stand down the cannon, men!" he ordered. "Helmsman, resume our course, and keep a distance from that thing.

"In the meantime," he told Quartermaster Tafari, "make no move of aggression. Get the men back to their jobs. Let me know if anything changes."

"What in God's name is it, sir?" Tafari asked.

"I'm not sure whose name it is in, Tafari. Or what it is. I am sure it could have sunk this ship with little effort, and our guns are helpless against it. If it is in God's name, then say a prayer, for we've just been spared."

Shortly thereafter, I went below deck to help Silver prepare the night meal. Later that evening, when my duties were completed, I went up top and observed the light from the eyes of the beast just below the surface of the water. It followed us league for league and knot for knot. Finally, I could no longer stay awake and went down to sleep. When I awoke in the morning, Long John told me it had disappeared during the night. I asked him what he thought it was.

"I've no idea, Jim. But I can be tellin' you this. If it be pirates or the like, the Crown 'ad better be afraid, for it seems there be no way of stoppin' it. If it be one or another of the Crown's ships, we old buccaneers be doomed."

GԼ✝35X△⋏   ✝J53∴✝XԼ

Chapter Twenty

Pirate's Cove

We arrived at Pirate's Cove about mid-day on the twenty-seventh of May. The actual town, if it could be called that, was located within an inlet to the northeast of the island of Espaniola. Pirate's Cove is the *nom de plume* given this destination by the buccaneers, whereas on most of the maps it is known as Schotsche Bay.

Captain Steele decided not to use the docks. My suspicion was he didn't want the name of the ship easily being seen nor bandied about. We anchored within the cove but near its outer markers, and then used the longboats to reach the town's docks.

I was called into Captain Steele's quarters and therein met with the captain, Quartermaster Tafari and John Silver. It transpired that Silver wanted me, and me alone, to accompany him into Pirate's Cove and help secure the map. He insisted I would be indispensable as an additional set of eyes and ears, and furthermore, that I was the only one he could trust in that regard.

Captain Steele seemed most displeased with this suggestion. After some deliberations back and forth, he agreed to this arrangement, but with a startling threat: if the map was not in his possession that very evening, he would track us both down and put us to death. That would be the end of it. He also

151

reminded us that there was no way out of Pirate's Cove except by water, and therefore escape was not an option.

I, for my part, was as surprised as the captain with Silver's request. It was true we had a history, and that he could trust I would not harm him. Still, given my ungracious attitude toward him on this voyage, it seemed out of place. However, it was not lost on me how exciting it would be to help with the search to find the treasure map, and be the first to lay eyes upon it. It was equally true that leaving the ship after crossing the Atlantic would be most welcome. Based upon these reasons, I gave no resistance to the suggestion.

Silver had one more request. It was for firearms, which the captain agreed would be wise for him to possess while in this lawless town.

While we were preparing to leave that evening, the captain granted the request of the crew who had voted for leave that night, with the caveat that we were to sail the next day, and all hands should return before then.

Pirate's Cove was a combination of dilapidated establishments as well as modern-day taverns and busy warehouses. The docks were mostly used to bring goods that had been liberated from their former owners, and then sold and reshipped out to legitimate dealers of such goods, either to the Americas, or back to Europe.

We arrived just as the bright red sky faded into darkness, contrasting with the candles and gaslights of the town. The eerie combination only heightened my feeling of danger and foreboding. As we walked through the streets, which were no more than dirt roads, the sights and sounds of the waterfront bowery were everywhere: laughter, yelling, screaming and pistols firing. Both men and woman lined the wooden walkways that doubled as sidewalks. I was very glad to have Long John by my side in this wretched place.

Silver made a few inquiries, and after some searching we finally found what he was looking for—"the Quiet Woman". It was located in the northeast part of the village. There were no words on the front sign. Rather, it was simply a picture of a headless woman. I suspected this to be a sarcastic form of buccaneers' humour at work. Once we entered I was reminded of Long John's Spyglass Inn in Bristol—gaudy, loud, and at the same time, with a certain gaiety pervading the smoke-filled room. Four or five barmaids were hastily running to and fro from the barkeep area serving steins of bumboo. Buccaneers were scattered about in small groups shouting and toasting to this or that: one to the greatest group of mates they ever sailed with, another to the death of some squire or other, while still another to his dead aunt's mother's sister's husband, or the like.

I found myself becoming increasingly attracted toward this buccaneer lifestyle—one seemingly devoid of all responsibilities, cares and worries. It was a simple life. Black and white. Having just spent three weeks crossing the Atlantic with a ship full of them, I also knew the other side of the coin. The dangers and risks they—we—faced daily. I started to understand, at least in small part, why they needed to partake in these debaucheries that the church and my parents had constantly warned me to avoid at all costs, in order to save my soul from Beelzebub's clutches.

"Come on Jim, me boy," said Long John, "let's take a table near the bar and see if we can learn something from this motley crew."

We found a small table a few feet from the main bar and took our seats. A barmaid approached us and asked what will be our fare.

"Thank you for asking, me fair lady. We've come a long ways and are parched for some grog, that's for sure. Perhaps you can bring me and me friend here your house's finest drink, a tasty one as there is, I'll wager."

She nodded, smiled slightly, turned and headed toward the bar. Long John surveyed the open area. He eyed each buccaneer as if trying to remember if he knew them, all the while smiling and animated in a jovial way.

"Jim," says he, "this here establishment reminds me of me own little tavern back in Bristol, it does. 'Twas a happy time for me then indeed; swappin' stories, spinnin' a yarn or two. Seems like such a long time ago."

I was about to respond with a sarcastic answer, when at that moment I noticed a couple of men walk into the Quiet Woman. The sight of them caused my throat to tighten up while my stomach wretched in pain. It was two of the buccaneers that I ran into on my way to Bristol, the ones who robbed me and left me for dead. I knew for sure I was right, for how could I forget that hooknose and eye patch of the one? They were laughing and slapping each other on the back. When I looked down at one of them, my suspicions were confirmed. He was wearing *my* boots.

Long John noticed my gaze fixed upon these miscreants and watched them also as they stumbled up to the bar—not a stone's throw from where we sat. By their appearance and gait, this was not the first drinking establishment they had visited that evening. Long John leaned over and whispered.

"Do ye be knowin' those two scallywags, Jim?"

"I've had an unpleasant run-in with them before," I replied.

"Do ye still have a problem with 'em?"

"I'd rather let it go and keep our attention on the matter at hand. I've crossed their paths before. It will happen again, no doubt. Then the score can be evened."

The barmaid brought our drinks and set them down upon the table.

"That'll be two shillings," she told us.

Silver pulled out a farthing and handed it to her. She took it in her hand. As she clamped down on it, Silver grabbed her entire fist with one hand and pulled her closer to him, smiling all the while.

"We'll be needin' some information as well, me dear lady. And I'm hopin' you can be the one that helps us. We're lookin' for a particular lady, one that goes by the name of Lady Blue, I'm told. Would you be knowin' who that might be?"

"I might."

"Ah, I be hopeful with yer response, I am. And would you be willin' to double the stake you now hold to remember if ye do or don't?"

She thought for a moment.

"I can tell you what you want to know. And if you make it thrice, I will have her come to your table here, if'n' you really want to see her."

"Me dear, dear woman," said Long John, "that would be worth the price, and a kiss to boot. Be off in speed and have this woman meet us here on the swift. I'll pay yer price."

As she left us, the two buccaneers at the bar started shouting at one another, arguing much the same as when they were deciding what to do with my nearly lifeless body over two fortnights earlier.

"Looks like our fortunes be assured, Jim. I'm getting a real good feeling about this here establishment. Drink up, me boy, drink up."

As Silver picked up his stein, one of the buccaneers took his mug and slammed it into the chest of the other, shouting some curse about his mother or something, and he started flying backward—right toward our table—and fell upon my lap. I quickly pushed him up and off me, and he fell to the floor with a hard thump, shouting out in pain.

On the ground he turned toward me and looked up with a fearful scowl gracing his cragged face, the same one I had seen much earlier. Only this time I was looking down upon him. He pushed off the floor, steadied his stance and then peered directly at me, seemingly trying to gather his thoughts. All effects of his brew seemed to suddenly subside as he growled:

"No one pushes me to the ground, mate, and leastwise gets away with it. I wants an apology, and be swift about it, or be prepared to suffer the consequences."

In an instant I found myself standing up, seemingly not of my own volition. My chair flew backwards and hit the floor with a loud thud. It was as if something deep within me had caused this reaction, quite opposite to the one I consciously wanted to pursue.

"I assure you, sir, I only deflected your fall, and had no intention of pushing you onto the floor—or anywhere, for that matter. There is neither an apology due, nor will one be proffered. Of that you can be sure."

"Not one be proffered? Proffered is it?" He turned to his buccaneer companion. "Seems like we have an *educated* buccaneer on our hands, indeed it does, matey." He turned his attention back toward me.

"So I say there is one due, and you say one will not be 'proffered', is it? Well stand to, and be prepared to suffer the consequences, and that's a fact, say I."

The swirly lot of buccaneers around us quieted up and started to slowly move away from our area in the tavern. I quickly glanced over at Long John. He had stealthily pushed himself back from the table, moved his crutch under his arm, and was starting to rise upon his leg.

"I can handle this!" shouted I to Silver. "There's no need for your interference."

He nodded and smiled, while standing straight up. I cast my gaze back toward that buccaneer.

"As to you, you'll get no mercy from me. So I'm warning you and giving fair notice, that I am well trained and considered quite capable with fencing swords. So I beg you to take your leave before I am forced to avail myself of these skills and gravely hurt you."

He stared at me, with a queer dumbfounded look for a few moments.

"What be the intentions and point of what this son of an urchin just said to me?" he shouted toward his drinking companion, almost in a sneer.

I must here admit that directly after this soliloquy there was a feeling of embarrassment, coupled with regret. It became immediately clear that there was more grog than self-preservation residing in these miscreants, and that no amount of reasoning was to avail. The mates in the surrounding area all turned full attention toward the ruckus we were making, some of them pointing and whispering to each other.

"I'm a thinkin' he wants to duel with you, Barton, with a fence of some sort or other."

He started laughing, spitting grog out of his mouth as he did.

"That's not what I said, gentlemen."

"Whoaaa, stop right there, urchin," said he, "there's where ye've been lead astray, and that's a fact."

He reached to his side sash and slowly pulled out his cutlass with his right hand.

"*Gentlemen* we surely not be, and to the devil with them that insults us with that title."

As the cutlass left his sash, he swung it toward me in a quick snap of his wrist. I kept my attention on his hand and anticipated something of the sort, and had already planned on moving back a pace or two. In my favour, it was an older type of cutlass, with the side being the thicker and duller of the blade being swung nearest me. It slightly glanced off the side of my head, leaving me none the worse.

I reached for the dagger in my sash, grabbed the handle and pulled it out. It looked decidedly small in comparison to his weapon, and it was then I realized I had not thought this through. I was clearly at a disadvantage. My first impulse was to throw it at him, hoping to wound his arm and thereby allow some time for my next move, of which I was even more unsure. However, by the time I had worked out this dubious action in my mind, the cutlass came round again on a reverse arc, and only the reflexive action of stepping back again saved me from a lethal head wound.

Silver moved quickly from behind the table and grabbed a cutlass from a buccaneer's sash standing next to him. While doing so, he rammed his elbow up and into the hapless fellow's face. As this poor wretch collapsed to the ground Silver tossed it to me.

"I don't be thinkin' yer goin' a be talking him to death," shouted Silver, winking, "so tries this!"

I fortunately caught it by the handle while tossing my knife to the side. All of this occurred within the blink of an eye. I nodded back at Silver, took my stance, and faced directly this vile and now proven unsavory buccaneer.

"So the urchin desires to meet his maker this very day, does he? To die like a dog, eh? I warned you!"

The buccaneer immediately went into a lightning group of slashes; a fiendish glow of bloodlust enveloped his seedy eyes. It was obvious this man had had some training, I thought, as I instinctively blocked each of the pounding jabs coming my way while I was backing up. Even though drunk, I could see he was very effective. I returned his volley in kind, and he was visibly surprised at my response. He shakily hastened a retreat at the force of my pursuit. His back hit the bar, and I hesitated a moment, perhaps due to the years of training and good sport I was taught in university. Even now I am not sure why. But it cost me dearly.

He reached toward the bar, grabbed a mug of grog, and tossed it into my face. A searing burning sensation closed my eyes and sent a wave of pain throughout my head. I held up my cutlass to ward off his blows and could feel his blade crashing into it as I quickly retreated, trying to get my bearings. I hit the back wall and gritted my teeth as I screamed with all my might. I leaned forward into his cutlass just as it hit mine, and with all my might pushed him back a few paces. I rubbed my eyes and commanded them to focus. I knew my life depended on them doing so. I could now make out the buccaneer, although still just a blur. His shock at my screaming and retaliatory reaction caused him to pause for a few precious moments—a move I vowed would cost *him* dearly.

An electric tingling feeling started to engulf my body, emanating in my chest and moving outward to all my limbs—a feeling I had never known before. Anger welled up within me in an instant. All I wanted to do was murder him. A strength that I had never known took over, while I watched myself in a detached manner advance ruthlessly and with wild and wicked abandon toward this focus of all my hate. I felt my face contort and fill with blood and my teeth clench. I swung away at him like a madman, pushing this beast of a human further and further back and into a corner. Cling! Clang! Cling! He could now only try to defend these vicious blows I was delivering to him, and for the first time I caught a glimpse of something like fear in his eyes, which seemed to escalate the welling up of pure animal hatred growing within me.

I redoubled my efforts, not with conscious thought, but instinctively; as if some inner part of my being knew I had him on the run. My thirst for vengeance and harm toward him grew in intensity, and I knew I would kill him. And yet, my conscious mind gave no objections in the least. He would die a deserving death. For I had no doubt he had shown no mercy to others like myself who were not so fortunate as to be able to put up a fight. I had already experienced that first hand.

We moved to the left and passed the table where Silver and I had sat. Long John was still standing and leaning upon his crutch near it. I could see with my peripheral vision that he was staring at me, a slight smile crossing his lips. I cared less, for I could focus on nothing but the task at hand.

159

Just at that very moment this vile buccaneer's drinking mate, the very one who pushed me into the fire that awful night, and who was still wearing my boots, lifted his leg and rammed his booted foot into the side of my right knee, sending a shock of pain through my body as it knocked me completely off balance. I fell toward my left, while at the same moment I raised my right arm, cutlass in hand, and tried to alleviate my fall through counter-balance. After two stumbles, I was able to right myself. I looked up to see the buccaneer I was fighting swinging his cutlass in a wide right hand arc aimed directly at my neck. I tensed my body for the deathblow I was sure to receive, filled with an anger beyond all measure I have ever known.

Bang!

A loud explosion rang out next to my right ear, sending a concussion coursing through my head. The buccaneer violently flipped backward, feet off the ground, and flew into the wall. A crimson hole appeared in the center of his brow as he crumpled to the floor in a lifeless heap. Blood started dripping down his face. I fell to my knees due to the force of the explosion and a loss of my equilibrium. I twisted my head to the right to see Silver standing with a smoking flintlock in his right hand, holding the deadly aim that ended that buccaneer's life. He tossed the gun aside and reached into his sash and pulled out another one in its place.

The crowd of buccaneers started to get angry at his stepping in at this point. Murmurs escalated into talk.

"Before anyone here be gettin' any ideas, let me speak my piece," Silver shouted. "Fairs be fair. We has a code we's all agreed to. Me mate here didn't sniff out no trouble or a fight, but he met it head on like a true buccaneer is honour bound to do's. I only evened the odds when his mate stepped in.

"And if there be any of you mates that takes exception to this, let him speak out, and you can take it up with old Long John Silver here. And you can be takin' it I'll give it a fair listen, by the powers. To a man say I, we've no use for mates who have no

160

sense of honour among us. We're not the barbarians the king's courts have made us out to be. We've oaths that say the difference. Shiver me timbers, we're not a band of cutthroats to our own."

Long John offered me his hand, while leaning down on his crutch.

"I could have taken him."

"Indeed you could have—and would have too, had you not been interfered with."

I reached up and used his hand to pull myself to my feet. He spoke lowly to me while I gathered my senses.

"But it be a lesson learned, Jim, me boy. Yer likely as not get a second chance with the likes of that type. Don't trust that a buccaneer will always be a fair and square. Although most of 'em abides by the code fer mates, there is the odd lot that don't. And you best assume none of them do, and you'll serve yourself well."

I stood there and shook off the dizziness I still felt. Silver turned to the buccaneer at the bar who kicked me.

"Now as to you mate, I'm sure you had yer reasons a plenty for interfering with a fair fight. Is that bein' the case here?"

"I don'ts answer to nobody. Especially the likes of scum like you, ye one-legged squid."

Long John smiled at him, while he eyed him like a snake does his prey.

"Don't answer indeed, is it? That be fair 'nough for this ol' sea dog, by the powers. I'm not your maker."

Long John turned his back to the buccaneer and hobbled a step or two away, and then turned his head slightly back toward him.

"But I'm a fearin' you'll be meetin' yer maker real soon, and then you can be tellin' *him* alls about it."

"What the he—"

He had not the chance to speak another word, for Long John had lowered his crutch from under his arm, and then swung it around his side, and by force of acceleration broadsided him squarely against the side of his head with a mighty force. This caused him to slide backwards along the bar railing a good four or five feet before collapsing in a crumpled heap against the wall.

My anger was still so welled up that I instinctively ran over and, with all my strength, kicked him in the gut where he lay. Long John grabbed me by the shirt.

"Calm down, Hawkins, you be needin' yer senses here."

He looked around at the crowd of buccaneers who were gawking at what they had just seen.

"This be a lessin' fer all of you. I'll not be hearin' no more of his kind a talk. Be there anyone else who sides with these pathetic swabs who disrespect our solemn codes?"

He held up his pistol so that everyone could see it plainly.

"For as sure as the tides, I've got another lead ball primed in wait for him that doesn't live up to 'em. And you can lay to that!"

Most of the buccaneers went back about their drinking business, and within a few moments, the place was as if nothing had happened. A couple of bar helpers moved the bodies out of the room. One of them picked up the pistol off the floor and tossed it over to Silver. We sat back down at the table.

"You be okay, Jim?"

"I still say I could have beat him on my own," I told him.

Silver grabbed his stein of grog, took a big gulp, and wiped his mouth with his sleeve.

"Of course you could have Jim. The fear of sharks was upon him 'til the last. I could see it plain as day. But you needs to know there be times to be takin' the help of a mate when disaster strikes... or circumstance warrants. You surprised ol' Silver tonight, Jim Hawkins. You've grown from the sardine I knew before to a full-dressed buccaneer. 'Tis a sight to behold, and you can lay to—"

"I heard you was looking for me… is that so?"

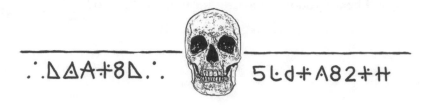

Chapter Twenty-One

We Meet Lady Blue

"**A**nd you would be?"

"Lady Blue I am." She gave a big curtsy with a mocking grin. Her bright red hair was piled under a lace cap, slightly askew. She was dressed in a red bustier which covered a slightly worn silk chemise and a bright red velvet outer skirt. White frilly pantaloons stuck out beneath everything. A bevy of silver bracelets jangled on her wrists.

"Lady Blue, be it? Well, my dear, I has a double message for you, one of thems be from old Jasper hisself," said Silver.

"Go on."

"He told me to send you his fondest and dearest greetin's, and I am also, in personal ways, sorry to have to tell you he has passed on from this life at a most inopportune time."

She crossed her arms.

"That so? Did he give anything to you for me?"

"Let's take a minute now to say our prayers for old Jasper's soul, yes indeedy." Long John took off his hat, bowed his head and winked at me. She didn't flinch. After a few moments he returned hat to head.

"Ahemmm. Now that that be done. It's on to business now, is it Lady Blue? Jasper told me straight that he left a certain something in yer charge, to be redeemed at a later time."

"Maybe he did, and then maybe again he didn't. I'm having a difficult time remembering anything right now, I am."

"Arghhh, I can understand that, me beautiful Lady Blue, yes indeedy I do. It's probable due to all the pain and sufferin' yer 'speriencing due to the news of old Jasper's tragic demise... so sad it 'tis... it's probable hard to remember anything at all. And that's a shame too, 'tis."

"And why is that?" she asked, slightly tilting her head.

"Ohhhhh. It's a shame 'cause he spoke so fondly of you, being the love of his life and all, and he gave me somethin' that looks like quite the 'trinket', he did, and that's a fact. Tolds me in no uncertain terms that I was to be given' it only to you, the 'Lovely Lady Blue' he called you, 'ceptin' of course, only if'n you should be holdin' something for him that he left with you and is to gives me. That's what he said, straight and square."

"Perhaps if you were to show me this 'trinket', I could move past me sorrows and me remembrances would start to return," she said.

"That's a thought," said Long John, "a solid one as ever I heard too. Are you supposin' there be a room we's could go to where it would be safe to bring it out and shows you?"

She motioned for us to follow her. We crossed the bar area and entered through a door into a room just to the right of the bar. Silver and I sat down at a table that stood in the middle of the room. Against the wall stood a settee day bed. The rest of the room was stark bare. Lady Blue remained standing.

"First of all, you owe Charlotte two more farthings."

She held out her hand, the noise of her bracelets emphasizing her motive. Silver reached into his pocket.

"Of course, and be sure to give 'er our gratytudes," said Silver.

He handed Lady Blue the coins, and she quickly put them in her brassiere.

"Now then, you were saying that Jasper left you something for me?"

"That be a fact."

"And you were going to show it to me, this trinket?"

"Ah yes, and here it 'tis."

Silver pulled out the coin with the Pharaoh's head and held it between his thumb and forefinger before the whale oil lamplight which glowed on the table. It glistened and shined like fire. He moved it around so that its golden brilliance danced about the drab and tattered walls of the room.

"You have something for me, Lady Blue?" asked Long John.

She quickly walked over to the settee bed, reached beneath, and pulled out a small, black, hard-cased shipman's bag. She brought it to the table and set it down, while not releasing her grip.

"Here is what you are wanting. Jasper left it in my care and said to give it to anyone who possessed that Pharaoh's coin."

Silver reached for the bag. Lady Blue stopped him with her free hand by slapping his, and then turned it over and spread-open her fingers. All the while she held an expectant and defiant stare upon Silver.

"Of course, Lady Blue, I almost be fergettin' the nature of our transaction."

He placed the coin in her outstretched hand. She clamped her fingers around it while releasing her hold on the bag, and stepped back.

She smiled for the first time, opened her hand and studied the coin.

"Good old Jasper. I'm going to miss him, As for you two, you've left me two bodies to get rid of this eve. This is very bad for business. So I'll ask you not to ever visit me again. That door over there opens to the alley. I suggest you use it. Stay as long as you like, although I'm not sure why that bag is so valuable. Nothing in it of any worth, as far as I could tell."

Long John and I simultaneously looked up at her.

"What? I didn't know if he or anyone would return, and was just checking my collateral. Making sure it was in good condition, and all." She stared directly at me.

"Too bad we didn't meet under different circumstances, my young one," she said with a wink. "Could have been a fun time for us both." She smiled. "Good night, gents."

As she reached the door, I found myself involuntarily asking a question.

"Lady Blue."

She stopped with her hand on the doorknob and turned her head toward me.

"Yes."

"May I ask why you arc called by that name?"

She opened the door and then smiled; with a jingle of her bracelets and a flip of her bustle she left and closed the door behind her.

We both sat and stared at the old black bag. I must say my heart sank on hearing Lady Blue's comment about having inspected the contents of it, and I could see Silver's crested brow fall a bit with mine. Outwardly, the bag did appear of no value, and yet I remembered I thought as much of Billy Bones' seaman's chest when I first laid eyes on it, and found later I was in error to the extreme.

"Well Jim, me boy, let's have a look in this here bag's insides, and see if we be chasin' sirens in the fog or if this treasure be real."

He stood up, grabbed the bag, opened it up and spilled the contents out onto the table: a seaman's compass, a shirt, a small whalebone-handled knife, a tobacco pouch, two rounded silver earrings, a small bottle of what looked like dark rum and finally, a deck of playing cards. Silver unbanded the string which held the cards, and spread them before us. Nothing unusual. He spread them further apart and studied them for any markings; there were none that I could see. He turned them over and after a few minutes we determined that there was nothing written on them. He took the bag, turned it upside down and shook it a couple of times while hitting the bottom with his hand. Nothing.

My heart sank further in disappointment. My mind raced through all the hardships I had endured on this voyage, at risk of life and limb; and now, seemingly, it was for naught—another old sailor's yarn that came to nothing. The worst of it was Steele. If we returned to the *Hispaniola* with no map, we were assured of a horrific death awaiting us.

Silver kept staring at the bag and continued sifting through the artifacts. He picked each one up and studied them once again. He finally picked up the shirt and spread it out upon the table, looking it over completely, as if maybe something were written on it. All of a sudden he smiled, shouted out loud to himself, "you old sea dog of a devil," and started laughing in an uncontrollable, boisterous way. I failed to see the humour, and so did not join him. When he settled down he looked my way.

"Jim, we're not done in yet," says he. "I still has a bit of me brains workin', and I be thinkin' I know what to do. Ol' Jasper, he don't wants to give up his secrets too easily."

Silver grabbed the whalebone-handled knife, opened the bag's top as wide as it would spread, and started to cut through the stitching at the top of the thick gauze lining the bag. He carefully cut one side and peeled it back; nothing there. He continued to cut the next side—the short one, and again it contained nothing. Again on the opposite long side, he peeled back the lining, and a smile enveloped his face. He slowly pulled out a piece of parchment, folded over numerous times, and held it up.

"Very clever, that ol' sea dog. But it takes more than a swabby before the mast to be pullin' one over on ol' Long John, and you can lay to that."

He carefully opened the map and laid it upon the table. My heart was throbbing in my chest. It was Treasure Island, sure and true. Skeleton Island lay to the south, Spyglass Hill clearly marked, longitude and latitude written in the legend area. All the mishaps and horrors associated with this island started to well up within me. And yet, the excitement of discovering this new treasure map overshadowed those feelings and instead, I could hardly wait to return there once again.

"Where is the treasure marked on the map, Long John?"

"I'm not sure, Jim. There be nothing apparent that I can see. There are strange symbols here," he points, "and here, of which I have no idea about. Over in the corner here is a pair of inverted 'v's', and an inverted triangle with a sort of squiggle within, but I confess I've no awares of what it all means."

He held it up to the lamp, very closely, as if he were almost trying to look through it. Finally, he started to fold it up. Then I noticed it.

"Wait," I shouted, "look over here."

I pointed to what could have been a slash mark on Spyglass Hill.

"That could be a mark, a blurred x of some sort," I said.

"Yer bein' right as rain, Jim. But look where it be on that hill."

"That doesn't make sense, does it?"

"No indeedy."

He studied the map for a few more moments, when we both heard crashing and shouting within the tavern connected to this room.

"We'll have to discover its secrets when back at the ship with that black-eyed Cap'n Steele," said Silver. "In the meantime, you take it back there. I'm going to see if I can find some of our mates and start befriendin' them, just in case, you know."

"You know what the captain said about that, Long John."

Silver started to pick up and throw the contents that laid before us back into the bag.

"Not to worry, Jim. I gaves me word, and I intends to keep it. I've a mind to fill up with a bit of the grog, seeing as our next stop will be Treasure Island, and I be suspectin' there's no taverns to be seen there yet. And, it don't hurt to be a good 'mbassador to the rest of the crew, now does it Jim?"

"No, I don't guess that it does."

"That's good, that's real good. Now go on back to the ship. Give that map straight away to the captain, and I'll be seein' you before the night be over."

He closed the bag, handed me the map and motioned for us to go toward the rear door.

"Tell me, Long John, how did you know the map was in the lining of the bag?"

"Clever he was, that old Jasper. He gived me a clue and I didn't even recognize it as such. But he did, by the powers. You see's, Jim, he had to cut out the lining in his shirt pocket to give me the gold coin in the jail cell. I figured he just had it there, for safekeeping and such. When I were looking at this here shirt he kept in his bag, I finally noticed a slit under the pocket's lining. That be another clue, 'twas. It be his way of tellin' me to look in the lining of the seaman's bag. Let's not be wastin' time here. If those two we took care of this evening had any other mates, they might be talkin' up a storm of trouble for us in that bar. We needs to be off with dispatch. You goes on now to the ship."

"I can go with you."

"Now, now, Jim, you don't have to worry 'bout ol' Long John. I still have one lead shot left if I runs into trouble. Take this bag back with you too."

He handed it to me and waved me off.

"Be careful," I offered as he took off in the opposite direction in the alley, realizing for the first time that I really meant it. He smiled back at me.

"I will Jim. Now get going. Shiver me timbers, lad, I don't want the captain to thinks we be up to no good."

– – – – – – – – – –

I arrived at the ship by rowing one of the longboats from the dock. There seemed to be no one aboard except for old Ben who was left to guard the *Hispaniola*. He appeared fast asleep. In truth, he was passed out drunk on the mezzanine deck from rum, by the smell of it, and snoring loudly. I crept by him to the captain's door and knocked. No answer. I suspected he was out purchasing stores for the next segment of our voyage. I knocked again to make sure, and thought I heard a muffled voice. I knocked again with more vigor. Again I heard the muffled noise, but this time it seemed as if... it was a sobbing sound. Very strange, thought I? Upon checking, I found that the door handle was locked, but that the door itself was not quite latched all the way. I pushed harder against it. It yielded, and so I let myself in.

The room was dark except for a small whale oil lamp that burned on the captain's desk. I slowly made my way toward his desk when I heard the sound again, this time a little louder. It seemed to be coming from inside the starboard side drawing room. I walked over and listened against the door. There was no mistake. I could clearly hear a voice crying from within the room. How utterly strange, I thought. Who or what could it possibly be? I turned the key that was protruding from the outside lock. When it made a loud clicking sound, the noise within stopped. I slowly opened it and peered inside.

At first I could see nothing. My eyes were not accustomed to the low light from the moon coming in through the starboard windows. Once my eyes adjusted, I could see a figure sitting in a chair in the corner, with their arms in an unusual position—up and over toward one of the ship's wooden beams. Suddenly, this person looked over at me and I could clearly see their face.

It is difficult to write what next went through my mind, heart and body. A series of conflicting feelings coursed through my entire nervous system—head to foot. I was frozen in my tracks, unable to even make a sound. There, before me, was Chloe.

My Chloe.

Chapter Twenty-Two

Escape from the Hispaniola

The incongruity of trying to comprehend how in the world she could be in the captain's drawing room in the middle of the Caribe was quickly outweighed by the unbelievable joy of seeing her. A joy only to be followed by abject terror. Before I knew it, I had slammed the door closed, and my body sprung into a full gallop across the room toward her. She turned away defensively from me, at first I suspect because she knew not it was me.

"Chloe!" I cried, "it is me, Jim!"

She blinked her eyes as in disbelief and started crying in earnest. I took out my knife and cut the leather straps that bound her to the spar with the metal rings. She fell into my arms, grabbed me tightly and cried my name. It seemed I could not hold her close enough to me, as she told me how glad she was to see me.

"I felt sure you were killed by those buccaneers, Jim, that some horrible villainy had been perpetrated upon you. I had no way of knowing if you were alive or dead. I had given up all hope of seeing you—or my family ever again. I am so happy to see you!"

She then kissed me with great fervor, pressing hard against my lips. I did not try to pull away. Finally, she stopped and rested her head back against my chest.

"Pray tell me, Chloe, what manner of adventure brought you to this ship?"

She told me the story of how she met Captain Smollett in Bristol, how they had joined together in the search for me and how he and the crew had gone off with some of the magistrate's men to find me.

"Once the ship was taken over by that Captain Steele, they decided to keep me prisoner because they thought I was Squire Trelawney's daughter. They believed no one of the Crown's fleet would fire on the *Hispaniola* if they thought the squire's daughter was aboard. I decided it best to say naught to their mistaken impression for fear of the consequences that should befall me if they learned the truth."

"But why would they think you were the squire's daughter?"

"It was that awful Long John you spoke to me about who suggested it, at first. I think since I was left behind, they assumed as much."

"Long John knew you were here?"

"Of course. Captain Steele swore him to silence upon pain of death. He didn't want the crew knowing I was aboard."

"Was the captain a gentleman?" asked I, fully expecting to cut him down and skew him like a mackerel on the end of a catch line if he so even as much as touched her in an inappropriate way.

"Yes, he was. In fact, a perfect gentleman in every respect," said she.

"We must get you off this ship at once. We sail the morrow for Treasure Island, and once there, even if they still believe this story, you will be in more jeopardy, for the captain and crew will surely be emboldened by the treasure they find, and there will lie no route for you to escape."

"To where, my Jim? I heard the captain speak about gathering stores for the voyage and then setting sail again. And are we not in Pirate's Cove, known throughout the civilized world as a dangerous place for Christians? Where could we possibly go?"

"I've got to think for a moment."

She was correct. The incident in the Quiet Woman earlier spoke volumes of the dangers that were to be faced there. A thousand and one thoughts, some too terrifying to even entertain, thrashed about in my imagination, each vying for attention. I felt I had to do something, and yet knew not what.

"Pray for an answer," I told myself.

I would think of one pathway out of this predicament, follow the train of logic through to its conclusion and quickly discard it, for it had no satisfying ending. The main obstacle lay in where we were located. A hornet's nest of buccaneers that not even the Crown's fleet dared sail into. A woman of good moral character was not safe within the depravity that flourished about this township. I needed more information.

I brought both of us into the main captain's quarters, and surveyed it. I found the captain's chart box, but it was unnecessary. He had a chart of the Caribe and the Island of Espanola already laid out on the table. I studied it carefully, and to my amazement I found a name I recognized, Esperanza. It was on the southwestern side of the island, a French protectorate. France and England were no longer at war; they had both signed treaties recently to improve trade and commerce. Perhaps, I reasoned, if I can get Chloe to that township, she could catch a ship eastbound for England with the help of the French magistrate, who most certainly could arrange safe passage for her under his seal. But it would cost.

"Have you seen any coinage in this room?" asked I.

"Yes, my dear Jim. The captain keeps—Captain Smollett that is—he kept coin in a secret compartment of his desk."

She walked to it, opened the second drawer on the left undercarriage of the desk and reached within. I heard a clicking noise that preceded the outward extension of the left top of the desk—a compartment usually reserved for letters and such. She pulled it out, and behind it she reached in and extracted a leather bag and tossed it to me,

I opened it and quickly saw it was a large sum of money in gold doubloons.

"I have a plan, Chloe, and yet I've not much evidence to base its success upon. Still, I feel it is more desirable to try for success than stay here and suffer perhaps a worse fate. Let us take half of this coinage, and leave it lay open the way it is. Where does the captain keep his clothing?"

"In his quarters, there," she said, pointing to a large chest.

I quickly opened it and rifled through.

"What you'll need is in here. Find some pants and a shirt and coat. I'll wait outside. As soon as you are changed, meet me on the main deck. And waste not time; it is now our enemy!"

I hurried out the door to the crew's quarters below deck and found a hat that would work for her. I raced back up the stairs and almost knocked her over.

"Sorry, my Chloe, we must hurry. Put on this hat and tuck your hair out of sight. Make haste behind me to the longboat. No matter what happens, stay with me."

I looked at old Ben passed out on the floor and devised a diversionary plan. I grabbed a belaying pin and tapped him on the head, causing a gash and blood to trickle down his face, and quickly tossed it to his side. We reached the longboat, and with all my might I rowed us to shore, sparing no pain in the process.

I only knew one person in that Godforsaken township, and therein I lay my hopes. I was betting on two things: empathy and greed. Of the latter one I could be sure.

We finally arrived at the Quiet Woman, and carefully, quietly, we entered the drawing room from the alley, through the same door Long John and I had exited earlier that evening.

While Chloe waited in the outer room, I walked into the main bar through the other door, sought out and found Lady Blue. I implored her to speak with me about a matter of a confidential nature. Her following me into the room was additionally premised upon the payment of another "trinket".

"Who is this?" she asked, eyeing Chloe.

"A friend of mine, in trouble," I replied.

"And what is this of me?"

"I have a proposition for you," I started. "My friend is in need of safe passage to Esperanza. There has been a falling out with a certain captain, one who would spare no pain to seek revenge. We believe the only way out is to get *her* there quickly," I said, and then wished I could take it back. I continued on instead. "Can you help us?"

"Us?"

"My mate and me."

"Why should I get myself involved in such an affair? If it were found out that I did, I would be on the outs with someone over it, and my business depends on not getting involved in anyone's affairs. I take no sides. Pass no judgments. You received that courtesy this evening. And this business of yours seems more than you state."

"Lady Blue, please, we've nowhere else to turn," say I. "We know no one here. Please at least hear my proposition."

She nodded an assent while staring at Chloe, who dipped down the rim of her hat to just above her eyes. Her baggy clothes seemed to droop even lower to the floor. I pulled out ten gold doubloons from my pocket.

"I'll pay you five of these now, and send the other five to you upon safe passage and arrival in Esperanza. This is a fortune, and no one will ever know you helped in any way."

"A fortune it is indeed, and yet of little value to me if this Captain Steele—that is who you are speaking of, I assume—finds out I in any way was helpful in a traitorous way. I'm aware of his reputation, and it spares not ladies. You'll need to take your leave, now."

Chloe lifted her head and looked to me, with sadness in her eyes. She slowly stood up and took off her hat, letting her hair fall down upon and over her shoulders.

"Miss Blue," Chloe started, "if you know of his reputation, then you know what fate must await me as his captive. I implore you, please show some compassion and mercy and help me escape from this awful man."

She stared at Chloe from head to foot.

"What is your name?"

"Chloe."

"Chloe," she repeated softly to herself. She took her eyes from Chloe and back to the table where I had dropped all the coins.

"It will be a difficult journey. Are you up for it?"

"I am strong and healthy and used to hard work. I will not be a burden," said Chloe.

Lady Blue turned and started to pace the room. We followed her with our eyes. It appeared she was going to head toward the door when suddenly, she stopped, took a big breath, and came back to the table.

"All ten of the coins *now*. I'll need part of them to arrange the passage. If ever I am asked, I will deny knowledge of who either of you are."

"Then you'll do it?"

"You agree to my terms?"

"Deal," said I.

"It will take a few hours to arrange," she stated. "I believe the best way would be the southern coastal route around the east side of this island. Trade between the townships is brisk, and I've a trusted friend who can make the voyage with no questions asked, for the right price. It will take about two days to get there. We'll need to cut your hair to discourage the chance of discovery of your sex. Do you have any other belongings?"

"No."

"Well, Chloe, I am not sure why I am helping you, but rest assured, I will keep my word and see to it that you get safely to Esperanza. From there, you are on your own."

"We'll be okay once there."

"Oh, this is for the both of you?"

"Yes."

"No," said I.

Chloe quickly turned to me, startled.

"What? What are you saying, Jim?"

"I can't go. It is too dangerous. If I am found missing from the ship, it will be unsafe for you. Once they have the map, you will be of no further interest to them. I must stay Chloe, and see this out."

"You'd better leave then, and quickly," said Lady Blue. "I want no one to see you here again. I will start to make arrangements."

She picked up the gold coins, and for the first time smiled warmly at Chloe; then she darted toward the door. She stopped, and turned back toward us.

"Bluebell," said she.

"Pardon me?" asked I.

"You asked earlier about my nickname here. My mother named me Bluebell. Now I am Lady Blue. You take care, Jim."

She closed the door behind her, and I could hear it lock.

"Jim, you must come with me. You simply must. Those buccaneers are dangerous, and that awful pirate captain cannot be trusted."

"Chloe, it is important that you listen to me. Our only hope for your safety is if I stay. I will be fine. The captain has grown to trust me, at least to a point, I suspect. Once he finds you have gone missing, he will realize that his 'trump' has been stolen from him. And you have no doubt seen his anger. But, he also knows, through that weasel of a buccaneer Morgan, that he has me to negotiate with. I am betting that once he has the map, and me, he'll not waste valuable time to search this township for you.

"Once you reach Esperanza, use the rest of the gold coins you have and buy passage back to England. Find Captain Smollett and let him know where we are going. Tell him it is back to Treasure Island. He will surely come to help."

"And what of you?"

"I am committed by word to stay on. If the fates are with me, and the captain keeps his word, I shall return this time a very wealthy man, and we can have a wonderful life together."

"Then you've become just like those... those pirates you used to so despise?"

"No, Chloe, I am not like one of them. But I must see this through. Yet, the thought of anything happening to you would weigh so deeply on my heart that I could no longer go on, especially if due in part to my actions. I believe that your going on alone will give us both a chance. I must go now."

"Jim."

"Yes, Chloe?"

She walked over and pressed herself into my arms, wrapping them around me, and then gently leaned up and we kissed. Softly this time. I found myself wanting in all ways not to leave her arms, for she felt safe, secure, right. I knew I wanted nothing more than to remain there, with her, forever.

"I've fallen in love with you," she whispered.

"I feel the same way," I replied.

"I know."

We were quiet for a few moments, when she suddenly pushed me out of her arms.

"Jim Hawkins," she said, "I told you when last together we would be married, and truer words have not been spoken. When next we meet, I shall expect you to ask me proper. Now go, make haste. Return to your pirate ship. And may our Lord and Savior watch over and protect you."

"As long as you are safe, I will be content," said I.

"Go, please. Get back to your ship."

I blundered out of the door and found myself standing back in the alley, making a multitude of excuses about why it was necessary for me to go back and see Chloe one more time, if only but for a moment. Weaving through the darkened alleyways, I found myself lost, and yet I cared not for my own safety. I could only think of Chloe and hers. I vowed to myself, with the full essence of my character and all that was within my heart, that when next Chloe and I were together, I would never leave her again.

As I rowed back to the ship in the longboat, I could see and hear a ruckus on board. I could make out Captain Steele's voice shouting, but little more.

When I boarded amidships I could see Captain Steele standing over Ben, who was holding his bloodied head, supplicating that he knew nothing about anything that was missing from the captain's cabin. When Captain Steele eyed me, he abruptly stopped and redirected his questioning.

"And where have you been, Hawkins, and where is that John Silver? You were in his charge. He was not supposed to lose sight of you on my orders."

"I left ahead of him, sir, whilst he stayed behind to have a few drinks with the crew."

"There has been treachery aboard my ship, this evening, Hawkins. Do you know anything about it?"

"About what, Captain? I've been with Silver all evening, and came straight away to the ship after our 'acquisition' was completed. Silver thought it ideal for me to get a certain paper back here safely and in haste. I know of no treachery."

"You've not heard the last of this, Ben. For I told you early on each must pull their weight. You will be given double the work the morrow and will be the quiet for it or face the whip. Hawkins, follow me to my quarters at once!"

As I followed behind him, I realized he was not going to mention anything about Chloe going missing from his quarters. Only he and Long John knew of her captivity. If he were to take it to the crew, he would be forced to disclose this secret and the fact that she robbed him and then subsequently escaped. Not at all flattering for a man of his stature and reputation. I hadn't thought this set of circumstances through earlier. Now, as I realized his plight, I at once became aware that Chloe would not be sought after.

He would not—could not—send out a search party, for to do so would undermine his standing and authority with the crew, and he could ill afford to allow that to occur. Relief flooded through me at this realization.

"What did you find?"

"Begging your pardon?" His question cleared my thinking and shook me back to the present.

"Come now, Hawkins, did you and Silver procure the map?"

"Yes sir, we did."

I took it out and handed it to him. As he grabbed hold of it and started its unfolding, I noticed for the first time a hint of a smile on his face, which quickly resumed its normal stoic demeanor. He set it down on his desk and studied the map carefully for a long time. Finally, he turned to me.

"You've been to this island before, yes?"

"Yes sir."

"Does this map speak true of its location?"

"Yes, it does."

"Are you familiar with any of these markings, here and here?"

"No, sir, and John Silver was perplexed as well. Said he's never seen anything like them before."

"Hmmm…very strange. I have seen symbols such as these before. But why they are here, on this map, is truly an enigma."

He picked up and studied it with a looking glass, and then lifted the map up and held it over his desk lamp, searching around the corners.

Without looking over he said, "Hawkins, when Silver arrives, I want you both to come back here at once. However, send Silver to me alone, first."

About two hours later, from my quarters, I could hear the crew singing in the harbor as they rowed their way to the ship. Silver was singing along with the rest, louder I might add, and proving that his sense of tone still left something to be desired. The boisterous mood of the men as they boarded the ship spoke well of the amount of grog that must have been consumed. I sought out Long John and told him of the captain's order.

Chapter Twenty-Three

The Treasure Map's First Secret

Silver was with the captain for well nigh an hour. I could imagine what must have been going on between the two of them, neither one knowing anything about the true facts. By this time the sun was starting to rise; a small crescent of gold broke the surface of the smooth Caribbean waters. The crew had gone straight to their quarters upon boarding a few hours before and were still fast asleep, except for Ben. He was pacing about the quarterdeck, talking to himself and holding the gash on his head with a rag. I confess I felt no remorse of conscience for having caused it.

Silver came out of the captain's quarters and motioned me to come closer.

"Everything all right with you and the captain?" asked I innocently.

"'Tis smooth as silk, Jim me boy," said Silver. "He's just 'misplaced' somethin' valuable and wanted to be knowin' if I were having any knowledge 'bout its whereabouts."

"Do you?"

"Oh no, no. I tolds him I was with you 'til you left for the ship. I've no awares where it could be, and you can lay to that."

"What is it?" I asked. "Maybe I've seen it—"

"Oh, I doubts that would be so, indeedy I do, Jim. And I thinks it be best to be puttin' the matter clear out of mind. Sort of lettin' it go, if you gets me meaning. Shiver me timbers, Jim, we's got ourselves a treasure to find, and the captain's wantin' us both in there."

Upon entering the captain's quarters, we found Steele absorbed in studying the map. Silver and I joined him in this effort. I noticed right away the leather pouch with the remaining coins inside that I had left upon his desk had disappeared. I surmised he and Silver had spoken about what had happened, and as I suspected, would make no mention of it to me, nor the crew. There was a whale oil lamp lighted on the map table.

"Did you notice anything queer about this map, Hawkins?" the captain asked.

"I didn't get a chance to study it very carefully, sir."

"That be a fact, there Captain sir... I had Jim here bring it straight aways back to the ship, knowin' how 'portant and all it be to all of us," said Silver.

"Well, both of you take a look at it now."

Silver and I studied it very carefully. As for myself, I knew not what to actually look for. So I tried to look at it anew. I at first noticed the material the map was drawn upon was not the usual color of parchment that I normally had access to in university. It was lighter in color and texture than I was familiar with. Besides the numerous strange symbols Long John and I had observed when earlier we looked at it, I also noticed something that seemed rather odd. The island was drawn out with the words written left to right parallel to the way you would view the map longwise, however, north was to the left, south to right and east at the top. What was queer was the compass drawn at the bottom that showed the cardinal points. The problem was this: they did not match the map's cardinal points. It showed north as pointing to the top of the map. It was misdirected by a total of ninety-degrees.

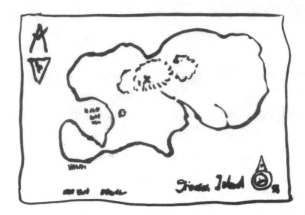

"It seems the paper is an odd type," said I, "but more importantly, I notice the compass's points seem to be misplaced."

"Indeed, Hawkins. It completely contradicts the latitudinal and longitudinal coordinates of the island as written. Are you sure these are correct?"

"Oh yes sir, by the by," offered Silver. "I've been there twice, and thems be the right ones, you can lay to that. But if I may speak more, sir."

"Of course."

"Well, the 'x' on this here map be confusin' to me. You sees, Jim and I both know that area, and I believes that it be nothin' more than craggy rock—and pretty high up too. That's why they calls it Spyglass Hill. Hardly seems the place you'd be burying even the dead, least any treasures and such."

The captain studied the map again.

"I'll agree with you, until we find out otherwise. But what is more perplexing to me are these symbols along the left side of it. I've seen them before, carved into stone in an old cathedral in Scotland. They are the signs that the Knights Templar used during the crusades. See this inverted V here? I believe it has something to do with stone masonry. But these others, I am at a loss as to their meanings. And we've no reference to go by."

"I's seen this here one before," said Silver, pointing. "'Tis the same as part of a tattoo on Redbeard's neck."

The symbol was an inverted triangle with a squiggle of some kind within.

"That may prove helpful once we start to decipher these strange symbols. Jim, as to your observation of the map's material, you are correct. This is not European parchment; it is from the Americas, probably those United States. It is of a type I have seen used by certain shipping companies for manifests and orders. I wonder..."

He pulled out a flint and lit a candle that was on the desk, opposite the side of the whale oil lamp. He picked up the map and studied the borders, much as Silver did at Lady Blue's, holding them about six inches from the candle as if he were trying to look through them. He then placed the bottom of the map near the compass almost in the candle's flame, and held it there.

"Careful, Captain sir," cautioned Long John.

"I know what I'm doing, Silver."

He held it above the flame for perhaps ten seconds, and then moved it a half inch at a time over the flame to a point next to the first one, almost until each little section started to burn. Then he moved it again another half inch. He started to smile.

"I thought so," said he.

He continued methodically in this way of almost burning the map for what seemed an interminable amount of time, and I also started to fear, like Long John, that the map could go up in flames at any moment. Finally, he blew on the map as if to cool it down, and then set it back upon the table, putting his gaze upon us both.

"Gentleman, look at what we've found."

Steele pointed to an area about three inches from the bottom of the map, and there appeared, where before there was nothing, a group of symbols printed and arranged in ten rows, colored in a kind of bluish green tint.

"By the powers! Where the blazes did that come from?" Silver blurted out before I had the chance to say something of the like.

"Simple enough," the captain said. "This was hidden by whoever made the map. We must assume that to be Redbeard. It was written in a special ink that, I would guess, was made up of zaffre mixed with aqua regia, and then diluted with water, since this is of a blue green tint. If cobalt diluted with spirit of nitre were used, it would appear more reddish. When the ink dries, it disappears, and none is the wiser. The only way to bring it back into sight is to heat it, which causes a chemical change and allows it to be seen again. It's very clever and used quite frequently by American shipping companies to hide manifests on their bills of lading, in case boarded by pirates or unfriendly countries intent upon taxing their goods. This type of parchment gave me a clue, since it is an American product."

"But, Captain, this here means," Silver started, "that—"

"This means that this is the original map, Silver, for a copy would not have picked up the symbols I've just revealed. It seems your Jasper must have made his copy and left it with Redbeard, taking the original with himself. Redbeard would be none the wiser, since these symbols we've just revealed would be unseen until they would be needed. He already knew what it said, so he had little need to reveal it himself."

"Old Jasper pulled one over on Redbeard? Now that's one for the yarns," laughed Silver.

"And since Redbeard is dead," the captain continued, "and this map supposedly lost, there is no one the wiser. We are indeed fortunate, for if we did only have a copy of the map, our efforts would have been in vain."

"Captain, what do these symbols you've uncovered mean?" asked I.

"They are a cipher of some sort. They convey a meaning that Redbeard wanted hidden from those who may have inadvertently discovered this map's secret or may have known of their existence. Very strange, indeed. No grammatical punctuations, a total lack of spacing and the like. It would provide an almost insurmountable challenge to the uneducated sailor. There are many different variations of this type of secret writing, but if my guess is correct, this should prove of a more simple variety."

He studied those symbols closely, moving his finger slowly over them.

"There seems no rhyme, nor reason, but that is the nature of a cipher, isn't it? The good news is this cipher was made by a man, and that means another man can, given the time and fortitude, unravel the mystery and meaning of it. Silver, how long do you estimate it will take to reach this island?"

"Perhaps four or five days, if the winds be favourable."

"Good. Send in Quartermaster Tafari on your way out. We'll have plenty of time to discover this map's secrets. In the meantime, we'll make haste for this Treasure Island of yours. Daylight will be fully upon us soon, and we've stores from the docks to load for the voyage. I want you to meet me here the morrow at mid-day. We will work some more on this intriguing map and see how quickly we can wrestle its secrets for our benefit. I will say this portends well for the bounty that awaits us upon deciphering it."

Silver begged his leave and we were alone.

"Hawkins, I want you to copy these symbols down very carefully, exactly the way they appear, with no input on your part in the least. We will work from that copy. Start on this right away. There is ink and paper upon my desk. I am hoping your education will be of importance in this matter."

Quartermaster Tafari entered.

"Sir?"

The captain took out his protractor and made a measurement from the map of the Caribe area that lay beneath the treasure map. He then checked his compass against the map.

"Wake up the crew, Tafari. I want this ship ready to sail within the hour. We will leave as soon as the stores have been loaded from the docks. I want to reach a heading of east southeast. When we hit latitude twenty-three, please notify me at once for further instructions. Then assemble the crew, for I'll wish to speak with them at that time."

- - - - - - - - - - -

I worked for hours on this task, yet after finishing the copying of these mysterious symbols and numbers, I was no more enlightened as to what they could possibly mean than from when I first viewed them. Here is what I copied:

ᒪꝪ†≈ᐱᐱᒪᒪ∴5ᐱᐱꝗ⊙ꝑℨᐱ†ᚺ
ꝑ≈Ҳꝑꝑᒪᐱ⊙ꝑℨᐱ†ᐱ∴Ҳꝑꝑᚈ
5ℨᏩᐱꝑᒪℨꝗҲᐱ∴ᚔ†ℨꝗҲᐱ∴
ꝑᐃᒪᐱᐱꝗᐱ∴ꝑᚔҲꝗᒪᒪꝑᚺᐱ
ꝑ≈ᒪᐃ5ᐃᐱ∴ᐱ5†ᚔ⊙ꝑᒪᐱꝑҲ
ℨᒪ5ᚺꝑᐃꝗᐱᐱᐱ⊙ᐱ∴ꝑᚔꝗᚈℨ
ᐃᒪᒪᒪꝑℨꝑℨᐃꝑꝑᐱꝗᏩᐱᐱꝗ✕
∴ꝑᚈᐃҲℨᚺҲꝗꝗ85ℨᒪᐱҲᐃ
5≈∴ᐱᐱ∴ҲꝗᏩ≈∴ᐃҲꝗᚈᐱҲꝑ
ꝑᐱ∴5Ҳᐱᚈᐱ⊙ꝗ∴∴ꝑꝑᐱꝗᏩᐱ

The captain's confidence in being able to discover these ciphers' meanings was assuring, and yet I did not share that same confidence. I am not sure why, but I had an ominous feeling. Maybe it was due to those strange symbols in the corners of the map. Perhaps because the treasure was from Egypt, a land famous for being mentioned in the Holy Bible and in Napoleon's triumphant adventures; a land filled with tales of wickedness and treacherous goings on. Perhaps there was even a curse on this whole venture.

It was true, however, that this feeling could have been due to my not concentrating on the matter at hand, for I was not for an instant able to release from my mind thoughts of Chloe and where she might be and what she was doing at that very moment. I was greatly assured that the captain was not planning to try to find her, yet there were still many obstacles she would face, and I wished with all my being that I could be with her to protect and guide her way. I struggled to keep the vision of her being safe and sound. I remembered the captain's words about my becoming whatever I wanted to, if I would only put my mind into it. That meant I could also put my mind to Chloe's safety.

My thoughts would be with her at every turn. Nothing else seemed as important. Not the map. Nor the treasure. Not even my own well-being. Nothing must befall her.

I was near exhaustion from copying the symbols and a general lack of sleep, and I found myself unable to stay awake. I went below deck to my cot to rest a few minutes. I pictured Chloe in my mind, her smiling face exactly as I remembered it upon leaving the Quiet Woman, and quickly drifted into a sound sleep.

GᏞᏎ35X△Ꭺ   ᏎᎫ53ᯞᏎXᏞ

Chapter Twenty-Four

The Battle

Upon waking early the next morning, visions of the treasure map and its ciphers danced about through my thoughts, and any chance of additional sleep were but fanciful wishes. I could hardly wait to see what we would discover that evening with Captain Steele. After cleaning up, I started to help Silver with the morning's meal, when our voyage took a startling turn.

"Ship off the starboard!" shouted the rear crow man.

Since leaving Pirate's Cove four days earlier, we had not seen any other vessels. The captain had put on extra watch, and I heard him speaking with Quartermaster Tafari about his concerns for the area. This part of the Caribe was known to be a haven for buccaneers. The various seafaring nations had been at a loss to protect their ships and stop the pillaging of their protectorates, and so they commissioned new war ships to the general area to combat the buccaneers in their own territory.

Captain Steele squinted as he looked through his spyglass, and after a few moments quickly snapped it shut. He looked to be enraged at what he saw.

"Turn eighty degrees starboard and head directly toward that vessel," he shouted to the helmsman. Quartermaster Tafari also spied the ship with his glass and approached Captain Steele.

"Respectfully, Captain, we don't need this fight. As far as they can tell, we are simply a merchant ship sailing these waters, and will no doubt ignore us."

"My orders are to sail toward them immediately!" he said as he pointed in the direction of the ship. He was getting visibly more agitated and angry.

The quartermaster nodded to the helmsman, who turned the ship's wheel toward the heading commanded.

I took out my glass from Jasper's bag and could see this ship was flying the colors of England. It was a huge ship, even from this distance and with the glass. Perhaps twice the size of ours. She had a triple layer of gun doors, and I quickly counted at least forty cannon on one side before the ship started a violent turn into the sea, causing me to lose my balance and slam into the railing.

"Captain!" shouted one of the buccaneers who was part of the buccaneers' council, "what be your intentions?"

"To sink that ship."

"Sir, it is not a merchant vessel nor is she attacking us."

"And your point?"

"We should have a vote as to what be our actions, according to the code."

"The code is not relevant here. I am captain, and I will say who and what we attack." He turned his attention toward the deck. "I want all guns powdered and shot ready," he shouted toward the master gunner. "Be quick with it."

"Sir," the quartermaster broke in, "we can easily outrun her, even if she has suspicions of who we are. There is no need to hit her square on in this way."

The captain continued to bark orders to the crew, ignoring the comment. Quartermaster Tafari drew nearer to the captain, and started speaking in hushed tones. I could hear him from where I stood.

"This is not right, sir. We have a treasure we are heading toward, the treasure of a lifetime, you stated. We are severely outmanned and outgunned. Even if we surprise them because of this ship, chances are not favourable we will prevail. Normally, I would not hesitate to follow you anywhere. Of my loyalty to you, this has been proven. But this is a fight we do not need, and may not win."

"Are you through?"

Quartermaster Tafari did not answer.

"Good. Now hear me Tafari. We are going to get alongside of that ship, and on my orders we will fire all cannon. My bet is they will be fooled into thinking we are merchants and will be caught unawares. If I am right, she will not be at the ready for a fight, and we will be able to get off at least another volley before she is able to react."

"And if you are wrong, sir, they will be at the ready and able to fire three score plus cannon at us broadside, and this ship is not able to withstand a barrage of that type. I beg you to make an exception this one time. Let this ship go."

The captain stepped to the foredeck and up against the railing.

"Are the cannons to the ready?"

"Aye, Captain," replied the master gunner, "ready and full."

"Men," started the captain, "we are going to attack and take that Crown's Man-o-war ship. I want you to be at the ready for boarding, once we cripple her. My orders are to search for anything of value and kill everyone aboard her. No exceptions. No prisoners. Our only advantage is the element of surprise. So I want you to look lively and work about as if nothing is amiss. They are no doubt using a spyglass on us now, and any hint of our intentions will be devastating."

I noticed a strained tone in the captain's voice. He seemed to be speaking to us, yet elsewhere in his thoughts and gaze— incongruous in nature. I could observe the men were as perplexed as I as to why we were going to attack this vessel, and quickly ran down to seek out Silver. I didn't have to go far, for just then Silver was hobbling up the stairs.

"What is it about up here, Jim me boy?" he asked.

I explained what the captain had said, and then asked him why we were simply not ignoring the ship and continuing on our voyage.

"Remember what I said about changing a leopard's spots. Jim? This be a concern of mine from the starts. A forty gunner, you say? That's no match for this guppy of a boat. Best be prepared for a fight, Jim, for if'n they don't sink us, the worst is yet to come, and you can lay to that, by thunder."

"What do you mean, Silver?"

A large boom rang out from the front of the other ship, and I observed a smoking trail following a ball that crossed the front of our bow and splashed into the water.

"She's signaling us, Captain!" shouted the quartermaster.

"I can see that," the captain stoically replied. "Continue to hold course, and be ready on the guns."

His stare was fixed on the other ship, and as we sailed closer, its immense size came clearer into view. For the first time I felt small and vulnerable on the *Hispaniola*.

"She's signaling us now with flags, Captain," shouted Tafari. "Do you want me to respond?"

"Hold your course, cannon ready, make no response."

The looks of Quartermaster Tafari and the crew told the tale. We were about to get into a battle we could not win. I found I was not scared, only numb and confused as to why we were entering into it at all. And I realized, as I am sure the rest of the crew did, there was no way to avoid it at this point.

Another explosion rang out from the front deck gun of the war ship. This time my gaze followed the smoking ball as it landed about fifty feet in front of our ship. The splash from its impact sprayed the side deck railing and myself, too.

"Hold steady our course," said Steele.

Both of our ships were heading directly toward each other. The wake from the warship shot high into the air, and put in perspective how large she was. It seemed madness to attempt to take her, and yet the determination and resolve of Captain Steele only seemed to temper in strength the closer we approached her. I inwardly feared this would be the end of our voyage.

"Hard turn to port!" shouted the captain. "Prepare to fire all cannon on my mark!"

The ship listed violently to the starboard side as the helmsman spun the wheel around into the turn. Everything that was loose on deck tumbled across and slammed into the railing. The *Hispaniola* quickly righted itself, and we were now broadside to this warship and in a position to fire all cannon toward her front and quarter starboard side.

"Fire!" screamed the captain.

Within moments all ten cannon exploded. We watched as the ten smoke trailing iron balls raced toward their target. Most of them slammed into its head and lower starboard side with devastating effect and force. Large holes appeared. Wooden pieces flew off the ship and into the ocean. The forward mizzen mast was cut in half and fell onto the deck.

"Re-fire at once!"

As Steele shouted the order, the other ship started turning to port, trying to get her side guns in position to fire broadside at us. However, because it was so large, it was slow to react. The next set of explosions of our cannon, which contained both ball and chain, were not fired in unison, and it seemed as if a succession of volleys were flying into this ship. She took more holes to the side, and her front lower sails were ripped to shreds.

Before she finished her turn, a half dozen of the forward cannon were fired toward us and slammed into the front of the *Hispaniola*. The shattered wood flew onto the deck, and the force of the impact caused the ship to shudder fiercely.

"Fire again and quickly!" Steele raged.

"Captain, we must try and get out of range of their cannon," shouted the quartermaster.

"Hold your course and fire those cannon at once!" Steele screamed even louder. I could see the veins of his neck bulging and his eyes glazed. He was focused and determined and would listen to no one.

Another volley of ball flew from our cannons, many of them hitting their mark, but now with little discernable effect. As she completed her turn, her size became frightening. I counted what I thought were at least five decks, and all of her cannon doors were up, and as I had surmised earlier there were at least forty of them. I'd never even dreamed of a ship that large. The horror of the situation suddenly became real for me, and as I looked about the crew the same thoughts must have entered into their minds as well. We had not a chance in this fight.

The captain ran down to the main deck toward the master gunner.

"Fire those cannon at once."

"Sir, I've sent men down for more powder."

"Explain to me at once how we have no powder—"

A thunderous explosion erupted from this monstrous ship, and as I turned I observed dozens of smoking cannon ball hurling directly toward us. I fell to the deck and braced myself for the hit. The whistling became louder. Suddenly, the ship listed violently to port as the helmsman spun the wheel to try and turn the *Hispaniola* directly into the line of fire. The winds cooperated. A half dozen of the fiery balls slammed into the lower deck of our ship, above the water line. We shook with great force, and the noise was deafening.

"Captain, we must try and get away," pleaded the quartermaster.

"We will not run from the likes of those cowards. We will take them or die trying. Turn about this ship at once!" he screamed to the helmsman. "I want all cannon firing at her at once!"

While he was yelling these orders, we heard another much louder explosion coming from the direction of this other ship, only this sounded different from the cannons firing. I and the crew turned toward her and could see it was… wobbling, for lack of a better description, and listed greatly to the starboard side. An eerie sound like the cracking of wood followed, and then she started to sink, with the head of the ship going in first. I could see men scrambling about in a panic above deck as the ship was being engulfed by the sea. They started to climb the masts as ants would on a wooden stick. Within a few more moments the main ship was under water and finally the masts disappeared into the engulfing sea. Not a man could be seen on the surface. The crew and I just stood there, transfixed by this most incredible turn of events.

"Shiver me timbers," remarked Silver incredulously. "I've never seen anythin' like that in all me days."

Suddenly, without warning, a bubbling appeared on the surface of the water near where the ship went down, and then, through the wake and turbulence surfaced the strange whale like vessel we had seen a week earlier. It plopped onto the surface and then continued on a course away from both us and the sunken ship.

The men broke out in a cheer, and the exuberance of the moment seemed to spread like wildfire. I found myself screaming at the top of my lungs, with both joy and relief, as I watched this strange benefactor disappear onto the horizon. The men calmed down, and, as if on a predetermined cue, we all turned toward the captain, who was spying the whale with his glass. He climbed the stairs to the upper deck and faced the crew, stoic and without emotion.

"It seems we now know whose side this strange monster has allegiance, men," he stated, "and we are the better for it. All of you showed courage and temerity today. Attend to the damage of the ship, and then let us take a day to rest and celebrate. It has been a good day." He turned his attention to the rear deck. "Helmsman, get us back on course. We have a treasure to find."

He walked down the stairs and into his cabin.

Later that afternoon, after the wooden patches had been put in place and other minor repairs had been made, the men were in the galley, drinking and eating. The mood was jovial; however, I was suffering the effects of being too close to what I perceived as my death. Fear still gripped my body, yet relief held my mind. I found it confounding how the men could shake off death so easily.

From my vantage point in the kitchen, I could hear a couple of the mates asking each other questions, and I detected a bit of anger in their voices.

"Why would he do such a thing?' asked one.

"No sense about it I can see," proffered another.

I looked within the galley to see the quartermaster enter down the stairs. He was plied with these same questions by the men as well. He motioned for them to quiet down, and then proceeded to speak to them in hushed tones.

"I've sailed with Captain Steele for the past twenty years. Many a ship we've plundered," he started. "Yet all the while, these Man-o-wars took priority over the rest. It took me quite a while to figure out why.

"You see, Captain Steele, the one you call 'black-eyed Steele' behind his back, is an educated man. Went to a number of fancy schools in England, he did. Part of the gentry itself. Then, after his father died, the Crown demanded its death tax on the family estate, they did. It was a considerable amount due, an amount that the family had not the means to pay. He pleaded his case for time with the courts, and was rebuffed. He then approached a certain squire named Alistair, and this squire persuaded him to become a privateer; to sail under his colors, with the proceeds to be favourably allocated to him. Aye, a fairer deal he could not have asked for. His papers were signed by no less than the King himself. In return, the squire would pay off his family's obligations, and the estate would be saved.

"Success soon followed him. He was sending great quantities of gold, jewels and goods to the squire's agents, and was near paying back the debt owed, when fate dealt an ugly blow to his plans.

"One of the ships he took belonged to a French company, and it had a great wealth within it. Just at that time, the kings of both countries signed a treaty, one of the many signed and broken through the years, and the French King demanded retribution for this ship.

"Aye, the King summoned the squire, who disavowed any knowledge of the act, and thereafter was ordered to sign and issue a warrant for the immediate arrest of Captain Steele, stripping him of the Crown's protection. A sad day it was for Steele.

"Squire Alistair then proceeded to call the deed on the family's estate, home to twelve generations of Steeles, it was. When they refused to leave, the squire sent in troops to evict them. In the process, a fire erupted, and all within the house perished an agonizing death. All of them, including his wife and children.

"This 'brave' squire of course disavowed any responsibility as to how it happened, and an inquiry ruled it be an accident. The squire then took possession of the family's property."

We heard a noise and all turned to see a pot rolling out of the kitchen from the ship's rolling. Tafari leaned in a little closer and continued in hushed voice.

"When Captain Steele learned of his being hunted, the squire's treachery and of his family's demise, he vowed revenge. Despite a price on his head and the dangers he faced, he found his way back to Scotland and tracked down this squire. A great fight broke out, a vicious one. The squire pulled out a small knife in the middle of it and stabbed Steele in the eye, but he would not be stopped. He ended up tying the squire to a tree and skinning him alive. It is said he lived for hours before dying, and the screams could be heard for miles. He then beheaded him. His head has never been found.

"After that he swore a vendetta, and as you are aware he has become one of the most ruthless, feared and cunning captains that has ever sailed the seas, and I can attest to that. Yet a fairer man I've also never met."

"How do you know of his story?" one of the men asked.

"I was a slave captive on one of the first vessels that Captain Steele took as a buccaneer. He spared my life and offered me a chance to join him. In Freetown he introduced me to his brother who later shared the tale. This brother was the last of his family and became a buccaneer on old Flint's ship. He was killed in a battle about ten years ago."

"Would that be Bart? Bart Steele?" asked Silver.

"That's right, Bartholomew Steele."

"By the thunder, he was killed in the same battle when I lost me leg."

The men sat there in silence after Quartermaster Tafari spun his yarn. I could see now the reason for his rage at that Man-o-war, and why he was willing to risk the treasure to take revenge upon her. It had been difficult to reconcile the demeanor and depth of character of the man I had dined with and the barbarous actions displayed within these past few days. Although understanding what he might have felt and why, he had still risked my life and that of the crew for his own selfish purposes. Silver was right all along. He had a side within him that was not to be trusted. I vowed to myself from then on to always be on my guard.

"The captain wants to see you and Silver at five bells." I turned around and saw the helmsman at the door speaking to me.

"Tell him we'll be there," I replied.

I had totally forgotten. The treasure and the cipher. We still had work to do. I thanked God, and whoever was within that strange whale vessel, that we were still alive to do it.

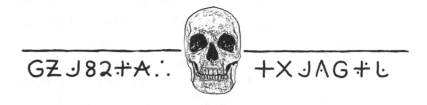

Chapter Twenty-Five

The Cipher

We met in the captain's quarters that evening at five bells, after we had fed the main crew. Captain Steele was absorbed in studying the duplicate of the map's ciphers I had copied, and then compared these and the symbols on the map. I also noted a number of pages with the same ciphers written in straight lines. He didn't seem to hear us upon entering, and so I cleared my throat.

"Ah yes, you are both here. Have you had any thoughts on this since yesterday morning?"

The entire day, after our near decimation, I had thought of nothing but this map, and of course, my Chloe. Silver had remarked more than once regarding my inattention to duties. He also must have been thinking about it for the men had complained bitterly about the excess of salt within their stew that evening.

"I've nothing to add, sir," said I. "The key seems to be—"

"Yes, Hawkins, we need the 'key' to unlocking this cipher's meaning."

He started to pace around the room.

"In most cases, the party making the map and the party who are to receive it would have the same key, which would assign a letter or some other value to each of these symbols. In a Caesar cipher, for instance, x equals A, y equals B, in that way. Unfortunately, there is no key for this that I am aware of. Did Jasper say anything to you of this Silver?"

"No, Captain sir. This be a complete surprise to me, and I am even wondering if'n ol' Jasper hisself was aware of it, by the powers."

"I am thinking he must have known," said Steele, "otherwise, there was no need to risk such a danger by taking the original and risking retribution for what he did. Redbeard was one captain even I would have been hesitant to cross. But back to the point, I have been studying this, and there seem to be a lot of symbols repeated, which gives me hope."

He returned to the map and picked up the copy I made.

"The first thing we need to determine is what language this cipher is written in. My guess would be English, since that is what Redbeard spoke, and the rest of all the names and locations are written in that language."

"Exceptin' fer the compass, Captain," Silver said, "that 'pears to be in the Latin script."

"You're right, Silver," the captain said, somewhat surprised. "But let us start on the presumption of the former, since it is easier to discern. If it is not English, we can then revert to the Latin and try that.

"Hawkins, I wish you to take this copy and count the number of times the symbols repeat, starting with the most frequent. In other words, which of these symbols appears the most? List them in their descending order. I've already noticed that this symbol (𝄐) looks to be the most plentiful without actually counting. In the meantime, I want Silver to go over with me in detail the various areas of this Treasure Island and the terrains that are located upon it, especially the harbor behind Skeleton Island and this Spyglass Hill."

It took less than an hour to count all the ciphers and make a list of them in their descending order as the captain desired. It looked like this:

$$\mathcal{A} - 27 \qquad \approx - 5$$
$$\mathcal{+} - 25 \qquad \uparrow - 5$$
$$\mathcal{8} - 14 \qquad \odot - 5$$
$$\mathcal{\therefore} - 12 \qquad \mathcal{H} - 4$$
$$\mathcal{C} - 11 \qquad \Delta - 3$$
$$\mathcal{Z} - 8 \qquad 3 - 2$$
$$5 - 8 \qquad \mathcal{d} - 2$$
$$\mathcal{A} - 6$$

Silver and the captain spoke about the block house Flint had built on the island. He was particularly interested in this structure and questioned Silver extensively to get an idea of its size and condition. I interrupted them with the news that I had finished.

"Good work, Hawkins," said Captain Steele as he grabbed the paper I had written it on and studied it. "Let's leave it at this and meet again tomorrow about the noon hour. More research on my part needs to be completed before we may proceed. In the meantime, I need to understand as much of this island as possible before we arrive. Jim, you may go. Silver, I desire you to stay and continue enlightening me as to every detail you know about it."

- - - - - - - - - - - - - -

The next day we met Captain Steele after he had finished his noon meal, and he seemed in high spirits, even being a bit cordial upon our entry.

"Gents," said he, "I have been studying the symbols uncovered within the map, and my hopes have been lifted with each passing hour. I am convinced, as I thought before, that this is a simple variant of a Caesar cipher, with letters transposed or substituted with symbols to mask their real values. Although the various symbols used may have some additional meanings, the first order of business is to try and ascertain what the underlying letters are and see if they make sense. To that regard I have some observations.

"Firstly, there are no divisions between any of the symbols. I believe this was by design. Had there been divisions, it would have been much simpler to unlock. For instance, it would have shown the shorter words, which there are far fewer of and can readily be discerned, and perhaps even exposed a single symbol, which would undoubtedly have been an *A* or *I*, and our job would have been much easier. But there are no divisions. That is why I had Hawkins count and list all of the predominant symbols in descending order.

"Hawkins, you may remember from your philology studies that there is a frequency of letters used in words within the English language. The most numerous is the letter *e*. From my studies these past few days, I have discovered that the rest follow in this order: *a o i d h n r s t u y c f g l m w b k p q x* and *z*. However, it should be noted that the letter *e* predominates within almost every sentence in the English language. Would you agree Hawkins?"

I thought about it for a moment, and came to remember such a statement from one of my professors, while in work groups constructing spelling tables.

"That is correct," I spoke. "It is definitely the most predominant and frequently used letter in written sentences."

"Well, then, with that knowledge we have a very good starting point, with more odds in our favour than a simple guess. The most numerous symbol, according to your count, Hawkins, is this symbol ⅄, and we shall assume for the present that this represents the letter *E*. I have written the cipher out on these papers in a single line and left room to put letters of the alphabet beneath them."

The captain wrote the letter *E* under each of the ✗'s, and then stared at the cipher for a few minutes.

"I believe we have made an error. If you look at this, you can discern there is a problem. The letter *E* is placed in positions where no English word can possibly be derived."

He paced about the room, then sat at his desk and was quiet in thought. Suddenly, he got up and looked again at the cipher.

"American English is different from Oxford English," he stated. "I remember now that American English can oftentimes contain an extraordinary number of the letter *T* in their syntax. So if we make that assumption and assume the cipher ✗ is a *T*, and then the ✠ as the *E*..."

He started to write the letter *E* below the ✠'s and crossed out the previous *E*'s under the cipher ✗.

"Aha! As you can see, when I have done this it makes more sense. One of the ways we can confirm if it is indeed our letter, is to look for repeats of it throughout the cipher, since the *E* often does repeat in words such as *speed, been, agree, tree* and so on. As you can see, it does so five times in this message. This is a good sign.

"So we'll keep assuming the ✠ to be *E*. Hawkins, what do you think is one of the most common words in the English language, written form?"

"I am not sure, perhaps *I*?"

"Using multiple letters."

"Then I should think the word *the* would be the answer."

"That's what I think too. So what we need to do is find a set of three repeating symbols, each perhaps starting with the ✗, and ending in ✠. These most probably would represent that word. Hawkins, would you search this out for me?"

I searched through the cipher symbols and found five such instances, and pointed each of them out.

"Good," said the captain. "Let's mark those in with the *T* and *H*. Now we have made great progress, for we have confirmed the value for the cipher ⅄ as a *T*, and can now mark the other areas that also have the symbols for the letter *H*."

"I notice Captain, sir," Silver interjected, "that there still be other sequences of repeating letters, here and here," he pointed. "What do you think those be?"

The captain studied them for a few moments, while I completed adding the *T* and *H*'s to the papers.

"I believe they are either the *S* or perhaps an *L*, since those are also very common repetitions, such as in *compass* or *hill*. You've made a good point, Silver. There is a repeat right at the beginning, with the very first letter being of the same symbol. It is highly unlikely, then, that this message starts with the *L*. I have a suspicion regarding this. We have found there is an **X** on the map upon what is marked as Spyglass Hill. Count the letters until reaching the end of that first repeating symbol, Hawkins."

I did, and they totaled eight. In my mind, I make the first letter and the two last letters, which are all ㇄ symbols into S's, and there it was:

S*****SS

"Spyglass," I shouted.

"I believe you are right Hawkins, and this makes our progress very great, indeed. Fill in the rest of the symbol ㇄ with an *S*, and let's see where it takes us, and add the *P*'s, *Y*'s, *G*'s, *L*'s and *A*'s as well."

The rest of the afternoon was spent in that manner, and by the evening bell, when Silver and I made way to prepare the crew's supper, we had clearly made progress; more than half of the letters were discerned, and there was great hope by the three of us that the rest would come the morrow.

- - - - - - - - - -

I took two of the pages and worked on them below decks on my own. We had found it much easier to discern words if we did the following: wherever there appeared to be a division of letters, such as when there were two **EE**'s together, we would search for a grouping that would support that combination, first and last. In this case, there was a **T✕EE**. If we substituted a dot for the symbol, like this, **T*EE**, it became easier to discern. In this case the word "tree". This would also give us another letter to distribute throughout the cipher, the letter **R**.

Near the afternoon, we again met and compared our notes. With some more deductions, and only a very few guesses, the captain wrote out the entire cipher in our new alphabet. We separated out the words:

Spyglass Hill twenty degrees twenty three minutes north by northeast to the crossed legs fifth limb western side follow the compass seven feet out to the mark drop coin straight through from tree thirty-two feet out.

"Well, Captain," said Silver, "it be a most perplexing set of words, them are. Although I believes you be right on course by the mentioning of that thirty-two feet."

"Why is that Silver?" asked the captain.

"I'm not bein' at liberty to 'xactly say why, yet."

"Oh, part of your insurance policy, is it?"

Silver just grinned.

"Not to mind, we'll find out soon enough."

I ignored their comments.

"I must agree, Captain," said I. "It still is a jumble of words that could contain a myriad of different meanings. How do we know where to separate them into meaningful sentences?"

"That has been confusing to me too. Part of this concealment was designed to be such. Remember when I said it was written in this way to make the job almost impossible for those without a key? However, I have also noticed that there are clusters of these symbols written closer together on the original map, almost as if the writer was overly trying to conceal their natural grammatical separation."

He put his pen to the paper, and while looking back and forth at the original map, puts dashes between certain words. Finally he stopped and set his pen down.

"I believe this will give us a good start. If I am off a word here and there, we will find out when we get to the island."

I looked at the text, and he had it separated as follows. I read it aloud:

Spyglass hill twenty degrees twenty three minutes north by northeast—to the crossed legs—fifth limb western side—follow the compass seven feet out to the mark—drop coin—straight through from tree thirty- two feet out.

"What do you think it means?" asked I.

"There is much to be discovered once we are there. But I believe it will become clear once we get to the spot marked on the map with this 'x' on Spyglass Hill."

"Then you be believin' the treasure can be found with these clues?" asked Silver.

"Indeed. As I mentioned before, a man conceived this secretive way of concealing the location of it, and therefore another man can surely unlock the mystery. We have been given a stroke of good fortune by possessing the original map and discovering its hidden secrets. We are well on our way to finding it. However, Silver, let me be clear. Up to this point, I have been a tolerant man with you regarding this supposed additional knowledge that Jasper entrusted to you. Do not test me with anything other than the truth when it is due."

"It was Jasper's wish to keep it unknown until it were needed."

"I see trust is a scarce commodity as far as this treasure is concerned."

"Well, Captain," Silver says, "I've always been awares that things sort of equalizes out when one of the parties needs something' of anuther—sort of vicey-vercy, by the by. Like if ol'

Ripley had been the one with the secret, he'd be with us this very day, by thunder."

The captain, although he tried to not show any reaction to this comment, could not control the visible reddening of his face.

"That would remain to be seen, Silver, for as I've told you before, map or no map, secret or not, treachery will be dealt with swiftly and with a sure hand. I would advise you to not bring up this Ripley matter again."

"Aye, Captain, I was just conjecturin' like. No offenses meant. You can be sure the knowledge to find the bundt will be all of ours alike at the proper time, since there be plenty enough for every last one when's this treasure be found, and you can lay to that."

The captain glared at Silver for a moment and then turned his attention back to the map.

"Captain, have you made sense of the compass on the map?" asked I, hoping to move the matter off that subject.

"No, Hawkins, I have not. The Latin written within the compasses circle translates as *the tree of knowledge*. It may be referring to the way the tree, branches and leaves within it are drawn or placed. As to its meaning and reason for being here, I am presently at a loss. But I have full faith that it will be revealed to us, if we keep an open mind to finding it."

"Land Ho!"

The lookout in the crow's nest yelled so loudly we could hear it plainly in the captain's quarters. I became so excited that I darted out of the room and out onto the main deck. The helmsman was sounding the bell. I could hear Long John hopping out onto the deck with his crutch knocking directly behind me. The crew bustled about like bees swarming from their hives, all jockeying for a position to look out past the ship's railing. I scanned the horizon.

And there it was.

In the distance, barely visible within the vastness of the deep blue waters of the sea, stood the island I had once vowed never to return to.

Treasure Island.

Δ5Ƶ卄∴5卄卄 ✝ƵdGƵ卄𝖠

Chapter Twenty-Six

Treasure Island

Captain Steele, based on Long John's stem to stern familiarity with the island and its waterways, had arrived at the most economical way to enter Flint Harbor, approaching around the outside of the reefs to the south and entering that passage by using the longboats to tow the *Hispaniola* in.

Excitement raced through the crew and was apparent everywhere. Some started singing old pirate tunes, and there seemed a certain kind of lightheartedness... not in any manner the same demeanor I was in when last I approached this part of the voyage.

The island was breathtaking. The three main high points of land, of which the tallest was Spyglass Hill, stood majestically near its center above the palm trees and other flora that graced the island.

It was getting late, and the tides were low. We were forced to wait for a morning high tide before we could row our way in. I found it difficult to sleep, although I was happy to be free to experience this adventure to the fullest, with no threat of skullduggery of the type that last occurred when I sighted this island nearly three years ago.

Racing through my mind was a concern about the captain's threat, or implied threat, regarding Silver. In point of fact, I was more than concerned. I was scared. Yet, I found myself hesitant to tell him. My thoughts were to wait until the last minute before I did, for fear of Silver laying some dastardly plan such as trying to turn the crew against Captain Steele, who, although ruthless, merciless and despicable in my mind now, was nonetheless fair in all other respects. I believed he would surely keep his word for all to share in the wealth we would find. Since I have not spoken about it, the dilemma lay in this: Have I waited too long in order to give Silver fair notice of Steele's potential threats and thereby inadvertently put him in more jeopardy? I did not know.

I made a decision to tell him in the morning, and then it would be off my chest. In the meantime, I vowed internally to do what I could to influence favourable light on Silver to captain and crew. In lieu of sleep, I kept visualizing my Chloe safe and sound, and sending thoughts of how deep my feelings were for her.

- - - - - - - - - -

"I want our ship anchored over in the east side of this harbor," the captain told Quartermaster Tafari. "Position it so her starboard cannon will be on even keel and parallel with the inlet. I want the blunt force of our balls to be received by any ship attempting to enter. Have our full stores of powder and balls brought to the main deck."

While the *Hispaniola* was being towed that morning into the harbor, I was one of the mates charged with carrying up the individual powder bag charges, while the black powder barrels and balls were to be brought up by three other mates. I wanted to finish my task with haste, for I had a plan in mind. I had not been able to speak with Silver in confidence since I decided to share with him the captain's thoughts and warnings from our last meal together. I vowed I would not be thwarted again before we reached the terra firma of Treasure Island. I observed my opportunity, slipped away in the midst of my assigned task, and caught Long John in the kitchen area. I approached him and motioned with hand to my lips to be quiet.

"I need to speak with you now, before we land on the island," I whispered.

"Well surely. What be it, Jim?"

"I'm scared—"

Silver stopped his cleaning and sat upon a barrel.

"Ah, Jim, I can understand you feelin' that way, bein' as yer last time ashore here was devystatin' to say the least. You've no need to be a feared with ol' Long John at your side. I'll be yer extra set of eyes and watch out for—"

"Not for me, for *you*!"

Silver looked taken aback.

"Arghhh. Why be that?"

I wanted to tell him in the most accurate way without inflating it by my own impressions, and chose my words accordingly.

"Captain Steele stated at our last dinners that once he confirmed the location of the treasure, there would be no need for you, and that he would need to make a decision about your fate at that point."

"Ah Jim, that's just captain talk tryin' to impress a young mind like yers."

"Maybe so. Maybe not. I got the distinctness of impressions that he would not be an ally if the crew should be of a mind to... well... you know most of the men are his, and Morgan's mates are not fond of either of us. I think we've got to make some plans to make sure, just in case that, well, just in case is all."

"Arghhh, Jim, plans be good, if they be solid, by thunder. Even if you don't end up needin' 'em. No harm in preparin' for the unexpected. A good buccaneer, if he's worth his salt, can be counted on to that end."

I didn't respond, but was lost in my thoughts to see if there was anything else that had led me to these feelings of mine. It was really more of an intuition, I reasoned, nothing solid to pin it on. And yet, it was a compelling fear that something could befall us, or rather Silver, with me being a secondary concern of theirs.

"There still be two bits of knowledge they'll need befores finding that treasure," Long John continued, "and I can be seein' meself parlayin' them for some time, and you can lay to that."

"I've got an idea, Long John."

"That be a fact, Jim?"

"Yes, I do. We need a place to hide if there should be reason to escape from them. No one on this ship but you and me knows about Ben Gunn's secret cave and its whereabouts. I say, when—and *if*—the time arrives when we are in danger, we make off for it and wait them out. Help is surely on the way."

"And why would you be thinking that help is on the way, Jim, me boy? Help from who? It surely not be lost on us that Ben Gunn would still be on that Godforsaken island if'n we hadn't stumbled 'pon it, knowin' what we did about where it was and what was hidden within. If we plays a dead hand, and they leave, we could be there 'til our dyin' days arrive."

"I don't have time to tell you right now, but you can rely on my word that help is rushing toward us as certainly as the sun rises. For now, we've got to bide our time until it does. And act as if nothing is the matter."

Long John pondered what I'd said for a few moments and then asked me to wait there. He walked over and into the black powder room, and then returned a few moments later, his hands black with powder dust.

He said not a word about it. Leaning closely, he told me, "Stay close to me Jim. If there be treachery afoot, then there'll be a time, a narrow sparrow of a moment, when opportunity will present herself for us to flee. Be aware always. Eyes and ears to the fore. We must watch each other's back at all times. Agreed?"

He held out his hand and I took it in mine. We grasped fingers together in a binding handshake. Something about it felt good to be on the same side again.

"We be a team now," said Silver, smiling.

"The captain wants you to help with the powder kegs, Hawkins," yelled Quartermaster Trafari. "Get to it!"

"Yes sir," I shouted back, startled.

Long John returned to the kitchen, and I saw him not again before bedtime.

That night I lay awake, deep in thought. After speaking with Silver, I felt much better having told him the truth. I purposely left out the part about loyalty, for I reasoned it did not relate to my fears for Silver. I also relayed in my mind the captain's accommodating attitude while we were uncovering the map's secrets. Still, he had shown himself to be two people, the likes of which Silver warned me about. I did not feel that Silver, or even myself for that matter, were actually in danger, at least not yet. Only that now that we had spoken, there was time to still plan, and hopefully, we would not be caught unawares if anything should try and befall us.

The thought of finding the treasure was bubbling within me and filling my mind with visions of grandeur. I realized we were on perhaps the greatest adventure ever attempted, and it was the chance of a lifetime for me. Being a part of it was thrilling in the extreme.

Concurrently, I could not for a moment take my mind off Chloe. I wouldn't let myself. I needed to keep the vision of her face clearly in focus, her blue eyes and warm smile predominating in this mental picture. Not until she could be in my arms again and I knew with certitude that she was safe, would I feel at ease.

I arose to get some water and heard muffled voices around the corner in the kitchen. I crept up to the other side of the wall to listen, and wished I had not, for on the other side I could hear Long John whispering.

"I've thought about what you spoke to me about in Pirate's Cove, Silver," said Morgan, "and hears me out. I am not going against the captain or anyone. Look what he's already done to me. He be a fair man. He kept his promise and Articles was signed, so I'll get me fair share. As to you, I've still a debt to collect, and pay it you will."

Morgan walked out of the kitchen, turned toward the hatch and proceeded up to the main deck. I hurried back to my cot and jumped into it as quickly as I could. Silver was up to his old tricks again, I thought, just as Captain Steele said he would be. The only good spin I could put on his actions was that Morgan rejected his advance. However, I was aware of a feeling of dread in the back of my mind that something would go awry. I prayed that I was wrong, and trusted that since we had gotten this far, all would be well.

Still, I feared I would never be able to sleep again.

- - - - - - - - - - - - -

Early the following morning, two longboats were launched with sixteen men, including Captain Steele, Long John and myself. We rowed toward a small opening on the shore bound by thickets of mangroves and landed on a sandy beach. It was the same spot I had landed when once before I was here. We beached the boats and commenced our trek inland.

"Which is the most economical route to the fort, Silver?" asked the captain.

"I believe it be to follow upstream to the west of Death Creek and then cut inlands a mile or so upwards of it."

"There is a short cut," said I. "We can head to the northwest over there past those palm trees and pick up a trail that directly gets us there."

"Silver?"

"I defers to Hawkins, sir."

The trail I mentioned was quite overgrown, but proved to be a timesaver. When at last we arrived, the fort looked much the same as we'd left it almost three years earlier. The eastern wood post wall had collapsed about midway and lost about twenty-five feet. No doubt due to a storm or such. As we entered the inner yard, I could see rusted flintlock rifles spewed about the grounds, left by us when shot and powder were naught. The block house was unchanged: a small wooden structure with a large center pole holding up a roof made of palm fronds. It appeared light was now easily getting through the boards, casting beams of sunlight into the dust motes drifting in from our boots.

The captain surveyed the entire grounds and block house, and returned to stand before it.

"This will do us quite nicely," said he. "Strategically sound, and wanting for nothing as far as our needs are concerned. I can see why Flint built it here."

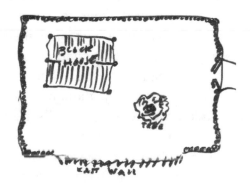

He ordered the men to set up an encampment in the yard. When he entered the block house, he mentioned how some of the men would stay inside through rotation. It started to rain slightly, and although temperate in nature, it promised to make for an uncomfortable and unpleasant evening if it continued, at least for those who would be sleeping outside.

It took most of the day to ferry the supplies and food stores from the ship and carry them from shore to the fort. I was sent with wooden cisterns along with four of our crew to a spot I knew of upstream of Death Creek where the water formed a shallow pool. This was about a mile to the northwest.

Daylight started to subside, and after a meal of dried mutton and biscuits, the rain started pouring down, followed by lightning and thunder.

Captain Steele decided Silver would be one of the first of the crew to spend the night indoors. He also picked me to join them; his stated reason was my familiarity with the island. I wondered at first why he did not suggest Morgan, who should be more intimate and knowledgeable with every part and detail of this island, since he spent a great deal of time on it. Upon reflection, it was probably a combination of his distaste for his coarse presence, and perhaps to keep me close in case of any villainies. In point of fact, Morgan and I had not spoken a word since we boarded the ship.

The captain lighted two whale oil lamps, and a fire was started in the fire pit in the middle of the room. All the men gathered inside the block house, either sitting or standing where they could to avoid the rain coming in through the roof.

"The first mystery we need to address men, is what this 'x' on the map refers to," Steele started. "Since we are all one in this venture, I want to share my thoughts. As far as I can ascertain, having no knowledge of the site itself, it must act as a starting point. Once there, we will discover if my surmise is valid, or if we need to readdress its meaning. As to the rest of this cipher and the underlying message, I believe it will all become clear as we progress and can study the actual sites. I am confident of our God-given abilities, as thinking men, to unravel another man's hidden message, and reap the rewards of such an effort."

He looked over at Silver and fixed his stare.

"The last piece of this most complex puzzle is still possessed by Silver, and I am confident as well of his forthrightness in giving it to us at the appropriate time."

"Where the time be right, Cap'n sir, ol' Long John will be the mate you cans counts on for gettin' our hands on that there treasure, and you can lay to that, sir."

"On my word, Silver, you've been warned before, the consequences that await you should you not be forthright would chill the bones of Redbeard himself."

He held his gaze upon Silver, and then continued.

"There will be no drinking tonight. We'll need clear heads and strong backs for the days ahead. Once we make our discovery, there will be plenty of drinking time for all. Quartermaster Trafari will assign duties and watches while here in the fort, and they will be shared in equal portion. Mates, we have come a long way. We are all in for a share. Tomorrow may very well prove just how lucrative for each of us this journey will become, and justify all the work and hardships. I ask each of you to visualize in your head and dreams the success of our adventure."

As I sat up in a dry corner of the block house watching the fire crackle and dance, and listening to the thunder roar in the background, my mind raced back through my journey so far; the voyage, the battle with the Man-o-war, the killing of Ripley, that most strange whale, the fight in the Quiet Woman, Chloe and the lightning striking me at the tree. These events and more came back full circle with facile as I balanced them all against the treasure we were to search for the morrow. It seemed any hope for sleep had abandoned me again, and yet my next awareness was of sunlight entering through the window openings and holes in the ceiling, and the sounds of men bustling about the room.

"Get up, Hawkins," said Long John. "'Tis time to be searching for our treasure."

Chapter Twenty-Seven

Spyglass Hill

Located close to the center of this somewhat oblong island, Spyglass Hill was its highest point, and the first landmark that could be seen from sea. It lay about two miles to the northeast of the fort. The distance between the two was covered in many parts with swamp and tropical vegetation, with the mangrove being particularly troublesome. The trip was slow and arduous, especially circumnavigating the swamps, for they contained a deadly black snake whose bite could kill a man in minutes. Bellowing black clouds spurted rain down happenstance on us, and coupled with the heat and winds, gave warning of a large storm brewing somewhere out at sea.

Captain Steele surprised me. He took to his machete with vigor, ferociously pushing ahead, side by side with the crew, with no sign of fatigue making itself known. Half of the crew remained at the fort for this initial trip, with only two men left on board the *Hispaniola*.

It was well into mid-day before we reached the west side of Spyglass Hill, which was too high to scale. We needed to go along the south perimeter and follow it to the southeast end and make our ascent from there, it being a more favourable grade to make a climb.

After we crossed a small creek, we started our trek upward. The sporadic rain made the coral incline slippery, and at times it was comical to watch the awkwardness of some of the seafaring men as they tried to maintain their balance on the slimy rocks. Long John, however, bounded up with his crutch as if no obstacle lay in his way, and was second to the top, behind the captain.

From atop Spyglass Hill, it was a commanding three hundred and sixty degree view. Reefs of various colors protruded from beneath the azure, white-capped sea. Light blue pools dotted the reefs where coral sand lay beneath. Even with the clouds and rain squalls, it was a feast for my eyes.

To the west lay the *Hispaniola*, berthed in Flint Harbor. The cliff face of Skeleton Island, from this perspective and height, did resemble the skull of a man. No other land was visible on the horizon.

When we reached the general area where the "x" had been marked on the map, we encountered a slight downward sloping toward the edge of the cliff. Thick vegetation of dark green and sprinkled with beautiful multi-petaled blooms that resembled, in many respects, the poppy, covered its edge.

"Spread out," said the captain, "and see if you can find any evidence of a carving or **X** on these rocks. It has been many years, so use care and look with diligence."

The area indicated by the mark on the map was large. Compensating for scale, it could have been within an area of perhaps four hundred feet along the cliff, and that much again from the cliff's face inward. After an hour or so passed, nothing had been discovered. The captain's demeanor remained calm and stoic. He walked along the cliff's edge, and periodically peered into his glass, searching outward upon the island in a methodical nature.

Steele ordered four men to clear the vegetation with the poppies back as far as was safe to the cliff's end, reasoning it might not have been there when Redbeard made the map. The cliff face on this side was quite sheer. The men hacked away at it with their machetes; clanging metal sounds reverberated from striking the hard coral rock that lay beneath. When the slope to the cliff's face became steeper, one man would hold another's waistband and lean back while the other would cut away at the growth for three to four feet. I was one of the men held by my waistband in this way. When I had reached the limits of safe working, I was pulled back and sat down upon its edge. I peered to my left to see the progress of a crewman and noticed a line, at least I thought it was a line, carved into the coral.

"Captain!" shouted I, "look at this!"

He walked over, spied it, and a hint of a smile graced his face. He bent down on one knee, brushed his fingers against it and followed it to the cliff's edge, where it revealed an arrowhead, pointing off the cliff.

"To where does this point?" I asked.

He leaned over and looked below and asked Long John for his crutch. Silver seemed bemused, but willingly surrendered it. The captain knelt upon both knees and used it to prod the cliff's foliage. He hit something solid.

"A ledge!" he shouted. "Men, hand me a rope at once."

Steele stood up and tied the rope about his upper chest, while three men tied a loop around themselves and stood about twenty paces back. Steele turned his face to the cliff's side and had them start to lower him as he maneuvered down the cliff with his feet, holding the rope with his hands. Perhaps seven feet down his boot touched a ledge of coral extending about two feet away from the cliff's wall beneath the vegetation. He had the men lower him another two feet, allowing the use of his machete to cut away and reveal the ledge as the vegetation fell down to the ground far below.

"There is an **X** on this ledge!" he shouted. "We've found the mark. Quickly, pull me back upward so I may stand on it. And lower a sextant and spyglass at once."

Once solidly footed, Captain Steele turned around with his back to the cliff. With my hands trembling from the excitement, I helped lower the instruments wrapped in a scarf. The rain had started to relent, and patches of sunlight miraculously shown through the cloud patched sky. Steele placed the spyglass in his waistband and started to look through the sextant, adjusting various levers and finding direction with his compass. He hung it on his belt after a few moments and pulled out the spyglass, pointing it in a specific direction.

All of us were transfixed on Steele. I kept telling myself to breathe as I watched the captain move his glass in a methodical manner. He used a pattern in which he slowly moved his spyglass to the right, then up and then to the left, each time extending its arc in small increments outward. We watched as he adjusted its focus, lowered it from his eye, looked beyond it and then peered into it again.

Suddenly, he let loose with a hearty laugh that echoed about us and, in my mind, surpassed the sounds of the wind and rain that was steadily increasing. It escalated into a boisterous affair. His chest heaved to and fro as he put the spyglass back into his waistband and shouted to be brought up. The site of his empowering figure on that narrow cliff-side laughing so heartily was both heartening and distressing, for I had hope afloat that he had discovered something of value, as opposed to a realization of folly connected with our adventure.

When he reached the top, he took out the map, compared it to the area he was looking at and started making notations upon it. He then took out his spyglass and looked in the same direction it was pointed when he started laughing, and finally placed it back in his waistband.

"Men, we've no time to lose," Steele said. "We need to get marks made down below."

Four men were ordered, in groups of two, to certain spots the captain pointed to about two miles away in an easterly direction, about a quarter of a mile from the ocean's shore. After descending Spyglass Hill, the first group of two headed toward the left of our position, and the other group of two made their way almost straight from our position. I could see that the shore beyond that area was sandy, and the water looked a deeper blue. There was a large grove of trees, perhaps of the evergreen variety, that the captain wanted them to get near. They were to light smudge pots once they arrived in the area. The smokier the better, he told them. Steele sent one of the men to fetch these pots from the fort.

After they left, Steele sat down against a slight overhang of the plateau, and I could contain myself no longer. The men crowded around with the same question on their tongues.

"Begging your pardon, Captain, but what was it you saw?" I asked.

"I be with the boy on this one," Silver added. The others agreed.

"A tree. A very special tree. One with crossed legs. This is proving to be most interesting. The originator of this map, if it is Redbeard, is more cunning than I could ever have imagined. I pray we need to keep our wits and senses about us. This treasure will not easily give up her whereabouts."

"What do you mean crossed legs? How can that be?" one of the men asked.

"An ironic reference, I suppose. From the cliff's face down below, at exactly twenty degrees twenty-three minutes north by northeast, a large tree stood atop the others in that grove. Attached to the trunk, high above the others, I am guessing by nails of some sort, are two femurs, placed in an **X** or crossed position, exactly as our Jolie flags are drawn. They are bleached white and easily seen when the eye is trained upon them. They have been placed in exactly that position for a reason. For when I marked the spot in my mind, and was brought to the top and again looked at that same tree, the bones were blocked by its upper branches, rendering them completely invisible. I was able to ascertain generally where this tree is located, but I believe it may be surmised that the bones are also invisible from the ground. I therefore have sent the men out to light the smoky fires in such a way that I can triangulate where this tree is in relation to the rising plumes. In this way, we can, with little effort, find this mysterious tree and see what next awaits us in order to unravel more of this secret message we have uncovered on this map."

"Can I have a look?" asked I.

"Of course."

Two of the men lowered me as I traversed the cliff's face in the same fashion as did the captain. I landed, turned around and pulled out my spyglass. The captain shouted instructions and directions to me, and within a few moments I was able to clearly see the crossed bones upon the upper trunk of the tree.

A shudder lurched through me, and I wondered who gave up their life, more than likely unwillingly, to end up being used as the mark for this tree. I shook it off, for I knew in my heart that this portended well for the success of our search.

It took the first team of men almost two hours to reach the spot designated and then light a fire. The second fire appeared a bit later. The plumes rose amidst the rainy drizzle that had started again and cast an eerie shroud around the island. The captain used his spyglass and then marked some notations upon the map. When he was satisfied, he put the map away.

"It's getting near dark, and it has been a successful day's hunt," said Captain Steele. "We will return to the fort and get a fresh and rested start back here early in the morning. Hawkins, I want you to follow both of the trails the men made and make clear markings where they are, and then you and the men out there can join us."

It took not more than an hour to accomplish this, although there were two swamps to navigate across, since the men had made a good trail through the brush. If not for the smoke as a reference point, I could easily have lost my way in the swamps, for there was no sun to follow for guidance, and the rain's intensity had again increased. I helped the men mark the area with cut branches inserted into the earth, and we arrived back at the fort just as darkness was enveloping the island.

In spite of the weather, it was a jubilant scene. Everyone was talking about our finding the "sign" we needed, and talk of palaces and ships and wenches aplenty filled the encampment. The outside fires were lighted, and some of the men were dancing and singing. One of them played some sort of accordion. I made my way into the block house where I found the captain sitting at a table studying the map and my written version of the message we had uncovered. Long John was next to him. He acknowledged my return and continued to peruse it.

"I am hoping this makes more sense when we arrive at that tree tomorrow. The reference to the fifth branch up on the western side is clear enough, but this business of the coin and thirty-two feet is perplexing."

"Maybe the branch is that high," said I.

"It is possible, but I am doubtful. If that were so, then just mentioning the branch would be enough."

"Begging the Captain's pardon, but perhaps the coin given me by ol' Jasper, bless his dear departed soul, has somethin' to be doin' with it?"

"I thought of that possibility, Silver, and made a copy of it as such in case it would prove important in this matter. But upon close inspection, I could discern nothing of any value that would help us here.

"No, whatever it all means, we will have the chance to solve it soon enough. In the meantime, extra rations for the men this evening, but no grog. Tomorrow promises to be a challenging day, and I need everyone's wits about them."

I must mention here a strange occurrence that at the time seemed out of sorts. After evening meal in the block house, I ventured out to the yard's encampment where all the men were gathered. There were boisterous goings-on, and I wanted to join in the merriment. However, as soon as I arrived, the men quieted down and spoke not a word to me. I asked if anything was the matter, and one of them answered all was fine. Still, silence ensued, and an uncomfortable feeling overcame me.

I bade them my leave and returned to the block house. At that time, I convinced myself that it might have roots with my being allowed to stay with the captain in drier quarters than they found themselves, and perhaps a resentment of sorts to this special treatment lay at the heart of it.

I was to find out soon enough how wrong I was.

GL⧾35X△A   ⧾J53∴⧾XL

Chapter Twenty-Eight

The Tree of Knowledge

The storm had made good on its threat and released itself in full fury that night, including frightening displays of lightning. The sound of thunder and rainfall at times became deafening, waking me up off and on throughout the night. I envisioned that the mates who were in the yard, even though tented, were having a rough time of it.

In the morning, the sun peeked out on the horizon from behind huge bellows of dark clouds and clothed the dawn in golden rays. A rainbow showed itself, and I imagined it was not only myself that thought it portended well for our day's activities. The rain had turned the compound into a field of mud. The heat and humidity, even this early, was already oppressive. After a quick meal of biscuits, the captain allowed that all hands should go today, with none left behind at the fort. We packed our implements and set off on our adventure.

Although it was sluggish and slow going through the muck, high spirits prevailed with all the men. It was a jubilant affair, with all of us singing, whistling and carrying on about this, that and the other. Long John was his usual merry self, and kept up with us step for step in spite of the obstacles that lay in our path.

We reached the more northern marker of the two sites first, and the captain made some calculations using his compass. He ordered me to accompany one of the men to find the other area where the fire had smoked, and to pace in a straight line out from it exactly 271 degrees, as shown on the compass. We tracked back toward Spyglass Hill, crossed over to the other path, and easily reached the site and remains of the fire. We determined the direction we were to move via my compass. At first, thick brush impeded our progress, but soon very few obstacles presented themselves. Presently, we could hear the captain and others coming toward us from a distance. We were now in a grove of large trees, although the trees were quite far apart. I had guessed yesterday that they were a kind of evergreen, and was correct, although of what tropical variety, I knew not. The canopies created a leafy roof and blocked out a majority of what little light was offered through the cloudy sky. The ground was dark. Only a few misty rays of sunlight broke through, creating an eerie and mystical effect. Different varieties of birds were sounding away from atop the branches, with flocks here and there flying off, startled upon our approach.

Once in this grove, my hopes were not elevated that the tree would easily be found, for the branches of most started very high and they all looked quite similar to my eyes.

We sighted the captain and headed toward him. When we met up together, he looked at his map and markings, and then walked past me to the left and stopped before a particular tree. He surveyed it, looking up, and then took out and observed it through his spyglass, but it was clear that he would not be able to see much above the foliage. On this tree, the first branch was about ten feet up. Its diameter did appear larger than the fellow trees surrounding it, but not so much as you would notice without close observation.

"This is the tree!" he declared breathlessly, and started to walk around and inspect it.

I sat down to rest and catch my breath. Not from exhaustion, rather, excitement. It seemed my body was aglow with energy, and I experienced a feeling of elation.

Steele pulled out his compass, plotted true north and drew its direction into the reddish sandy ground with his cutlass.

Fifth limb western side—follow the compass seven feet out to the mark—drop coin—straight through from thirty-two feet out.

"Hawkins!" he called out. "Do you think you can climb this tree?"

"Of course sir," I shouted, and jumped up and ran over to where he stood.

"You are the lightest and nimblest of the group. I want you to climb up on this side, to the fifth branch, and then call down to me. I do not see it with the glass, but assume it is right above the tree's lower canopy. Use your compass for reference. The branch must be on the west side of the tree."

"Yes sir."

"Men, help him up to the first branch."

Steele grabbed my hand and placed a gold coin upon it.

"Hold on to this. It may come of use."

I placed it in my pocket and walked up to the tree. Two of the men made a kind of step by interlocking their arms, and upon my standing on it they lifted me, with the help of a few more hands, to where I could grasp the first branch and pull myself up upon it. This branch faced north. I carefully made my way up until I reached the first branch that appeared to face west. I shimmied over to it.

"First branch sir," I shouted.

"Continue on, Hawkins."

Up I went to the next, and then the next branch. These were more to the south, and I finally reach what I assessed was the second branch to the west.

"Second branch."

"Good job."

I could no longer see the ground clearly below. I made my way upward, passing two more branches that were in a westerly direction, until I finally reached the fifth branch. I checked and confirmed it with my compass.

"Made it, sir. I am on the fifth branch."

"Now Hawkins, I want you to approximate, in your mind, the distance of seven feet out from the trunk. See it in your mind and make a mental mark of where it is, and carefully crawl out and reach that mark. Then call down to me."

"Yes sir, I'll do it."

I did what he asked and made my mental mark. The branch appeared sturdy. It was at least six inches thick at the base where it met the tree. I straddled the tree limb as if on a horse, and progressed slowly outward in this way until reaching what I had guessed to be the distance of seven feet.

"Here sir."

"Are there any marks in the branch?"

I looked but found none.

"No sir."

"Continue outward another foot, Hawkins. The distance you judged may be short."

I started to move forward and realized I needed to traverse a small branch that protruded out from the main one on which I was sitting. As I lifted my leg to go over it, I lost my balance and found myself swinging to the right, losing all sense of bearing. I could feel my legs release their grip on the limb. As I swung around I instinctively held my hands above my head, which was now facing downward, and let out a huge scream as I fell. My arms wrapped around the next branch below me, but my grip was not sure, and it only managed to slow my descent slightly. I continued my fall through the canopy of foliage and saw another limb racing toward me. I reached out with one arm and hooked it. My arm wrenched as my fall was violently halted. I was determined not to lose my grip as I swung below it. The tree's bark had painfully scrapped my arm, and I could feel blood dripping down from it toward me. I looked below and observed my feet dangled precariously as I held on and assessed my next move. I could see the men staring up at me, although slightly obscured through the foliage.

"Hawkins, are you all right?"

"Yes sir!" I cried, "Give me a minute sir to secure my position."

With all my strength I swung my legs up and around each side of the limb I was hanging from and wrapped them tightly. I started to feel a little more secure. I was now parallel to the branch, and needed to make my way back to the trunk, where I would safely be able to use my legs to turn myself around and stand up on the branch. I moved to the main trunk as a possum would, and finally reached the trunk where another branch lay not two feet away and below me to the right. I released my legs from their grip and stretched them until I could feel the branch under my feet. I moved inward with my hands and was finally able to let go and stand up. My breath was heavy with exhaustion. Fear still gripped me as my heart raced. And yet, I felt a certain elation at the thought of not letting death's grip take hold of me.

"I've reached the trunk again, sir."

"Did you see any marks before your fall, Hawkins?"

"No, Captain. There were none to be seen or found. Do you wish me to return and look further, sir?"

"Stay where you are and catch your wits, Hawkins."

I could now see the captain from this vantage point and heard him speak with little difficulty. I sat down straddling the branch and started to attend to my arm, which was badly cut and bleeding. I cut away a piece of my sash with my knife and wrapped it around the cut and tied it, hoping to arrest the loss of blood. It began to work.

"This is most perplexing," I heard the captain say to the men, and Long John in particular. He studied the map, looked up at the tree and paced around it. He oriented to his mark of true north on the ground, put his back up to the tree and then started to pace out, walking in a westerly direction. He ended up atop of a coral outcropping that bordered the west end of this grove of trees. He then rejoined the men.

"It is clear I have made an error in where I put the break within this sentence of the cipher. It is not thirty-two feet down, but rather, if I break it here..."

—fifth limb western side—follow the compass seven feet out to the mark—drop coin—straight through from tree thirty-two feet out.

"...then it means thirty-two feet *from* the tree. But it matters not, for anywhere west of this tree ends upon the coral rocks, where, it is clear, no treasure can be buried. So we have a dilemma that seems to have no immediate solution."

"Beggin' your pardon, Captain."

"Yes Silver?"

"Well sirs, there be enigmas and mysteries aplenty with this here treasure, and that's a fact. But one thing be clear. We've broken part of it, and the rest is ours for the takin'."

"Get to the point Silver. Is this the last part of the secret you're supposed to let us know about? The one *ol' Jasper* imparted to you as your, what did you say, insurance policy? For if it is and you're not telling us—"

"Well no Cap'n, it's not that I be speakin' 'bout. As to what you speak, it will be plain as the morning sky soon enough. But as to this, I'm thinking maybe it be the reference to the compass that be the key."

The captain looked again at the map and studied it with concentration.

"I'm listening," said Steele, without looking up.

"Aye. Well Cap'n sir, the Latin 'scription upon it says *The Tree of Knowledge,* and I'm thinkin' it refers to this here tree, I do. But that's only the half of it. That compass on the map ain't no way aligned with the true cardinal points. And based on that cipher and such, I'm thinkin' it ain't no mistake at all. No sir. By the powers, I'm thinkin' that when the cipher said 'follow the compass', it means—"

"Of course, Silver!" he exclaimed. "It means follow the compass that's *drawn on the map.* Not the true cardinal points. We must use the west that is indicated by the compass on the map."

"That be my thinkin' too, sir, by thunder."

"You surprise me, Silver."

"Still 'ave a few of 'em left, Cap'n sir."

Steele studied the map for a few moments.

"As we already discovered, the compass is exactly ninety degrees to the west of true north. Hawkins, climb back up, but this time it will be five branches from the south."

"On my way, sir."

I determined south by the compass, got a visual reference to my surroundings and started to make my way back up the tree, branch by branch.

"Second branch, sir,"

"Be careful Hawkins, and yet make haste."

I continued my ascent, and my heart raced again, but with excitement this time. I struggled to hold my balance. I had to wrap myself against the tree while at the same time lift my leg to the next branch. It seemed more arduous than the first climb, perhaps because fear of falling was now near the top of my thoughts. After a few minutes, I could see the branch I was searching for. It was about two feet higher than the previous branch I was on to the west, and although pointing toward the south by the compass, it was off about ten degrees.

Upon reaching and straddling it as I had done before, I mentally made a determination of where seven feet would lie. I started my journey outward, again wrapping my legs tightly and shimmying slowly toward the mental mark I had made. When I had reached what I guessed was six feet, I could see a sort of round cutout in the branch ahead on its top, and excitement coursed within me. I reached that spot, and there, inlaid about a half of an inch within the branch, lay a gold doubloon.

"Captain! Captain!" I shouted. "I found it! I found it! There is a gold coin set atop the branch, right where you said it would be! It's here, Captain, it's here!"

The excitement that raced through my body almost tickled, and I could feel a smile stretching from ear to ear. I could also hear the men murmuring in a joyous way. The captain had to quiet them down.

"Hawkins, can you hear me clearly?"

His voice echoed at that height.

"Yes sir."

"Hawkins, I think I understand what we need to do at this point. Steady yourself. Grab hold of your concentration. I want you to dig the coin *out* of the limb. When finished, call down."

I reached for my knife and wrapped my legs tighter around the limb. I carefully put the tip of the blade on one side of the coin's end and pushed outward ever so slightly. Back and forth I went. It started to move. I then took the knife's blade out and inserted it under the opposite end of the coin, and worked it in the same manner. It moved sufficiently that I was able to slide the blade underneath that edge and lift it slightly above the branch. I released my other hand from its grip on the branch, which had been used to steady me, and grabbed the coin. I put my knife away with my other hand, and resumed my grip on the branch with it.

"I have it in my hand, Captain."

"Good Hawkins, very good. On my word, I want you to drop the coin directly from where you took it out. Hawkins, it must be parallel with that exact spot. And do this from the right side of the branch, which would be toward the west. Do you understand?"

"I do, Captain."

"Do it now."

I placed my hand next to the hole where the coin was resting, lined it up and then let it go. I followed its descent as it tumbled straight down. There were no major branches to impede its free fall. I saw it pass through the canopy of foliage and then heard the men break out in shouts of joy.

I scrambled down as quickly as safety would allow, jumping from the last branch onto the ground, and found the captain placing a large branch end carved into a stake next to the coin. The wind and rain, which I had not been aware of through the climb, had picked up considerably. The wind especially was blowing fiercely.

The captain walked to the far side of the stake away from the tree and sighted it. He walked back to the tree and pointed.

"I want a rope nailed into the tree at this exact spot."

One of the men brought an eyebolt and proceeded to pound it into the tree about a foot above the ground. Another pushed a rope through its eye and tied it into a knot. I walked up to the captain, along with Silver. He folded the map and put it away.

"When I changed the sentence break, Hawkins, it now reads thirty-two feet from the tree 'through' the coin, where it dropped. In other words, when you start the rope from the closest point of the tree to the coin and run it in a straight line over the coin, it is a geometrical line of two points. If the coin were to fall from anywhere else, the two points would end up giving us a false angle, and we would have no hopes of finding the treasure. That's the last of it. I believe this mystery has been solved."

We pulled the rope straight from the tree and walked it past the stake, touching it slightly and then laid it down upon the ground.

"Count out thirty-two feet from the tree, using this as a straight line," he told the ship's mariner.

The mariner did this, and when he stopped the captain placed another stake in the ground, hitting it into the terra firma with fervor.

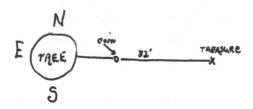

"It is done!" he shouted in a triumphant voice, holding up the hammer. "And as I predicted, we have used our God-given abilities to break this most mysterious cipher and solve this enigma. The treasure will now be ours for the taking! Men, light torches, for it will soon be dark, and we can still work for an hour or more if weather permits. Nothing can stop us now!"

"Captain, beggin' your pardon," said Silver, "I needs to speak to you, private like."

"Your insurance policy has come due now, has it Silver? Looks as though we've found it without your help."

"Please Cap'n, a minute of yer valuable time, if'n you will. There's danger a plenty if you know not of what I needs to tell you."

"So be it. Light those torches, men. I'll return shortly."

Long John and the captain walked out of earshot, and I could observe Silver telling the captain something with his arms animatedly moving about. This caused the captain to turn and pace around him for a few moments. He appeared to ask some more questions, Silver answered and then he returned to our area.

"You and you," he said pointing to two mates, "will stand guard in this spot tonight. I caution you, do not commence in any digging activities. Food and shelter will be sent. Men, we will return tomorrow."

He took off toward the fort, and all of us followed him. I hurried to catch up with Long John.

"What happened? What did you tell him?"

"I told him the warning from Jasper, as I promised I would," he whispered. "We'll talk later."

He looked around and smiled, but the crew was tired, wet and not outwardly pleased with this delay. By the time we reached camp, it was nightfall. The captain sent two men with provisions for the two left at the treasure site, and then retired into the block house.

At camp, the mood turned decidedly upbeat, once food and rest had set in. The men were laughing amongst themselves, talking about the coin and how the treasure was hidden, and a jovial mood seemed had by all. Even I was unable to master my thoughts; the treasure occupied them all.

As I returned to the block house, I could hear the captain and Long John in raised voices, with Steele telling Silver that he'd get no signed Articles until what he said proved to be the truth, and that was the end of it.

"You be a man of your word, Cap'n, I'll give you that," Silver replied. "And I'll be trustin' it to the fullest."

"Let us hope, for your sake, that this is the last delay in our quest. My patience with you has reached its end."

The rest of the evening I had not the chance to speak with Long John in private. I put it out of my mind as to his conversation with Captain Steele and let the doctor attend to my arm, which had deep cuts and needed sewing. He had me drink a cup of grog, and then placed a thin wooden dowel between my teeth. I turned my head and suddenly felt a sharp pain and screamed as he sewed the largest gash with catgut. When over, I took another few drinks and tried to forget the excruciating pain in my arm.

Later, as I was falling into an almost inebriated sleep, lost in visions of a life filled with all the riches that were surely awaiting me, Captain Steele walked by and squatted down next to me.

"Hawkins."

"Yes sir."

"You did well today, very well."

"Thank you, sir."

He pulled out the gold doubloon I found in the tree and tossed it upon my chest.

"This is yours, Hawkins. You found it, and you deserve it."

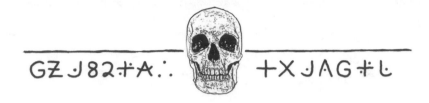

Chapter Twenty-Nine

Silver's Secret Revealed

Most of the men huddled in the block house the next morning to wait out the storm that had unleashed its fury throughout most of the night. We were not able to leave for the treasure site before noontime. I had the chance to see Silver alone outside under the east eve of the block house. I told him of the captain giving me the coin, and then asked what he had told him the evening before that stopped all work.

"Jasper told me two things, Jim, he did in fact. The first were to 'go half again back the distance told and dig ten feet to stop the flood'. It became clear to me once the Cap'n discovered the distance and all from the tree. I figures it must be meanin' we goes back sixteen feet and digs down ten, and see what's there waitin' fer us."

"And?"

"Aye, that's all."

"You said two things."

"Did I? Aye, the other be me concern, and will be apparent soon 'nough. As to the former, I am unawares as to its full meaning other than if not heeded, the treasure surely will be lost."

The storm was waning as we arrived at the treasure site. The captain had the mariner pace out sixteen feet from the tree, or half again as much as thirty-two feet, and place a stick marker upon the spot.

"We'll start to dig here," said Captain Steele. "I want a hole at least five feet in width, and we'll go to a depth of ten feet. I also want a ramp to the west side here so we can have ingress into and egress from the pit. I'll start digging with the men in the first shift. Every hour we will rotate our efforts amongst us."

"Why we be diggin' here, Cap'n, when the treasure be over there?" asked one of the men.

"It seems that Jasper gave Silver a grave warning, one we must follow up with. Although the labour will be difficult, and it seems to be double the duty, if he is right it will be worth our every effort."

Steele grabbed a shovel and started to dig. Four other men joined him, creating a circle with all of them digging toward the center. Within an hour's time great progress had been made. Five others, including myself, were assigned the next shift of the digging. All shirts came off quickly as the weather, although improved, still bore down on us with heat and mugginess, causing sweat and fatigue with every shovelful we removed. Within another hour's passing we had gone perhaps seven feet down, since I could no longer see over the rim of the hole. The next crew started digging, and just short of their allotted time, they hit a hard structure.

"Cap'n, we found something!"

He ran down the dirt ramp, jumped into the pit and ordered them to clear the sand and dirt covering what they had found. When cleared, it was seen to be a large wooden covering, resembling a door and measuring three feet square. There were eight pieces of wood lengthwise, with two pieces that transversed it, acting as cross-bracing to hold the other eight pieces in place. With great effort, the men lifted this piece of wood up from one side and leaned it against the wall of the pit. Beneath it was found a large wooden four-walled box with a floor about three feet deep. The part removed appeared to be its lid.

Inside, the only thing visible was a large wooden lever. It went through a hole at the floor of this box with a piece of rounded metal attached to the floor and passing through the wooden lever, attached with bolts to the bottom. It seemed to me that this lever's length protruded some distance below the box. The captain studied it carefully from all sides and was not quick to move it.

"All of you men get out of the pit at once!" he ordered.

They quickly scurried up the ramp and onto the sandy soil above. I was leaning over the side of the pit looking in.

The captain put his feet on either side of the box above ground, squatted down, placed his hands firmly around the lever and slowly pushed it in the opposite direction of its leaning. He exerted great effort, and it moved slowly. A sort of grinding noise could be heard, but it was difficult to distinguish its nature because of the thunderheads that rolled over the horizon. He finally moved it fully to the other side, and within moments, water started to rush into and fill the box. The water then leached over the wooden sides. The captain just stood and watched it as it covered the lower part of his boots. He started to move to higher ground as it rose further. Within less than an hour it was up to the surface of the ground and started to spill over the edge.

The area from the tree toward the stake ran slightly uphill. The water started to flow the opposite way, or eastward, toward a channel we had not noticed before—a slight indentation in the ground with rounded edges. It flowed into this channel, which snaked behind the tree and continued out and down a slight hill toward the ocean. The captain reached down, touched his fingers to the water, tasted it and then stood up.

"Fresh water," Steele said. "It seems Silver's insurance policy was real. Although I am not sure what this is about, I believe we will now have full and unfettered access to the treasure. Let's start to dig the actual treasure site in much the same way we did this hole, and start with the last crew."

Suddenly, a huge bolt of lightning followed by thunder erupted from above and rain poured down as if from a waterfall upon us. The captain yelled for all to return to camp, and we drudged our way back, soaked to the bone. The heat made the trek quite miserable, but I was determined not to let anything upset my jubilant mood. The treasure was within our grasp, and no swamp heat nor rain or thunder could deny what was now our due, at least in our hearts and minds. We arrived at dusk.

After dinner, Silver and I were assigned to the night watch at the fort. It was a thankless task, and, for no point of security that I could ascertain. The *Hispaniola* in the harbor assured no uninvited visitors, and there appeared no enemy upon the island.

Late that evening I needed more pitch for the torches and walked to the block house, where it was kept in dry storage. As I was about to enter I heard one of the men talking, in low voice.

"He be not one of us, that's what I say, and I've no taste for him sharin' in anything we find."

"And what if'n he didn't tell us about that water lever?" added another. "We were always at his mercy."

"I gave my word," I heard Captain Steele say, "and on my word I'll keep it. A contract of Articles promised is a contract he'll get. He kept his part of the bargain."

"Aye, but we all know the tales of his treachery to 'is own kind," spoke another, "and there's no evidence to show that his villainous ways be changed. Tales be spoken how he's killed his own mates, which is against the code if there be no reason."

"We gets us a vote, Cap'n, since there be no contract in place now. And that's the code. Until it is signed, he's subject to a vote for the Black Spot."

"I can't deny you that, or your vote," said the captain. "But be aware, the consequences may be great."

"I says we gives him the Black Spot and be done with 'em," I heard another one shout. "He's been workin' up part of the crew, with all his niceties and charmed ways, his this's and that's, always tryin' to 'pear doin' no harm, but still attemptin' to plant seeds of dissent amongst us. And like Perry said, we knows it's true he murdered crew before, him and Flint, and that's a fact. Cold blooded it was too."

"Aye, but we've all killed men before," said another, "and that's no call for a Black Spot."

"But not fellow crew, say I. And that breaks our code."

"And what if we don'ts Black Spot him," I could hear Morgan say. "I don't want to always be lookin' back wondering if he's gonna kill me next, unlooked for, like the Devil at prayers."

"We needs a vote, Captain."

"As you wish. I will abide by the vote. I'll start it then. I vote no Black Spot."

One by one, the men voted. At the end, the captain said it is one more in favour of giving Silver the Black Spot. I quickly walked into the room.

"I also get a vote, do I not? I have a contract with the crew. Am I not entitled to a say?"

Hushed murmurs from the men filled the room.

"Yes you are," said the captain.

"This is not fair, Captain, and you know it. Long John has kept his word, and this is a traitorous way to reward him for it."

"Are you going to vote, Hawkins?" asked the captain.

"Yes sir. I vote no. No Black Spot."

"There's a surprise."

I looked over and found these words came from Morgan, who was in the corner and covered with shadows. He stepped out into the fire's light.

"You two have always been like father and son, and now the son is voting for the father. All even it is now, is that it, Captain?"

The captain nodded an assent. Morgan reached in and pulled out a piece of paper.

"Seems like I also gets to vote, being as the captain kept his word and made me an equal partner with the crew. Long John can't vote. There be twenty-two of us all in, and if my calculation be correct, that's ten for, and ten against."

A sinister smirk enveloped Morgan's face as his eyes squinted, blocking out any reflection from the fire's light.

"I vote yea, Black Spot him," said he, "and then he can be killed. And if it pleases the captain, I would be honoured to be chosen for this... *sad* honour."

He started laughing.

"It'll be a day without the sun rising high in the sky before the likes of you be havin' a chance to send ol' Silver to Davy Jones locker, Morgan, and you can lay to that!"

We all turned and saw Silver standing in the doorway, leaning on his crutch, soaking wet. He hobbled into the room and stopped.

"Black Spot and kills me, is it? After what I's done to help you find this treasure? If not for me, there'd be no treasure, and that's a fact. Black Spot ol' Silver, eh? By the powers, that's been tried before by gentlemen o' fortune, and you can bet the devil is not holding his evil breath for me arrival, although thems that's tried be at his side this very minute, and I'm none the worse for it, by thunder."

He hobbled a little closer toward the fire.

"When I thinks of Jasper in his cell trustin' me to do right, to make sure his family gets the fair part they deserve, and me keepin' me promises and such, well, I wish he were here and not me to see the greed in yer eyes and hearts."

"More'n likely you killed him, Silver," said Morgan. "I've seen your ways. You remember Tom and Alan? And you would have killed me given the chance."

"And I still may, Morgan," Silver said with a scowl.

He moved closer to the fire and near the captain.

"Captain, is this how you keeps yer word to ol' Long John Silver? Is this the great Captain Steele's way of commandin'?"

"I voted for you Silver, on my word, but you know the code. A vote is entitled to every man. All are equal. And the vote is binding."

"Equal 'tis?" He looked toward all the men.

"You to a man, who voted against me, brings disgrace to our traditions. Remember this well. There's never been a man to look me between the eyes and seen a good day a'terwards, you may lay to that."

Silver stealthily moved closer to the fire, leaning upon his crutch as he slowly stared at the group.

"And mark me words. None of you gentlemen will ever lay a hand on that treasure."

"Aye, a condemned man's rants and raves sendin' forth empty threats, like the coward he is," replied Morgan.

"Coward?" roared Silver. "Long John Silver never backed from nothin' fair. Coward I am now? I take 'ception from no man, and especially from no rats of yer ilk. By the powers, you know this here to be wrong, and as far as I be concerned, there'n no rules left for the likes of them that has the gall to condemn the man who brought them riches. That's what I say, and you may lay to that."

I watched Silver's eyes as he quickly locked gazes momentarily with each man in the fire's light as he spoke, all the while slowly walking backwards toward the door.

"To the devil with you all, say I!" he shouted.

He reached into his pocket, pulled out a small bag of what looked to be black powder and tossed it into the fire's flames, while he turned around quickly and...

An explosion threw all of the men near the fire backwards as a ball of flames shot out into the room. Silver started to run out and grabbed my hand.

"This be the moment we needs to 'scape Jim. We've got to be off. Follow me."

We raced through the door and out toward the section of fencing that was collapsed to the east. I looked back as men raced from the block house with their clothes afire and rolled in the mud and water puddles upon the ground.

Silver was surprisingly nimble with his crutch, using it to hurdle the fence and all manner of objects that lay in our way. In short time, in spite of the darkness, we were a fair and safe distance away from the fort. We stopped to rest and catch our breath.

"Silver, I tried to stop them."

"I heard your vote, Jim, and I 'preciate yer spoken words. We needs to get to Ben Gunn's cave. Gets out of the rain and formylate a plan. Do you think you can find it from here, being dark and all?"

"I do, Long John. We've got to cut back around and behind the fort. If we do that, it's only a couple hour's walk at best. Do you think they will come after us?"

"Nay, not tonight, Jim. I don't believe they've a mind to venture out into this storm nor the dark of night, riskin' life and limb, for the likes of me. No, me boy, I think they'll be lookin' 'pon our leavin' as good fortune, providence in fact, and put their attentions on the treasure. They knows we can't leave the island. Nor can we cause them great grief. Their ship be well guarded. And they believes they has the key to the treasure now, and me value is used up. I thinks we'll be safe and sound for a day or so. We can make plans and such once we gets dry and some rest."

It took us the better part of two hours to finally reach the cliff below Ben Gunn's old cave. The weather presented some formidable obstacles, not the least of which was a lack of light. We climbed up the ten feet or so onto a ledge and entered the cave. Once inside, we found a torch by feeling about, and Silver wrapped some dried moss from the cave's entrance around the top and used one of his pistol's flints to fire it. Once light flooded the cave, I looked around. Much of the furniture Ben Gunn made was still in its place, and there were three piles of bedding lying about that still had soft moss as a cushion.

"We'll take inventory in the morning, Jim. 'Til then, get some rest. We'll devise a grand plan together, I promise you that. Yer ol' Long John still has a trick or two that's got us a chance to work this here problem out."

"Good night," said I, tired beyond words.

I was soaked and exhausted as I finally lay down upon one of the beddings and tried to think. But alas, my mind would not cooperate. I realized that in an instant my life had changed from having a share in the treasure and a life assured, with all the results I had envisioned and dreamt about, to being an outcast stuck on this inhospitable island, and death the only sure prospect I could see. And what of my Chloe? My dear sweet Chloe. What was I to do? If she had gotten away, and was able to return to England, then perhaps help was on the way. But that could take months, and the treasure would be long gone by that time. I needed to sleep, to gather my thoughts with a fresh view. At that point, all seemed hopeless.

Long John extinguished the torch, and I remember nothing more beyond falling fast asleep.

Chapter Thirty

Negotiations

The sound of water gently dripping off the outer cave's entrance awakened me the next morning. I shook myself, stretched like a barnyard kitten and then the horrible realization struck me that the previous night had not been a terrible dream; that in fact, Silver and I were stranded in Ben Gunn's cave on an abysmal island in the middle of the ocean. I also remembered how we, at least I, by my actions, had created enemies of our former crewman and captain. I noticed Long John was awake and sitting down, staring out the cave's entrance. I arose and sat down next to him.

"Mornin' Jim."

"Silver."

"Jim, I've been thinkin' here, and it's a fierce mess we's into, and that's a fact. No use putting shellac on it. We've no food, provisions and only our cutlass and two pistols, for which, at least, I do has plenty of powder and a dozen balls for them. And thems the easy parts. I'm a sorry I got ye into this here fine mess, Jim, I truly am."

251

I didn't say a word. He was right, we were in dire straits, and I believed in my heart of hearts that it was, at its core, somehow his fault.

"Ands I can understand how yer feels, Jim. And I wants you to know how proud I am at your stickin' by me side. Hand and glove we be. Warms me heart to be thinkin' of your carin' so much, and that's a fact, 'tis."

"Here's another *fact*, Silver," I interrupted. "We're stuck on an island with cutthroats that want to kill us and we've no way off."

"Now, now, Jim, that there's takin' the worst of approaches to it. I'm not through yet."

"Oh? Perhaps I have missed something. What exactly is your 'grand' plan' you mentioned last evening, Silver?"

"Well Jim, here it be, bare. I say we holes up here, for awhiles. It's dry and safe. We needs to get some food and fill up the cisterns with water, which seems easy enough with this here storm. Once our supplies be full, we'll be snug and secure."

"And then?"

"Wait."

"Wait for what?"

"For that sly ol' Captain Steele to make us a deal."

I picked up some small stones off the cave floor and started throwing them out the entrance.

"In case it is lost upon you, Silver, the Black Spot is upon you and now probably me too. He'll make no deal, and you of all people know that to be true. His honour and word will get the best of him."

"Just wait, Jim, just wait. Presently, let's go out and see if we can gets some fruit fer nourishment. It's always best to be belly full when makin' plans and such."

We left the cave and found some bread fruit and papaya nearby, wrapped as many as we could in my shirt and brought them back to the cave. I went out and gathered moss from under the nearby cliff faces, which shielded them from the storm's water. Long John started a fire near the cave's entrance, which we used to dry the moss sufficiently so as to wrap it for burning on our torches. The cave was situated pointing east, and there was no fear of discovery or being seen from the fort or treasure site, since neither offered a position to see the fire's light. The cloud cover offered shelter from discovery for the smoke we generated. By the end of the day, we had sufficient food stores, water and torches to last a good while. We didn't speak much to each other that day, and I was not unhappy about it.

The stark reality of my situation started to bear down on me like the oppressively humid air that permeated this island. The more I thought and tried to reason a way out, the more the inevitable conclusion etched itself in my mind that there was no escape—no way out of this terrible predicament. In my mind, our only hope was rescue by Chloe's efforts. And in that, at least in the short term, I had little faith.

By darkness, I was too tired to continue with this train of thought, nor even care. I only wanted to find a way off this accursed island and back to the life I had left behind. I missed everything about it. What seemed mundane at the time, when viewed from the present, looked like a king's ransom to me now. I missed the Admiral Benbow and all her patrons. I missed my mother coming to wake me up in the morning. My mother: I had forgotten all about her and how she must have felt, not knowing where I was, or even if I was alive. How selfish I had been. I truly regretted leaving that life of mine that I had so often taken for granted.

Hopelessly, I finally fell asleep after a meal of fruit.

- - - - - - - - - - -

Long John was standing and staring out the cave's entrance, a pistol in hand, when I awoke the next morning. Then I heard voices.

"Silver, are you in there?"

It was Captain Steele. How could he have known where we were?

"Long John and Hawkins, if you are in there, make yourselves known. We need to speak with you."

"I forewarned you the treasure would never be yers!" shouted Silver. "And now ye knows the truth of it. Traitorous ways gets no rewards from ol' Long John Silver, by thunder."

I quickly jumped up and ran to his side.

"How did they find us?"

"Mus'n been Morgan. We overlooked his bein' on this island. There be three beds in here, and I'm suspectin' it was he and the other two mates that made 'em when we's left 'em here."

"I want a parlay, Silver!" shouted the captain. "We need to speak."

"Speak if you will, but from no closer than where you stand, or a ball will be your reward."

A long silenced ensued as Silver and I exchanged glances. He gave a slight smile.

"The crew was wrong, Silver," Captain Steele said. "They took another vote, and to a man, they voted you right and took back the Black Spot."

"Even my good ol' dear friend and former shipmate Morgan, is it? Did he votes me right?"

"Every man Silver, on my word."

"Well then, that truly be a heartwarmin' tale, Captain Steele, it surely be. And if I've ever a mind to join the likes of you swabs again, it pleases me no end to know I'm welcome with open arms, and that's a fact. But I be happy 'n content here with me mate Jim, and we'll just be stayin' all comfy like in this fine cave until ye hears otherwise."

Another silence follows. *"What is he doing?"* I asked myself.

"Silver, you know there is no treasure at that spot. We dug down over ten feet, and all we found was a small chest with fifteen doubloons and a dozen dead men's bones. Where is it?"

"Oh, so that be it? No treasure? Well it looks like ol' Silver has the last laugh on you, it does."

Silver laughed and it echoed around the cliff.

The captain's voice raised in pitch, and I could see even from my vantage point in the cave that he had become red with anger.

"There will be no waiting 'until we *hears* otherwise', Silver!" Steele shouted. "We have come for the treasure's location, and I promised you I would provide no mercy for treachery. We voted the Black Spot off, and you are welcome to join the crew again. However, you will receive no share of the treasure. It is your life only that will be spared. Hear me clearly. I will not be thwarted by you. If you do not cooperate, if you refuse, then if I have to, I will resort to any means that I think will work. And I am a very clever man in that regard."

"What about Hawkins, here, Cap'n. What be his fate?"

"He sided with you. His fate is your fate. The contract does not protect a traitor. It is only his life that we offer. There will be no share."

"That not be much of an encitin' offer, Cap'n. Fact is, it seems short on fairness, it does."

"Silver, if your treachery continues, you're a dead man. And we'll only be negotiating the method. You know what I am capable of. You will tell me what I want to know, I can promise you that, or suffer consequences even you cannot imagine."

"Aye Cap'n, maybe what you say be true. Maybe you'll get it out of me, and maybe not. But sure as the tide rises and sets, if you're thinkin' of comin' up here, the first bullet will be between yer eyes, and the treasure'll be of little worth to you."

"Silver, maybe you'll care about your 'son' there, and what we will do to him? I can kill him slowly in front of you, and you can watch him die, save only for your truthfulness. Or, you can tell me what I want to know before I kill you, and it will become his parole. I will keep him alive until what you say proves true. If not, he will die a more tortuous death than I have ever bestowed upon a man."

Silver stood silent, thinking. The only sounds heard were the drippings of water into the cave's stony entrance.

"You be speakin' horrors I needs to think about well and good, Captain. The way you puts it, I am thinkin' that rejoinin' the crew, now that the Black Spot's been lifted, could be my— our—best advantage."

"That offer is short lived, Silver. The consequences of which I have spoken will prevail if you choose unwisely."

"Can you give me 'til the evenin', Cap'n?"

"Till the evening then. I would request that you remain here until my return. I am putting some guards out here, just in case you should decide to change your residence before then."

"Cap'n Steele?"

"Yes?"

"Will ye be puttin' all this here in a contract all affy-davy like, and bringin' it with ye for me to sign?"

"Silver, have your answer ready upon my return. And may God save your soul if you choose wrongly."

Four of our former crewmates were posted below the cave, about fifty feet out, muskets in hand. We retired within the cave and sat near the fire pit.

"What are we to do now?" asked I.

"We've bought some time. Now we needs to think this out."

"What's to think, Silver? We can be back with the crew and, who knows, maybe still get a share in the treasure if you tell them what they want to know."

"No Jim, we can't. There be no treasure for us. The captain were firm as rock on that point. So I thinks that be off the table, negotiatin' wise. But there be more, for I fears this be a ploy, and the end aim be not in our best interests."

"What? You're worried about Morgan?"

"Morgan? No, he's the least of me worries. You noticed how the captain would not lay to his word to a signed contract? There be reasons for that. I'm thinkin' this whole votin' off the Black Spot is sugar to coat their real intentions."

"You mean he is lying to us?"

"I just don't be knowin'. He's a hard one to read, that captain. But I do know that he's honourable to the code. What I don't know is if he be in on a treachery to trick us into thinkin' they has welcomed us back in. If they hasn't, all that he threatened can still come to pass."

"Was this your plan all along? That they would come seek us out and negotiate?"

"No, it weren't. I were hopin' they's would be true to their word and give me a fair shake and share. But once treachery became aflame, I did rely on this here to be me last bargainin' chip. I knew once they didn't find the treasure, their greed would get the best of 'em, and maybe we could negotiate a way out of here. That's why I wanted to wait 'til the evening. Greed's a funny thing, Jim. It grows and causes all sorts of changes in swab as well as gentry, and in the end you can sometimes make a deal with the devil hisself if it means you get yer hands on the gold. We'll just have to wait and see if they wants to make a real deal, hopefully involving a share, even if it be smaller."

"And if not?"

"Then it's the pistols and a fight we are in for. And I'm not so sure the crew be havin' the stomach to die for what I has. No Jim, I thinks we has a fair shot at workin' thru this here dilemma, as you call it, to our 'vantage."

The next few hours were tedious, with nothing to do and being unable to leave. The storm had reached a lull, and a rainbow could be seen over the azure sea once again. This one I did not think portended well for us.

I implored Long John to tell me the story of how he met and received the knowledge of the treasure from Jasper while he was in jail, if only to pass the boredom. I had my notebook with me, and wrote it down word for word. This helped greatly to pass the time until evening.

As night approached we lighted a torch and started to eat some fruit, staring silently upon it. I was scared, not knowing what to expect. Long John seemed calm and assured enough, with no outward signs of distress. I wished I could also feel that way.

Suddenly, a ball of flaming pitch bounced into the cave, with black smoke bellowing from it. It began filling the cave with a horrible and oppressive smell. Both Long John and I started coughing, our eyes burned, and we were unable to catch our breaths.

"Time's up!" we could hear Captain Steele shout.

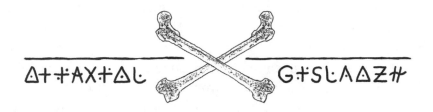

Chapter Thirty-One

Discovery

"**W**e decided to try another way, Silver!" Captain Steele shouted. "I'm afraid the devil is now waiting for you both."

I panicked. What were we to do? It was getting harder to breathe, and I could barely make out Long John's silhouette through all the smoke.

"Come out now, Silver. Tell me your secret. We'll put it to the test, and if it is true, I'll make it a quick death for you and that traitorous Hawkins."

Silver fired one of the pistols through the smoke and out through the cave's opening.

"I'll take me secret to Davy Jones before I gives it up to the likes of you, you scurvy traitorous one-eyed dog."

"Silver!" I pleaded. "Come please, we've got to get to the back of the cave where we can catch a breath."

Silver fired the other pistol, grabbed our torches and we hurried toward the rear of the cave. The air was not yet sullied there, and I could finally catch my breath as I filled my lungs with clean, sweet air. Another pitch ball landed in the cave and rolled further toward us. The smoke rose and drifted forward toward the cave's entrance.

I observed this, but the fact was incongruous to me. How can that be, I thought to myself? How could the smoke be blowing *out* of the cave?

I took the lighted torch from Long John and observed the flame. It too was leaning away from the back part of the cave. I moved it slowly against the back wall, which was perhaps six feet tall to the rock ceiling. As the torch neared the top of a large boulder resting on the floor, the flame was pushed away from the wall.

"Long John, there is air coming out from somewhere over here. Hold this torch."

I leaned my back against the boulder and, using my legs, pushed with all my might. It budged only slightly, and then stopped. I grabbed a handful of fine gravel from the floor and threw it on the opposite side of the boulder in the direction I was pushing it, hoping it would help it slide over the coral floor. I pushed again. Nothing. After a Herculean push it finally moved a slight bit.

"Here, Jim, let me be helping."

Long John set the torch down, sat down with his back to the rock alongside me and dug his one foot into the ground. He looked over at me with fierce determination.

"Ready Jim?"

I nodded. We both put our backs into it. The boulder moved ever so slightly. I found strength anew and pushed again with all my might. I could feel Silver's help. It moved again, this time another foot, then two, and I then had no more reserves. I fell to a sitting position and felt a cool, fresh breeze upon me. I looked over, and there was an opening, a small one, measuring no more than two feet in height and half again as much in width. I peered within and saw only darkness.

"We must get through this and see where it leads if we are to live, Long John."

"Aye. I'll be gettin' more torches."

He hobbled up upon his foot, picked up his crutch, went into the smoky abyss, and returned shortly with three more of the ones we had made earlier.

"Give me one of the torches and I'll go in first to see where it leads," said I to Silver.

I slid down upon my belly and put the torch ahead of me as I tried to see where it led. As I slid into this claustrophobic opening my shoulders and back barely cleared the ceiling. Darkness only lay ahead, as far as I could see. I noticed it slanted decidedly downhill, which made it easier as I slithered my way forward. My progress was hindered and made more difficult by the constant breeze of fresh cool air that blew the flames of the torch toward me. I had to keep it well ahead of me for fear of catching fire. After what I estimated to be fifteen or twenty feet, the torch exited the tunnel, and as I also did, I could see I was within a large cavern. I stood up and held the torch aloft. It was breathtaking. Stalagmites as tall as trees and stalactites extending far down from the ceiling, all of them possessing a reddish glow with rings of various florescent colors that danced about them from the light of the torched flame.

"Jim, do you be findin' anything?"

I had forgotten for a moment the danger behind me, and quickly planted the torch in the ground and kneeled into the tunnel.

"Long John, come in quickly! This tunnel empties into a huge cavern."

"Aye Jim, I'll be on me way. They've pitched another ball and it's almost next to me."

While Silver made his way back, I took another look at this most magnificent cave. I could hear waterfalls somewhere in the distance, although they could not be seen. The ceiling looked to be over fifty feet in height, and I judged it to be twice that long, at least. The columns of limestone gave the impression that they were part of a grand forest. The light of the torch created a dreamlike feeling that both scared and intrigued me.

"Come on, Jim, give yer ol' Silver a hand here, will you?"

Silver was almost to the end of the tunnel. I reached down and helped him and then up and onto the cave's floor. He had two fresh unlit torches with him. He reached in and pulled his crutch out from within the tunnel.

He looked around and said not a word about our surroundings. I imagine he was as much in awe as I was at the sight.

"Shiver me timbers, Jim, I can feel the air blowin' in from somewhere," he finally said. "And where there be air, there be an equal chance of 'scape, says I."

He reached into his jacket's pocket and pulled out another full charge bag of black powder. He ripped the end of it with his teeth, and started to pour a trail starting at the tunnel's exit and extending two feet out.

"What are you doing?"

"They'll soon discover that we are not to be found in the cave, Jim. This will hopefully give us a permanent 'scape. It's a chance of faith we be takin', you can lay to that. But I sees little other choice. We can neither make anew nor mend our sityation here. Are you with me?"

I nodded an assent.

He bent down and poured the black powder a little way into the tunnel, and then emptied some of it into a small pile, leaving the remainder in the bag. He scooted back, got up upon his crutch, and then leaned down and pulled out one of his pistols.

"Run Jim, let's get aways from here fast."

He pulled the trigger, and the flint produced a spark that lighted the line of powder he left in front of the cave. We were twenty feet away when the powder exploded with a resonance that rang throughout the cavern and knocked us both to the ground with its force. The echo was deafening, and continued to repeat itself until my head and ears were ringing.

When it finally subsided, I stood up and used the torch to look back at the tunnel area. It had caved in on itself. Rocks blocked the entire area. There was no way back. I hoped then that Silver was right about another exit.

We found a small stream that ran almost in the center of this cavern, and decided to follow it to its source. We walked along the side for what I estimated to be half of a mile, and observed that the cavern's ceiling was descending. Finally, we found ourselves facing an opening about as tall as a man, which we needed to pass through if we were to continue on. We stepped into the stream and followed it into the opening, and exited into a cavern so large we were unable, even with the aid of our torch, to see the ceiling. I might add that the water was extremely tepid.

The stalagmites in this new cavern, which reached heights of over twenty feet, sparkled like glitter when the torch passed near them. Upon closer inspection I observed they were embedded with little crystals of various colors. The stream wound its way through these giants, and it seemed at every turn the colors became more brilliant and wondrous. We both remarked how we were going uphill at a slight rate. We also observed that there was still a markedly cool breeze coming at us from somewhere upstream. Our enthusiasm and energy were great, and we never once slowed down our pace nor progress.

We came upon a small waterfall. On the left side of it was another tunnel with an upward direction from the ground. We decided to try that before attempting to climb up the rocks on which the water cascaded down in order to follow the stream in that way.

As I was walking in this tunnel, I suddenly lost my footing; or rather, the soil gave way beneath my soles. My feet went out from under me, and I fell down and started to slide. I could see from my torch that I was heading for a cliff of some sort. I reached out my left hand to try and stop my descent, to no avail. Over the edge I slid. I instinctively let go of the torch and tried with all my might to find something to hang onto. I grabbed at soil on the side and it simply broke off and gave way. As I continued to descend, I finally felt a ledge and grabbed it with both hands. I looked down and could see the torch falling, and falling, until it disappeared from sight, not hearing any sound from its touching bottom. My breath was heavy and my heart beat so loudly they were the only things I could hear in my head. My hands ached, and my fingers were extremely sore at having to bear the brunt of my entire weight.

"Hold on Jim!" Long John shouted as his voice echoed about two or three times. I heard him slide onto the ground and then saw him peering over the rim of the cliff with his torch, his leg slightly over the edge. I looked down and saw my legs dangling above the bottomless abyss, and my fright escalated into terror.

"Help me, Silver. Please, help me!" I screamed.

"Hold on Jim. Just be holdin' on, by thunder!"

He slid back, away from my sight, and from his shadow I could see him brace his leg against a rock. I then saw his crutch hang down over the edge of the cliff from where he was sitting.

"Grab onto me crutch, Jim, and I'll pull you up. Just grab it with your hands. I'll do the rest."

"I can't, Silver. I'm hanging on to a ledge with both hands. I cannot do what you ask."

"Jim, you can do this. Trusts me. Grab me crutch and hold on. It be yer only chance. Don't let dragons and demons grab hold of yer with their fear. Ye gots to fight 'em. Focus on just gettin' yer *one* hand on it."

I gritted my teeth, took a deep breath, and in one motion I reached up and was able to get one hand on the crutch. This evenly distributed my weight between the ledge and his crutch. Long John started to pull on it, and I moved up about a foot. I could hear the strain in his voice.

"Silver, hold up. I only have one hand on this. I need to get them both on."

"I'll feel it when ye do, and by the powers I'll pull you up then, Jim."

I took a breath, counted to three and then swung around and grabbed the crutch with my other hand. The extra weight caused the crutch to drop slightly.

"Silver!" I screamed.

"Hold on Jim, we can do this."

Up he pulled me another two feet, and I could then rest my knee on the ledge. I stood up on my other leg upon this small ledge and now reached out for Silver's hand. He grabbed it, and with his leg braced against the rock and his back to the wall, he used all his strength and pulled me up and over the edge of the cliff. I lay on my back a few moments to catch my wits about me, and struggled to breathe again normally.

"You in one piece there, Jim?"

"Yes, I think I am."

"Shiver me timbers, Jim. That be a close one, as close as I've seen."

"I don't think there is a bottom to it, Silver. It probably goes straight down to Hades itself."

"Aye, well, we'll not be finding that out today. Here, grab the torch whilst I stands meself up."

He picked it up from near him and handed it toward me. When I moved I noticed that my right leg was full of sharp pains, and I let out a scream.

"What be troublin' ye, Jim?"

"My right leg. I think I sprained it."

"Well, if that on'y be the case, it should be fine with some rest."

While I continued to reach for the torch, I noticed the pain in my fingers was worse than I had thought, and as he handed the torch to me, it slipped through them and slid onto the ground. We watched, helplessly, as it slowly rolled down and then over the edge. As it fell within the abyss, the fiery light dwindled to nothing, and we were engulfed in pitch blackness.

"Oh my gosh Silver, I am sorry. It just slipped out of my fingers. Where is the other one?"

"It be back a ways where I left it when ye fell. Let's catch our senses first before we lays out to find it."

My eyes were still used to the torch's light, and it seemed that they saw only spots of white circles for a few minutes. Gradually, the spots diminished. Then a sight that at first confused me made an appearance.

Light.

Not the kind from the sun, nor from fire or oil lamps. Rather, the kind of light a bright starlit night might produce, and yet more. I looked around and saw that all the stalactites and stalagmites were aglow, and the ceiling of the cave was also completely aglow in a bright luminescence. Millions of little lights covered everything within this cavern, and I could clearly make out Long John's features and even his eyes, which were darting around as were mine.

"Silver?"

"I sees it, Jim, but me mind says me eyes be playin' a deceivin' trick on me."

"What are they?"

"Must be the same type of creatures as produces the silver tides. Phosphoresce I thinks they calls it."

"It's beautiful."

"That it be, Jim, and you can lay to that."

I just lay there, drinking this scene in with all my senses and soul. I held out my hand, and could see it as clearly as if on a cloudy day, although there was a slight greenish tinge to the light. I started laughing.

"We sure cheated death again. And now it is I who owe you one, John Silver."

"Nay, Jim. It be nothing. You owe me naught, and that's a fact."

"A debt is a debt. I intend to repay it."

"Jim, it is I who owe you."

"We'll see," said I. "After we're out of this predicament, we'll have to make an accounting. It is ironic, though, because the reason I am even here was to try and save your life."

"Pray tell, what are ye speakin' about?"

"Why I came to find you in the first place."

"That do brings up a question I's been havin' for you for quite a spell, Jim. And that be this: how was you happenin' to be in the wagon when we arrived at the camp after I was rescued? Surely you weren't being with Morgan, and Captain Steele showed no knowledge of havin' ever known you. I've been wrestling with that question for this 'ole time."

"As I said, to try to rescue you."

"Rescue me, is it?"

I told him the story of the buccaneers coming to the Admiral Benbow, and hearing of his sentence to be hanged. He asked me to describe them, and he shared with me that he knew who they were. I then relayed receiving his letter and how I felt it my duty to try and put in a good word with the magistrate, since I made a promise to do so before he escaped the last time. I shared the adventures I went through, including the lightning strike, and finally of my being rescued. I did not tell him about meeting Chloe and how I intended to marry her.

"When in Bristol," I continued, "while waiting outside the jail to try to speak with you, I happened upon the men who were creating the means for your escape, and in a moment of fervor jumped into the back of the second wagon and went with you and the buccaneers."

"I had no awares of your motives, Jim. You went through all of that to help ol' Long John, is that it?"

"I did."

"Pray tell, why?"

"Because you're my friend, and I made a promise to you. A promise made, is a promise kept."

"Aye, Jim, but when I left the ship on me own, you were not honour bound by any promise you made."

"That's what Doctor Livesey said, but I felt differently. You would do the same for me, wouldn't you?"

"Well, Jim, that there be an interestin' question… Of course I would, yes indeedy. Dooty is dooty. Don't even have to think on that one, no sir. If me Jim be in trouble, well then, the two of us is in it, and to the end too, and you can lay to that as fact."

"I knew it," said I. "The doctor and my mother both said you were of no account and not worth it, but I said they were all wrong about you. I even went against my mother's wishes to come here—well at least to Bristol."

"I be truly touched by your friendship. Imagine that. Long John Silver has a true friend. Touches me heart to the core, it does."

He sat back against the wall and closed his eyes with a smile gracing his scraggily bearded face.

"Although good in intention, I fear it could all end for naught, with both of us dead and no treasure to share."

He shook himself to sit straight up again.

"It could end like that, yes indeedy, it truly could. Dire's the outlook at this latitude. But they can't kill us 'til they knows the secret I still has. They's come too far for that. I'm a thinkin' there still be room aplenty for negotiations, although the terms could be a might less favourable right now."

"Less favourable than a horrible death at the hands of Captain Steele? I must say, you're much more of an optimist than myself, Silver. I think they are mad enough at us to do just about anything to hasten our demise."

I picked up a small stone and threw it over the cave's ledge.

"Plus, they don't know at this point if we are even alive."

"Yer right as rain on that point. And that be in our favour."

"If we can just hole up here and keep ourselves fed, there is a chance that help might be on the way," I told him. "But even if it arrives, we'd be unaware of it, for in here I fear we'll never be found."

"Speak your mind, Jim. This be the third time ye've mentioned that. What 'xactly do you be referring to when you says help be on the way?"

"From Chloe."

"Who in tarnation be this here Chloe yer speakin' 'bout?

"The girl in Captain Steele's quarters."

"The squire's daughter?"

"She is not his daughter."

"But how in the seven seas would ye be knowin' her?"

"She is my fiancée."

Once the shock of this statement wore off, I explained to Long John how she was the one who found and nursed me back to health after being robbed and left for dead by those buccaneers. The same ones, I now told him, that we killed at the Quiet Woman. I then relayed how she explained she was looking for me when teaming up with Captain Smollett, and how he insisted that she stay on the ship while he and the men were searching for me. I finished by sharing with him how I accidentally discovered her and arranged for her escape.

"So Lady Blue helped you, she did? That's one for the yarns, by thunder. But if all you be tellin' me be true, then shiver me sides, it will still be months before she can get backs to England and arranges a ship to sail here. And that be the start of the hurricanes upon us too. I think our best chance be layin' in outsmartin' Captain Steele and winning our freedom, and a share of the treasure to boot, if'n skies be clear and fate our friend."

"The chances of outsmarting him are very slim, Long John. He seems to know what we think before we do. A smarter man I think I've never met."

"Smart or not, he'll not find the treasure without me knowledge."

"What is it he needs to know?"

Silver scooted closer on the ground toward me and leaned close.

"Aye, Jim, you've earned the right to know me last secret, and ye shall," said he with a smile. "You see, ol' Jasper told me that Redbeard was all fixated about certain numbers, something about a group he belongs to. Anyways, he holds a particular respect for one of them, the highest sacred one of this group, says he, and that the treasure is buried at that depth."

"What is the number?"

"Thirty-two."

"That's the same distance from the tree that was in the cipher."

"Aye, that's when I knowed Jasper had spoken the truth. They be at the right spot, but I am suspectin' that this chest with the fifteen coins and dead men's bones about it he were speakin' 'bout was on'y a diversion, to stop any further diggin' if'n you didn't know the truth. They stopped short with their diggin', by thunder. The treasure is still below them."

"If we tell them, Long John, might'n they leave us alone? After all, once they have the treasure, we'll be of no value to them."

"From your lips to God's ear, Jim. But as ye've mentioned before, that captain be a might honourable man, he be. With him dooty is dooty. And I don't be thinkin' he takes lightly what we've done by leavin' and 'barrasin' him in front of the crew."

"Leaving him?" I shouted. "He was going to let them kill you."

"That's a fact. Still, he's got his honour to defend. And as I mentioned, he's dangerous and unpredictable as a scorpion, and just likes a scorpion, could very well end his own life in order to defend and hold his honour."

"We've got to try something, Long John."

"I agrees, Jim, I agrees wholeheartedly with you. But let's take care with thought and action. We's safe now. Let's take our bearings first and see what is ours for the taking here, and refresh ourselves with food and rest. Then we'll make our plans."

Tired to the core, I rested while Silver went about looking for food. The stream and waterfall were nearby, and within it he found and caught two of the oddest-looking fish I ever laid eyes upon. In fact, that was why they looked so odd. They had no eyes. And they were transparent, whereby you could see completely inside of them as if they had no body. Silver was able to gather moss and light it with his flint, and we were treated to a delicious portion of this strange fish. After our meal, we sat silently together within our own thoughts.

"Do you ever get scared, Long John?" asked I.

"Of course, Jim, like all mates I s'pose."

"You never show it, leastwise not that I've ever seen."

Silver stuffed his pipe and lit it slowly, taking large breaths to start it.

"Well, that's a fact, and I'll tell ye why. Once I did, and it ended up costin' me me leg in the process. Ye got to learn that when some men, the really evil ones, smells fear on ye, they seems to feed off of it. So's I learned to fights it. Like that old King George of lore and his Knights of the Roundtable. These Knights had fears a plenty when havin' to face their dragons, even knowing they couldn't win. But they knows that if they showed any fear, the dragon could get awares of it and kills them. That be their strength."

"So you're saying by fighting your fears, my fears—"

"What I be sayin', Jim, is all men has fears. It's them that fights 'em and wins that are the lucky ones. You needs to fight yours. Slay them dragons once and fer all. It will serve you well."

After eating, we both felt rested and full. I lay back and all troubles seemed distant. The waterfall's gentle sounds, mixed with the wonderfully relaxing lights of a million small creatures and the cool breezes still blowing past me, all blended and obscured the seriousness of the threat we faced in the cave only hours ago.

GԼ+35XΔA ᛭ J53∴+XԼ

Chapter Thirty-Two

Daylight Again

Without benefit of the sun or moon for reference, I had no idea if it had been days or weeks since we ventured within those huge underground caverns. We took perhaps a dozen or so meals. I had slept quite often. Long John found an opening near the rear of the next cavern where, he said, we could exit with some minor difficulty. He ventured out once and gathered some fruit. My leg had started to heal, and I began to place my weight upon it when standing, although it still hurt to walk any distance. The gentle quietness around us became comforting. Calmness started to dwell within me as a constant companion.

Our predicament did not seem so dire and forlorn. The surroundings were pleasant, and circumstances were still in our favour. Although not a fortune, I reasoned I did have a good deal of capital at home, the remains from my earlier adventure here. My education could still be successfully completed, and after my studies, the practice of medicine would provide for a comfortable existence for Chloe and me. And hopefully for the family that would follow. The thought of losing a share of the treasure did not weigh as heavily on my heart as it had only days earlier.

There was also every possibility that the buccaneers would never find the treasure, based on their not knowing the true facts of its whereabouts. And if they did not, it could still become mine; mine and Long John's, and wouldn't that be putting lipstick on a sow?

My thoughts then turned to Captain Steele and his crew, my former shipmates. It was equally not likely they would have given up their search and desire to find the treasure, at least not easily. The journey and costs had been too great. In point of fact, they possess all the time they could desire to continue their search and dig, which is what I guessed they would do. Food and game were plenty. Water was available, and but for the storms, which would surely abate with time, there was no reason for them to discontinue their pursuit.

And what of Long John and me? Were we in danger from the cutthroats? I reasoned that the explosion in the cave would give them pause. Are we alive, they must be wondering? No one, not even Morgan, would know of this cavernous system. The likelihood of our accidental discovery was remote.

Collectively, these thoughts brought me to the conclusion that if we stayed here and out of sight, and left no evidence of our having survived the explosion in the cave, then time was on our side. We could wait them out, with no cause or concern for food, nor drink, in high style and comfort, even. All we needed to do was be aware of their activities in a stealthy manner, and once they gave up and left, the island and treasure would indeed be ours.

Knowing that Chloe would send help when she reached the proper authorities gave mortar to my thoughts, and I could reasonably expect it would be only a matter of a few months before help should arrive.

I shared my thoughts with Silver upon his return, and he listened intently.

"Aye," said he," it be a good knot of reasoning and a fine plan. And nary a hole in the entire cloth you've woven your logic into, I might add. The only problem I see is if your Chloe doesn't reach the proper authorities."

"Do not speak of that," I snapped back.

"Now, now, Jim, I wasn't sayin' it be true, was I? Nay, I only be speculatin' to that possibility, that's all. No harm be meant on me behalf."

"I know she made it. In my heart, I just know it."

Long John stared at me a while, as if he could not understand what I was saying, and then he hopped up and onto his crutch.

"Well Jim, as I said, your plan be sound as a rock, and I say we takes our first venture out and take a look at what these scallywags be up to, that's what I say."

"Do you think that wise? We are safe here."

"'Tis true, we be safe and all. But I've a mind to see what those swabs be doin', and if'n we're goin' a need to spend the rest of our days in 'ere," Silver replied.

"Do you have any idea what time of day it is?"

"'Twas mid-day when last I checked. Me guess would be nigh morning again. But we'll see soons enough. Is your leg favourable for travel?"

I stood up and said yes, I was ready to go. My leg was still hurting, yet my determination—and curiosity—overrode the pain. I used all manner of effort to solidify my wobbly walking.

"Then let us go and see what be going on in the outside world," Silver said, smiling and pointing with his arm.

As we made our way to the opening at the rear of the cavern, a most interesting site we beheld. We followed more closely the stream running through these caves, and as we rounded a turn, there before us stood a pool of multi-colored water, as if glowing from below. And it was bubbling. I reached down to it, and it was hot to the touch. As my hand disturbed the water, the colors changed as if they were a moving rainbow. How very mystical that was, I thought.

I could finally see the light of the exit we were looking for, when suddenly the area within the cavern we were in went black, followed by the beatings of a thousand winged creatures swirling about us. The screeching they made increased to a feverish pitch as we both ran off of the ledge and fell to the ground while trying to cover our heads from this onslaught. They seemed to fly an interminably long time. Finally, it became quiet, and I looked up and saw a long shadow of them heading for the opening and flying out. I waited for a few moments, and then started to get up.

"Arghhh," said Silver. "By the thunder, I hate bats. Filthy creatures, they be."

As he said this, I noticed that the ground was, well, slushy and smelled like ammonia. When I stood up I could feel this 'mush' was all over my shirt and hands, and face. I tried to shake it off.

"By all the Saints!" I shouted. "Bat guano."

"I be covered in it too, Jim," Silver replied, while fruitlessly trying to shake it off his hands. "Let's make our first stop at the stream."

The opening to the outside world, although level to the cave's floor on the inside, was situated about ten feet above the ground on the north side of Spyglass Hill, or what would be thought of as the backside according to the way the map was drawn. In all my previous wanderings around the island, I had never been here before. From the ground looking up at the opening, it would appear as if it were but a small craggy indentation of the hill, and gave no sign of what lay within. The opening was about three feet wide and not more than two feet high, and took some effort sliding on our sides to get out. Fortunately, a small ledge gave support, and we were able to make if safely to the ground. This ledge and its slight incline also assured our ability to return.

After cleaning up at the stream, we made our way to the east side of the hill, and decided to go by way of the longer trail that was cut into the foliage by the crew when Steele had ordered the fires lit. We reasoned that it was not convenient enough to be used by the crew, and that it would offer us cover and not attract any attention. Hopefully, we could get close enough to see what they had been doing in our absence and then return to the cavern unnoticed. We finally made it down to the beach, followed it south for a distance and then turned inland toward the treasure site. We could see that no one was around the area. Upon getting closer, we observed at least a dozen large, deep holes throughout the area, with soil and sand piled high all about. All of these diggings ventured outward from where the original hole must have been dug, for the stake marking it was lying on the pile near where we had paced out the original distance to dig.

Suddenly, we heard a noise in the bushes. We jumped to our feet and began running back toward the beach. Long John was navigating over some tree roots almost at the sand's edge when he hit his leg and tumbled. His crutch flew away some distance and a yelp of pain erupted from him. I ran back to help.

"Come on Silver, get up. We must keep moving."

"Go on Jim, get away. No use the both of us gettin' caught."

"I won't leave you," I whispered loudly. I ran over to get his crutch. As I bent down to pick it up a large boot stomped on it. I looked up, slowly and with fear.

"How touching."

It was Captain Steele. I looked around and saw four other crewmen, including Morgan, whose sinister gaze and smirk sent shivers through me. Steele pulled out his pistol and kicked me in the chest back over toward Silver. I held onto his crutch and it flew with me. My ribs started to ache.

"Get some rope and return at once," Steele shouted to one of the crew.

He strutted and circled us like a barnyard rooster, his gun pointing with iron grip and precision.

"I had hopes you were not killed in the cave," he started, "if only for my own selfish desire to kill you both myself. You've tried my patience beyond its limits. Your time has run out."

He stopped, squatted down and leveled his gaze directly at me.

"You are my biggest disappointment, Hawkins. With your mind and education, you could have become anything you desired. However, loyalty and actions are what count, and you have placed your loyalties with a cripple who will now watch you die like a dog and is helpless to stop it. I would say you've made the wrong choice."

That feeling of rage that I tasted in the Quiet Woman began to coarse through my breast, and I was emboldened to speak my mind.

"No, it is you that have made the wrong choice, Captain Steele. For as you've said to me, it is a man's *actions,* and not his words, that tell the tale of his character. And your actions regarding Silver were not honourable in the least. It is you who disappoint me, with your talk of belonging to the Gentry class and having been forced into this life. What a ruse. You are no better, and in my mind worse, than these pirates; and I fear the truth of the matter is you derive pleasure from killing and hurting others. You can be sure that my choice was true and straight, and if given a second chance would surely choose Silver over the likes of you. You disgust me to my core."

"Are you through?" snapped Steele. I could not tell if he was angry or amused, his look so confounded me.

"No, I am not. I no more fear you than I fear a fly. Kill me if you please. I only pray that you make my death quick, so that I may meet my maker with honour.

I stopped, mainly to catch my breath.

"That will be entirely up to your *friend* Silver," Steele finally responded.

The mate returned with a rope. Captain Steele continued to hold his stare on me a few moments longer, then stood up and pointed to a tree with branches leaning over the sandy beach.

"Throw it over that high branch, and make a noose in it for our Mr. Hawkins here."

"Leave the boy alone, Steele," pleaded Silver. "There be no use killin' someone for no cause. I has what ye needs to be gettin' the treasure, by thunder, and if you wants it, you've gots to let him be. 'Tis me yer wantin. Me and me alone!"

"And it is you I'll have, Silver, of that you shall have no doubt. But only after you watch your," he looked to Morgan for a moment, "what did you call him, Morgan, his *son*?" Morgan nodded. "After you watch your son hang until he is dead. Then, if you have not come clean with what I want, I'll cut his carcass into pieces and use them for chum on our way home."

"Captain!" shouted Long John. "You know he's the favourite of Squire Trelawney and Captain Smollett, and you'll be losin' a bargainin' chip sure as the tides. They'll never let you live in peace after killin' this boy."

"I do not live in peace now, Silver. The Crown has seen to that. I've heard this tale of yours before. There seems to be no reason to hold on to this *chip* as you call him. No one is coming to rescue him, and there's no ship in sight that is threatening us. I'll not be fooled by your simple-minded rhetoric or feeble logic."

Steele laughed to himself and then pointed toward me.

"Put the noose around his neck at once."

They tied my hands behind my back and slipped the noose loosely, at first, around my neck. Then they cinched up the knot tightly, causing my throat to constrict. The rope's coarse hairs dug into my skin.

"Now, Silver, do you have anything to tell me before we stretch his neck? I can make it quick, or slow, the choice is yours. The truth about the treasure, and I promise it will bode well for your death too."

Silver looked around at the men, held each one's gaze for just a moment while he scratched his cheek with his hand and then smiled.

"I don't know anything more, Captain sir. I only said I knew more to try and buy us some time. It be a mystery to me—"

"More lies!" Captain Steele shouted as the veins in his forehead pulsed with anger. "Does the truth have any home within your miserable body? Have you no sense of any dignity or concern for anyone but your pathetic, worthless self?"

"Cap'n, I'm only tellin' the truth, plain and simple, and you can lay to that."

"Enough!" he said holding his hand up to make his point. "It is too bad, for I had hoped, for the sake of Hawkins here, for a quick death."

He unleashed his cutlass from his sash and walked toward me, fire in his eyes.

"Silver!" I cried.

What happened next seemed to me as if father time himself had slowed down. Long John moved his forefinger over his lips and made a signal as if for me to be silent. I found myself not afraid to die so much as angry. Anger not only toward this villainous Captain Steele, but also toward the one man I had come to trust and love as if he truly were a father to me; who now had a hand he could play that would lessen the pain of my death. Yet he refused to do so. I could not think of any reason for his actions and decided to take matters and my fate into my own hands and have done with it.

"Are you buggers, Silver? I'm going to tell them myself and get this whole business over with quickly!"

"No Jim!" Silver shouted. "Don't ye be doing it. Trust ol' Silver."

"What?"

"Don't give in yet!"

BOOM!

A loud explosion could be heard followed by a whistling sound, and then an area not more than ten feet away erupted in a violent explosion, sending particles of sand and flame flying in all directions. Steele and the men were frozen in their steps. Slowly they turned toward the ocean behind me. A second boom, followed by a whistling sound preceded another explosion to my right, close to Captain Steele. It propelled him off of his feet, and he dove and rolled away quickly from the flying debris. He shook his head and then managed to regain his footing, though visibly dazed.

Long John jumped up on his crutch and reached me in seconds. He fumbled and finally pulled the noose from around my neck.

"Back to the ship, now!" Steele ordered.

Long John and I took off running in the opposite direction, toward the beach, my hands still tied behind my back. I turned and observed Captain Steele stop, aim his pistol at us and fire it. I felt a burning pain in my right leg.

Another explosion erupted further into the jungle, persuading the captain to scurry off quickly after it landed close by. They disappeared down the trail leading past the fort and toward the beach where the *Hispaniola's* longboats still rested. I fell down onto the sand. My leg was hurting frightfully. I looked down and saw blood on my pantaloons, about midway up my thigh. I caught my breath and turned to see where the shots had originated. Before me, about a half-mile out, was a beautiful tri-masted frigate with smoke rising from her gun portals. It was heading for the inlet between Skull Island and Treasure Island.

Long John untied my hands and reached down to pull me up from the ground. I refused his hand.

"You were going to let them kill me like a dog!" I screamed. "Why didn't you—"

"Jim, quiet 'er up! I be trying to tell you to remain silent to buy us some time. I could see the ship, and was of hopes help be on the way. Shiver me timbers, lad. Come on, get up."

He stretched his hand out again. I reached up and let him hoist me to my feet.

"You didn't think ol' Long John would let them get you, did ya, Jim?"

"You certainly waited to the last minute, if that was your plan."

"By the powers Jim, look. They's be waving at us from the deck."

I looked at the ship closely and tried to focus my eyes. I could make out Captain Smollett on the deck, along with what looked to be his first officers, who were also waving. Smollett was looking through a spyglass toward us. I jumped up from the sand and waved back, my enthusiasm and joy at the eminence of rescue overshadowing any pains or doubts I had housed. I was elated greatly. Then, I saw someone else on the deck next to the men, waving madly and shouting something inaudible.

It was Chloe.

My heart skipped a beat.

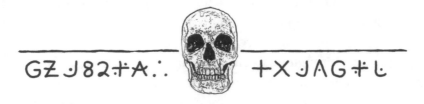

Chapter Thirty-Three

The Ships Battle

The new ship continued heading into the inlet between Skeleton Island and ours. Instead of longboats, oars were lowered and they pulled the ship through the narrow depths. High tides had been favourable, and the ship progressed with speed and ease. Silver and I decided not to return directly to the caverns, but rather, to find a vantage point where we could have a view of the *Hispaniola* and Captain Kidd's Harbor. Such a spot I remembered visiting, and we were able to make it to this point in about a half hours' time, even with my injured leg. It was a rather minor, though painful, flesh wound on my thigh. Silver had wrapped it in a piece of cloth torn from my shirt. We spied Captain Steele and his remaining crew from the fort on the beachhead loading into the longboats, getting ready to launch.

Upon reaching the plateau, I could now make out the new ship's name as The *Morningstar*. It had passed Skeleton Island and started to enter Captain Kidd's Harbor. The *Hispaniola* launched a volley of ten guns at her with a deafening roar. I could see Quartermaster Trafari giving the orders to fire. Many missed their mark. However, one of the balls hit the lower arm of the *Morningstar's* mainmast and snapped it off, with rope and wood falling resoundingly to the deck. Another ball ripped into the head of the ship, sending splinters and wood pieces flying into the air and falling onto the bay. The oars kept a steady pace as the ship started to turn toward starboard, which would offer her favourable positioning to be able to fire her cannon. The *Morningstar* fired a ball from her front gun, and it slammed into the middle deck of the *Hispaniola*. The sounds of crushing wood echoed all the way up to our vantage point.

A return volley from the *Hispaniola* was unleashed, and this time half of the loads were filled with chains. The sails took a savage thrashing, as the metal links flew into them en masse, ripping them like paper and leaving them fluttering about. One of the balls slammed across the top deck and knocked out a massive part of the ship's outer railing. The *Morningstar* headed toward a parallel position so it could return fire from its main starboard guns toward the *Hispaniola*.

Simultaneously, as it finished its turn in the water, twelve of her guns unleashed in rapid succession. The plumes of black smoke attached to each ball formed trails as they traveled toward the *Hispaniola's* upper decks in a slight arc. They hit their mark with devastating and deadly accuracy, knocking out three of the upper deck cannons and ripping through the side railings.

The two longboats carrying Captain Steele and crew were by this point but halfway to their ship, and I could observe, but not hear, Captain Steele shouting orders to Trafari and moving his arms about in a frantic manner.

Five cannons fired from the *Hispaniola*, and two of the smoke trailing balls slammed into the *Morningstar* just above the waterline, creating a loud crackling noise and rocking the ship from side to side, like a cork bobbing in the water. Smoke started to rise from out of these holes.

Seven canons returned fire toward the *Hispaniola*, and the smoke from the balls showed that they were headed toward the upper deck. They hit slightly below it, ripping into the floor of the deck and throwing all manner of boxes and barrels high into the air as the crew started to run toward the rear of the ship. I could not at first ascertain why, until I saw a large flame erupt on deck, and then a sight and sound ensued, the likes of which I could not have imagined.

Black tinted and cloudy flames surged from the upper deck, in the manner of a volcano's spewing forth its inner lava. The ship lurched and tilted backward toward shore, and then the entire side of the ship facing us exploded in a huge ball of flame, ripping itself from its main spars to at least the water line. An explosion followed that almost knocked Silver and I down to the ground. The side piece of the ship flew into the air, and then fell onto the ocean, laying flat side on the water's surface. The impact created huge concentric waves that rushed outward, especially toward Captain Steele and his boats. They quickly tried to turn the longboats around, and as they were sideways to the oncoming waves, they were broadsided. The longboats flipped over, throwing the men out and into the water like bugs being shaken off a leaf.

The *Hispaniola* listed greatly toward its port side, which was now the heavier side because of the starboard side's being blown off. It sank rapidly into the bay, completely engulfed in flames. The masts fell onto the shoreline as she slid down until all that could be seen were the masts lying slightly at the water's edge. Sizzling sounds and smoke were rising from among the bubbling waters atop the ship's resting place, I could see no men emerge from the wreckage, and knew that no crew who were aboard the *Hispaniola* could have survived such a blast.

On the deck of the *Morningstar*, I could see Captain Smollett yelling ferociously at his crew, animated and gyrating wildly about as he paced the decks.

It appeared that Captain Steele and most of the men in the longboats reached the shore, and after crawling out of the water quickly disappeared into the mangroves.

The *Morningstar* continued into the bay, and about midway I saw her drop anchor. Almost at the same time, they were readying two longboats on the side for launching.

"What happened?" I asked Silver. "Why did the *Hispaniola* blow like she did?"

"The powder kegs, I be suspectin'. Remember the captain had us bring 'em up to the main deck? Smollett knew that ship like the back of his hand. He were tryin' to avoid the powder room belows deck. But he didn't know Steele had most of the black powder moved to the main deck, and that's what blew. Mighty fine waste of a grand ship, and you can lay to that."

"We've got to hide until Smollett gets here, Long John. Let's get back to the caves and wait until they deal with Captain Steele and his crew."

"That be smart thinkin', Jim. After you."

He pointed with his crutch, and we took off down the hill. I decided to take the same path back from the treasure area that we arrived from. Although longer than a more direct route, my hope was to avoid being seen by any of Captain Steele's men.

After we turned inland from the beach, we made great progress, and within an hour's time we had reached the bottom of Spyglass Hill. We were ready to turn right and head around the back to the cavern's opening when, out from the foliage emerged two crewmembers. They stepped directly in front of us with flintlocks in hand. Long John hit one of them with his crutch, crumpling him to his knees, while the other mate slammed his rifle into the side of Long John's head and knocked him down. He took aim at Long John's head and slowly started to pull the trigger.

"On my word, hold it right there."

I looked up to see a disheveled Captain Steele walking down the side road on Spyglass Hill, the same one that we had ascended when first starting our search for the treasure. He had his spyglass with him, staring in contempt at the both of us.

"I thought I would be able to see your progress from a higher vantage point, and it turns out I was right." He swept his arm toward Long John. "Pick him up," he ordered the men.

The mates grabbed Long John and brought him to his feet, his face bloodied.

"Seems you were correct after all, Silver," Steele sneered. "I *will* need Hawkins if we're to get off this island. Very prescient of you."

He pointed toward both of us.

"In the meantime, bind their hands, and let us return to the block house. We'll let this captain of the *Morningstar* find us there. I believe it is Smollett, the former captain of the ship they just sank? Is that right, Hawkins?"

I stared at him with contempt; hate and anger boiled within.

"I told you I had made the right choice," said I. "Now, because of *your* actions, you are in a bad way. No ship, no treasure and facing the musket balls of a crew your equal and more. And I'm having the laugh on it, you can be sure. But know this: you and what is left of your crew will never leave this island alive. Of this there is little doubt, for I know the character of Captain Smollett *and* his actions, and they will be true and honourable, unlike yours."

"It is of no matter what you *know*," said Steele, with no outward sign of emotion. "I am sure this Captain Smollett will be interested in seeing to your safety, and a deal will be reached."

He turned his attention to Silver with a malicious smirk.

"As to you Silver, your fate is still sealed with me. You will give up your secret, and then you will die."

Chapter Thirty-Four

The Captains Meet

We were forcibly escorted to the fort, where Captain Steele put Long John and me under guard in the block house while he met with the remainder of his crew in the yard. I felt more than solemn. Long John had not spoken a word, and there was not even the hint of his usual optimism. I stood up to walk around and try and relieve some of the cramping and pain in my leg. When I ventured near the door, I could barely hear the captain. What I heard did not portend well for us, or Captain Smollett's crew. He relayed how they would agree, under the pretense of duress, to anything that Smollett demanded. Then, when they had their first chance, they would murder Smollett and take the ship, even if it were within moments of their agreement.

I returned and relayed what I had heard softly to Long John. He seemed to turn more somber.

"This be news of a dour nature for ol' Long John, Jim, and that's a fact. Seems either way it goes, me neck gets stretched good and far."

"What do you mean?"

"Yer Captain Smollett will surely see to me hangin', if we ends up with them. And death's also the reward for Captain

Steele prevailin' in this sityation. Avast. There be no good outcome for Silver in this battle, win or lose."

"I'll stand up for you with Smollett," said I. "After all, you were going to save me from being hung by Steele, right?"

"Oh, that's a fact, Jim. Your Captain Smollett just beat me to it."

"And you saved me in the cave."

"No denyin' that."

"Well see, then? I can relay those events to him."

"Would ye? You'd still help yer old friend here like that?"

"Of course."

"Well then, Jim me boy, you speak up plucky like that and I've got a chance, by thunder. Of coursin', that be predycated on no villanies being perpetrated on Smollett by Captain Steele."

"We've a duty to help prevent that from happening."

"Indeeds, we do, indeeds we do."

Silver's eyes seemed to roam about like a plan was formulating in his mind.

"It be our dooty for sure. Looks like we be fightin' some more of them dragons, Jim, but if we don'ts lose our heads and gives fear a chance to be visitin', we has a chance, and you can lay to that."

Silver's mood improved after our talk, and he even whistled once in awhile.

For my part, I could only think of reuniting with Chloe.

"This is Captain James Smollett, of the ship *Morningstar*. I am commanding you who are in there to come out now and show yourselves."

The captain looked at his mates, winked knowingly and walked to the door.

"This is Captain Graham P. Steele, captain of the former ship *Hispaniola*. I demand a parlay if you wish to speak with me. I also have someone with me who may be of interest to you."

He turned to me.

"Say something to *your* Captain Smollett."

"It's Jim, Captain, Jim Hawkins."

"Hawkins? Are you harmed in any way?"

"No sir."

"A parley you have, Captain Steele."

I was moved outside with Captain Steele by two of his men and could see it was now early evening, with the sun beginning to set behind Spyglass Hill. Long John was also escorted with one crewman on each side. Captain Smollett crossed over where the fence was broken and was backed by perhaps a dozen well-armed men.

"You have heard of me?"

"I have," replied Smollett.

"Then you know of my reputation."

"I know you are a cutthroat of the lowest form. And as to your reputation, it is of no concern to me."

Captain Steele put his hands to his hips defiantly, surveyed Smollett and tensed his facial features.

"Well hear me clearly. As you see, I have your Hawkins here, and am willing to make a deal with his life if you will grant safe passage for myself and crew."

Captain Smollett displayed no emotion as he eyed his adversary.

"Captain Steele, your situation seems to have escaped you. You are on an island and have no ship. There is a twenty gunner in the harbor and a full crew ready to kill you and your crew for piracy. I am thinking it is I who will decide if a deal is to be made, and what, if any, terms will be proffered. However, if the boy remains unharmed, the terms may be more favourable than the immediate death you and your crew have earned."

"There is also the matter of the treasure to discuss," said Steele.

"Have you found it?"

"Yes."

"Then you have compounded your difficulties, being that you have no way to get it off this island."

"I might point out Captain, that my not having a ship is entirely of your doing."

"That it was my cannon that sank her you speak the truth. But you are surely responsible for stealing her and all the consequences that followed from such an act. And it is you I hold to account for its destruction."

"It appears we have a disagreement," responded Steele with a slight smirk. "So I will state my demands and terms with crystal clarity: safe passage to Pirate's Cove for myself and my crew. We will additionally retain fifty percent of the treasure."

"A disagreement, is it?" replied Smollett incredulously.

Captain Smollett stared at Steele for a few moments, leaned over and whispered into the ear of his first mate; then he returned his attention to Steele.

"And if I refuse to meet these terms?"

"The death of you and your entire crew, starting with Hawkins here."

"Stern words from your position, Captain Steele."

"You know I do not speak lightly, and that I do as I say."

"Perhaps we can make some other arrangements."

"Such as?"

"Putting you and your crew in irons, sail to the nearest crown post and then hang you all together from the gibbets."

Steele walked behind me and put his hands upon my shoulders, shielding him from Smollett's line of fire.

"That does not sound like much of a compromise, Captain."

"I am not here to compromise, Captain Steele. You have stolen and destroyed my ship, kidnapped a citizen of the Crown and murdered untold innocent people. You are a pirate of the worst sort, and the mercy I am showing you is a few more weeks of life instead of beheading you all this very day."

Captain Smollett looked behind us and spied Long John.

"And as to John Silver, there is no deal to be made of any kind. I want his head, and I will surely have it no matter the outcome of our parlay here."

"He is of no concern to me, Captain Smollett. You can have him now, as a token of my negotiating in good faith."

Silver violently shook loose of the men's hold on him.

"What!?" shouted Long John. "I be not a bargainin' chip here!"

"No!" I shouted to Captain Smollett. "You cannot harm him, Captain."

"Jim, please stay out of this," replied Smollett. "Captain Steele, you have heard my terms. What do you say?"

"I think these terms are not acceptable, Captain Smollett. In fact, I think today is the day you and your crew will die."

Captain Steele pushed me to the ground and reached into his sash to pull out his pistol.

Long John raised and slammed his crutch into the side of one of the buccaneers on his left side and grabbed a cutlass from the other man to his right. He swung around and held the cutlass up to Captain Steele's throat, precariously balancing himself, his hands still tied together. Steele's pistol was not completely pulled out of his sash.

"Trade me, will you?" Long John snarled. "We'll see if them's cards gets played out, by the powers. Drop that pistol and order the men to stay put."

"I will not."

"Stand down, or he dies," shouted Silver to Steele's men.

The men stood their ground.

"I should have killed you a dozen times over, Silver," said Steele.

"Aye, you should have, by the by, but what's done can't be mended. And that will cost ye dearly, says I, and you can lay to that." Silver kept his gaze on Steele as he yelled, "Captain Smollett, you can have this sorry mate. For as sure as the tide rises and falls, you saw how he was plannin' on treachery for you and yer crew."

"Silver," Captain Steele said tersely, "today will also be your death, on my word. You will stand down at once."

"But, Captain," Silver responded with a menacing smile. "I sort 'ave gotten used to holding this here cutlass on yer throat, by thunder. Makes me feel all safe and secure, it does."

Steele made a particular clicking sound with his tongue and teeth, and I remembered exactly where I heard it before—at the camp, when he called his men from the forest.

"Silver!" I shouted as I stood up.

"I remember, Jim," said he.

"Kill him and the boy!" Captain Steele shouted to the crew.

The rest of the men exited the block house and came running toward us. The mates nearest advanced with cutlasses at the ready. Steele screamed and gurgled in anger as Silver leaned into the cutlass he held and sliced through his throat. Steele's pistol fired aimlessly into the ground as he slumped backward toward the terra firma, dead by the time he hit, his head almost severed.

Silver winked at me and threw his cutlass, which I caught in my hand. He reached down and pulled Steele's cutlass from his crumpled body, turned and swung at my hands, freeing them from their rope bond. I swung back and released him from his. The pirates were momentarily in a state of shock, seeing their captain dead on the ground, almost headless. This gave us a moment's edge. Long John swung his blade and cut one of their arms in a deep gash.

They suddenly rose to attention as the rest of the crew from the block house reached us with blades raised and pistols firing. Captain Smollett ordered his men to advance and enter the fight. By the time they arrived, we were swamped with men swinging cutlasses, while they took pistol shots at Smollett's men as they ran toward us. I was fighting two men at once, and with an aggression that pushed them both backward toward the block house. I lanced one in the side, while the other swung at my arm and slightly gashed it. One of Smollett's men stepped in and took over the fight as I turned to see...

...Morgan, coming up behind Long John, who was fighting three of the pirates, and with the upper hand. I shouted to Long John, who turned to see Morgan advancing toward him. As he did, one of the pirates he was fighting knocked the cutlass out of Silver's hand. He was now facing Morgan, unarmed. Smollett's men engaged the three pirates Silver was fighting. I noticed no fear on Silver's face, only unadulterated rage. Morgan raised his cutlass to deliver Silver's death blow. Screaming at the top of my lungs, I reached Morgan just as he was about to swing it, and skewered him clear through his back to his gut. He shuddered, dropped his cutlass and turned to see it was me who did it. With a look of horror and bewilderment, he reached behind himself, grabbed the cutlass and yanked it out of his stomach through his back, and then fell down, never to get up again. I picked the cutlass up and looked over at Long John.

"We're even now!" I shouted, and tossed him my cutlass. He turned and continued the fight. I picked up Morgan's cutlass, but it was not necessary. Their numbers and spirits had already dwindled, and there was no fight left in them. They dropped their weapons and surrendered. When the tally was taken, ten of the pirates were dead, including Captain Steele and Morgan, and another four were injured. None of Smollett's crew died in the fight, although many injuries were sustained, including some from pistol shots.

Smollett walked up to where Long John and I stood.

"Very brave, Silver," said Captain Smollett. "I am surprised."

"'Tis nothing sir, only protecting me Jim here and doin' me dooty."

"You've probably saved a lot of my crew's lives, and for that I owe you a debt."

Chloe came running up to me. She practically smothered me in a hug, and kissed my face all over.

"Oh Jim, my Jim, you are safe and sound."

"Aye, Chloe it be," said Long John. "I am glad to be finally knowin' yer name. And it's Bible true that you be the only one he spoke of the whole time we's together, and that's a fact."

He looked over and winked at me, while sporting a huge grin. Chloe ignored everyone else there and added more pressure to her hug.

"I told you I would return," said she.

Captain Smollett was speaking to two of his officers in whispered tones. Suddenly, the two of them grabbed Long John's hands and shackled them.

"What are you doing?" I shouted.

"I cannot take any chances," replied Captain Smollett. "He's a wanted man and cannot be trusted. This is the way it will be, Jim."

Chapter Thirty-Five

The Treasure

A full day and night was needed for me to finally start to feel my normal self. Sleep was a great help, and I partook of it in quantity. After the fight and Long John's arrest, Chloe brought me back to the *Morningstar*. For the first time in months, I was able to lie upon a bed, a luxury I appreciated dearly. The superficial nature of my leg wound was confirmed by the ship's doctor, and Chloe tended to it by changing the bandages and dressing it regularly. The rest of the injured crew were also brought aboard ship, and although many were in pain, the overall mood was one of optimism. I learned that Captain Steele's crew, what was left of them, along with Long John, were being kept and guarded at the fort.

During my time convalescing, Chloe shared with me the tale of her escape, and how she came to get to Treasure Island so quickly. Lady Blue, it turned out, did much to acquire her safe passage out of Pirate's Cove, and cared for her personal safety as well. She accompanied Chloe from the Quiet Woman to a ship called the *Esperia*, captained by a man named Ethan. Chloe relayed how Lady Blue gave her back the coins we had exchanged for passage, and warned the captain that no harm should befall Chloe lest he answer to her. They left the next morning, a day early, for a dry goods run to Miramar, which was within a day's journey of Esperanza.

The trip was uneventful, the captain a perfect gentleman, and they arrived four days later. She then hired a small boat to take her the rest of the way. When she arrived in Esperanza, she immediately contacted the governor, a certain Frenchman who took to her story with great interest, especially when he found that Captain Steele was involved. Chloe learned that the outposts under his jurisdiction had been terrorized by Captain Steele for years. He invited her into his home, and his wife took it upon herself to help her in all possible ways.

As it happened, Captain Smollett returned home from Bristol and relayed the tale to Squire Trelawney of how the ship had been pirated away. They learned of Chloe's capture and captivity upon the *Hispaniola* by the note Captain Steele had left behind on the dock for him. Squire Trelawney purchased a twenty-four cannon frigate, the *Morningstar*, and authorized Captain Smollett to set sail with no delay for the Caribbean area to find and capture the *Hispaniola* and return her and Chloe to safety. It transpired that the *Hispaniola* had been spotted in Africa loading supplies, and was presumed to have set sail for the Americas after that. They were unaware at that time that I was aboard the ship.

When Smollett arrived in Esperanza, he also had checked in with this same French governor, and told them he would be harboring at Havana, no more than three days away. The governor sent a boat to summon Smollett, and he returned a few days later. Chloe told them of all that had happened, that I was aboard the *Hispaniola*, and where we were heading—Treasure Island, a place he was intimately familiar with. They set sail forthwith, and as they were arriving, placed eyes upon me through their spyglass with the noose around my neck on the beach, and took appropriate action with the cannon.

Captain Smollett came to visit me often during the days I was unable to move about freely, and I shared with him a number of adventures we had been through. When able, I was invited, along with Chloe, to his table for dinner.

Present at this dinner were Smollett and his two first officers, Avery and Nigel, who were most interested in one of my tales—specifically, the vessel that resembled a whale I had witnessed with the men upon her. I gave a vivid and unembellished account of our first encounter and the subsequent battle and sinking we witnessed. Even when I was relaying it after all this time, the hair stood up upon the back of my neck, the memory was so clear. After my tale, these officers explained how a certain botanist claimed to have been taken captive aboard such a vessel, and traveled around the world within it. Twenty-thousand leagues, this botanist claimed. He stated further that it was a metal underwater ship of some kind. It had already sunk at least five Man-o-war ships, with all aboard killed, and there was a high price for the capture or destruction of it. The odd part of it, one of the officers continued, was that this botanist relayed that the captain of this vessel, which he called the *Nautilus*, claimed his name was "no one" in Latin.

"You mean his name was Nemo?" asked Captain Smollett.

"That's what he claimed, sir."

They asked further about what our coordinates were for both when we first observed it, and the sinking, all the while taking notes.

The account of how Silver and I retrieved the map, and Captain Steele's discovery of the secret cipher, captivated them all. They were aware of the use of this type of secrecy in commercial shipping, but were unaware of the difficulty in bringing it to light, and especially the type of coding used and how to decipher it. I then shared how I climbed the tree, found the coin and how we paced out where the treasure lay. On many occasions throughout these tales, either the officers or captain stopped and pressed me for additional details, and truth be told, I was quite happy to be the center of all of this attention. I continued with the discovery of the lever and water, and finished by telling them of how we ended up within this wondrous cave system, and how we were so close to death throughout our stay there.

"You mean to tell me Jim, that this Captain Steele did not discover the treasure?" Captain Smollett asked.

"No sir, he did not."

"But he told us he had it."

"It was a lie sir, a ruse to placate you and do you harm when they could find opportunity."

"I see."

"So it is still there?" asked Nigel.

"I believe so."

"What was the secret Silver kept all that time?" asked Smollett.

"He said this Jasper told him in order to find the treasure it was necessary to dig thirty-two feet down. The pirates never seemed to go below ten or twelve feet. I am guessing they were fooled into thinking that the depth of that lever and the box of fifteen gold coins indicated the depth of the treasure, too."

"That is odd," said Nigel.

"Go on," Smollett urged.

"Well sir, Hawkins here said the limb was the fifth one up, and that he needed to go exactly seven feet out, and that the pace was thirty-two feet out from the tree."

"Yes?"

"Well, those numbers, five, seven and thirty-two. Do they sound familiar?"

"Now that you mention it," said Avery, "they are numbers commonly used by the Knights Templar; the first two are prime, and the last the highest degree of their order."

"Does this mean anything to you, Jim?" asked the captain.

"No, it doesn't," said I. "However, when Silver was relaying the tale to me of how he met Jasper in the stockade jail, he stated Jasper mentioned something about a group called the Knights of the Golden Circle. He said that Redbeard was part of this group."

"What would they have to do with this whole business?" asked Smollett.

"Not sure sir," Avery broke in. "However, I have heard about this group called the Knights Templar. Some say they were founded in King Solomon's time in Babylon. A very secretive society, they are. The knights themselves, in addition to protecting pilgrims traveling to the Holy Land, were charged with trying to find the Ark of the Covenant, and it is said they searched all over the Middle East for it. I am not sure what or who these Knights of the Golden Circle are. My guess would be an offshoot of the Templars. Perhaps exclusive to those American States, based on Redbeard's involvement, and their founding father's passion for the whole Masonic movement."

"Do you think that the treasure, being from the Egyptian lands, has anything to do with this society?" I asked.

"It seems significant that it originated there," Avery continued, "but as you have related, Jim, this Jasper fellow stated that it was intended for the other side of the conflict in those United States, the North. It seems that Redbeard stole it in order to keep President Lincoln and his forces from getting it. It does paint an intriguing picture. But as to what the ultimate canvas reveals about it, I am unsure."

"However, back on point," said Smollett, "this information about the depth of the treasure implies that the treasure has not yet been discovered, and that it still awaits being brought to light. Would you all agree?"

We all nodded an assent.

"Well then. We have traveled a great distance. Fought a sea battle and lost a valuable ship. The crew has been loyal, and I think it advisable to use all of our resources to see if we can discover this treasure ourselves. I am sure, if put to a vote, the crew will readily agree. I say we share the rewards to a man, in sufficient quantity to make this trip worthwhile and profitable. The squire will get his share, and if the wealth of riches is as great as has been spoken of, we should all find ourselves in a position that only pharaohs and kings of past have enjoyed. Are you all game?"

There was no question of the outcome. We all agreed whole-heartedly.

The captain called a meeting of the crew and shared the major details, and a plan was formulated. Captain Smollett and his first officer decided to move the ship to the mouth of Captain Kidd's Harbor, and position her in such a way that no vessel could get around her if it entered the reef channel. He explained, when I asked him, that this assured that no ship could come about to broadside her, and at the same time prevented a surprise of the sort that confronted the *Hispaniola*.

The next day, seven of us went to the treasure site and surveyed the area. The original hole was obvious to me, and I pointed it out. The problem to be solved was how to dig down and excavate to a depth of thirty-two feet without the walls caving in. We reasoned that it was possible, since it was dug that deep in the first place, and hence we only needed to replicate how it had been done. One of the men, an engineer, suggested that we make the diameter of the hole much wider at the top, and then bring it in concentrically as we went down—in effect, digging a shape like a funnel. This was agreed upon. The diameter chosen to start with was fifteen feet.

The next question was access. How would we get the dirt out of the hole and us, the diggers down into it? We decided that a branch from a nearby tree would serve well as a joist, with block and tackle used to bring up the soil in buckets and lower the men in to dig. When all of this was resolved, all agreed to start the next day when tools and tackle could be put into place.

I asked that Chloe be brought back from the ship, and she arrived about an hour later. I took her to the caves and showed her the glowing worms that made it seem almost daylight inside. I marveled in Chloe's delight upon seeing the beauty of the stalagmites and stalactites glowing in forests of phosphorescent light. We could hear the misty waterfalls gently tumbling throughout the caves. Being with Chloe helped me rekindle the wondrous feelings I had upon discovering this magnificent creation of God. Later, we walked hand in hand about the island, and if pushed for truth, I would admit that this was one of the happiest days of my life. All seemed hopeful and full of promise. That night, aboard the ship, we affirmed our love for each other, and our commitment to stay by each other's sides the rest of our lives.

The following day, we were up by the first morning's light. It hadn't rained for the past two days. A blue sky with whispery clouds ensconced by the golden light of the sun greeted us upon the deck. Most of the crew came ashore to participate in the dig, and I suspected no orders to the contrary from the captain would have mattered. It took two trips with the longboats, before our full contingency finally reached the site. The engineer took charge and barked orders to the crew. He divided us into three main groups: the first were responsible for the actual digging, the second group for winching and dirt removal from the pit and the third for moving the soil from within the area to outside its perimeter. It was decided that we would work two shifts this day of approximately four hours each, with a meal break in between. Most of the men, at least at first, wanted to skip the mid-day meal altogether.

The work was arduous with the heat bearing down on us from the noontime sun. The humidity seemed to drench us like rain. I was part of the first group, and the widening of the hole to a fifteen-foot diameter just to the depth that had already been accomplished by Captain Steele and his men, took almost the entire four hours of our first shift. While still near the surface, we threw the soil onto the sides of the hole, and the third group shoveled it into buckets, moved it about thirty feet away and poured it out, then returned and refilled them. When we went deeper than we could throw the soil, the buckets and winches came into operation. We filled the buckets directly, the second group of men then raised the buckets by pulleys and tackle and the third group would then take them off, empty and replace them for the next load of soil. In this way, although we could have gone faster by simply throwing the soil willy-nilly, we were assured of clear access and an orderly way to excavate the treasure, if and when we found it.

By the time the mid-day meal was prepared, most of us agreed it would be a wise decision to take a rest and replenish our energies. Chloe helped to cook and serve the food, and I caught more than one set of eyes gazing upon her with a smiling look. Enthusiasm was elevated. Talk of what we were to find began to escalate until we were all convinced that the Crown jewels themselves lay beneath our feet. Captain Smollett, although not participating in the endeavor physically, was still a source of inspiration and encouragement with his comments and suggestions.

We returned to work that afternoon, and by the end of the first day, we measured down almost twenty feet. The engineer declared it to be a good day, and as excited as we were, we also envied the thought of getting a meal and a good night's rest so we could start afresh the next day.

I had asked Chloe earlier if she could save some food, for I wanted to take it to Long John and have a visit with him. It had been four days since I had laid eyes on him. With permission of the captain, I left to meet with him.

I arrived at the fort just at dusk. Long John was being kept within the block house, along with six other of our former mates from the *Hispaniola*. I knew the guards, who promptly let me enter. He looked tired and older than I remembered, and I felt a pang of pity when I laid eyes upon him sitting there. When he saw me, he smiled.

"Jim, me boy, what have you brought yer ol' Silver? Shiver me timbers, it looks and smells good, it do. Please, sits down and tell me how you be these last few days, fer news of anythin' has been scarce as mermaids here."

I relayed to him of our plans and progress in digging for the treasure, and how we thought that maybe the day after morrow we might find it. He asked many questions, and I told him all.

"How have you been, Silver?" asked I. "I mean I am sorry about what the captain is doing to you. It's not fair and I have repeatedly told him so."

"Arghhh, Jim, I be at the sunset of me years. And a good life 'tis been, and you can lay to that. Fact is, I've been sittin' here thinkin' of me life, and it be seemin' like a good time to be makin' a change, it is. Seems like ol' Beelzebub has played a joke upon me, and justs when I's be seein' the light, he's laid plans on snuffin' it out. A bit of the irony, I be thinkin', and you can lay to that."

"There's still a chance, Silver. As long as I can breathe, I will do all I can to make sure no harm befalls you."

"Ah, still tryin' to fight them dragons, are ye? By the powers, Jim Hawkins, yer a true friend, indeedy, and of that I be truly grateful, I am. But this time, I thinks the shallows has run out and there be no more chances given."

I returned to the *Morningstar* with a heavy heart, feeling sad after my visit with Long John. After walking the deck and relaying to Chloe the details of my conversation with Silver, I went to bed. Although planning on thinking about all manner of thoughts, I promptly fell fast asleep.

We started earlier the next morning, since all of our implements were waiting for us at the site. I observed that all of us moved slower than the day before, aware of the shear brutality of the work we were performing and the toll it would take. By the noon hour, we were down another six feet. While taking our mid-day meal, we celebrated our progress with congratulatory toasts and extra portions. The rest of the afternoon we dug. With a formidable effort, aided by the men singing and shouting to one other, we reached close to the thirty-foot level. It was already getting dark, and we elected to go back to the ship and start anew in the morning.

By this time the crew was elated, and I myself could almost visualize the wealth that lie only a few feet from our shovels and pickaxes. I did not see Silver that night. My exhaustion ran to the core of my bones. After a quick meal, I bid goodnight to Chloe and slept.

Dawn was breaking when we arrived at the site the following morning, having left the ship while quite dark. The engineer took some measurements, and then instructed us on the angle we were to make that day to the outside walls in the treasure pit. The soil was much more solid as we dug deeper, so the likelihood of the walls collapsing was slim. However, he wanted to take no chances. He also formed two new crews: one that was charged with making a sort of walkway from the area where we were digging and extending out to the beach. He started to use the soil we were excavating at this level for a foundation. The other crew started to cut thick limbs from the surrounding trees. The purpose of this was unclear to me. We simply followed the orders of the captain and engineer.

Suddenly, about two hours after arriving and starting to dig, one of the men shouted.

"Captain, I have hit wood!"

Everyone stopped what they were doing and ran to the side of the pit. From this position, I had a sense of how deep it was. To fall would certainly have caused great injury. I could see four crewmen brushing off the wood they were speaking of. When cleared, it appeared as a door very similar in construction to the one in the first hole where the lever was found. Only this one was much bigger, perhaps five feet square. When all the sand and soil was removed, we could clearly see a symbol of sorts. It looked like some sort of a tool that might be used by a builder, but exactly what it was I did not know. There were words below it, in English.

The captain demanded to know what it said.

"It says: *Beware if you do not know the Square, for yours will be a fate worse than death.*"

"Is that all?"

"Yes, Captain, that is all."

He turned to his officers.

"Any idea what that means?"

"Other than the obvious curse upon us, I perceive no meaning."

"Nor do I," said Avery. "However, it may be referring to the fate that awaited one if they did not know about the lever and water."

"Perhaps you are right," says Smollett, thinking for a moment. "Well, curses be damned. They are for idle minds and superstitious simpletons. Remove the door, and let us see what lies beneath."

One of the men put a pickaxe under the side of this door-like structure and used it as a lever to lift it up. It slowly moved. When the side of this cover was visible, another crewman put a shovel under it and helped raise it. The planks that constructed it were thick and heavy. Great effort was mustered to bring it over and lay it on its side against the wall. Finally it was done. Below, in the box was a Jolie flag—skull and crossbones—draped flat. The crew called for a rope, and the men in charge of the block and tackle lowered one with a hook. They wrapped the rope around the door, and attached the hook to it. The men raised it, pull by pull, until it was out of the pit and pushed to the side.

A crewman lifted the pirate flag, raised it up and over and then a set of eyes were looking... staring... upon all of us. They were bathed in a golden glow that seemed to light the entire pit and even beyond. It was a pair of eyes attached to the most wondrous golden bust of a goddess that I could ever have imagined. These eyes were oriental in nature, with some kind of green stone glowing from within. From my vantage point I could see a headdress that rose above it and a large, half-moon shaped piece of blue or turquoise jewelry that covered the upper chest. The statue ended about mid-chest.

There was not a sound to be heard from any of the men. We all simply stared at this golden goddess who lay upon her back and looked up at us. The electricity running through me would have nurtured my running a hundred miles if directed that way. I could not take my eyes away from hers. Finally, one of the men took off his hat in the pit and started yelling and screaming. And within seconds all of us were screaming and jumping up and down with joy, hugging and slapping each other's backs. Captain Smollett was caught up in our merriment too and fired his pistol into the air.

"We've found it!" I shouted. "We've found the treasure!"

GᏝ✞35X△⩕   ✞Ꮣ53∴✞XᏝ

Chapter Thirty-Six

Unexpected Visitors

Many hours of work were expended before we were able to finally get the statue of the Egyptian goddess up and out of the pit. It was tenfold heavier than any of the dirt buckets, and a double block and tackle system was needed to be hung in order to support the additional weight. It was even more intriguing once we all could see it plainly. The golden sheen of its surface lighted up the entire area, and upon closer inspection it was found to be encrusted with jewels and stones of various kinds: emeralds, sapphires and bright red rubies. There were strange types of ciphers or glyphs on the back of the statue which no one knew the meanings of. One surprising aspect of this goddess's eyes was that no matter where you stood, they looked directly at you. We moved it with great difficulty, using levers, to a position about ten feet away, and continued to excavate what lay below in the treasure pit. All the while, her ever-watchful eyes gazed upon our activities.

Bucket after bucket of treasure came forth, each one bearing more and greater riches. There was every sort of jewelry imaginable: rings with diamonds, long intricate golden earrings with rubies and emeralds, bracelets with pearls, gold and silver headbands of various sorts and solid gold animal statuettes of different species, many I could not recognize.

Jewels and stones of great size were next, endless buckets of them. This went on for the rest of the day, and still no bottom to the riches could be determined in the pit.

The captain and engineer decided to put effort into a separate project that would facilitate the loading of these riches onto the ship. The first problem they discovered was the treasure's great weight. It was determined that most of the treasure should be stored in the hold below deck, discarding the lead and rock that had been used to create weight for the ballast and draft of the *Morningstar*. They also decided to move the ship straight away offshore, in line of sight from the dig. Due to the coral reefs, this put her into deep water, which turned out to be about a league from the beach. The men were reluctantly pulled from the job of bringing up more treasure and conscripted to build a rail system from the edge of the forest over the sand and down to the water. This was the use the captain and engineer had in mind for the branches that we had chopped off a few days earlier. They then had us build a sort of dock that stretched into the water about ten feet.

Another group of men built rafts from the local trees by tying the logs together with ship's rope. This took two days to complete. What we had constructed was an elaborate yet secure way to move the treasure from the site. First, we moved the goods over the sand on the tree rails that were laid upon the sand, much like how a train uses its rails. This was accomplished by using round logs that would roll upon the rails until they reached the dock. The treasure was then slid from off the dock and transferred onto the rafts. Using poles, it was moved by men standing on the rafts over the shallow reefs until they cleared them. A rope was then brought by long boat from the *Morningstar* to meet the raft. From there, the men would pull on the rope, which moved the raft across the next expanse and brought it alongside the ship. A pulley and winch system was used to lift the treasure aboard, where it was painstakingly taken below deck and exchanged with the rocks and lead the ship used for ballast, which were unceremoniously tossed overboard.

Once the mechanics of transporting the treasure were completed, the first load was readied, and it took almost half a day to complete the trip from treasure site to ship. This was also due to waiting for favourable tides.

Concurrently, it was decided that much of the smaller items would be put into wooden boxes, which were built onshore out of spare ship's wood. They were about two foot square when finished, and were filled to their tops with loose jewels and small golden trinkets.

When digging resumed in the treasure pit, we encountered another wooden door. When this was opened, many thousands of gold coins lay beneath. Below these were found hundreds of gold bars, stacked neatly in rows forming a sort of platform. Each bar was extremely heavy, and only one or two at a time could be brought up.

After working all morning, I decided to take a rest from the activity during the noon meal, and implored Chloe to join me in a trip that ended with us alongside Captain Kidd's Harbor. I wanted to dive down to the *Hispaniola*, and thought it would be enjoyable for Chloe as well. We easily reached the shore where she rested, and could see her upper deck through the clear rippling water, which was perhaps ten feet below the waterline at low tide. I threw off my clothes, down to my pantaloons, and jumped in. Chloe was afraid to join me, however, for unbeknownst to me, she did not know how to swim.

I skimmed along the surface, caught my breath and then dove down to the upper deck. I had a two-fold purpose for my visit. I remembered the compartment in the captain's quarters where the gold coins were hidden, and I also desired to rescue the original treasure map. I found the door to it unlocked, opened it and swam in. Everything within was strewn about by the tilting in the water, except the desk and map table which were bolted into the floor. It was an eerie sensation seeing fish swimming in there with me. Diffused sunlight flooded in through the windows, casting rays of light that danced about the room. I first swam to the desk and tried to open the lower drawer. It was jammed, and by the time I had loosened it, my breath was low and I returned to the surface, gulping in fresh air as quickly as I could. Chloe shouted for me to be careful, and I assured her I would.

I resumed my dive and went straight to the captain's desk, opened the drawer, and then released the upper part that held letters and retrieved the bag of coins. This accomplished, I went back to the surface and swam over to Chloe, handing them to her.

"I don't understand you, Jim Hawkins," said she. "This is nothing compared to the gold and riches we have already discovered."

I admit here she was right. But, I had an ulterior motive I did not want to share with her at the time. However, the more important treasure I was looking for was the map.

I dove again down into the captain's quarters, and searched around for where the map might be. I looked in the drawers of the desk, and found nothing of import. I was getting short of breath again when I looked at the map table. I thought I saw something sticking out of the slightly open drawer. I swam over, opened it completely and therein lay the treasure map, folded in half. Although my lungs were starting to hurt, I carefully lifted it from the table and started my ascent. My lungs felt as if they were ready to burst, and my head was getting a bit dizzy.

I felt something touch my back and turned to see Tafari, floating behind me. His eyes were wide open, staring at me. I screamed out of instinct reaction and jerked back. My last bit of air reserves left me. I then could see he had no lower body. He was just floating there. My lungs were burning, and I thought of nothing else but getting out of this macabre room. My head was getting light and darkness enveloped my sight. I pushed myself backwards further away from Trafari's body and finally exited the captain's quarters. I could see the surface, but my mind was getting foggy. I willed myself to push up from the deck toward the sunlight that awaited me on the surface. It seemed as if time were slowing down. The closer I was to the surface, the longer it felt to go any further. Finally, I burst through the surface and gasped for air. I could see Chloe motioning for me and could hear her saying something, but my ears were plugged and could not make it out. I gathered my wits, swam over to shore, crawled out and laid the map upon the sand, for my fingers never lost their grip on it.

Chloe ran over and met me, pointing toward the dig site.

"Jim, Jim, did you not hear? There was a cannon shot a few moments ago."

I had not heard it, but I knew it could not portend well. I quickly rose, dressed, carefully folded the wet map and put it into my sash, and we rushed in the direction of the treasure site.

When we arrived, there was a quiet tension in the air. The captain and his men were on the beach. Smollett was intently looking through his spyglass. I looked out, but saw nothing.

"What is it?" I asked.

"Another ship coming," said one of the men, pointing, "over there."

I looked with my hand shadowing my eyes, and observed a small dot on the horizon.

"Can you see anything, Captain?"

"Not much," he replied. "We need to wait for it to come closer before we know whether it is friend or foe. In the meantime, we must prepare for the worst. I want all guns to the fore, and all men to dig in at the sand line. We've no fear of cannon fire onto this beachhead with the *Morningstar* out there, and unless they are willing to risk a loss of ship, I doubt a fight in the ocean will ensue either. We are safe here. First officer Nigel is on board and well trained to handle what may come. He no doubt was the one who ordered the cannon shot to warn us of the incoming ship.

"Avery, I want another six men aboard her to handle the cannon. Also, when you arrive on board, tell Nigel that I want the ship moved out to deeper water immediately."

This dot of a ship grew larger as it continued toward us. The men pushed out on the raft and finally cleared themselves beyond the reef. They were met with a longboat and taken to the ship. As this mysterious vessel sailed closer, the captain became bewildered. He could see through his spyglass two flags: the Southern United States flag, called the "*Dixie*", and a Skull and Crossbones. Neither he, nor any of the officers or men, knew what it meant, nor why the two would be flown together in these waters. The *Morningstar* had by this time moved out about a half mile further into deeper water.

"Are we going to give the sign to fire on her?' asked one of the crew.

"No," replied Smollett. "She has not made a malevolent move, and even though the Jolie is flying, we also have to consider the other flag. We will wait to see what her intentions may be."

This unexpected visitor was a large ship, of the frigate class used by the America's military in battle. With two main masts and a mizenmast, it was fast and sleek. It also was not heavily armed. We had an evenly matched number of cannons aboard the *Morningstar* for every one this ship had. However, ours were longer ranged and shot heavier ball. It slowly sailed around the outside of the *Morningstar* by two leagues, and cut into the channel between Skeleton Island and ours. No cannon or signal flag of any kind was forthcoming from her. We followed the ship along shore and observed a long boat being launched, and it started to tow her into Captain Flint's Harbor. After a few hours, it was inside and had been towed almost into the middle of the bay before it dropped anchor. Another longboat was lowered.

The two combined boats totaled a dozen and a half men. They started to row toward shore.

The captain and a like amount of us rushed to meet them on the shore where they were to land. We stood upon the coral ground where the sand ends, and observed them as they continued to row—headed directly toward us. The captain had also placed men to the sides of the landing area on higher ground and had them armed with muskets. These strangers landed their boats and started up the beach to meet us.

A large man, with a fiery red beard, led the group. They stopped a few feet from where we stood and stared directly at us.

"Who are you, and what are your intentions here?" asked Smollett.

"I am here for what is mine."

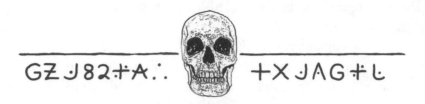

Chapter Thirty-Seven

We Meet Stuart Jackson

The man before us was a fearsomely commanding figure. He stood over six feet tall, and was above average in girth. However, it was his stature, or more precisely his *presence*, that demanded attention. His eyes were stern, weathered and penetrating, his face leathered. On his neck was a tattoo of a circle with something I could not clearly make out within except for an inverted triangle with an eye beneath. There was a certain amount of weariness in his look, and yet I felt as if he had the cunning of a panther, ready to spring at any moment.

"There is nothing of yours on this island," Smollett told him sternly. "You are welcome to get water and provisions, but I have claimed this as property of the Crown, and you have no rights to anything on it."

The man stared at the captain and then cast his gaze upon each of us separately. He then turned his attention to the higher positions, where the men were standing with muskets, loaded and aimed.

"I assume you are the captain of this crew?"

"That is correct. Captain James Smollett."

"Well, Captain Smollett, I am Captain Stuart Jackson. I have left some valuable cargo upon this island, and I intend to retrieve it."

There were gasps from most of our crewmen. I heard one say in a low voice that it was impossible. Captain Smollett also looked startled.

"That cannot be," Smollett said. "The man whose name you claim to be is dead."

"Apparently, those reports of my death are premature."

"It is of no matter. Whatever was left upon this island is no longer yours."

"Do not try my patience, Captain Smollett. As you are no doubt aware, it is a commodity I have a very short supply of."

"Redbeard, isn't it?"

He nodded.

"I have been known by that name."

"As I stated to you before," Smollett continued, "if provisions are your need, then you are welcome to them. But that is all."

"You know what I have come for. My spyglass has told me of your discovery. It is mine, and I intend to be in full possession of it. Mark my words carefully, Captain. I will do anything to accomplish that objective."

"Anything, is it?"

"The means are of no concern to me. Only the ends."

"Because if it is your intention to try and sink my ship, and through some quirk or fancy, carry it out, a good portion of the cargo you seek will be lost forever, for our ship has moved to deep water."

He was silent as he purveyed us all.

"There is a bigger purpose for my being here than the mere recovery of 'cargo', Captain. A greater cause transcends our own wishes. Myself, and each one of my men, are willing and prepared to die for such a cause. The fate of a future nation is at stake, and I would willingly kill a thousand men and sink a hundred ships to retrieve what lay within this island."

"You are out-gunned and out-manned. Unless some sort of an arrangement is accommodated between us, you will not only lose your cause, but your lives and ship as well."

"Captain, since you have indeed discovered my secret here, you are an intelligent and resourceful man. A man such as I thought did not exist. So I will speak to you frankly. We are here to retrieve the treasure I left here many years ago. It is for a noble cause, and, as I have already stated, we *will* leave with it. If it means death to us all, then so be it. I would rather die trying, than capitulate."

Captain Smollett eyed his adversary as he walked a couple of feet closer and then stopped, pistol at the ready by his side.

"Redbeard, let me be as frank. You are a pirate of the worst sort. Although it is clear you are also an educated and clever man, you have chosen to kill and murder innocent people to further enrich yourself. I cannot envision any cause that you would be connected with that would give impetus for me to change my mind. You should be in chains for the crimes you have committed, and I will see to it that you are not rewarded for your ill-gotten gains."

"Then it appears we have a difference of opinion, Captain; what the French call a *tete-a-tete*, yes?"

"Indeed it does."

He was silent while he eyed our men again with measure, and then looked back toward his crew. After a few moments he turned back, resolve in his eyes, shaking his head in an affirmative manner.

"For now, we will take you up on your offer for provisions and water. By morning's time, I will expect an affirmative answer from you as to my demands. If not, then all consequences resulting from such a refusal will be upon your hands."

"Do I have your word of honour for peaceful actions while on this island until the morrow?"

"You do. I will move my men to the fort and camp there."

"The block house is occupied with prisoners. My men will be guarding them."

"That is your affair. I will camp outside of the east wall. There is a clearing there that will serve us well. In the meantime, I will have my men hunt goats and bring water to the ship."

"You will no doubt understand that my men will be watching and on guard."

"I would expect no less and would do the same. We will return within the hour."

Redbeard and his men walked back to their longboat and returned to their ship. We headed back to the fort, well ahead of them. I rushed into the block house to tell Long John all that had transpired.

"This here news of Redbeard bein' alive is dire indeedy, Jim. He be the worst of the worst, he is, by thunder. Me minds still disbelevin' it be true. For if ever a mate needed to be scrubbed from the seven seas, he would be the one. Made Flint look like an orphanage mistress, he did. You must bewares of whatever he said, for a more dangerous man I've not seen exist."

Captain Smollett entered and heard the last part of Silver's words.

"We'll take care of Redbeard, Silver, and without your help. He appears to be reasonable, and I think the best option is to negotiate with him. After all, we did not come here for the treasure in the first place. Our hulls are full, and there is more than enough to pay for the *Hispaniola* and take care of the men's welfare. There is still more than we have even seen yet to be taken. We'll play a bluff with him, and if my guess is correct, they will take it."

"Beggin' the Captain's pardon," Silver interrupted, "but there be hundreds of men in Davy Jones locker who thought that ol' Redbeard could be reasoned with, and I am a witness to a

317

good lot of 'em. The man has no remorse of conscience. But mark me here. He takes negotiatin' for weakness, and he be merciless to the extreme. It is Redbeard's *actions*, not the fancy words he speaks, that you needs to lay on, Captain Smollett. He's naught to leave man, woman, child nor animal for witness against him, and you can lay to that."

"This will be different, Silver. He does not have the upper hand. Still, we need to know how his thinking is going and what to expect tomorrow."

"Them's death words, Captain," warned Silver.

Smollett ignored the comment. I volunteered to stealth my way over to the outside of their camp, once darkness fell, to see if I could learn of anything that may help. Smollett agreed it would be a good plan. After he left, Long John beckoned me closer.

"Jim, me boy, I begs you not to do this. You needs to get Chloe and you to the caves. Smollett has no idea who he be dealin' with, and if'n he'd been half a man, he should 'ave cut Redbeard down when he first laid eyes 'pon him. Ye remember me stories of him? You know I mentioned he and I had differences. Well then, he vowed to kill me in ways I shudder to repeat. By the by, he'll do the same to all of you. I don't know how he will do it, but I knows his nature, and it be evil. Do ye hears me Jim? By the powers, I knows him. Sailed with him. Left him finally, for his brutality finally tore even me to the core."

"Silver," said I, "maybe I can get some knowledge that will help. I must say I side with the captain on this. Redbeard seemed, well, tired, almost weary. Perhaps after all these years, he has not the fight left in him. I must at least try. I will use caution to spare. If it turns out to be true what you say, then I will come and get you and Chloe and we will all return to the caves."

"Be careful, Jim."

"I will."

- - - - - - - - - - - - -

Chloe and I returned to the ship with the captain, and had our evening meal together. I relayed the day's events, and she agreed with Silver as to the dangers involved. I had already given my word to the captain, and she resigned herself to the fact of my going. Captain Smollett was busy making tactical arrangements with the officers for the morning, should his plans not grow into positive fruition. The main one was to right the ship into firing position so Redbeard's ship could not leave without coming under attack. I heard one of the officers mention that the position Redbeard took in Captain Kidd's Harbor prevented us from firing upon it from our present position; Skeleton Island blocked a clear trajectory of any ball or chain reaching it.

That evening, Captain Smollett ordered armed men to be stationed at the treasure site and extra watch at the fort. I took a longboat in from the *Morningstar* and landed to the south of the treasure site. I reasoned that traveling to the fort through the regular pathway would give notice of my arrival, thereby spoiling the surprise and giving knowledge of my visit. Cautiously, I snaked my way through the trees, carefully trying to remember where the marshes were located. I was hoping to be helped by some light from the moon, but it was partially hidden behind clouds and only offered a slight advantage in my quest.

Suddenly, I slipped off a bank and fell into a marsh. I righted straight up and chastised myself for being so negligent. I did not move, for fear of sending vibrations to one of the black snakes that lived within and that I should end up as food for these deadly venomous creatures. After moments that felt like hours, I very slowly and carefully started to back up when I felt it. Something brushed against my leg. Oh my God, thought I, my heart pounding in my throat. I must remain still. My breathing became heavy, and I feared it alone would cause the waters to ripple. I ever so slightly started to move my leg toward the shore area where I slipped in. Nothing. That is good, I thought. I moved my other leg, and now was only a couple of feet away. At that moment I felt another brush against my leg and could stand it no longer. I took a deep breath and then jumped as hard as I could manage toward the shore. My knees touched the bank and I scurried the rest of the way and finally stopped, resting on the ground.

I turned upon my back, gathered my wits and made a mental mark of where the marsh was located. I continued upon my journey while veering a little farther to the south of the marsh than necessary, which impeded my progress because of the mangroves. I minded not, as long as I did not risk the chance of falling in that deadly water again.

Finally, I found the light of Redbeard's campfire. I lay upon my belly and crawled forward with my elbows. I dared not get too close, and yet I could barely hear their words. Some low bushes provided a boundary and safety between where I laid and their camp area. The talk that I was able to discern was much of the ordinary, with some laughter interspersed. But on the whole, I surmised they were a solemn lot, and talk of what may come tomorrow percolated throughout the camp.

I could see Redbeard sitting near the fire. The fire's light and shadows played a sinister trick by making his pronounced features, especially his brow, appear more diabolical than earlier in the day. He seemed lost in thought. Suddenly, he yelled for someone and waved them over. A man soon joined him. He stood up and motioned for him to follow. They started in my direction, and my heart started to beat rapidly. I slowly wriggled backwards with my elbows as they continued walking toward me. They stepped over the low shrubbery I was hidden behind and almost stepped upon one of my hands. I was frozen still, afraid to breathe. A slight breeze and the rustling of branches were in my favour. They finally stopped not more than a few feet away. I lay deathly still upon my stomach and prayed to be silent.

"Have you decided upon a plan of action, Stuart?" the man asked Redbeard.

"This does not bode well for us, William," he responded. "I made no plans for encountering anyone on this island. We are short of men and ammunition. It will present difficulties that we have not the time for."

"Agreed. Time is what we have precious little available. The troops are in need of money. Our last reports before sailing were not hopeful. Unless we are able to obtain ammunition and supplies from our South American allies, our cause will be greatly hurt. If we get into a battle with these men, and should lose, it will be a greater loss than simply our lives. Perhaps thousands will die too."

"I realize that, William," replied Redbeard. "And were it not for that, we would have been fighting from the moment we landed, and to the devil with the consequences. Having some Crown's 'pretty boy captain' taking what is rightfully mine does not sit well with me, William. Not well at all."

They remained in silence for a few moments.

"I do not want the men to know of our plight, William," Redbeard continued solemnly. "They must be ready to fight, and die, if necessary. If they thought our cause was in this much danger, they might not put their hearts into it, and that must not happen. This captain is hard to read. The fact that he was able to find our treasure without the cipher is surprising."

Redbeard walked in a small circle rubbing the back of his neck, and then faced his mate.

"Somehow, he must have gotten a copy of the map's compass and unlocked the symbols hidden within it. But where such a copy came from, I am at a loss."

He was silent for a few more moments, and I could see his brow furl.

"He must be more cunning than he appears to let on," said Redbeard.

"I took him to be a simpleton," responded William.

"I as well. But actions speak otherwise. I will ask to speak with him privately in the morning. All is not lost. I am not sure he and his crew want to die over this matter. He is right about our being outgunned and outmanned, yet ours is a just cause, which gives us the advantage. If a fight is the result, we will take it on the square with determination to win. If one can be avoided, so much the better. Either way, let us go and have drink with the men, William, and toast to the South's rising again in all its glory. For tomorrow may be our day to die, and a good one it will be!"

Redbeard slapped William's back as they turned and walked toward the fire with me lying on the ground between them and their camp. I tried to make myself as small as I could, and they did not become aware of my presence as they walked within a foot of where I lay. I stayed there long enough for them to return to the fire and to catch my wits, for fear had gotten hold of me and my breaths were short. I finally snaked my way back far enough to stand and leave undetected. I hurried toward shore and rowed the longboat to the ship.

I awoke the captain, who summoned his officers to his cabin. They had me relay every detail of the conversation I had heard. However, I decided not to include the comments referring to Captain Smollett's intelligence being in question, judging that it added little to the matter at hand, and could offend him into some unwarranted actions not justified by the whole of the information I had learned.

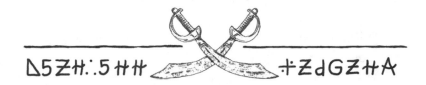

Chapter Thirty-Eight

Deal With the Devil

Captain Smollett and his officers stayed up into the night discussing their strategies, and after almost falling fast asleep several times, I excused myself and went below deck to my bunk. I awoke at times during the night, due in large part to anxiousness for tomorrow's outcome and how it could affect Chloe and myself. At some point I must have fallen fast asleep, for the first bell startled me awake. I scurried up to the main deck to meet Captain Smollett. When all the men on board had gathered, he told us:

"I have decided, gentleman, to meet with Redbeard alone, and thereupon see if an arrangement may be negotiated between us. Although I am in hopes of a positive outcome, if I should fail, and treachery or worse should become my fate, I am ordering you to sink their ship with no regards for her crew and at all costs. Avery will be responsible for seeing this order carried through. As to the men on shore, use wise judgment in waiting for them to return, but do not risk this ship nor lives aboard her in hope. You must escape at any cost.

"Jim, I am ordering you and Chloe to remain on board for your own safety until my return. I am asking all of you for your prayers that this plan works, and that in the end all will fare well.'"

"God's speed to you, Captain," one of the officers pronounced.

"I will need it."

Smollett disembarked onto a longboat and was rowed toward shore, whereupon he was dropped off, and the men returned. During his absence, the ship was repositioned closer to the channel between Skeleton Island and Treasure Island, where the master gunner established our balls could reach their ship with full force and accuracy, whilst theirs would surely fall short.

- - - - - - - - - -

After hours that seemed like days had passed, the captain signaled and the longboat returned to shore to bring him back to the ship. The crew greeted him warmly, most of us taking it as a good sign that he was returning at all. Without a word asked he told us that a compromise had been reached, and all would be well. The men cheered and whooped about the ship. The captain asked me to join him and the officers within his cabin.

"Upon meeting Redbeard," Smollett started, "the talks began in a contentious nature, as would be expected. However, soon they proceeded exceedingly well. Jim, your reconnaissance and information as to their intentions played an exceedingly important part of my strategy, and I should venture to say was pivotal in helping bring it to a positive outcome."

All of us asked for more details, which were readily forthcoming.

"Redbeard and I walked down to the treasure site alone. I ordered the men there to leave. He was most interested in what we had accomplished, how we knew about the lever and water, and was begrudgingly complimentary in our ingenuity in discovering it.

"I sidestepped his questions and explained further that only a portion of the treasure was on board in the hold of our ship, and that was necessary to replace the *Hispaniola*, which was destroyed in a battle related to this adventure. He asked if I was referring to the ship's remains in the harbor, and I acknowledged it so. I did not offer further details of how or why, and his disinterest in the matter confirmed my not doing so. I showed him our method for moving the treasure to the shore, how it was loaded and then taken out to the ship.

"I then relayed how it would be an advantage for both of us not to get into a gun battle with our ships, since chances would be great one or both would be destroyed. I suggested that we keep what we have, and that we will load one more box, which was already filled and waiting on the dock, ready to move.

"In return, we will leave all equipment and conveyances in place, and agree to leave the island in two day's time, after securing game, fruit and water for our trip back to England. I agreed to not stop between here and England and report his existence or the location of this island, assuring him of uninterrupted access to the rest of the treasure and safe passage away from here.

"His crew will start their excavations of the treasure the morrow, and we will supply him with the prisoners we have to help him work until we set sail to leave."

"Remarkable negotiations, Captain," one of the officers remarked, "splendidly executed."

"I agree," said another, "a most favourable outcome, given the circumstances and whom we are dealing with."

"Agreed," responded Captain Smollett. "That is not to say we will in any way lower our guard nor open ourselves to foul play. But I believe, given what we know of their needs, they will stick to the bargain made. There was one rather strange request that Redbeard made, however."

"Pray tell, what was it?" asked Nigel.

"He relayed that he had heard from men at the camp that we were holding a prisoner who was of particular interest to him, a certain one-legged ship's cook named John Silver."

"Yes, we are," I told him.

"He must be delivered to me," said Redbeard, "as part of the bargain."

"And you agreed?" I asked in disbelief.

"Of course. What is he to us? Saves the Crown the cost of a rope and hanging."

"But Redbeard is a murderous barbarian," I interrupted, "capable of the most heinous acts of brutality imaginable! You know of his reputation. Silver told me he promised him the most torturous death he could devise when next they met."

"It's probably what he deserves," one of the officers stated.

The others laughed at this comment.

"I won't have it. It is not right!" I said, pounding my fist on the table.

"Calm down, Hawkins, compose yourself," Smollett said sternly. "Silver is headed for certain death upon our return. His fate is sealed. As far as I can see, Redbeard is doing us a favour."

My next recollection is standing up, storming out of the room and slamming the door behind me. This was beyond my limits of anger. I could not comprehend the captain so callously agreeing to such a fate for Silver, no matter what his crime. My mind was so enraged, I was unable to think clearly. I paced violently across the upper deck, unaware of my surroundings and caring less. Tears started to force themselves upon me, and I fought back with all fortitude to hold them in abeyance.

I made a decision then and there.

I hurried to the ship's side and stepped over. Down the ropes on the side of the ship I climbed, and I jumped into one of the longboats. With reckless abandon I found myself rowing toward the shore. I heard Captain Smollett shouting at me to return. I heeded it not. I focused only upon each stroke of my oars, pulling as surely and swiftly as possible and would not entertain any thought unless it would hasten my arrival to that despicable island.

After landing, I ran with full force of will toward the fort. This took perhaps fifteen minutes. Past the guards I ran and into the block house. There I stopped in front of John Silver, winded, my body twitching with energy. He was sitting on the floor chained to a post in the middle of the room. He looked up, startled.

"By the powers, Jim, what be it? Are you and Chloe all right?"

I looked around to make sure no guards were near. They seemed to not care what I was doing in there, for they remained outside. I crouched down low and close to him, and in a whispered voice told him to be ready to escape from this place when the time presented itself and that we would hide out in the caves.

"Why, Jim boy, what be the matter?"

"Just be ready, Silver. I'll work out a plan by then."

"Redbeard?"

"I've no time for stories. As you've told me before, we must make our chances and take them. We'll not have another."

I heard Captain Smollett yelling at the guards as to my whereabouts, and I guessed correctly that he had followed me upon my leaving the ship. Smollett walked into the block house and stared at Silver and me. He motioned for me to join him outside the door. We walked beyond the front gate and onto the road leading to Captain Kidd's Harbor.

"What did you tell Silver?" he asked.

"I told him nothing."

"I am ordering you, Jim, to relay exactly what you spoke with him about."

"It is my concern, alone. And although I am assuredly under your command, I will neither comply with your request nor share with you any of what was said between us. Do with me what you will."

He grabbed my shoulders.

"Hawkins, I want you to understand that I have the ship and crew, including you and your Chloe, to consider in all of my decisions. I could not, and will not risk all of that for the likes of John Silver."

"I promised him, Captain. He saved my life—"

"And you his, if I remember correctly."

"I am aware of that. But he, he... he is my friend. And I cannot, and will not, let him be butchered by the likes of Redbeard. It is true, as you say, his fate is sealed upon return to England. I can only try to help him avoid the gibbet at execution dock. But if he succumbs to it, it will be a dignified death, a proper death. And by waiting until then, I will be able to keep my promise to him. It would be better to give Silver a pistol and let him end his own life, rather than an abysmal death at the hands of Redbeard."

Captain Smollett released his grip on me and started to pace around in a circle. He stopped, looked directly at me and I could see a visible difference in his demeanor.

"Jim, I had no idea of your feelings toward John Silver, at least not in the way you have just stated them. I am sorry. But Redbeard was unwavering in his insistence of getting Silver as part of the deal. I doubt he will retreat from his position or relent at this stage. I will try. But I will not risk the arrangement that has been negotiated, for the good of all, simply to save his life from a fate he will most likely meet in a month's time."

Smollett became silent as he took measure of what had just been spoken between us.

"I want you and Chloe to join me tonight for supper. In the meantime, you need to help our mess officer find the most advantageous place to hunt for goats. You mentioned once that you learned of such a place through old Ben Gunn. I will see you later this evening, and if further talk of this matter is necessary, it will be then."

As I walked away, I observed Captain Smollett enter the block house and squat down near Silver.

- - - - - - - - - - - - -

That night at dinner was a solemn occasion. I had little heart or desire to speak, and my thoughts would not focus. I tried as best I could to participate in the idle chattering of the officers, but was unable to muster the ability to do so. Finally, I excused myself and went to the upper deck to get some air. Chloe joined me and asked no questions nor mentioned my behaviour. She just stood next to me, put her arm through mine and looked off into the sea with me. I did not share with her my thoughts about Silver. For one thing, I wanted to keep her out of danger and felt that if she knew of my plans, it would expose her to such. However, it is also true at that point I had no definite plans. Nor had I any idea of what plans were needed or how to make them. I only knew that I would not give up. I would fight those dragons, as Silver urged me to do. There was always a chance. Surely an opportunity would present itself, and when it did, I would act.

We stayed on the deck for at least an hour, and were interrupted by the sounds of the captain speaking with two of his first officers, Nigel and Avery, who were carrying boxes. They stepped over the side with whale oil lamps in hand, and down into a longboat. We could hear them rowing toward shore.

I kissed Chloe goodnight, and went to my bunk, knowing that sleep would be but a wishful thought.

Chapter Thirty-Nine

The Exchange

Dawn was of a superlative nature. The golden and red rays of color from the sun's orb that peeked over the waters and bounced off the wispy clouds dotting the horizon gave no hint of the dangers that I believed lay ahead that day. During the past day and night, I was unable to clearly devise a plan. I had no way to foretell how the events of the day would transpire, and could therefore not proceed any further in my deliberations, other than to take the first opportunity that presented itself and act accordingly. Act accordingly. What that meant both intrigued and frightened me. For it could involve danger to myself and crew. And Chloe. I knew I would not risk anything happening to her, and yet I did not know how far I would go to fulfill my inner desire and promise to make sure Redbeard would not get his hands on Silver.

I had insisted that Chloe and I accompany the exchange. On the boat trip over to the island, I was quiet in my thoughts.

The crew had been focused on bringing the ship's stores to capacity with fresh meat packed in salt, water and fruit. We were to leave today at the high tide, which was near the noon hour. The last acts were to pick up the prisoners, exchange Silver and bring the remaining meat stores back with us. The final box of the treasure, as negotiated between Redbeard and Smollett, had been loaded upon the ship yesterday. The captain brought a dozen men, armed with pistols, musket and cutlasses. He said that although it appeared Redbeard was living up to his side of the bargain, it was unwise to assume, that if the chance presented itself, a shark such as he would not hesitate to feast upon a bloody fish.

We arrived at the fort, and Redbeard was not there. Two of our crew were guarding Long John. All the other prisoners were away at the treasure site to help Redbeard and crew with their digging. We had passed that area on the way in, and the work was proceeding with great fury.

Smollett had the crew move into key positions around the fort to wait.

"I need to go in and say goodbye to Silver," I told Chloe.

"Why do you carry that pistol with you Jim?" she asked. "I have never seen you with one before."

"It is for the exchange, Chloe. Captain Smollett ordered all the crew to carry them."

This was a half-truth, and I promised to make it right later. It is true Smollett asked the men to carry weapons. He did not extend that order to me. Once I was inside, Long John sat up on the floor, still chained to the center post.

"Why Jim, have you come to say goodbye to yer ol' Silver?"

"Quiet Silver, and listen closely."

I handed him the pistol and coin bag I took from the *Hispaniola*.

"I will try and create a diversion. I know not what. But—"

"Jim, you do not be needin' to help me. Do not risk your life. Ye's got a future, a bright one, by thunder. I'll be fine, ye can bet on that. Ol' Long John has been in dicier sityations than this here, and lived to tell the tale, and you can lay to that."

"Just be ready," said I. "Take the chance when offered. Go to the caves. No one will find you there. I will spread the word when we return home that there is additional treasure located on this island, and liberally give out the coordinates. I would bet there will be quite a few ships here in great haste."

"Jim, I'm tellin you, by the powers, you need not be a part of anything to bring risk to yerself."

"I've made my choice Silver, and that is that."

There was a long silence between us. I didn't know how to say what I really felt. Silver seemed lost in thought, and then a smile graced his face.

"Jim, I wonders," said Silver, "is your Chloe out there?"

I nodded yes.

"Well, I wonder, Jim me boy, if I could meet your Chloe again, and wish you both good fortunes for yer futures. Could you do that for this ol' buccaneer, Jim?"

I nodded, ran out the door and brought Chloe in with me. She walked over and knelt down on one knee next to him.

"Glad to make yer aqyatence agin, and this time in a more favourable light, Miss Chloe."

"Thank you Mister Silver, although the circumstances are not so favourable for you. I will not soon forget how I met you, and how you convinced the captain to save and protect me from harm."

"You be most welcome, and that be a fact."

"My Jim sees a different man than I and the rest, a part of you that others do not. He cares for you deeply. Although the tales tell a different story, I trust his judgment. And so I wish you God's speed and His divine protection."

"Thank you miss, that warms me heart, it does. Knowin' that such a fine wunderful woman such as you, be me Jim's reward for the rest of his life, well, it surely makes this here whole adventure we've been through worth it, and you may lay to that."

"Jim," said Silver, "I'm glad things worked out the ways they did. You'll be bein' a rich man, and a family life is part of yer future. One of us is the lucky one, and by the powers you can be bettin' it's me that's glad it be me mate Jim Hawkins."

"Hawkins, Chloe."

We turned around to see Captain Smollett standing at the door.

"It is time."

He walked over and unlocked the manacles around Silver's wrists. I helped him up to his feet and fetched his crutch. He stretched out and hopped on his leg a few times, as if giving it life again.

"I wonder, Jim, if you and Chloe could walks out with me, sort of give me a little strength in what 'tis I be facing. Could ye do that for ol' Long John?"

"Of course," said I.

We walked through the door, and there, arms on his hips, stood Redbeard, along with six of his men. Our crew was also out in the yard, at the ready. Captain Smollett's first officers were standing to our left. We continued walking out into the yard and stopped.

"We have come for our prisoners, as we agreed upon," said Smollett to Redbeard.

"If it is all the same to you, Captain Smollett, your prisoners would like to stay with our crew."

"I have no problem with that. Saves the Crown a lot of time and money."

Redbeard turned his attention toward Silver and sported a malevolent smirk.

"It's been a long time, Silver," said Redbeard.

"It be that and then some, Stuart."

"I always knew one day we would meet again, and now that day has come."

"You always was one fer seein' the future. Although these here circumstances were not ones I foreshadowed on meself. Especially thinkin' ye was restin' in peace with ol' Davy Jones hisself."

"Sorry to disappoint you, Silver. I think you will regret that I am still alive."

"Well, don't be countin' yer coins before ye lay hands on 'em, you dirty scoundrel of a pig."

Silver pushed me away, pulled out the pistol and then grabbed Chloe. He raised the pistol to her head. Redbeard looked to his men and they drew arms. Captain Smollett's men simultaneously drew their pistols and muskets and held them on Redbeard's crew.

"What treachery is this?" shouted Redbeard, looking at Captain Smollett.

"Captain Smollett," pleaded Silver, "I demands to be goin' with you on yer ship, or I am going to kill this girl, as surely as we stand here, and the devil to the consequences."

"Kill them both!" shouted Redbeard.

"No!" commanded Smollett. "Order your men to stand down this instant, Redbeard, or the consequences will be dire."

Redbeard looked around at our crew, guns at the ready, and observed he had not a chance to prevail. He eyed his men and nodded for them to stand down.

"Let her go, Long John," I screamed. "Let her go this instant. This is not what I planned. Not like this. Not with my Chloe."

"Sorry Jim, I be seein' no other way."

"You know my feelings for her. I demand you let her go *now*, Silver."

He stood still. I did not blink nor move my gaze from upon him.

"Now!" I shouted.

He kept the gun to her head, and looked directly at me. I pulled out my cutlass and stepped toward him.

"Silver, you will let her go. If you harm her, I will kill you dead where you stand. Make no mistake of my intentions. If you need someone, take me and let her go."

"You'd risk your life for hers?"

"I told you I would, remember?"

Silver remained motionless. I raised my cutlass and put it toward his throat.

"Either let her go, now, or you will surely die, right here, right now. Do not test me, Silver, for my resolve is firm. I am not bluffing."

He hesitated for a moment, surveyed the men around us and then slowly lowered the pistol and let her go.

"I'm sorry Jim, I, I…"

Chloe ran away from him and into my arms. I took her in my arms and looked over at Silver. The two first officers grabbed Silver by the arms and took the pistol.

"This is the most egregious insult to decency I have ever witnessed, Silver!" shouted Captain Smollett. "You show no remorse of conscience nor concern for anything sacred, taking a woman hostage. I have had enough of your ilk to last a lifetime. I will act now as I should have done three years ago, when your first treacheries were inflicted upon me and my crew."

Smollett eyed the officers who were holding Silver. His normally reserved demeanor had grown in intensity to outward anger.

"Bring him into the block house at once!" he commanded them.

"What are you doing, Captain?" shouted Redbeard. "He is mine by agreement."

"He is still mine until I say so. You will have him soon enough."

The officers dragged Silver toward the block house with force, almost causing him to lose his crutch, while Captain Smollett walked behind them. Silver looked over toward me.

"I… I be sorry Jim. I didn't mean no harm."

My fists and mouth tightened as I thought of him putting Chloe in harm's way, and I found myself not so much angry as hurt. I pulled Chloe tighter toward my breast and simply stared at him as the officers and Smollett continued to take him into the block house and then disappeared inside.

"May God have mercy upon your wretched soul!" Smollett shouted.

"No, Captain, no!" cried Silver.

Two loud shots were heard coming from within the block house. Smollett walked out with two pistols in his hands, smoke rising from the barrels. He looked over toward us.

"I didn't want your Chloe to see his death, Jim."

I was confused, hurt and angry. But mostly numb. I simply looked at Smollett, unable to even utter a word. Such was my state. I felt empty. I realized, as angry as I was, that I had lost something dear to me, a friend, one the likes of which I'd never had before.

The two officers carried Silver out, by his foot and hands. Blood was all over his chest, his crutch lying across it.

"Take him out to the cliffs and throw his carcass to the sharks. Let them taste of his foulness."

Smollett looked over toward Redbeard.

"Unless you still want him?"

Redbeard simply laughed.

"A fitting funeral, I'd say."

The officers carried Silver out past Redbeard, who spat upon him as he passed and laughed again. He then walked over to Captain Smollett.

"You've denied me my revenge, Captain Smollett, yet I see we're not so different, you and me. You're ruthless as well as cunning. Traits I admire."

Redbeard turned to his men.

"Let us leave and continue our digging."

Smollett's men lowered the pistols that were previously trained on Redbeard's crew. As Redbeard reached the gate, he turned back to Smollett.

"I learned from your prisoners about Captain Steele's involvement in discovering my treasure, Captain Smollett. I had misgivings about who you were. Today you've proved me wrong. I think you'll go far in the Crown's service."

"You'll pardon me if I do not respond favourably to a comment from you, Redbeard, even one as gracefully misgiven as that."

"I understand, Captain. Our business is concluded. Let us hope we never meet again."

"A hope I also share."

He turned back around, and his men followed him toward the treasure site. I turned to Chloe, who was still in a state of shock.

"Let us leave this awful place at once," said I.

We walked away toward the longboats, leaving Smollett and crew there.

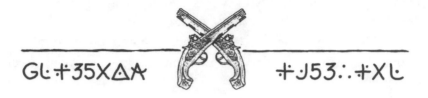

GL✝35X△A   ✝J53∴✝XL

Chapter Forty

The Final Voyage

My activities were limited aboard the *Morningstar* the first week after we set sail for England. Not by assignment, rather, by choice. My hunger was minimal. I had not the energy or reserves to spare save for awaking each morning and performing minimal duties in and around the kitchen. Chloe volunteered as additional kitchen help, and she would lighten the load for me whenever it was possible.

Her demeanor was forever elevated, and she always had an extra smile gracing her face whenever our eyes met. We would often small talk about this, that and the other. Truth be told though, I was not paying much attention to what she was saying most of the time, not that I did not care. No. More to the point, it seemed as if there were a giant fog within my mind, and her voice sounded distant and difficult to focus upon.

My thoughts were consumed by the image of Silver's lifeless, limp and bloody body being carried past me. I was startled awake on many occasions by the image of his being tossed into the sea and being ravaged by sharks. An unfitting and degrading end to his life.

I felt guilty and responsible. The reasons for these feelings were unclear to me. Perhaps if he had been allowed back on our ship, I may have prevailed in my quest to save his life. Perhaps I would not. But, I would have had my say, and my conscience could be at rest knowing I had kept my promise and tried.

Captain Smollett took that chance away. I was angry at him to my core. His refusal to try and intervene with Redbeard was not only a direct rebuke to Silver, but to me and my requests for leniency and mercy from his fate at Redbeard's hands. He could have at least pretended to care, but then it mattered not to me. His actions, including what I perceived as his murdering Long John Silver, were more than I could forgive. I could not stand to be in his proximity, and I put little effort into masking how I felt about the matter. The thought of leaving the *Morningstar* and his presence grew in intensity, and I counted the days left until this desire would be achieved.

One night, two weeks into our voyage, Chloe asked me to meet her above decks after the evening meal and clean up of the kitchen was completed. We sat under a moonlit sky, the warm tropical breezes still pushing us easterly toward England. It was some time before we spoke.

"Jim Hawkins," she started, "you have been acting a mullet head and creating a ruckus on board with your behaviour, and I am asking you as your fiancée to stop it at once."

"I am sorry, Chloe."

"It is not about being sorry, Jim; it is about you, and us. We have an opportunity lying before us, one that only royalty have ever known. Our share, your share, of the treasure aboard this ship is beyond description and imagination. It will provide a life for us, our children and even their children. I am asking you to focus on our future, and let the past be on its way. It does no good for you to remain lost in it and in this forlorn mood of yours."

I stood up and walked to the railing, wanting to get some air into my lungs and gather my thoughts.

"Chloe," said I, "it may be hard to understand, but Silver was more than just a... I felt as a friend would feel for him. Maybe more so; perhaps even as a son."

Chloe arose, walked over and grabbed my hands, looking me directly in the eyes.

"He was not your friend, Jim, nor your father, and he proved this at the end. He was prepared to kill me. His actions have resulted in your having almost been killed more than once. He has used you for his own personal gain, and still you have these feelings for him? I don't understand."

"He could have let me die in that cavern, Chloe, and no one would have been the wiser. Yet, he risked life and limb to save me. For no gain other than how he felt for me. There was more to him than you know."

"Perhaps you are right," she said, "and I have nothing but thanks for him saving your life. And he is responsible, in an indirect manner, for our having a part of this wonderful treasure. But he is gone. No matter how hard you wish it, you cannot change or alter that outcome. I do not want to tarnish his memory. But please remember that all that has befallen you, all of the calamities, have been his fault in one way or the other."

I sat back down and remained quiet for a few moments. I wanted to share with Chloe exactly how I felt and what I had discovered about myself. I had resolved there would be no secrets between us for the rest of our lives.

"No, Chloe, that is not so. From the beginning it has been my choices that are to blame. If I had not acted so selfishly, so... it is I who am responsible for all that has transpired, and I know I must accept fully the consequences that have resulted from my actions. I see it clearly now. As much as I would have blamed Long John in the past, I am not at liberty to do so in the present. Long John's death, ultimately, I am a part of. And I regret it dearly."

She sat next to me and was silent as she looked into my eyes.

"Do you regret meeting me?"

"Chloe, how could you ask that? You are the most important and wonderful part of this whole adventure. I could give it all up, including my share of the treasure, if it only resulted in our being together."

She threw her arms around me, and for the first time since we sailed, I felt warmth and love toward her. Felt anything. The numbness had left me. Tears welled up in my eyes. We kissed, tenderly, and then sat wrapped in each other's arms.

"I cannot compete with a ghost, Jim Hawkins. I need you to be with me. Can you do that? Can you let his ghost be free?"

"I can Chloe, and I will always be with you. I promise."

Something changed within me after that night with Chloe. A new perspective arose. Although still sad about the death and loss of Silver, it was now a memory that no longer activated any hurt when recalled. I put myself wholeheartedly into my work and found the balance of my free time being spent almost exclusively with Chloe. We discussed everything regarding our past and future together.

Smooth waters and calm seas prevailed and created a pleasant and serene environment, and soon the days flowed into one another without thought or regard as to time. I still avoided Captain Smollett whenever possible, for as much as Chloe had helped me realize how anger would not serve me, I still held him in contempt for his actions regarding Silver's murderous death.

It was not only I who felt lighthearted on this return voyage. With my new outlook, I could now understand and relate to the rest of the crew. They were full of hopes and high spirits. Laughter and songs filled every evening. More than once I overheard my fellow mates yarning each other as to who would spend the most for this that or the other.

"I thinks I'll purchase a great estate outside of Sussex, I will, with three large sleeping bedrooms and a huge barn to keep all me horses in as well, and they all be heated at night with fire.

341

Only three bedrooms, is it? My, my. How cramped you should feel in such tight quarters as that. No, that will not do for me. I am going to have a palace with no less than six bedrooms, and a barn that will hold a dozen horses, and not one less."

And on and on it went each evening, with the size and numbers of bedrooms and castles being purchased rising to such grand and lofty expectations that I feared the Queen herself would have to sell some of her estates to fulfill their dreams.

Talk was racing aboard the ship regarding our imminent arrival in Bristol, when Captain Smollett surprised me with an invitation for Chloe and me to join him for an evening meal in his quarters. He accomplished this by first inviting Chloe, who then extended the invitation to me. How could I refuse her request? I promised myself to be cordial, yet would offer no form of conversation or pleasantries of any kind.

We arrived at his quarters just at sunset, and met Captain Smollett at his table, where also sat the two officers that had helped carry away Silver's lifeless body from the block house at the fort. A feeling shot up within that surprised me. I thought I had contained the anger that I previously entertained, throwing it into the wind and never looking back. I was wrong. It had only lain dormant, awakened by the sighting of these three together in the same room at the same table. Every effort was used by my will to restrain and not let it overflow, especially not in front of my Chloe. I wished at all costs to avoid any unpleasantness with her by my side. Still, the blood rushed to my neck, and I could feel the warmth of it coursing as I remembered all the horrible events that transpired when last all of us were together.

Captain Smollett mentioned at the beginning that we should be arriving in Bristol by tomorrow afternoon, should the winds remain favourable. We had passed to the south of the Shetland Islands, having sighted the north of Scotland two days earlier.

During the meal, nothing much was said. Smollett maintained the conversation with his officers and would occasionally ask me a question. I would return with a terse and short answer, followed with a pithy smile. Chloe would give me a certain look, which I took to mean that she was not happy with my behaviour. Yet I did not want to interact with these three and wanted even less to be there in the first place.

Near the end of the meal, when coffee and cognac were served, the captain excused the men who were helping serve the meal and we five, the captain, first mates, and Chloe and I, were alone in the cabin. Smollett held up a glass for a toast.

"Here's to the successful conclusion of a great adventure, and to our future health and prosperity."

"Hear, hear!" the other two officers shouted.

I tapped my glass with Chloe's and we drank. I did not normally drink, excepting the occasional grog as a lad at the Admiral Benbow Inn when my mother was not observing me. And of course, there was that one time in the Quiet Woman with Long John. However, I had never drunk hard liquors. This burned my throat, and I let go of a deep gasp as it choked me. It seemed to have no ill effects on Chloe.

"Are you all right, Jim?" asked the captain.

"Yes, sir," I replied, although I was not really sure. It still burned.

"I have one more toast, then, so pour yourself another one all around."

One of the officers grabbed the bottle and filled our glasses.

Smollett stood up, held his glass high and motioned for all of us to stand with him. We did, and raised our glasses in the same manner.

"Here's to Long John Silver. Thanks to him, we have our futures assured, and may the Lord look after his soul."

That was all I could stand. I threw my glass against the wall, and it shattered with force. My mind went into a rage. How could he even suggest such a thing?

"You are toasting the man you murdered? Have you no honour or sensibility in the matter? As far as I am concerned, you are no better than the murderous and bloodthirsty barbarians you profess to abhor. I can no longer stand here with you and pretend that nothing has happened. It has, and I despise you for it. I will have nothing further to do with you!"

I grabbed Chloe's hand, and observed the look of abject shock gracing her face. My voice had risen in pitch, and I knew that I was shouting. Yet, I did not care.

"Come, Chloe, let us leave at once."

"Sit down Hawkins. That is an order, not a request!" shouted Captain Smollett."

I wanted to run out. Curse him. Be anywhere or do anything but remain in that room. I looked toward Chloe and could see from her eyes that my behaviour had embarrassed her. I could see myself through her eyes, and for a moment felt a flush of humiliation for my behaviour and actions. I resignedly sat down in my chair, folded my arms and waited.

Captain Smollett looked to the two officers, as if waiting. They nodded their heads in approval to something unspoken, and then he turned back toward me.

"What I am about to share with you may never be spoken of again outside of my quarters. I am swearing you both to an oath of silence, on your words of honour, to accede to this request. Do you both agree?"

"I do," said Chloe.

"What is this concerning?" said I.

"I said, do you agree, Hawkins?"

"Yes sir, I agree."

"Pray tell, whatever are you speaking about, Captain Smollett?" asked Chloe.

"John Silver."

He looked at me, and I started to feel a shiver running throughout my body. And a foreboding as well.

"I have waited until this day to speak with you about this matter and purposely invited your Chloe to join us, in respect and anticipation of your future nuptials and not wanting to bind you to a secret that might come between yourselves."

"Go on, Captain, for I cannot imagine where this is going," said I.

"You remember I mentioned to you my negotiations with Redbeard, and his insistence on Silver being part of the negotiated settlement. I was not in agreement with his request, but as I mentioned to you, the crew and ship's safety were uppermost in my mind. I agreed, not giving the matter too much forethought.

"After speaking with you, Jim, I realized that as horrible a man I thought Silver to be, and although I had no doubts he would be strung up and hung from a gibbet upon our return to Bristol for his past crimes, it was against my conscience and all I believed in to hand him over to as barbarous a pirate as Redbeard. You made me realize that a deal with the devil was to be avoided, if at all possible. At that moment, I started to formulate a plan of action to avoid, for me personally, such a distasteful and undesired outcome.

"I knew Redbeard would never relent in his insistence for Silver. He wore his pride on his sleeve too clearly. I realized I needed to create a diversion that would not challenge it, lest all our negotiations achieved to that point would be in jeopardy.

"After our talk when you left him in the block house, I went to see and speak with him myself. I shared with him my thoughts, and we made a bargain. He also shared with me what you had spoken of with him, of which I hold no ill will.

"That night, after all had gone to their quarters, I enlisted the help of my first officers here at the table, and we decided to proceed with the plan I had concocted. We gathered supplies of foodstuffs, included a small part of the treasure and they rowed back to Treasure Island. As planned, they deposited these near the entrance of the cavern system you and he discovered.

"The morning you and Chloe went to see him, our plans had to change. Originally, Silver was to grab one of the officers, remove his gun and threaten to kill him if I did not take him on the ship with us. All of this was to be accomplished in front of Redbeard. I would promise to take him with me, and when he released his hold, would order the men to take him inside of the block house.

"It seems Silver improvised, since the original plan could be in danger because of you two showing up. He used Miss Chloe here for the purpose, which although more effective for the dramatics, was not what I would have wished upon her, and I apologize to you now for his doing it, Miss Chloe."

"Thank you for your concern, Captain Smollett," Chloe said.

"Your ordering Silver to let her go, Jim, was more than I could have hoped for, and I am now convinced that Silver knew what your reaction would be, and in fact, counted on you reacting in this manner. I am assuming you gave him the gun?"

"Yes sir, I did."

"The plan for what was to occur within the block house did not change, and inside we went. I fired the two pistols into the back wall of the block house, and then had Silver carried out for all to see."

"I saw he was dead," said I. "There was blood all over him."

"You saw what I wanted you, and Redbeard, to see."

"It was goat's blood," said one of the officers. "We hid it in the block house when we went that night."

"I had them carry Silver away, purposely in front of Redbeard, and they released him when safely out of sight of Redbeard and his men."

"Released him?"

"Yes, Hawkins."

"Are you telling me that John Silver is not dead?"

"That is correct."

"So he is in the caves?"

"I presume so. He was to wait there until Redbeard sailed from the island. Thereafter, I assume he will move to the block house at the fort. We provisioned him for an extended stay. I will release the location of Treasure Island upon our return to England, and I've no doubts that soon enough, once the stories of the treasure found there swirl through the pubs of Bristol, there will be plenty of ships heading toward that island. He is resourceful enough to find passage away from it and to his home once they arrive."

I sat dumbfounded. All anger and energy had left my body. I looked at Chloe, and her look reflected what I guessed mine to be.

"I, I don't know what to say, Captain. I feel... I feel like such an oaf in the way I have treated and thought of you these past weeks."

"Understandable, Jim, and I take no offense, for you could not have felt any different. I would no doubt have shared these same emotions had the situation been mirrored. I purposely led you astray, and did not share this with you sooner, because I wanted the crew to believe he was truly dead. If you had acted in any manner other than the way you did, then suspicions might have been aroused. As it is, when we do arrive in port, the talk will be of our treasure find *and* of how Long John Silver was murdered in front of Redbeard and before their very eyes! He will be free to meet his fate.

"In return for this mercy shown, Silver made a solemn promise to return to his home and wife and live out his remaining years in quiet solitude, an ending much more dignified and agreeable than his other choices. One perhaps, that is more than he deserves."

"Captain, I, I want to apologize to you, from the bottom of my—"

He motioned me to stop with his arm.

"There is no need Jim. As I've mentioned, if I were you, I would have no doubt entertained many of the same thoughts. I gave you no choice but to think them. I have made no secret that I do not share the same feelings as you toward John Silver, and if given the chance would have brought him back here to execution dock to hang. And you must know, I also hold him partially responsible for the sinking of the *Hispaniola*.

"However, the positive side of the ledger contains his finding the treasure and our having a good part of it aboard this ship, and of course seeing to it that no harm should befall you. On the whole, I am satisfied with my decision and can live my life with no remorse of conscience regarding the way events have unfolded."

He stood up and held his glass.

"I am holding you both to your promise, and will never speak of this matter again once outside of this room, except as to how it appeared to the rest."

"I will keep my promise, on my word of honour, Captain."

"I expect you will."

"And I too," said Chloe.

The captain smiled and raised his glass.

"And now, I trust, you will join me in my toast to John Silver?"

A new glass of cognac was poured for me, and we all picked up our glasses.

"To John Silver," said Captain Smollett, "may he find the peace he is searching for, and may he have long life."

"To John Silver!" I shouted as tears ran down my cheeks.

We clanged our glasses and drank. It still burned my throat, and yet it bothered me not.

"I suggest you both get some sleep. For tomorrow, when we arrive in Bristol, I expect there will be crowd's aplenty and questions a mile long once the news of our discovery and adventure spreads through the local drinking establishments."

"Captain, I, I want to thank you," said I.

"As I already stated, Jim, I am happy with the outcome. There is no need for thanks. I did what I thought was right. Good night, Miss Chloe. I hope now to be invited to your wedding."

"Oh, Captain Smollctt," Chloe blushed, as she rushed over and gave him a big hug.

"You sincerely are invited. And thank you from me... for giving me back my Jim."

For the first time ever, I saw Captain Smollett smile down at Chloe as if smitten.

I knew that feeling well.

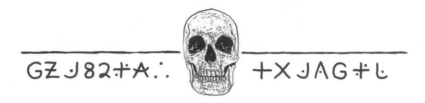

Chapter Forty-One

Saying Goodbye

As I walked upon the upper teak decks of the *Morningstar* after that meeting, hand in hand with my lovely Chloe, the night sea air seemed particularly fresh and invigorating. I could feel the blood course through my entire body. I was aware of every beat of my heart, every breath of sweet air I inhaled. My thoughts and chest were filled with love for Chloe, and my future lay before me in all its glory. I could see it clearly before my eyes. I felt totally alive for the first time in my life.

Staring up into the heavenly skies, lighted with millions of twinkling stars, a sense of awe overcame my being. I felt as if I were a part of it, and yet small in nature, and I prayed for this feeling of humbleness and joy to remain with me the rest of my life. The stars reminded me of the caves Long John and I discovered, lighted by millions of little creatures expending their luminous selves as if only for our benefit. It all seemed right.

I imagined he was looking up at that ceiling at that very moment, and that somehow, by us both concentrating intently, we had connected through the thousands of miles that now separated us. I hoped that through forces unknown, he sensed I was thinking of him.

I shared in my thoughts how happy I was that he was alive. Long John was still alive. I could now go on with my life, knowing that his was secured. There was no ghost left to haunt me. I was free! It seemed that my quest had not been in vain. Although circumstances had veered in directions completely unforeseen, the result I envisioned—my intent of saving Silver from hanging—had been attained.

I will never forget you, Long John Silver. Never.

God's speed, my friend.

Afterword

The winter season has finally passed since we've returned from Treasure Island. The sun and gentle sea breezes have mixed with spring's first blooms, filling the air with sweet smells and warmth—a much needed respite from the harsh winter we've just lived through.

I now look back at how our lives changed dramatically upon our first landing in Bristol. News of our discovery traveled like wildfire, and soon we were inundated with queries of all types. It would be no stretch to state that we were "the talk of the town". Truth is we became the *Cause du Jour* throughout all of Great Britain, Scotland and the Colonies too.

Captain Smollett and Squire Trelawney were charged with the dispensing and selling of our treasure and the distribution of the proper shares to our crew. However, upon assay, it was found to be of such vast wealth, that much of it had to be divided as it was found, in lieu of pound sterling notes, for the treasury would surely be burdened if required to pay that sum at one time. Inquiries started to arrive from all of Europe, and as far away as Asia, for purchase of our individual holdings of artifacts and jewels.

After a few days in Bristol, I accompanied Chloe to her farm. She made apologies with her family for running away, which they were quick to forgive, for they were greatly relieved to see she had returned unharmed. They showed great enthusiasm upon the news of our planned nuptials and welcomed me into their family as if one of their own—including her little brothers.

I traveled from there directly to the Admiral Benbow Inn, where I found my mother absorbed in her work, a typical sight before the evening meal. Upon laying eyes on me, she ran over and smothered me in hugs and kisses, which I admit I had craved and longed for. I could feel the smile etched into my face at all the attention.

I made it my aim, as I had promised myself I would many times on my adventure, to apologize profusely for my selfish acts. In spite of my wishes to the contrary, I broke into tears upon seeing her, and while she hugged me, I told her how sorry I was to have worried her. But she would hear none of it. My return was an answer to her daily prayers, she said, and that was gift enough for her.

Dr. Livesey came 'round that evening as he did every night for his meal. I was glad to see him, and he related how he had heard the tales already from travelers through the area of the great treasure find and adventure to Treasure Island, and that he was profoundly happy at my well being and good fortune. He requested a full accounting of the story, and it was nigh the morning sunrise before I reached the end of the tale. Not a soul left our tavern before I finished. As word spread of my adventure and telling of this tale, greater crowds came to the inn nightly, and within a fortnight we were packed every night with visitors, some who had traveled days to reach us, all requesting that I repeat the tale. I needn't mention that business was the best it had ever been, and that additional help was hired to accommodate this profitable turn of events.

The portion of the treasure that I received was beyond description, since it included many of the jewels and artifacts besides gold and money. It would do no good to mention the total amount here, since the number has no meaning to anyone other than royalty. I pleaded with my mother to give up her job at our inn and fare well in her older years to do whatever and travel wherever her pleasure would take her. Nay, she said. Working and running the inn is what she loved to do and would continue to do, until her dying day. It is what makes her happy, she told me. I realized that this was one argument in which I could not possibly prevail, and I gave up on the idea. Although, I must add, she seemed very happy with the additional help staff and newer equipment I had installed.

Chloe and I were married on the 14th day of February, 1863. It was for me the happiest day of my life. A most wondrous day. All of my friends and relatives traveled to Bristol, and Chloe's entire family joined us there too—over fifty of us in all.

We decided to have the ceremony aboard the *Morningstar*, in honour of the fact that it was upon her that we first avowed our love for each other. Captain Smollett, alongside our local parson, officiated. When I laid eyes upon Chloe, coming out of the captain's quarters in her flowing white gown, I was struck by just how beautiful a woman she was. Anxiety also reared itself at the same time. For I prayed that her beauty and my joy at this event would not tongue-tie me at the appropriate time of my verbalizing my "I do". My prayers were answered, for the words came out with ease.

The wedding reception afterwards was a gay affair, with dancing and all types of food and drink, and took us well into the morning hours. It is still being spoken of to this day as an affair of great beauty and charm. Our families have become the best of friends, and I am now blessed with wonderful in-laws, including new brothers and sisters.

Speaking of family, Dr. Livesey informed us that ours has already started, and I am over the moon with the joyous news. I've put my medical studies at the University on hold so as to be with Chloe as much as possible every day, between the business dealings that I now find myself attending to. I plan on resuming these studies after our "bundle of joy" appears.

We have taken a home midway between the Admiral Benbow and Chloe's parents' farm, so that Chloe will have the support of both of our mothers through her pregnancy. If it is a boy, we want to name him John.

Additionally, we have purchased a large piece of property in Scotland, near the area where my relatives originally settled in Elgin. An architectural firm in London was hired to design the estate, keeping in mind that it will be not only ours, but also our future generations—a place where our children's children will be able to live a life commensurate with the riches we now possess. Chloe is very creative in this respect, and I have deferred all decisions to her regarding the main features of our future home. I look forward to our raising our family there.

I finish this Afterword with the acknowledgment that I have lived a lifetime of adventures this past year, and on the whole am grateful and thankful for the experience. I have been blessed beyond all measure, both in wealth and with family and friends. I pray that my life ahead will be full, and that providence will continue to smile upon me and my family.

Signed,

James Hawkins

James Hawkins

Post Script:

A week after writing this, a packet arrived at the Admiral Benbow addressed to me. It contained a rather unusual enclosure: a medallion made of solid gold. There was a hole in it that allowed a chain to thread through and hang around the neck. On one side was the shape of a dragon inlaid with abalone shell. The design was quite intricate and beautiful to the eyes.

On the other side was an inscription:

Chase your dreams and slay ye dragons. JS

I wear this medallion always as a reminder of my adventure to Treasure Island and as a symbol of our remarkable friendship.

May you chase your dreams too, John Silver.

As per my promise to you, the reader, at the beginning of this narrative:

Treasure Island Location:

Latitude: 18° 19' 04 N, Longitude: 64° 36' 47 W

Acknowledgments

I wish to thank, with all of my heart and being, my friends, past and present, distant and close, who offered words of encouragement and a smile when I really needed them.

I love you all and hope to prove, through my work, that your faith was well placed.

www.RedBeardsCode.com

If you would like a copy of the Original *Treasure Island* by Robert Louis Stevenson, either as a free download or a beautiful matching book, please go to

www.TreasureIslandBook.com

Appendix

Glossary of Terms

Bundt - *treasure*

Stone - *a unit of weight, equal to 14 pounds (6.3503 kilograms)*

Nigh - *near*

Fathom - *a unit of length used to measure the depth of water or the length of a nautical rope or cable, equal to 6 ft (1.8288 m)*

Score - *twenty years*

Espaniola - *present day Puerto Rico*

Bumboo - *a drink made from rum, water, sugar and nutmeg*

Frigate - *a ship with three masts, a raised forecastle and a quarterdeck. This ship carried anywhere from 24 - 38 guns.*

Goddess Moira - (Greek) *the female deity who assigns to every man his lot. The goddess of fates.*

Philology - *the study of linguistics and written language, especially historical and comparative linguistics*

Tafari - *Ethiopian name meaning he who inspires awe*

A man before the mast - *a sailor without rank, not an officer*

Belaying Pin - *a short, removable wooden or metal pin fitted in a hole in the rail of a boat and used for securing running gear*

Supplicating - *to pray humbly; make humble and earnest entreaty or petition*

Black Spot - *the mark of death*